U0050465

NEW
GEPT

新制全民英檢

10回試題完全掌握最新內容與趨勢！

中級 寫作&口說 題庫大全

○ 解析本 ○

全書MP3一次下載

http://booknews.com.tw/mp3/9789864542833.htm

「iOS系統請升級至iOS13後再行下載，
下載前請先安裝ZIP解壓縮程式或APP，
此為大型檔案，建議使用WIFI連線下載，以免占用流量，
並確認連線狀況，以利下載順暢。」

全民英語能力分級檢定測驗的問與答

財團法人語言訓練中心（LTTC）自 2000 年全民英檢（General English Proficiency Test, GEPT）推出至今，持續進行該測驗可信度及有效度的研究，以期使測驗品質最佳化。

因此，自 2021 年一月起，GEPT 調整部分初級、中級及中高級的聽讀測驗題數與題型內容，並提供成績回饋服務。另一方面，此次調整主要目的是要反映 108 年國民教育新課綱以「素養」及「學習導向評量（Learning Oriented Assessment）」為中心的教育理念，希望可以透過適當的測驗內容與成績回饋，有效促進國人的英語溝通能力。而調整後的題型與內容將更貼近日常生活，且更能符合各階段英文學習的歷程。透過適當的測驗內容與回饋，使學生更有效率地學習與應用。

Q **本項測驗在目的及性質方面有何特色？**

整體而言，有四項特色：

(1)本測驗的對象包含在校學生及一般社會人士，測驗目的在評量一般英語能力（general English proficiency），命題不侷限於特定領域或教材；

(2)整套系統共分五級--初級(Elementary)、中級(Intermediate)、中高級(High-Intermediate)、高級(Advanced)、優級(Superior)—根據各階段英語學習者的特質及需求,分別設計題型及命題內容,考生可依能力選擇適當等級報考;

(3)各級測驗均重視聽、說、讀、寫四種能力的評量;

(4)本測驗係「標準參照測驗」(criterion-referenced test),每級訂有明確的能力指標,考生只要通過所報考級數即可取得該級的合格證書。

Q 「全民英檢」與美國的「托福測驗」(TOEFL)、英國的測驗(如FCE 或IELTS)有何不同?

IELTS的性質與TOEFL類似,對象均是擬赴英語系國家留學的留學生,內容均與校園生活與學習情境有關,因此並不一定適合國內各階段英語學習者。FCE則是英國劍橋大學研發的英語檢定測驗中的一級,在內容方面未必符合國內英語教學目標及考生生活經驗。

其實近年來,日本及中國大陸均已研發自己的英語能力分級測驗,日本有STEP測驗,中國大陸則有PET及CET等測驗。由此可見,發展本土性的英語能力分級測驗實為時勢所趨。

Q 本測驗既包含聽、說、讀、寫四項,各項測驗方式為何?

聽力及閱讀測驗採選擇題方式,口說及寫作測驗則採非選擇題方式,每級依能力指標設計題型。以中級為例,聽力部分含35題,作答時間約30分鐘;閱讀部分含35題,作答時間45分鐘;寫作部分含中翻英、

引導寫作，作答時間40分鐘；口說測驗採錄音方式進行，作答時間約15分鐘。

Q 這項測驗各級命題方向為何？考生應如何準備？

全民英檢在設計各級的命題方向時，均曾參考目前各級英語教育之課程大綱，同時也廣泛搜集相關教材進行內容分析，以求命題內容能符合國內各級英語教育的需求。同時，為了這項測驗的內容能反應本土的生活經驗與特色，因此命題內容力求生活化，並包含流行話題及時事。

由於這項測驗並未針對特定領域或教材命題，考生應無需特別準備。但因各級測驗均包含聽、說、讀、寫四部分，而目前國內英語教育仍偏重讀與寫，因此考生必須平日加強聽、說訓練，同時多接觸英語媒體(如報章雜誌、廣播、電視、電影等)，以求在測驗時有較好的表現。

Q 口說及寫作測驗既採非選擇題方式，評分方式為何？

口說及寫作測驗的評分工作將由受過訓練的專業人士擔任，每位考生的表現都會經過至少兩人的評分。每級口說及寫作測驗均訂有評分指標，評分人員在確切掌握評分指標後，依據考生的整體表現評分。

Q 通過「全民英檢」合格標準者是否取得合格證書？又合格證書有何用途或效力？

是的，通過「全民英檢」合格標準者將頒給證書。以目前初步的規畫，全民英檢測驗之合格證明書能成為民眾求學或就業的重要依據，同時各級學校也可利用本測驗做為學習成果檢定及教學改進的參考。

Q 全民英檢測驗的分數如何計算？

初試各項成績採標準計分方式，60分為平均數，每一標準差加減20分，滿分120分。初試兩項測驗成績總和達160分，且其中任一項成績不低於72分者，始可參加複試。如以傳統粗分計分概念來說，聽力測驗每題2.67分，閱讀測驗每題3分，各項得分為答對題數乘上每題分數，可以大概計算是否通過本項測驗。實際計分方式會視當次考生程度與試題難易作調整，因此每題分數及最高分與粗分計分方式略有差異。複試各項成績採整體式評分，使用級分制，分為0~5級分，再轉換成百分制。複試各項成績均達八十分以上，視為通過。

Q 採標準計分方式有何優點？

考生不會受不同次測驗中考生程度與試題難易之影響。

Q 國中、高中學生若無國民身分證，如何報考？

國中生未請領身分證者，可使用印有相片之健保IC卡影本替代；高中生以上中華民國國民請使用國民身分證正面影本。外籍人士需備有效期限內之台灣居留證影本。

Q 初試與複試一定在同一考區嗎？

測驗中心原則上會儘量安排在同一地區，但初試、複試借用的考區不盡相同，故複試的考場一律由測驗中心安排。

Q 請問合格證書的有效期限只有兩年嗎？

合格證書並無有效期限，而是成績紀錄保存兩年，意即兩年內的成績單，如因故遺失，可申請補發。成績單申請費用100元，證書300元，申請表格備索。

Q 複試是否在一天內結束？

不一定，視考生人數而定，確定的時間以複試准考証所載之測驗時間為準。

Q 報考全民英檢是否有年齡、學歷的限制？

除國小生外。本測驗適合台灣地區之英語學習者報考。

Q 合格之標準為何？

初試兩項測驗成績總和達160分，且其中任一項成績不低於72分者，複試成績除初級寫作為70分，其餘級數的寫作、口說測驗都80分以上才算通過，可獲核發合格證書。

Q 初試通過，複試未通過，下一次是否還需要再考一次初試？

初試通過者，可於二年內單獨報考複試未通過項目。

Q 考生可申請單項合格證書

另外，證書核發也有新制，除了現在已經有的「聽讀證書」與「聽讀說寫證書」外，也可以申請口說或寫作的單項合格證書，方便考生證明自己的英語強項，更有利升學、求職。

★關於「全民英語能力分級檢定測驗」之內容及相關問題請洽：財團法人語言訓練測驗中心

中心地址：106台北市辛亥路二段170號 (台灣大學校總區內)

郵政信箱：台北郵政第 23-41號信箱

電話：(02)2362-6385~7

傳真：(02)2367-1944

辦公日：週一至週五(週六、日及政府機構放假日不上班)

辦公時間：上午八點至十二點、下午一點至五點

本書特色與使用說明

1

依最新出題趨勢，精心撰寫 10 回寫作及口說模擬試題，題本編排 100% 與全民英檢正式考試相同，可作為準備全民英檢初級複試、老師課堂使用及在家自修。

2

夾帶於本書內頁的試題冊可剪下，而後面的答案紙也完全模擬正式考試格式，以方便您實際練習，並檢視與記錄自己的測驗結果。

3

試題冊每一回的口說測驗右上方會有一個QR碼，提供「口說測驗考場真實模擬」的MP3音檔。隨時隨地用手機一掃就可以開始進行測驗。

全民英語能力分級檢定測驗

中級口說能力測驗

T05.mp3

請在 15 秒內完成並唸出下列自我介紹的句子：

My seat number is（座位號碼後 5 碼）, and my registration number is（考試號碼後 5 碼）.

第一部分：朗讀短文

　　請先利用一分鐘的時間閱讀下面的短文，然後在二分鐘內以正常的速度，清楚正確的讀出下面的短文，朗讀時請不要發出聲音。

Speaking｜全民英檢中級口說能力測驗 🎧

第一部分 朗讀短文

T05P1.mp3

Life is short and sometimes in a messy and ever-changing world. Precious things can easily become lost. Frequently, circumstances out of our control cause loss, and our own choices may cause us to lose the things that mean the most. Each of us has different needs and priorities in life, but we share one thing in common: the absence of certain things in our lives can make us feel that our lives are incomplete.

第二部分 回答問題

T05P2.mp3

1. Have you ever been to a night market? What food or drink do you like best there?

你去過夜市嗎？你最喜歡那裡的什麼食物或飲料？

`答題解說`

題目第一句的 "Have you ever been to...?" 是「你曾經去過…嗎？」的意思，關鍵字詞 night market 是「夜市」。而第二個問題則……你，可以回答一種自己最愛的夜市美食或是飲……多食物的英文名稱，說錯了反而扣分。可以自……錯。像是比較簡單的 stinky tofu（臭豆腐）……potato（地瓜）、sweet potato balls（地瓜球

第三部分 看圖敘述

T05P3.mp3

4

解析本每一回的口說測驗有三個Part，可以用手機掃描每一個Part標題最右側的QR碼，聆聽並學習母語人士的標準語調及正確發音。

5

精心設計的題目，符合時下日常生活的相關主題內容，並提供最完整、最具效率的答題策略。以逐句說明方式，讓你清楚了解正確翻譯一個句子的程序。不僅讓你知道翻這句時要用哪一種句型，同時提供該句的關鍵字詞或表達用語。

6

可以參考「譯文範例」，檢視自己的翻譯是否符合「信達雅」的完美境界，爾後你在中翻英的考題必能快速下筆，獲得高分。

第一部分 中譯英

一般對於單身或結婚的選擇有著各種優缺點的爭論。這個爭議性話題最常被討論的是陪伴、責任和生活方式這三方面。在過去，很少人會否認「婚姻是人生必經之路」的說法。而如今，這句老話已受到許多不婚族的挑戰。他們認為婚姻，甚至有無自己的後代，都只是一種人生的選擇。

答題解說

第一句可以用「There be + 主詞」的句型來陳述。主詞是「爭論」（debates/disputes），後面接介系詞 about（對於…）再接「單身或結婚選擇的優缺點」這個名詞詞組。「優缺點」可以用 advantages and disadvantages 或是 pros and cons。第二句的主詞當然就是「這個爭議性話題」，可以用 this controversial issue，而「最常被討論的是…這三方面」可以解讀為「最常被以…的觀點討論」，可以用 in terms of（就…而言）。第三句的架構是「很少人（few people）＋ 會否認（would deny）＋…的說法（that...）」，「必經之路」可以用 the road one must take 或是 the only way one must go 來表示。第四句的主詞是「這句老話（this old saying）」，動詞是「已受到挑戰（has been challenged）」，後面接 by 後再接名詞「許多不婚族（many people among the Never-Marry group）」。關於「不婚族」或「獨身主義者」的英文說法，比較正式的是 celibate(s) 或 bachelorist(s)，如果沒把握寫得正確，只要用「釋義」的方式來表達即可，你也可以寫 those who have decided not to get married for their lifetime。最後一句則用 They think/believe 或 They hold the view that 開頭，that 子句內的主詞可以用「婚姻，甚至連帶著有後代」或是「婚姻以及有後代」，注意前者要用單數動詞，後者因為主詞有兩個東西（getting married and even having offspring of their own），所以要用複數動詞。請注意 offspring 是不可數名詞，不要寫成 their offsprings 了，你可以用最簡單的 their kids/children 來表示也可以。「一種人生的選擇」可以用 a (kind of) choice in your life 或是 one of the choices in your life。

譯文範例

There are generally debates over the advantages and disadvantages about the choice of being single or being married. This controversial issue is most commonly discussed in terms of three most commonly aspects: companionship, responsibilities, and lifestyle. In the past, few people would deny that "Getting married is the road one must take in

---

回答範例 2

Of course, I used to go there, though I don't like night markets much. Night markets are normally crowed, especially on holidays or on weekends, which makes me feel like a fish out of water. However, I like a night market's pearl milk tea, which reminds me of the good old days when I was still a university student.

當然，我去過，雖然我不太喜歡夜市。夜市通常很擁擠，尤其是在假期或週末，這讓我感到渾身不自在。儘管如此，我喜歡某夜市的珍珠奶茶，它讓我想起我大學時代的美好時光。

關鍵字詞

night market n. 夜市　**fried chicken** n. 炸雞　**stinky tofu** n. 臭豆腐　**crowed** adj. 擁擠　**feel like a fish out of water** phr. 感到渾身不自在　**pearl milk tea** n. 珍珠奶茶　**remind sb. of sth.** phr. 使某人想起某事

延伸學習

跟外國朋友聊天時，想要介紹美食、小吃英文給對方卻詞窮嗎？以下繼續為您補充一些常見的美食英文。
Taiwanese salt crispy chicken（鹽酥雞）、fried chicken cutlet（炸雞排）、pork belly bun/gua bao（刈包）、Taiwanese oden（甜不辣）、giant meat dumplings（肉圓）、scallion pancake（蔥油餅）、pepper cake（胡椒餅）、meat-based geng noodle（肉羹麵）、pan-fried bun（水煎包）、grilled

---

7

「答題範例」提供兩個觀念不同的回答，無論你是學生族群或是上班族，無論你保持肯定或否定態度，都可以看到與自己意見相符的回答。

8

「延伸學習」是透過與題目本身有關的觸類旁通學習法，讓你練習完整本書的試題之後，你的實力已經進入中高級程度的水準了！

自我檢測

每次完成練習後，可以利用以下指標和表格檢視自己是否準備充裕：

☐ 我都能在時間內完成作答。

☐ 在寫作測驗中，我能做出正確的動詞變化。

☐ 在寫作測驗中，我能正確使用 5W1H 疑問詞。

☐ 在寫作測驗中，我能分辨詞性以及重組句子。

☐ 在寫作測驗中，我能理解短文寫作的題目並寫出符合字數的短文。

☐ 在寫作測驗中，我能根據短文寫作的相關圖片提示做答。

☐ 在口說測驗中，我能複誦出我所聽到的每一個單字。

☐ 在口說測驗中，我能正確唸出試題中的所有單字。

☐ 在口說測驗中，我能回答出確切的答案（Yes / No）。

☐ 在口說測驗中，我不會停頓太久且能很快開始回答。

☐ 在口說測驗中，我能避免使用 uh, umm, ah... 等無意義的單字。

學習進度表

記錄自己的成績曲線，幾天後再複習一遍，檢視學習成效。

回數	第一回	第二回	第三回	第四回	第五回
寫作測驗					
口說測驗					
扣分原因					
註解					

回數	第六回	第七回	第八回	第九回	第十回
寫作測驗					
口說測驗					
扣分原因					
註解					

進度表怎麼寫？

例 1：扣分原因。可記錄自己最常扣分的部分，像是「句子改寫」中沒注意到動詞要跟著做變化。

例 2：註解。作答時間是否超過，或口說回答問題時，是否每一題都有回答。

CONTENTS

目錄

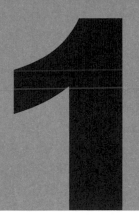

1

GEPT
全民英檢

中級複試
中譯＋解析

第一部分 中譯英

請將下列的一段中文翻譯成通順、達意且前後連貫的英文。

陸地上的大眾交通工具在我們日常生活中扮演著極其重要的角色。在台灣，它是數百萬人彼此之間每天相互聯結的生命線。同時，它也建立起繁榮的社區、創造了就業機會、緩解了交通擁擠並造就更清潔的環境。比較普遍的交通運輸工具包括火車、公車、捷運、輕軌、計程車、接駁車等。這些運輸工具除了方便，也更環保。此外，在高油價的時代，乘坐大眾運輸工具也是個不錯的選擇。

答題解說

中譯英是許多考試中常見的題型，最重要的一點就是要有足夠的單字量來應付，因為不夠的話就會遇到你不知道該用什麼單字去翻譯的狀況。比方說第一句的「大眾交通工具」的英文，有 public transport 和 public transportation 兩種說法，而且要注意的是，它們都是不可數名詞，屬於「集合名詞」，不能在前面加冠詞 the，如果要表達可數的話，可以用 "...means/ways of transportation"。另外，「陸地上的」可以用 on land 加在 public transportation 的後面。接著，「在…方面扮演著極其重要的角色」可以用 play a key role in... 來表示。第三句的「建立起…、創造了…、緩解了…並促進…」可以用 4 個對稱結構的「V + O」來表示。其中「繁榮的社區」可以用 "thriving communities"；「就業機會」可以用 "job/employment opportunities"；「交通擁擠」可以用 "traffic congestion" 來表示。第四句的「比較普遍的交通運輸工具包括…」可以用 "The more common ways of transport include..." 來表示。第五句的「除了…也…」可以用 not only... but also... 的句型，因為這裡的「方便」以及「更環保」比較簡單的陳述方式是用形容詞，所以千萬別寫成 "In addition to convenient..."，不過你也可以寫成 "In addition to their convenience, these ways of transport..."。最後，要記住「搭乘」交通工具的動詞要用 take，「乘坐大眾運輸工具」是 "take public transport(ation)"。

譯文範例

Public transportation on land plays a key role in our daily life. In Taiwan, it is a lifeline for millions of people to connect each other every day. Meanwhile, it builds thriving communities, creates jobs, eases traffic congestion and helps build a cleaner environment. The more common ways of transport include trains, buses, MRTs, light

MRTs, taxis, and shuttle buses. They are not only convenient but also environmentally friendly. In addition, it is a good option to take public transportation during a period of high-priced gasoline.

延伸學習

所謂「陸上交通工具」也可以用 land/ground transport(ation) 來表示，而「水上交通工具」以及「空中交通工具」可以分別用 water transport(ation) 以及 air transport(ation)。另外，transit 這個字也有「運送，運輸」的意思，而「大眾運輸」也可以說 mass transit，它也是個不可數名詞，常用於 in transit（運送中）這個片語。例如：My ordered furniture was damaged in transit.（我訂購的傢俱在運送過程中受到損壞了。）

第二部分 英文作文

請依下面所提供的文字提示寫一篇英文作文，長度約 120 字（8 至 12 個句子）。作文可以是一個完整的段落，也可以分段。

提示

每年找工作的人多如過江之鯽，尤其是在畢業季。除了本身學經歷之外，要找到一份理想的工作，面試時的表現是最重要的。有時候，一份好的職缺會吸引眾多競爭者，因此第一步就是撰寫一份完善的履歷，否則連第二關的面試、考試的機會可能都沒有。如何在求職過程中有好的表現、脫穎而出，您認為應如何做足功課，或者有哪些秘訣呢？

答題解說

本題主要針對求職的成功提出自己的意見。而題目已提示你，可從「履歷 + 面試」這兩個階段去陳述。不過你也可以再加上「面試後的積極跟進」。

❶ 一份好的履歷（CV or resume）必須是「結構及內容完整」（well-organized with sufficient content）的。比方說，最上方要放自己的連絡資訊（contact information），接著是學經歷（educational background & work experience），然後是自我介紹（self-introduction），其他是個人特殊專長（personal skills），但要一直記住的是，你寫的每一件事情都要符合這份工作的需求（meet the requirements）。

❷ 在面試（interview）前，準備好可能被面試官拷問的問題（prepare some questions the interviewer might ask you），可以從別人的經驗或上網爬爬文，獲取一些有用的資訊（surf the Net for some useful information）。接著，面試時，你得讓面試官留下良好的第一印象。例如，當他／她出現在你

第 1 回
第 2 回
第 3 回
第 4 回
第 5 回
第 6 回
第 7 回
第 8 回
第 9 回
第 10 回

面前的那一刻開始，你就要面帶微笑，當面試官對你提出任何問題時，盡可能從容不迫（take it in your stride），並充分展現自己的專業能力（show a high level of proficiency in...）或說話中夾帶一些專業用語（speak occasionally with professional terms），以及對於這份工作的自信（confidence）。

最後，如果時間允許，可以補充面試後的跟進（follow-up），試著展現自己的誠意（show your sincerity），以及想要一份工作的積極態度（aggressive attitude），有時候會是讓你成為 best candidate 的最終關鍵！

作文範例

To land a suitable job, first of all, you should prepare a well-organized resume with sufficient content. The top of the document should contain important contact information, and a summary that introduces yourself, and shows your experience and achievements, while the rest of it is there to provide as many relevant details as necessary to convince the reader that you're the perfect fit for the position. Then if you're lucky to receive an interview invitation, prepare some questions the interviewer might ask you. During the interview, always put on a smile in front of the interviewer(s). Try to be calm and unhurried when you answer the interviewer's questions. If possible, speak occasionally with professional terms to show a high level of your proficiency in certain field. Lastly, try to follow up if you haven't been informed of a job offer.

要想找到一份合適的工作，首先，你要準備一份結構完整且內容充分的履歷。這份文件的最上方應包含重要的聯繫資訊，然後是一篇自我介紹的摘要，展示您的經驗和過去的成就，而其餘部分則提供盡可能多的相關細節，讓閱覽者相信你非常適合這個職位。接著，如果你有幸收到面試邀請，準備一些面試官可能會問你的問題。面試時，在面試官面前始終保持微笑。回答面試官的問題時盡量表現從容不迫。如果可能的話，偶爾用專業術語說話，以展現你在某領域的高等級專業程度。最後，要是還沒接獲錄取通知，可以試著跟進看看。

延伸學習

除了以上提及的事項之外，面試之前你還可以搜尋公司相關資料（search for information related to the company or organization）、練習自信的身體語言（practice the body languages that make you look confident）、站在鏡子前練習回答面試的問題（practice answering interviewers' questions in front of a mirror）等相關技巧。另外，相關用詞還有面試者（interviewee）、正式服裝（formal attire）、特殊技能（special skills & competences）、具備…資格條件（qualify for...）、相關領域之成就（accomplishment in related fields）、推薦人（references）、錄取通知（be informed of a job offer）…等。

第一部分 朗讀短文

T01P1.mp3

請先利用 1 分鐘的時間閱讀下面的短文，閱讀時請不要發出聲音，然後在 2 分鐘內以正常的速度，清楚正確的讀出下面的短文。

Every year in Taiwan, about 200,000 students graduate from colleges or universities, with the average age of them 22 to 24. Approximately twenty percent of these graduates will study further for a master degree or go abroad for further studies, while 60% of them will enter the workforce, though nowadays the job market has always been competitive.

****

Mr. Roberts went to a fancy restaurant last week to have a date with a pretty lady he was recently acquainted with. It was crowded inside and they had waited for about one hour before a waitress took them to a table. When the lady made her orders, hesitantly and slowly, the waitress looked annoyed and impatient. This made Mr. Roberts a bit upset, because he thought the waitress should not bear such an impolite attitude. He decided to make a complaint with the restaurant owner.

答題解說

朗讀文章時，請注意以下標有顏色的單字，盡可能唸得比較響亮，並注意抑揚頓挫，別讓語調太平淡。再者，文章中出現「|」的地方，請稍作停頓，會讓人聽得更清楚，且不會給人感覺你很緊張或急躁，否則會扣分的。另外，字與字之間應該「連音」（或「消音」）的部分（以下畫底線），像是 age of、percent of、has always、have a、a bit upset、make a... 等，也要多加注意。

Every year in Taiwan, | about 200,000 students graduate | from colleges or universities, | with the average age of them | 22 to 24. Approximately twenty percent of these graduates | will study further | for a master degree | or go abroad for further studies, | while 60% of them| will enter the workforce, though nowadays | the job market has always been competitive.

****

17

Mr. Roberts went to a fancy restaurant last week | to have a date with a pretty lady | he was recently acquainted with. It was crowded inside | and they had waited for about one hour| before a waitress took them to a table. When the lady made her orders, | hesitantly and slowly, | the waitress looked annoyed and impatient. This made Mr. Roberts a bit upset, | because he thought the waitress | should not bear such an impolite attitude. He decided | to make a complaint with the restaurant owner.

短文翻譯

每年在台灣，有約二十萬名學生從大專院校畢業，他們的平均年齡為 22 至 24 歲。有大約 20% 畢業生會繼續升學，攻讀碩士學位或出國念書，而有 60% 的畢業生將投入職場，儘管現今職場競爭性一直是非常激烈的。

****

羅伯茲先生上週去了一家高級餐廳，與他最近認識的一位漂亮小姐約會。餐廳裡面人潮相當多，他們等了大約一個小時，一位女服務生才把他們帶去座位。當這位小姐猶豫不決、慢吞吞地點餐時，女服務生看起來很煩躁且不耐煩。這讓羅伯茲生有些不高興，因為他認為女服務生不應該表現出這種不禮貌的態度。他決定向餐廳老闆投訴。

關鍵字詞

graduate n. 畢業生　**be acquainted with** phr. 與…（某人）相識　**average age** n. 平均年齡　**make one's order(s)** phr. 點餐　**approximately** adv. 大約　**hesitantly** adv. 遲疑地　**study further** phr. 升學　**annoyed** adj. 惹惱的　**master degree** n. 碩士學位　**impatient** adj. 不耐煩的　**go abroad** phr. 出國　**upset** adj. 惱怒的　**enter the workforce** phr. 進入職場　**impolite** adj. 無禮的　**competitive** adj. 具競爭性的　**attitude** n. 態度　**fancy restaurant** n. 高級餐廳　**make a complaint with** phr. 向…（某人）投訴　**have a date with** phr. 與…（某人）約會

第二部分 回答問題

這個部分共有 10 題。題目已事先錄音，每題經由耳機播出二次，不印在試卷上。第 1 至 5 題，每題回答時間 15 秒；第 6 至 10題，每題回答時間 30 秒。每題播出後，請立即回答。回答時，不一定要用完整的句子，但請在作答時間內儘量的表達。

1. **Where is the best city you have ever been to?**

   你曾經去過最棒的城市是哪裡？

   答題解說

   首先，要聽懂題目重點，答題才能命中要害，讓人理解。本題重點是要聽懂 "have ever been to"，是「曾經去過」的意思。而「最棒的（best）」，可以針對風景、特色建築、美食小吃、宜居性…等作說明。開頭第一句，可以用「某城市 + is the best beautiful city I have ever been to.」開頭。但千萬別只答了一句話就不說了，答題時間是 15 秒，如果只用一個句子回答問題，後面就愣住的話，分數可能連一半都沒有喔！如果你覺得有個很棒的城市，但是你沒去過，也可以如實說明。接著，你可以進一步提到什麼時候去的、為什麼會去那個地方，以及這個城市為什麼讓你感覺最棒。比方說有什麼著名的地標（landmark）、風景名勝（tourist attraction），或者遇到友善的人等，且未來希望可以再來一次等。

   回答範例 1

   I think New York is the best city I have ever been to. When I was 18 years old, I visited there for the first time. There are specially-designed buildings, facilities, and exhibition halls where I learned much and enjoyed myself a lot. I expect to go again!
   我覺得紐約是我去過最棒的城市。我 18 歲那年第一次去。那裡有特別設計的建築、設施和展覽館，我在那裡學到很多東西，也玩得很開心。我期待可以再去！

   回答範例 2

   Seattle has long been known as one of the most amazing cities in the world. In my opinion, Seattle is the best city in the world though I have never been to. The reason I want to go is that, there are plenty of great places to visit. I want to go shopping at Pioneer Square. Besides, I also want to go to Discovery Park where there are some species of wildlife you're unable to see elsewhere.
   西雅圖長久以來一直被認為是世界上最令人驚豔的城市之一。在我看來，西雅圖是全世界最棒的城市，雖然我還沒去過。我想去的原因是，它有很多很棒的地方

第 1 回
第 2 回
第 3 回
第 4 回
第 5 回
第 6 回
第 7 回
第 8 回
第 9 回
第 10 回

可以參觀。我想去「拓荒者廣場」購物。另外，我還想去「探索公園」，那裡有一些你在別的地方看不到的野生動物。

關鍵字詞

have (ever/never) been to... phr.（曾／從未）去過… **for the first time** phr. 第一次，首度 **specially-designed** adj. 特別設計的 **facility** n. 設施（慣用複數） **exhibition hall** n. 展覽館 **in one's opinion** phr. 就某人看來 **plenty of...** phr. 滿滿的，非常多的… **species of...** phr. …的品種 **wildlife** n. 野生動物 **elsewhere** adv. 在別的地方

延伸學習

❶ plenty of...（大量的）用法：
   plenty 當名詞時，是不可數名詞，後面常接 of，形成 plenty of...（充分的，豐富的）的用法，意思相當於 a lot of，可接可數或不可數名詞。另外，plenty 也可當形容詞用，例如：There will be <u>plenty things</u> to take care of.（會有很多事要處理。）

❷ in one's opinion（依某人之見）的說法相當於 from one's point of view、according to 某人，但要注意，沒有 according to my opinion 的用法喔！

2. **What is the movie you've seen recently? What do you think about it?**

   你最近看過什麼電影？你覺得這部電影如何？

答題解說

題目問「最近看過的電影」，要先有個認知：不一定是去電影院看，在家看小螢幕也算。那如果最近都沒看過什麼電影，可以如實說 "I haven't seen any movies recently."，然後說明為什麼沒看過電影。也許是太忙（too busy）或是沒興趣（have no interest in...）、沒人陪伴…等，或是可以提到以前看過很棒的一部電影。但絕對不能簡單的說 I haven't seen any movies recently, because I have no interest in movies.，然後就等著下一題。閱卷老師不會去調查你是不是誠實回答，所以很多回答可以根據你會說的詞彙、表達用語，當場編造也沒關係。而對於電影的看法，也可以回答「從一開始就吸引我注意（capture / catch my attention from the beginning）」、主角演技絕佳（... is a super actor/actress）、電影特效（special effect）、電影手法很棒（The cinematography was amazing.）、結局很精采（have a great ending）…等。

回答範例 1

I love Marvel Movies. The best movie I've seen recently is *Spider-Man: No Way Home*. I love it because, first of all, the plot is complex and interesting. Next, the leading role

Tom Holland is very attractive. He is brave and funny. Finally, the film director focused much on special effects. Frankly, the movie is really amazing.

我喜歡漫威電影。我最近看過的電影是《蜘蛛人：無家日》。我喜歡這部電影是因為，首先，劇情複雜有趣。接著，主角湯姆霍蘭德十分吸引人。他既勇敢又好玩。最後，電影導演對於特效十分重視。說實在，這部電影真的很精彩。

回答範例 2

It's been a long time I haven't seen a movie. Maybe that's because I've been busy with my work. But several years ago, I went to see *Sense and Sensibility* with my boyfriend in a theater. It was directed by the world-known director, Ang Lee, and it was adapted by the novel of the same name. The story is a perfect combination of wonderful characters and romantic storylines. So, don't miss it.

我很久沒看電影了。也許是因為我一直忙於工作。但幾年前，我和男朋友一起去電影院看《理性與感性》。它是由世界知名導演李安所執導，且是由同名小說改編的。故事完美結合了精彩的人物的和浪漫的故事情節。所以，千萬不要錯過了。

關鍵字詞

spider n. 蜘蛛 **plot** n. 情節 **complex** adj. 複雜的 **leading role** phr. 主角 **attractive** adj. 吸引人的 **director** n. 導演 **focus on** phr. 聚焦於 **special effect** phr. 特效 **amazing** adj. 令人驚奇的 **adapt** v. 改編 **sense** n. 理性 **sensibility** n. 感性 **combination** n. 結合 **character** n. 人物 **storyline** n. 故事情節

延伸學習

當我們要舉例或以條列方式說明一件事時，通常會用 first、first of all、next/second(ly)、third(ly)、 then、finally…等副詞，擺在句子開頭。如： First, I grabbed a spoon. Second, I ate the cereal. Third, I drank the milk. Finally, I tossed the bowl in the dish washer. （首先，我拿了一個勺子。 其次，我吃了麥片。 第三，我喝了牛奶。 最後，我把碗扔進了洗碗機。 ）

3. **What festival do you like most? How do you usually celebrate it?**

你最喜歡什麼節日？你通常怎麼慶祝呢？

答題解說

festival 是「節慶、節日」的意思，聽不出來或聽錯意思，基本上這題就沒了。台灣的節慶很多，從農曆春節（lunar Chinese New Year）、元宵節（Lantern

Festival）、端午節（Dragon Boat Festival）、中秋節（Mid-Autumn Festival），到接近年尾的萬聖節（Halloween）、聖誕節（X'mas）…等、而對於如何慶祝，原則上根據不同節慶會用到不同的詞彙，但如果沒有把握的話，盡量以自己可以立即脫口而出的用詞，因為「如何慶祝」本來就是依個人的習慣，沒有一個標準答案。比如說，開車出遊（go on a driving outing）、去登山、健行（go mountain-climbing）、「辦個烤肉派對（have a BBQ party）」，或者你想展現自己的字彙能力，可以說去賞花燈（enjoy fantastic lanterns）、參加變裝派對（attend a cross-dressing party）…等。

回答範例 1

I like Halloween most, and I usually celebrate Halloween by holding a cross-dressing party. And yes, I may also go to a similar party. I think I will wear a scary costume and go with some of my friends there. During the party, we will watch horror movies, play frightening feel box and ghost hunts.

我最喜歡萬聖節，且我通常舉辦變裝派對來慶祝萬聖節。是的，我也可能去參加一場類似的聚會。我想我會和幾個朋友穿著恐怖的戲服去參加。我們會在派對上看恐怖片、玩恐怖箱和捉鬼遊戲。

回答範例 2

My favorite festival is lunar Chinese New Year, because I can have a long period of holidays. I'm always busy at work, so during this period, I can sleep for a full day or watch many movies at home, enjoying the leisure of being a couch potato.

我最喜歡的節日是農曆新年，因為我可以有很長一段時間的假期。我工作總是很忙，所以在這段期間，我可以好好睡一整天的覺，或者在家看很多電影，享受窩在沙發看電視的悠閒。

關鍵字詞

scary adj. 恐怖的、可怕的　**costume** n. 戲服　**social** adj. 社交的　**occasion** n. 場合　**invite** v. 邀請　**favorite** adj. 最愛的　**leisure** n. 悠閒　**couch potato** n. 窩在沙發看電視的人

延伸學習

「享受窩在沙發看電視」其實就是「耍廢」的意思。英文裡有 veg out 的說法，veg 是 vegetable（蔬菜）的縮寫，vegetable 除了「蔬菜」的意思，有時候還可以指「植物人」，所以 veg out 這個動詞片語推測可能是從這個意思延伸的，就是指「像植物人一樣一動也不動」，後來就演變成我們常說的「耍廢」。例如，I'm going to veg out at home this weekend.（這個週末我要在家耍廢。）

4. **What's your favorite hobby? How does it benefit you?**

   你最喜歡的嗜好是什麼？它給你帶來什麼好處？

   答題解說

   hobby 是「嗜好」的意思，也就是在學業或工作之餘，自己培養出來的興趣或活動，也許是釣魚（go fishing）、看書（reading books）、上網（surf the Net）、畫畫（painting）、運動（sports），或是看電視等。雖然個人最愛的嗜好可能也不只一個，但可以自己挑一個來講即可。本題的重點還是在第二個問題：你認為這個嗜好給你帶來什麼好處（benefit）。比方說，釣魚讓你培養耐性（cultivate patience）、園藝（gardening）、畫畫讓你養成一技之長（be proficient in a particular field）、運動讓你更健康（more healthy）...等。當然，如果覺得自己沒什麼嗜好，只喜歡上網、看電視，那也算是嗜好，可以朝增廣見聞（broaden your horizons）的方向去講。另外也可以說明自己為什麼或在什麼情況下培養出這樣的嗜好。比方說，因為家住在海邊附近，培養出釣魚的嗜好…等等。

   回答範例 1

   One of my favorite hobbies is fishing. When I was still a child, I often went fishing with my grandpa because we lived near a pond, in which there are many kinds of fish. I was very excited when a fish swallowed my bait and got hooked, even though I had waited for a long time. From this, I learned that sometimes happiness is something worthy of a long time of waiting.
   我最喜歡的嗜好之一是釣魚。我還小的時候，我經常和爺爺一起去釣魚，因為我們家附近有一個池塘，裡面有很多種魚。當一條魚吞下我的魚餌上鉤時，我非常興奮，儘管我已經等了很久。由此，我明白，快樂有時候是值得長久等待的。

   回答範例 2

   I like to go traveling by train, though I've got a car. And I consider it one of my favorite hobbies because I can see many amazing views on the train. Next time, I want to invite some of my best friends to go abroad and get on a train to watch more astonishing mountain scenery.
   我喜歡搭火車旅行，雖然我有車。而我認為這是我最喜歡的嗜好之一，因為我可以在火車上看到許多令人驚嘆的景色。下一次，我想邀請我幾位好友一起出國，坐上火車，去看看更多令人驚嘆的山景。

第 1 回
第 2 回
第 3 回
第 4 回
第 5 回
第 6 回
第 7 回
第 8 回
第 9 回
第 10 回

excited adj. 感到興奮的　**swallow** v. 吞下　**bait** n. 誘餌　**hook** v. 上鉤　**worthy of** phr. 值得…　**amazing** adj. 令人驚奇的，精彩的　**astonishing** adj. 令人驚豔的　**scenery** n. 風景

延伸學習

❶ 「go+Ving」常用來表示「從事某種活動」，特別是指休閒活動。例如：go shopping（去購物）、go hiking（去健行）、go mountain climbing（去爬山）、go bowling（去打保齡球）、go camping（去露營）、go cycling（去騎單車）、go dancing（去跳舞）、go picnicking（去野餐）、go skating（去溜冰）、go sightseeing（去觀光）、go surfing（去衝浪）、go fishing（去釣魚）、go skiing（去滑雪）、go swimming（去游泳）、go traveling（去旅行）……等。

❷ invite 當「邀請」的意思時，其後受詞為「人」，後面再接「to + 地方／活動」。例如：invite some friends to the show（邀請幾個朋友去看表演）。而 invite 後面的名詞也可能是「事物」，表示「徵求、招致」，例如：invite questions from you all（請大家提出問題）、invite accidents（招致意外事件的發生）。

5. **What type of food do you usually eat for lunch? Why do you choose it?**

   你午餐通常吃什麼類型的食物？ 你為什麼選擇這樣的食物？

   答題解說

   本題問的是，通常午餐吃「什麼類型」的食物，所以你可以提到 Chinese-style（中式）、Western-style（西式）、Japanese-style（日式）...等「大範圍」的字眼，或是一些比較簡單的字詞，像是漢堡（hamburger）、炒飯（fried rice）、去吃自助餐（go to a self-service restaurant）、買便當（go buy boxed meals）…等。因為有 15 秒的答題時間，通常需要講 3-4 個句子才算完整回答，所以可別以為回答個 I usually eat XX for lunch. 就結束了。至於「為什麼吃這類型的食物」，你也可以強調「視情況」而定（It depends.）。比方說，因為工作都很忙，通常買便利商店（convenience store）的東西可節省不少時間（save much time），或是可能從家裡帶便當（bring my lunch box / eat a boxed meal），在外面買便當（go buy a boxed meal），叫外送（order delivery），但要注意的是，雖然中文有「吃便當」，英文可別說成 eat a lunch box，好像要把這個容器給吞下去了！

回答範例 1

In fact, though I'd love to eat a variety of food, I usually bring my lunchbox on weekdays. My mother prepares it for me. Sometimes it contains some leftovers from the dinner of the previous day, and sometimes my mother would cook more for my lunchbox.

事實上，雖然我喜歡吃各式各樣的食物，但平常工作日時我會自己帶便當。我媽媽會幫我準備。有時便當包含一些前一天晚餐的剩菜，而有時我媽媽會特別為我的便當煮更多菜。

回答範例 2

I usually order delivery for lunch, because I am always busy with my work. I don't have time go out to buy a boxed meal or takeouts. But on weekends, I'd like to go to a fancy Western-style restaurant with some of my best friends.

我通常在午餐時會叫外送，因為我的工作總是很忙。我沒有時間出去買便當或買外帶。但在週末，我會和幾個我最好的朋友一起去高檔西餐廳吃飯。

關鍵字詞

a variety of phr. 各式各樣的　**lunchbox** n. 便當　**weekday** n. 平日，工作日　**leftover** n. 剩菜剩飯　**previous** adj. 先前的　**order** v. 訂購　**delivery** n. 遞送，訂貨　**be busy with** phr. 忙於　**boxed** adj. 盒裝的　**takeout** n. 外帶（的飲食）　**fancy** adj. 高檔的，精美的　**Western-style** phr. 西式的

延伸學習

❶ 「便當」的英文也可以用 bento 或 bento box。所以雞腿便當可以是 chicken thigh bento（chicken thigh with rice 也可以）。因為此說法是來自日本，所以如果你跟在日本或台灣待過一陣子的外國人說這個字，像是 I need to go buy a bento.，他會懂你的意思。

❷ 關於「吃外面」：我們中文會說「我要去買個便當」，不過在英文裡，你只要說 I need to go buy lunch / dinner. 就可以了。如果是「買外帶」，可以說 I need to buy（some）takeouts. 如果是「叫外送」，就是 I need to order delivery.。

❸ 如果是事先在家裡先準備好的餐點，可以用 prepare a packed meal 或是 a packed lunch。例如：My mom made me a packed lunch.（我媽媽幫我做了午餐便當。）

6. **Have you ever argued with someone? What did you do when you got a fight or quarrel with someone?**

你曾和人爭執過嗎？如果你和某人發生爭執或爭吵，你會怎麼處理呢？

答題解說

argue、fight、quarrel 都是與「爭吵、爭執」有關的字彙，要聽出來並不困難，但要注意的是，本題問的是過去的經驗，所以要用過去式來回答。建議預先想好「爭執的對象」（可能是朋友、家人、同學或同事等），以及爭執的內容，然後說明當時如何處理、因應。當然，你也可以憑空捏造，只是不要找些太為難自己的故事就好了。如果發現是自己錯了（find it's my fault），就誠懇道歉（sincerely make an apology），如果是對方錯了，也會試著讓對方有台階下（give... an out），或者可能盡量先傾聽對方的想法（try to listen to his/her complaint）、耐心地與對方溝通（patiently communicate with him/her），也許是先讓彼此冷靜一下再討論（let both calm for a while/moment）…等等。那如果你真的從來沒有和人爭吵過，也可以從「如果我遇到與人爭執的情況，我會怎麼做」的方向去回答。最後，小提醒：本題開始答題時間為 30 秒，您需要比前 5 題多說一些話，所以千萬別留下太多空白的時間。

回答範例 1

Of course, I used to have a fight with someone. Last month I argued with my supervisor at work. I disagreed with his suggestion that I don't think will make a profit for the company. Still, I tried to patiently communicate with him and told him what I thought and what we should do for the benefit of our company. At last, he accepted my suggestion and we created a very good project.

當然，我曾經和人吵過架。上個月在工作中我和主管起了爭執。我不同意他的建議，我認為那樣做不會為公司帶來利潤。儘管如此，我還是試著耐心地和他溝通，告訴他我的想法以及為了公司的利益我們應該做些什麼。 最後，他接受了我的建議，且我們創造了一個非常棒的專案。

回答範例 2

Yes, I often have a quarrel with my father about my school grades. Last week he said my poor grades were due to my failure to study hard and my playing too many cellphone games. I sincerely apologized for that and promised I'd play less games, spend more time on homework and concentrate more in class and take notes, and will be well prepared for every exam in the future. I hope this won't make him angry too often.

是的，我經常和父親因為我的學校成績發生爭吵。上週他說我成績不好是因為我

不用功和玩太多手機遊戲。我對此表示誠摯的歉意，並承諾我會減少玩遊戲、花更多時間寫作業，以及更專心上課並做筆記，並為未來每次考試做好充分的準備。我希望這不會讓他經常生氣。

關鍵字詞

argue v. 爭論　**quarrel** n. 爭吵，吵架　**fight** n. 打架，吵架　**supervisor** n. 主管　**disagree** v. 不同意　**suggestion** n. 建議　**patiently** adv. 耐心地　**cope with** phr. 處理　**communicate** v. 溝通　**accept** v. 接受　**grade** n.（考試的）分數　**failure** n. 失敗，未能做到　**sincerely** adv. 誠摯地　**apologize** v. 道歉　**promise** v. 答應，承諾　**concentrate** v. 專心　**complaint** n. 怨言　**calm** v. 冷靜

延伸學習

在英文裡，「爭吵」有幾種常用的說法。首先，可以用 quarrel 這個字。它可以當動詞也可以當名詞，像是「quarrel with + 人 = have a quarrel with + 人」（與某人爭吵）。fight 也很常見，同樣可以用於「fight with + 人 = have a fight with + 人」。fight 不一定指拳腳相向的打架，也可以指口頭、言語上的爭吵。而 argue 也有類似意思：「argue with + 人 = have an argument with + 人」。另外，如果要表示「為某事」爭吵，可以用介系詞 about 或 over，用法是 have a(n) fight/quarrel/argument over + 事情。

7. **Who is the most important person in your life? In what ways you think he/she is such a person?**

   誰是你生命中最重要的人？從什麼方面來看，你認為他／她是這樣的人？

   ### 答題解說

   本題其實有點難度，若無事先準備，可能會說完「某某人 is the most important person in my life.」之後，就不知道要說什麼了，本題主要是要針對 in what ways（從什麼方面來說）來說明，其實你只要針對「為什麼這個人是最重要的」來說明即可。也許是在生活上、工作上、學業上，或是可以舉出讓自己變得更好的某人，以及這個人如何幫助你變得更好之類的事。

   ### 回答範例 1

   I have an older sister, and she is the most important person in my life. We are very close. I usually share my troubles with her and she always listens to me patiently, giving me useful suggestions. Although sometimes she doesn't have an answer to my problems, I appreciate her listening to me. This actually blows off my uneasiness, so I think she is someone I can trust.

我有一個姐姐，且她是我生命中最重要的人。我們感情很要好。我通常會跟她分享我的煩惱，而且她總是很有耐心地聽我說，並給我有用的建議。雖然有時候對於我的問題，她也沒有給答案，但是我感謝她聽我傾訴。這確實讓我不安的情緒獲得釋放，所以我認為她是我可以信任的人。

I think my grandma was the most important person in my life. Sometimes when my mom or dad said no to me, I knew I could go straight to my grandma for almost everything I wanted or needed, but I would have to earn it. Because she always told me that I have to earn my way in life, and nothing is ever given. These words later have impacted my life tremendously because now everything I get comes from my working hard. I will cherish more what she has told me.

我認為我奶奶是我生命中最重要的人。有時候，當我的媽媽或爸爸拒絕我時，我知道我可以直接去找奶奶，我幾乎可以得到我想要或需要的一切，但我必須自己爭取才行。因為她總是告訴我，我必須靠自己的努力來獲得，因為沒有什麼東西是本來就應該有的。這些話對我日後的生活產生了巨大的影響，因為現在我得到的一切都來自我的努力。我會更加珍惜她對我說過的話。

關鍵字詞

close adj. 親密的　**patiently** adv. 耐心地　**appreciate** v. 感激　**listen to** phr. 傾聽　**blow off** phr. 吹熄，趕走　**uneasiness** n. 不安　**earn one's way** phr. 爭取自己要的，謀生　**ever given** phr. 理所當然給你的　**impact** v. 衝擊　**tremendously** adv. 極大地　**cherish** v. 珍惜

延伸學習

effect、influence、impact 在英文裡都有「影響」的意思，但其實它們的使用時機不太一樣。

❶ effect 屬於「立即見效」的影響，通常是做了某項實驗或執行新的措施而看到事物的轉變。例：Please be aware of the side effect of this medicine.（請注意這藥物的副作用。）

❷ influence 屬於「潛移默化」的影響，隨著長時間醞釀，來自周遭環境，或別人對你個人所產生的影響。例：Frequent fights between parents have negative influences on a child's development.（父母間經常爭吵對孩童發展有負面影響。）

❸ impact 屬於「當頭棒喝」的影響，通常是比較激烈、刺激的事件，讓人深深領悟並開始改變。例：The outbreak of the scandal greatly impacted his political career.（醜聞的爆發大大影響了他的政治生涯。）

8. **What weaknesses do you think you have? What are you going to do about it?**

你覺得自己有什麼缺點？你打算如何處理它呢？

答題解說

這裡的「缺點」weaknesses 當然是最關鍵的字，沒聽出來就沒辦法回答了。缺點可以提及的範圍很廣，它也可能是個性方面的，也可能是一種養成的壞習慣（bad habit）。比方說，沒自信（have no confidence）、缺乏耐性（lack of patience）、忘東忘西（forgetful）、抽菸喝酒（smoking & drinking）、孤僻或不擅與人交往（a lone wolf / not good at socializing）、愛生氣（be prone to angry/upset）、容易緊張（tend to get nervous）…等。至於打算如何處理的部分，比方說不擅與人交往，你可以說，我會多參加社交活動，培養自信心等，如果是天性使然，你也不知道如何處理，也可以如實說明，你只要針對問題來回答即可。但可別只說 I don't know what to do about it. 就結束了，記住本題要你回答 30 秒的時間喔！

回答範例 1

Well, let me think about it. I think one of my weaknesses is my tendency to get nervous, especially when I need to speak in public. Once, I had to go on stage to speak in front of more than a hundred people. I kept stuttering as I spoke. Actually I don't know how to kick my nervousness. Maybe such a tendency will naturally disappear when I have more social experiences in the future. I'll try my best to make myself better.

嗯，我想一下。我認為我的缺點之一就是容易緊張，尤其是當我得在公開場合發言時。有一次，我得上台在一百多人面前演講。我說話一直口吃。其實我不知道如何消除我的緊張感。或許以後社會閱歷多了，這樣的傾向自然就會消失。我會努力讓自己變得更好。

回答範例 2

One of my personal weaknesses is that I am inclined to forgetting things. I frequently forget somebody's name and call him/her the wrong name, and they may get angry. Sometimes I forget my umbrella, or even my wallet somewhere. This used to cause me big troubles. I know I need to get rid of my forgetfulness, so I'll try to be more cautious in the future.

我個人的缺點之一是容易忘記事情。我經常忘記某人的名字並把他/她的名字叫錯了，且他們可能會生氣。有時我把雨傘忘在某處，甚至錢包忘了帶走。這曾經帶給我很大的麻煩。我知道我必須戒除健忘，所以我以後會盡量謹慎一些。

第 1 回
第 2 回
第 3 回
第 4 回
第 5 回
第 6 回
第 7 回
第 8 回
第 9 回
第 10 回

weakness n. 缺點　**tendency** n. 傾向　**nervous** adj. 緊張的　**stutter** v. 口吃　**be inclined to** phr. 傾向於　**cause sb. troubles** phr. 給某人帶來麻煩　**get rid of** phr. 戒除　**forgetfulness** n. 健忘　**cautious** adj. 謹慎小心的

延伸學習

中文常說「缺點要改」，或說「改善缺點」，但英文一不小心就會說成 improve one's weakness/shortcomings 了！因為這樣說反而是要表達「將缺點的程度再提升、改良成更好的缺點」，所以別被中文給誤導了！所謂「缺點要改」就是「把缺點改掉／消滅掉」，因此英文可以用 get rid of 或 give up 等。又例如，「這個問題將獲得改善。」，如果說成 This problem will be improved. 那可就會被外國人笑掉大牙了！因為它的意思變成「這問題變成一個被加強的問題。」正確說法是 This problem will be solved. 。

9. **Are you popular in a group? How do you get along with people around you?**

你在團體中受歡迎嗎？ 你如何與周遭的人相處？

答題解說

第一個問題雖然是個是非題，但其實你不見得一定要回答 Yes, I am popular... 或是 No, I am not popular...，你也可以回答說 I'm not sure if I am popular nor not, but I...，然後就直接針對「如何與人相處（how to get along with people）」來做說明。也許你可以說「我經常幫助別人」、「我會為別人著想」，或是「有些同學或同事不好相處」、「我喜歡獨來獨往，不在乎是否受歡迎」…等。

回答範例 1

Yes, I think I'm popular in a group and I always get along well with most of the people around me. I seldom get angry with people, and I always keep smiling. I always greet my neighbors when I see them. We have a good relationship. I am not good at socializing, but I think I am a likable person. It's important to understand that nobody is perfect and to learn to accept people the way they are.

是的，我想我在群體中是受歡迎的，且我跟身邊大部分的人都相處得很好。我很少生別人的氣，而且我總是保持微笑。當我看到鄰居時，我總是跟他們打招呼。我們的關係很要好。我並不善於交際，但我認為我是個討人喜歡的人。重要的是，明白沒有人是完美的，並學習去接受他們原來的樣子。

回答範例 2

I'm not so sure if I'm a popular person in a group, but I think I have no problems with interacting with my friends. Indeed, some persons are really hard to get along with. They always complain and blame others when something goes wrong. Once, I had a big argument with one of my colleagues because she tried to put the blame on me when it wasn't my fault at all. I guess some people are just terrible. I try to ignore such people as much as I can.

我不是那麼確定我在團體中是不是個受歡迎的人，但我想我和朋友之間的來往是沒有問題的。確實，有些人真的很難相處。每當事情出差錯，他們總是在抱怨，並且把錯怪在別人頭上。有一次，我和一位同事起了很大的爭執，因為她想把完全不是我的錯來責怪我。我想有些人就是很糟糕。我試著盡量不理會這樣的人。

關鍵字詞

popular adj. 受歡迎的　**get along (well) with** phr. 與…相處得好　**get angry with** phr. 對…（某人）生氣　**be good at** phr. 擅長 …　**socialize** v. 參與社交　**lik(e)able** adj. 討人喜歡的　**interact with** phr. 與…（某人）互動　**argument** n. 爭執，爭論　**put the blame on** phr. 歸責於…（某人）　**fault** n. 錯誤，缺失　**ignore** v. 不理會

延伸學習

the way 可以當副詞用，後面接「句子」（其後省略 in which），相當於 how 的用法。例如：That's the way we like it. = That's how we like it.（那就是我們喜歡的方式。）在這樣的句子中，the way 也被視為「連接詞」的一種，可以用來表達 as（像…一樣）、if（如果…）的意思。例如：The way you are practicing now, you won't make much progress. = If you practice like this, you won't make much progress.（如果照這樣練習，你不會有多大的進步。）

10. **If you were not feeling well today and you needed to ask for leave, what would you say to your teacher or your boss through voicemail?**

如果你今天感覺不舒服且得請假，你會在透過語音留言你的老師或老闆說什麼？

答題解說

本題是個「情境考題」，需要您將自己帶入這樣的情境中來回答問題。就本題來說，你可以想像自己請病假時應該要說些什麼。首先，請聽清楚題目最後的 "through voicemail"，也就是「透過語音留言」來你請假。你可以用 "Good morning, XXX. It's XXX.""I'm sorry, but I..." 開頭，然後開始表達自己生病了（suffering from / coming down with + 疾病）、有什麼症狀（symptoms）。另

外，如果是上班族的話，通常請假時都會跟主管或老闆交代一下工作上的事情，讓他們覺得你是個工作負責的員工，這樣的答題也會比較完整，分數才會高喔！如果你是學生的話，可以跟老師說後續你會做什麼事情，讓老師不用為你擔心。

回答範例 1

Good morning, Miss. Lin. It's David. I'm sorry, but I won't be able to go to school today. I have been suffering from diarrhea since last night and I'm still feeling weak now. I guess I might have had something bad for my dinner yesterday. I'll go to a doctor 10 minutes later. By the way, I've asked Brian to take notes for me. I think I'll be able to go to school tomorrow and catch up with the lesson for today.

林老師早安，我是 David。很抱歉，我今天無法去上學。我從昨晚就拉肚子，目前仍感到很虛弱。我猜可能是我昨天晚餐吃了不乾淨的東西，我十分鐘後會去看醫生。對了，我已經請布萊恩幫我作筆記。我想我明天可以上學，並且趕上今天沒上的課。

回答範例 2

Hi, Mr. Smith. It's me, Jennifer. I think I'll need to ask for leave for a few days. I've kept coughed since I got up this morning at six and I got a heavily sore throat. My COVID-19 rapid test was positive five minutes before, and I've sent you a photo of my RDT reagent. I'm now prepared for a virtual appointment. I'll keep you posted as soon as possible.

嗨，史密斯先生。是我，珍妮佛。我想我得請個幾天假了。我早上六點起床之後就一直不停地咳嗽，而且我的喉嚨很痛。五分鐘前我的 COVID-19 快篩結果呈陽性，而我有用 LINE 傳給您我快篩試劑的照片。我現在正準備進行視訊看診。我看情況如何會盡快讓您知道。

關鍵字詞

suffer from phr. 承受…（疾病等）之苦　**diarrhea** n. 腹瀉　**weak** adj. 虛弱的　**catch up with** phr. 趕上（進度等）　**leave** n. 請假　**cough** v. 咳嗽　**sore throat** n. 喉嚨痛　**RDT reagent** n. 快篩試劑（**RDT = rapid diagnostic test**）　**virtual appointment** n. 視訊問診　**keep sb. posted** phr. 隨時通知某人最新消息

延伸學習

生病時，不要只會說 "I'm sick!" 或 "catch a cold" 喔！如果要表達「身體部位」的疼痛，可以說「have a pain in + 身體部位」，例如：I'm having terrible pains in my back.（我的背部好痛。）另外，有些「身體部位 -ache」的字彙，也可以記下來，像是 headache（頭痛）、stomachache（胃痛）、toothache（牙齒

痛）…等。在口語中，也常用 hurt 來表示「痛」，但須注意句子的主詞必須是身體部位。例如：I hit one of my knees on the corner of the table. It is hurting a lot!（我的一邊膝蓋撞到桌角。好痛的啊！）而「酸痛」的說法也很常用 sore 這個字。例如：sore eyes（眼睛痠痛）、sore throat（喉嚨痛）、sore neck（脖子酸）。最後，還有一些很常見與身體病痛有關的表達：itchy eyes（眼睛很癢）、have a runny nose（流鼻水）、have a blocked nose（鼻塞）、sneeze（打噴嚏）、bloated stomach（胃脹氣）…等。

第三部分 看圖敘述

T01P3.mp3

下面有一張圖片及四個相關的問題，請在 1 分半鐘內完成作答。作答時，請直接回答，不需將題號及題目唸出。

首先請利用 30 秒的時間看圖及問題。

提示

1. 照片裡的人在什麼地方？
2. 照片裡的人在做什麼？
3. 照片裡的人為什麼會在那裡？
4. 如果尚有時間，請詳細描述圖片中的景物。

第 1 回
第 2 回
第 3 回
第 4 回
第 5 回
第 6 回
第 7 回
第 8 回
第 9 回
第 10 回

這個大題的答題祕訣就是針對英文的「5W1H」（who、what、when、where、why、how）來說故事，不過題目一開始已經先提示你從 where、who、why 開始說，其他再根據你剩下的時間去發揮。所以不是要你一次把看到的東西都說完，否則一分半鐘的時間，你沒有那麼多東西可以講。以下就針對提示進行解說：

1. 照片裡的人在什麼地方？

   你可以說 "on the grassland in a park"（在公園的一塊草地上）或是 "on a forest land"（在一片林地上）。但如果只是說「他們在戶外」（They are outdoors.）之類的，分數會打折扣喔！

2. 照片裡的人在做什麼？

   提到「人」的部分時，你可以先提到有多少人，以及他們可能的關係，並稍加描述特徵或其他重點。例如，你可以說 "The man and the woman might be the parents of the two kids."。

3. 照片裡的人為什麼會在那裡？

   可以從現場的小帳篷（small tent）、背包（backpack）、小盒子以及水壺（kettle）等物，判斷他們正在野餐（picnic）。接著你可以更深入一點補充，野餐也許不是最重要的，而是他們正在享受一個悠閒（leisurely and carefree）、愜意的午後時光（enjoy a relaxing afternoon time），同時增進親子與家庭之間的和樂。

4. 如果尚有時間，請詳細描述圖片中的景物。

   例如，從照片中的，你可以繼續補充說，Thanks to such a nice weather, they can go together to have a picnic... because the parents are usually busy…。

回答範例

From what I can see, this picture was taken at a grassland in a park. There are four people in the picture, including a man, a woman, and two kids, and they might be family. They are sitting on the grassland and reading a picture book together. One of the kids is pointing his finger at certain part of the book. He seems to ask some questions or tell the other persons that something is very interesting. They are having a leisurely and carefree afternoon, enjoying the warm breeze and the fresh air. From my point of view, they spend their time together, perhaps on a holiday, which is the most important part of the picnic for them. Maybe the parents are busy on weekdays and they don't have much time interacting with their kids. Next time, they might go mountain climbing together and walk deep into a forest to enjoy a green shower!

就我看來，這張照片是在一個公園的草地上拍攝的。照片中有四個人，包括一名男子和一名女子，及兩個小孩，而且他們可能是一家人。他們坐在草地上，一起看著一本圖書。其中一個孩子正用手指者著書的某個部分。他似乎在問一些問題或告訴其他人某個東西很有趣。他們享受著暖風和清新的空氣，度過了一個悠閒無憂的下午。在我看來，他們在一起度過時光，也許是在假期，這對他們來說是野餐中最重要的部分。可能父母們平日工作繁忙，沒有太多時間與孩子互動。下次，說不定他們會一起去爬山，走進森林，享受一場森林浴呢！

關鍵字詞

meadow n. 草地　**grassland**(**s**) n. 較大、空曠的草原、草地　**woodland**(**s**) n. 林地，森林地帶　**forest** n. 森林　**finger** n. 手指　**leisurely** adj. 悠閒的　**carefree** adj. 無憂無慮的　**breeze** n. 微風　**interact** v. 互動　**green shower** n. 森林浴

延伸學習

本大題開頭第一句可以幾個句型來發揮：

❶ From what I can see, this picture was taken in a... （就我所看到的，這張照片是在…（什麼時候、地方）拍攝的）

❷ If I'm not mistaken, this picture was taken in a... （如果我沒有弄錯的話，這張照片是在…拍攝的）

❸ The first thing that caught my eye is... （第一個吸引我目光的是…）

❹ It is pretty obvious that this picture was taken... （很明顯，這張照片是在…拍攝的。）

MEMO

2

GEPT
全民英檢

中級複試
中譯＋解析

第一部分 中譯英

一個人的溝通協調能力，往往是能否將問題有效處理的關鍵。這不僅包括與他人交談時的態度，還有自我情緒控制的能力 — 千萬別輕易地情緒失控。善於溝通的人往往在職場上也更容易成功，且在各種社交場合中也會是個較受歡迎的人。

答題解說

第一句的「是…的關鍵」可以用 a/the key to...，且 to 後面要接名詞或動名詞。至於「溝通協調能力」，可以用 "communication skill(s) and capable in coordination" 或 "the competence in communication and coordination"。第二句的「這不僅包括…還有…」可以用 "This includes not only... but (also)..." 這個句型，其中「自我情緒控制」可以用 "self-control of emotions" 來表達，而「…的能力」可以用 "the ability to-V" 或 "the capability of..."，「情緒失控」可以用 "lose one's calm"、"lose control of one's emotions" 或是 emotionally unhinged。第三句可以用 "Those who... are more successful." 來表示，「社交場合」則是 social occasions。

譯文範例

One's competence in communication and coordination is always the key to effectively dealing with problems. This includes not only the attitude shown during a talk with others, but also the ability to control your emotions — never lose your calm easily. Those who are good at communication are more successful in the workforce, and are more popular on various social occasions.

延伸學習

「善於…」最簡單的說法是 be good at...，at 是介系詞，後面要接名詞或動名詞。但其實在很多地方，我們也會看到 be good in 的用法。例如，He's good in English.（他的英文很好。）事實上，good at 和 good in 意思差不多，大部分情況都可以互換。另外，be good with 要表達的是「處理人的能力」。例如，My wife is good with children, so she opts to work as a kindergarten teacher.（我太太很會處理小孩子的事，所以她選擇了幼稚園老師的工作。）

第二部分 英文作文

第 1 回
第 2 回
第 3 回
第 4 回
第 5 回
第 6 回
第 7 回
第 8 回
第 9 回
第 10 回

提示

隨著全球疫情逐漸趨緩、邊境解封以及各種防疫措施的鬆綁，國內熱門餐飲店或特色餐廳等，也都看到人潮的回籠，有些餐廳甚至會遇到一位難求的狀況。請分享過去在餐廳用餐的美好或不愉快的經驗。

答題解說

本題主要針對自己過去到餐廳用餐時，經歷過好的，或不好的事情，敘述一段經驗，所以時態要用過去式喔！首先，可以先提及當時到某餐廳的原因為何（也許是慶生、聚餐等目的），接著可以提到餐廳本身的類型或特色，也許是中式（Chinese-style）餐廳，也許是西式（Western-style）或義式（Italian）餐廳，或親子餐廳等（kid-friendly restaurant）。接著可以先設想好要寫愉快或是不愉快的經驗，但務必注意的是，一定要寫跟餐廳的人事物相關的體驗，否則很容易就離題了。

❶ 好的或愉快的經驗：燈光美，氣氛佳（The lighting around was beautiful and the atmosphere was great.）；服務生態度良好（The waiters/waitresses were friendly and polite.）、餐點精緻（delicate meals）、料理豐富，吃得好飽（The food was a feast and I was so full.）、價格實惠（They were generally affordable.）、享受了一頓開心的午餐（enjoyed a hearty dinner）

❷ 不好的或不愉快的經驗：基本上只要把上述好的經驗變成否定就可以寫很多了，當然你也可以再自己發揮喔！

作文範例

Last Sunday I organized a birthday party for my friend in a fancy restaurant. I ordered spicy chicken and beef fried rice, and my friend ordered beef noodles. We were assured that our meals would be ready in ten minutes. However, our meals weren't yet served after alwost an hour. My friend was mad. After hastening the waiter's response for a couple of times, we finally got our food. But to our further madness, the beef noodles seemed not fresh and were tasteless while the spicy chicken was so hard that it's difficult to swallow. When I reported this to the restaurant manager, he turned out to just say, "Sorry, but we are now very busy. Please wait a bit." Then we waited again for another long time, and finally had our food changed. But we've been hungry to the point where we were not hungry!

上週日我在一家高檔餐廳替我的朋友安排了生日派對。當時我點了辣味雞肉和牛肉炒飯，而我朋友點了牛肉麵。服務生保證餐點會在十分鐘之內準備好。然而，

我們的餐點在快一個小時之後還是沒來。我朋友很生氣了。向服務生催促多次之後，我們終於可以用餐了。但令我們更生氣的是，牛肉麵似乎不新鮮且索然無味，而辣味雞肉如此生硬且很難下嚥。當我向餐廳經理反應時，他竟然只說「不好意思，我們餐廳現在很忙。請等一下。」然後我們又等了很久，最後才更換了食物。但我們都已經餓過頭了。

延伸學習

我們常常會用「CP 值」很高來形容購買的東西或服務等，但其實在英文裡，CP 值（cost-performance ratio）是一個用於經濟領域的專有名詞，如果你對外國人說 "I bought this, see? Its CP value is high!"，對方可能會聽得一頭霧水，不知道你在講什麼。相較於剛才提到的詞，price-performance ratio 也許是更常在生活會話中看到的用詞，因為你將「專有名詞」用在一般生活對話中，會顯得奇怪又不自然。所以如果你要表達「CP 值很高」，可以說 "It's a bargain/great deal." 或是形容「好像是偷來的一樣便宜」的 "It's a steal."。那如果你要表達「CP 值很低」，可以說 It's a rip-off.（好像被搶了），稍微正式一點的說法：It's overpriced.。

第一部分 朗讀短文

T02P1.mp3

第1回
第2回
第3回
第4回
第5回
第6回
第7回
第8回
第9回
第10回

The so-called "youth" shouldn't be just considered the time in someone's life when they are young. It is actually not just a time of life, but a state of mind; it is not a matter of rosy cheeks, red lips or flexible limbs; it should be full of strong will, creative imagination, rich in vigor of love; it should be able to keep you curious and energetic. The "youth" state of mind can be cultivated by embracing curiosity, creativity, and a passion for learning.

****

Everyone may have some moments in life when they miss someone so much that they just want to take them from their dreams or memories to the real life, and hug them for real! Dream what you want to dream; go where you want to go; be what you want to be, because you have only one life. Don't let fear or doubt hold you back from experiencing all the beauty and wonder the world has to offer.

答題解說

許多考生在朗讀文章時，因為過於緊張，使得語調平淡，毫無抑揚頓挫，聽不出情感的成分在內。以下標有顏色的單字，請盡可能唸得比較響亮，除了句與句之間的句點（.）及分號（;）出現「|」的地方，請稍作停頓，試著讓自己融入短文的情境中。最後，請注意字與字之間該連音（或消音）的部分，像是 is actually、not a、but a、state of、keep you、energetic about、moments in、what you、want to、have only…等。

The so-called "youth" | shouldn't be just considered the time in someone's life | when they are young. It is actually not a Just time of life, | but a state of mind; it is not a matter of rosy cheeks, | red lips or flexible limbs; it should be full of strong will, | creative imagination, | rich in vigor of love; it should be able to keep you curious and energetic about things. The "youth" state of mind | can be cultivated by embracing curiosity, | creativity, | and a passion for learning.

****

Everyone may have some <u>moments</u> in life when they <u>miss someone</u> so much | that they just <u>want to</u> take them from their dreams or memories to real life, | and hug them for real! Dream <u>what you want to</u> dream; go where you <u>want to</u> go; | be <u>what</u> you <u>want to</u> be, | because you <u>have only one life</u>. Don't let fear or doubt <u>hold you</u> back from experiencing all the beauty | and wonder the world has to offer.

<u>短文翻譯</u>

所謂「年輕」，不應該僅是指某人年輕的一段時間。實際上它不只是一段生命中的時光，也是一種心境。它不是玫瑰色的臉龐、紅色的唇或是靈活的手腳。它應該要充滿強烈意志、創意想像力以及豐富的感情。最後，它應該要可以讓你保持好奇心與活力。「年輕」的心態可藉由擁抱好奇心、創造力和學習的熱情來培養。

****

每個人在生活中都可能曾經有過非常想念一個人的時候，他們甚至想把自己思念的人從夢中或記憶裡帶到現實生活中，真正地擁抱他們！去做你想做的夢；去你想去的地方；去成為你想成為的人，因為你的人生只有一次。不要讓恐懼或懷疑使得你無法經歷這個世界所要提供的所有美麗和奇蹟。

<u>關鍵字詞</u>

consider v. 視為　**actually** adj. 實際上　**state of mind** n. 心態　**rosy cheeks** n. 紅潤的臉頰　**flexible limbs** n. 靈活的手腳　**imagination** n. 想像力　**vigor** n. 活力　**curious** adj. 好奇的　**energetic** adj. 精力旺盛的

第二部分 回答問題

T02P2.mp3

1. **Have you ever bought things on the Internet? Talk about your experience of online purchase.**

   你曾經在網路上買過東西嗎？談談你的網購經驗。

   <u>答題解說</u>

   第一個問題是個 Yes/No question。一開始可以用 "Yes, I have (ever bought things on the Internet)." 或是 "No, I haven't (bought things on the Internet)." 或

第 1 回
第 2 回
第 3 回
第 4 回
第 5 回
第 6 回
第 7 回
第 8 回
第 9 回
第 10 回

"No, never." 來回答。大部分人應該都有網購的經驗，知道在網路上和實體商店購物的差別以及好壞處，如果你真的從來沒上網買過東西，至少也聽過別人的經驗，也可以如實回答，或當作自己的經驗談談。以下是一般網購的優缺點：

❶ 優點（advantages）：非常方便（convenient）、價格更優惠（lower in price）、更容易比價（easier comparison of prices）、不必接觸人群（尤其是在疫情的時代）（no need to have contacts with people）

❷ 缺點（disadvantages）：無法先看到實體物品、無法確認商品的品質、無法試用（unable to make sure if the product is good or bad, or unable to give it a try）、容易被詐騙（fall victim to fraud easily）、退貨程序可能複雜且漫長（It might take long to apply for returns.）。

回答範例 1

Yes, I have ever bought things on the Internet. Actually, I often make purchases on some popular sites such as MOMO, Shopee, PChome and Yahoo. Almost every product I bought is 10-30% cheaper than the same item sold in a physical store, and the quality of them is good. I'm usually busy and have no time going outside to shop, so I think shopping online is a good idea.

是的，我曾經在網路上買東西。事實上，我經常在 MOMO、Shopee、PChome 和 Yahoo 等一些熱門網站上購物。我買的每件商品幾乎都都比實體店賣的同款商品便宜 10-30%，而且品質還很好。我平時很忙，沒有時間出去購物，所以我覺得上網購物對我來說是個不錯的想法。

回答範例 2

No, I've never done that before. I don't like to buy things on the Internet because I'm not able to see and touch what I want to buy. In other words, I can't examine the quality, so I am afraid that I might get a faked item or find a sale is just another case of fraud. Therefore, online shopping is not a wise choice to me.

不，我沒有做過那樣的事。我不喜歡網路購物，因為我無法親眼看到以及親手碰到我要買的東西。也就是說，我無法檢視看商品的品質，所以我擔心我可能會買到假貨，或發現這筆銷售本身就只是一場詐騙。因此，網路購物對我來說，並不是一項明智的選擇。

關鍵字詞

make a purchase phr. 購物　**physical store** n. 實體商店（= **brick-and-mortar store**）　**examine** v. 檢查　**faked** adj. 仿造的，冒牌的　**item** n. 項目，品目　**fraud** n. 詐欺，騙局

「網購」的英文，一般稱為 online shopping，而在各個購物平台的首頁裡常見的單字有 Cart（購物車）、Today's deal（今日優惠）、Order（訂單）、Checkout（結帳）、Place an Order（下單）、Customer Service（客服）。通常看完商品後如果沒有要馬上結帳，我們會先將商品加入購物車，英文的說法是 "add to cart"，逛完以後一次付費，稱為 "pay for all the items"，如果要將物品從購物車移除，可以說 "remove the items from the cart"。另外，與運送／運費有關的字詞有：free shipping（免運費）、standard delivery（標準運送）、express delivery（快速運送）、direct delivery（直送）等。

2. **What type of TV program do you like most? Why do you like it?**

   你最喜歡什麼類型的電視節目？為什麼你會喜歡？

   答題解說

   題目問「最喜歡的電視節目」以及「為什麼喜歡」。一開始就可以將兩個問題用一句話來回答："I like... most because..."、"... is my favorite because..." 或 "My favorite program is... because..."。接著你要想到有哪些電視節目類型，常見的有 news（新聞）、cartoon（卡通）、sports（體育）、movie（電影）、variety show（綜藝）、drama/TV series/soap opera（連續劇）、music（音樂）、documentary（紀錄片）、talk show（談話／政論）等。至於喜歡的原因，則依照不同類型節目性質去發揮，像是新聞類的話，可以說 "... let me keep informed of what's happening around the globe"，卡通類的話，可以說 "I can accompany my kids and interact with them" …等等。

   回答範例 1

   Definitely! My favorite TV program is cartoon. Whenever I watch cartoons on TV with my son, I feel like I'm having my second childhood. Besides, I work as an animation designer, so I can learn more from those programs. Cartoons can train and inspire my endless imagination.
   當然！我最喜歡的電視節目是卡通片。每當我和兒子一起看電視的卡通片時，我都覺得我正在經歷第二個童年。此外，我是一名動畫設計師，所以我可以從這些節目中學到更多。卡通可以訓練和激發我源源不絕的想像力。

   回答範例 2

   I like to watch news report programs most because they let me have the opportunity to know about what is happening around the globe. Besides, I can train myself to develop the ability of critical and independent thinking, so I won't be easily fooled around by some fake news.

我最喜歡看新聞報導節目，因為它們讓我有機會了解全球正在發生的事情。此外，我可以訓練自己培養思辨能力以及獨立思考的能力，所以我不會輕易被一些假新聞愚弄。

關鍵字詞

animation n. 動畫　**inspire** v. 啟發　**endless** adj. 無盡的　**imagination** n. 想像力　**opportunity** n. 機會　**critical thinking** n. 思辨能力　**independent thinking** n. 讀立思考能力　**fool** v. 愚弄　**fake** adj. 假冒的

延伸學習

在英文裡，「看電視」是 watch TV，「看電視正在播出的某節目」是 watch...(programs) on TV，千萬別用 see 來看電視喔！用 see 的話意思會變成「看見」某個地方有一部電視機。而「看電視頻道中的電影」可以用 watch a movie on TV，但是到電影院看電影的話，要說 go to a movie 或是 see a movie。其他像是「轉台」是 changep/flip/switch channels；將電視音量「調大、調小」可以說 turn up、turn down，而電視的「打開、關閉」則比照一般電器用品，用 turn on、turn off，千萬別用 open、close 喔！

3. **What do you spend on most every month? How do you manage your money?**

你每個月花費在什麼上面最多？你如何理財呢？

答題解說

雖然本題主要針對的是上班族或社會人士來問，但如果你還是個學生，也可以談談自己一個月有多少零用錢（pocket money）以及花費的情況，可以針對大方向來說明，例如食物、交通費（transportation fare）、通勤費（commuting fee）、手機帳單（cellphone bill）、房屋租金（house rent）…等。至於第二個問題 — 如何理財（money management）— 的部分，假如你還是學生，每個月沒有多餘的錢可以理財，也可以說未來自己出社會之後，可能的理財方式有儲蓄（bank savings）、定存（fixed deposit）、買股票（invest in stocks）、買基金（invest in mutual funds）…等投資（investment）方式。

回答範例 1

I spend most on house rent, which alone takes up a third of my monthly expense. Besides, food and drinks account for one fourth. After spending what I need on transport and daily necessities, I have very little left for money management. But I'm trying to save at least 10% of my monthly salary.

第 1 回
第 2 回
第 3 回
第 4 回
第 5 回
第 6 回
第 7 回
第 8 回
第 9 回
第 10 回

我支出最多的是房租，單單是房租就占用了我每個月花費的三分之一。此外，飲食的花費佔了四分之一。扣除需要花在交通和日常必需品之後，我沒剩什麼錢可以理財。但我正努力把至少月薪的百分之十存起來。

回答範例 2

I'm still a student and my father gives me pocket money that is just enough for me to spend on my daily necessities. I spend most of it on food, drinks and transport. I hardly have anything left to buy more things I like. In the future, I hope I can make some investments if I have some money left every month.

我還是個學生，我父親給我的零花錢只夠我生活必需的開銷。我把大部分錢花在食物、飲料和交通上。我幾乎沒有剩下的錢可以買更多我喜歡的東西。以後如果每個月還有點錢，我希望可以做一些投資。

關鍵字詞

rent n. 租金　**take up** phr. 佔了⋯（多少分量或比例）　**expense** n. 花費 **account for** phr. 佔了⋯（多少分量或比例）　**transport** n. 交通，運輸　**daily necessities** n. 日常必需品　**money management** n. 理財　**monthly salary** n. 月薪　**pocket money** n. 零用錢　**investment** n. 投資

延伸學習

「花費」的英文可以用 spend 這個動詞，它的受詞可以是「金錢」或「時間」，但要注意的是，spend 的主詞必須是「人」，其慣用句型是「人 + spend + 金錢／時間 + 『on + 名詞』／『in + 動名詞』」。例如：

❶ She spent NT$1,200 on a new backpack.（她花了 NT$1200 買了一個新背包。）

❷ I spent an hour playing with the kids.（我花了一個小時和這些孩子們玩。）

4. **Do you often make a mistake? How would you apologize for it?**

   你經常犯錯嗎？你會如何表示歉意？

   答題解說

   所謂 "To err is human."（人都會犯錯。），所以如果回答說 "I can't answer this question because I never make a mistake." 或是 "I won't apologize for any mistake I've made."，是不切實際的回答！不過針對第一個問題，你可以回答 "Yes/Of course, I make a mistake sometimes."。接著在回答第二個問題（「道歉（apologize 或 make an apology）」的方式）之前，你可以舉例曾經「犯了什麼錯」，然後如何表示歉意！也許是「遲到（be late for...）」、「忘記某人

的生日（forget about someone's birthday）」、「誤會某人（misunderstand somone）」、「發脾氣（throw a temper）」…等，那至於道歉的方式也有許多種方式可以講，像是「親自打電話道歉（make a phone call in person）」、「傳訊息（send a texting message）」、「送禮物表達歉意（send a gift as an apology）」…等，都是可以派上用場的說法。

第 1 回
第 2 回
第 3 回
第 4 回
第 5 回
第 6 回
第 7 回
第 8 回
第 9 回
第 10 回

回答範例 1

Of course I do, but not very often. When I make a mistake, I would sincerely apologize for it by sending apologetic messages or emails to someone I've caused trouble to. If necessary, I'll make a phone call to them in person.
當然，我會犯錯，但不是很頻繁。當我犯錯時，我誠懇地表示歉意，方法是發送道歉訊息或電子郵件給讓我造成麻煩的人。若有必要，我還會親自打電話。

回答範例 2

Yes, sometimes I make some mistakes. Last Sunday was my wife's birthday and I forgot about it. This made her very angry. Then I went to the department store at once to buy a necklace for her. Plus, I wrote an apologetic card attached to this gift. She finally forgave me for that.
是的，有時我會犯一些錯誤。上週日是我太太的生日，而我忘了，這讓她很生氣。然後我馬上去百貨公司給她買了一條項鍊。另外，我在這份禮物附上一張道歉卡片。她終於原諒了我。

關鍵字詞

sincerely adv. 誠懇地　**apologize** v. 道歉　**apologetic** adj. 致歉的　**cause trouble to** phr. 給…（某人）帶來麻煩　**make a phone call to** phr. 打電話給…（某人）　**in person** phr. 親自　（be）**attached to** phr. 附在…　**forgive** v. 原諒

延伸學習

日常生活中若有發生一些小錯誤時，可以用 My fault!（我的錯！）來向對方表達歉意，這在現代美語口說中很常聽到，也就是 I admit (that) it's my fault 的意思。此外，你也可以用 It's my fault/mistake! 來表達歉意。而我們最常用來表達歉意的 sorry，則可用在不同程度的錯誤，比如當我們不小心撞到人，或較嚴重的錯誤，都可用 I'm sorry / Sorry about that.。另外，如果要指出對什麼事情感到抱歉時，可以用「for + 原因」。for 為介系詞，所以後面需加名詞或動名詞。例如：I'm sorry for being late.（抱歉，我遲到了。）

5. **Do you like to go traveling? Would you make a plan beforehand?**

你喜歡去旅行嗎？ 你會事先制定計劃嗎？

答題解說

本題看似兩個很簡單的 Yes/No 問題，但可別回答 Yes, I do. And Yes, I would make a plan beforehand. 這樣兩句簡單的回答就結束了。其實本題主要是希望你回答「如何計劃旅行」，題目的 beforehand 就是 in advance（事先）的意思。當然，有些人確實出遊不帶計畫，走馬看花也很開心，那也可以如實說明。總之，請記住，1-5 題是 15 秒的答題時間喔！

回答範例 1

Yes, I like to go traveling, especially with some good friends. I would drive, so I always make a wonderful trip plan in advance. I would also go online to look for popular tourist attractions and make a record of the best routes.

是的，我喜歡去旅行，尤其是和一些好朋友一起去。我會開車，所以我總是會事先擬定一個美好的旅行計畫。我也會上網尋找熱門旅遊景點，並記錄最佳行進路線。

回答範例 2

Sure, I like to travel, but I don't like to travel on weekends or holidays because most popular spots are always terribly crowed. Besides, the accommodation fees are higher. I usually plan to take one or two weekdays off and go on a domestic trip by train, so that I can enjoy a more carefree and "higher-quality" trip.

當然，我喜歡旅行，但我不喜歡在週末假日去旅行，因為大多數熱門景點總是人潮爆滿。此外，住宿也比較貴。我通常計劃在工作日請假一兩天，搭火車國內旅行，這樣我就可以享受更無憂無慮和「更高品質」的旅行。

關鍵字詞

beforehand adv. 事先，提前（= **in advance**）　**go traveling** phr. 去旅行　**tourist attraction** n. 觀光景點　**route** n. 路線　**accommodation** n. 住宿　**take... day(s) off** phr. 請…（幾天）假　**domestic** adj. 國內的　**carefree** adj. 無拘束的　**higher-quality** adj. 高品質的

延伸學習

說到「旅行」的英文，**travel** 是意義最廣的，統稱各種旅行。例如 travel abroad（出國旅行）、travel alone（獨自旅行）、travel the world（環遊世界）…等。travel 除了當動詞，也可以當名詞。安排行程時需要準備的護照、機票等文件，英文是 travel documents，有時也必須找旅遊書 （travel books/guides），或請

旅行社的專員（travel agent）協助，還能參考旅遊部落客（travel bloggers）的意見。最後，旅遊保險（travel insurance）也很重要喔！**trip** 通常用於有明確目的地的旅遊。例如 We're taking a trip to southern Taiwan this summer.（我們今年夏天要去南臺灣旅行。）但如果還沒想到要去哪裡，那就需要 some trip inspiration（一些旅遊靈感、建議）了！還有一個字是 **tour**。tour 通常是觀光的旅遊行程（sightseeing tours），常見的套裝行程（package tour）是市區觀光（city tours），許多大城市都有免費的徒步觀光行程（free walking tours），喜歡單車遨遊就可以參加 bicycle tours（or cycling tours）。最後還有一個字是 **journey**。journey 常用於一趟行程，會和某些固定用詞一起，最常用於祝福對方旅途愉快：Have a safe journey！或 Have a pleasant journey！除此之外，journey 也很常用來表示長途旅行：I need to rest after this long journey.（長途旅行之後我需要休息。）這種 long journey 未必是時間長或距離長，也可能是旅程太辛苦而感到心累的 tiring journey（疲累的旅行）或 difficult journey（辛苦的旅行）。

6. **Are you satisfied with your appearance? Have you ever done anything to make a change?**

   你對自己的外表滿意嗎？你有沒有做過任何改變？

   答題解說

   每個人都自己的外表或多或少都覺得有需要改善的地方，比如身高（height）、胖瘦（fat, chubby, thin, skinny...）、髮型（hairstyle）、穿著（clothes/clothing）…等。如果你滿意自己的外表，或是不在乎他人的眼光（No worries about how others think of you），覺得「自然就是美」（Nature is beauty.），也可以如實說明。建議可以說一些比較正面的話，例如外觀並不是最重要的，要接受自己，對自己有信心之類的話。

   回答範例 1

   I guess everyone has their own strengths and weaknesses, whether in their characters or appearances, so I'm not dissatisfied with my look. Although I am not the best-looking person in the world, I don't see there's any need to improve my appearance. I think it is important to accept what you are and feel confident about ourselves.

   我想每個人都有其優缺點，無論是個性在或是外表方面，所以我並不會不滿意我的外表。雖然我不是世界上最好看的人，我也不認為有任何改善外表的必要。我認為接受自己原本的樣子，並對自己有信心是很重要的。

Not really. I wish I were taller and thinner. I think I am a little plump so I would like to lose some weight. I would also like to make my eyes bigger and my nose smaller. However, I haven't done anything to make a change, but I'm considering undertaking plastic surgery. I'm now trying hard to save some money and hope this dream can be fulfilled as soon as possible.

其實不是很滿意。我希望我可以再高一點，再瘦一點。我認為我有點發福，所以我想要減肥。我也想要把我的眼睛變大一點，鼻子變小一點。然而，我尚未開始著手去做任何改變，不過我正考慮做整形手術，而且我正努力存錢，希望可以盡早完成這個願望。

關鍵字詞

strength n. 優點，強項 **weakness** n. 缺點，弱點 **character** n. 個性 **appearance** n. 外貌 **dissatisfied** adj. 不滿意的 **best-looking** adj. 最好看的 **improve** v. 改善 **confident** adj. 有信心的 **plump** adj. 豐滿的，胖嘟嘟的 **lose weight** phr. 減重 **undertake** v. 進行 **plastic surgery** n. 整形手術 **fulfill** v. 實現

延伸學習

有哪些描述人物外貌特徵的形容詞可以使用呢？你如何用英文跟人介紹你或別人是什麼類型的人呢？以下例句可供參考：

❶ I am a sporty/athletic guy.（我是個運動型的男生。）

❷ She's sweet and approachable, just like a neighboring simple girl.（她很體貼又很有親和力，就像鄰家女孩一樣。）

另外，除了高矮（tall, short），胖瘦的說法還有：slim/slender（苗條的）、stubby/stocky（矮胖的）。下面還有一些用語也很實用喔！

average-looking / plain（長相平凡的）、muscular（有肌肉的）、smartly-dressed（穿著得體的）、well-dressed（穿得漂亮的）

7. **How long do you surf the Internet a day? What's your usual purpose of doing that?**

   你一天花多久的時間上網？你通常上網做什麼呢？

   答題解說

   現代人幾乎離不開智慧型手機，當然也離不開網路世界了，特別是許多年輕人，每天上網的時間可不短，即使很少用手機的人，也會使用電腦來上網，尤其一般上班族，在工作上更是離不開網路，因此本題應該是很好發揮的！不會有人回答

I don't surf the Internet. 或是 I don't go online to do anything. 吧！針對第一個題目（How long...?），你只要回答一個簡單的數字加上 hour(s) 即可。甚至你也可以說自己除了睡覺時間之外都在使用網路。而第二個題目 usual purpose 表示「通常的目的」，也就是問你「通常上網做什麼」。你可以從工作以及休閒兩個面向去說，例如發送電子郵件、找資料（search for / check out information）、視訊會議（video conference）、上網採購（go online to make purchases）或購物、訂房（book a room）、訂車票（book a ticket）、瀏覽新聞（browse the latest news stories）、玩網路遊戲（play online games）…等。因為本題給你 30 秒的時間答題，如果還有時間，可以再補充使用特定上網功能覺得其便利性以及應注意的事項等，千萬別說完兩句話就結束了。

回答範例 1

I spend about two hours on the Internet a day, primarily at work and occasionally at leisure. I often I use the Internet to check out the information I need for my assignments, or to enrich my common sense and knowledge. Besides, I like to chat with my friends on LINE or through the Meta messenger. Even though we live far away from each other, we still can meet by way of online video chat to keep in touch.

我每天花大約兩小時上網，主要是在上班時間，偶爾在休閒時也會上網。我經常使用網路查找工作任務上需要的資訊，或更加豐富自己的常識與知識。此外，我喜歡在 LINE 上或通過 Meta Messenger 與朋友聊天。 雖然我們相距很遠，但我們仍然可以透過線上視訊對談來保持聯繫。

回答範例 2

Actually I've never calculated the time I spend on the Internet a day... maybe six to eight hours a day. Oh. My! That seems too long and too crazy. I like to play online games with some of my good friends. Sometimes I forget to eat lunch or dinner when I do that. I think I need to be moderate in using the Internet.

其實我從來沒有算過自己一天花多少時間上網…也許一天六到八個小時。噢！我的天！ 似乎太久、太狂了。我喜歡和我的一些好朋友一起玩線上遊戲。有時我玩遊戲時會忘記吃午餐或晚餐。我想我需要節制使用網路了。

關鍵字詞

primarily adv. 主要地　**at work** phr. 在上班時　**occasionally** adv. 偶爾　**at leisure** phr. 在休閒時　**assignment** n. 作業，任務　**enrich** v. 使變得豐富　**common sense** n. 常識　**online video chat** n. 線上視訊對談　**keep in touch** phr. 保持聯繫　**calculate** v. 計算　**play online games** phr. 玩線上遊戲　**moderate** adj. 節制的

在這個網路發達以及智慧型手機日新月異的時代,人們雖然感受到便利性,但也承受了不可逆的衝擊。我們經常聽到所謂「低頭族」、「網路成癮」、「重度沉迷」等,來形容那些過度使用手機或網路的人。而關於「成癮」,在英文裡有幾種說法:

❶ -aholic:以 -aholic 為字尾的單字通常都有「癮」的意思,最常見的用法除了購物狂(shopaholic)之外,我們會稱酒鬼為 alcoholic,工作狂為 workaholic。

❷ -maniac:如果說以 -aholic 結尾的字是比較中性的,那 -maniac 這個字尾所代表的通常是較為極端的。例如,egomaniac(利己主義者;非常自我主義的人)、megalomaniac(自大狂)。

❸ addict:通常用於複合名詞。例如,一個人有毒癮,我們會說他是一個 drug addict;如果是每逢空檔就拿出手機來滑的人,他們就是 smartphone addict,也就是俗稱的「低頭族」。

8. **If you have the chance of studying/working abroad, would you take it? Why?**

   如果你有機會出國留學或工作,你會接受嗎? 為什麼?

   答題解說

   首先,題目中的 abroad(出國,在國外,相當於 overseas)一定要聽得出來是什麼意思,否則會答非所問喔!無論是主觀或客觀條件的考量,每個人對於這個問題回答的理由不盡相同。如果你嚮往到國外留學(study abroad)、出國深造(go abroad to study further),英文可以嚇嚇叫(more fluent in English),以及未來會有薪水更優的工作(a job with better pay),或是覺得想當個外派人員(expatriate),可以領比較多的薪水,也都可以如實說明,或者想待在國內(at home)念書或工作,也可以針對兩方面的優缺點去陳述。

   回答範例 1

   I think I'll take it. I have long wanted to work abroad, because I don't have a boyfriend now and my parents used to encourage me to do that. In addition, as an expat, I can earn an amount of salary at least double my present monthly salary. What's more, I can make use of my holidays to travel in that country. I love to interact with people from different cultures.

   我想我會接受的。我一直想要到國外去工作,因為我現在沒有男朋友,而我的父母也曾鼓勵我出國。此外,外派人員可以獲得比目前工作多出至少一倍的薪水。

再者，我可以利用假日在那個國家旅遊。我很喜歡跟來自不同文化的人們互動。

回答範例 2

Hmm... I'd have to think about that for a minute. Some of my friends are, indeed, eager to go to the U.S. to study further because they think they will definitely speak fluently in American English. But I wonder if I will get used to the food and the climate. I went to Europe for two weeks last year, and I missed Taiwan. I missed my family, my friends and all the things that I am familiar with back home. It's all right to go on a tour but I don't think I want to study abroad.

嗯…這我得稍微思考一下。我一些朋友確實非常渴望去美國深造，因為他們認為他們一定會說一口流利的美語。但我不知道我是否能習慣那裡的食物和氣候。我去年到歐洲兩個星期，結果我很想念台灣。我想念我的家人、朋友和所有我在家鄉熟悉的所有事物。去旅行是沒什麼問題，但是我不想要到國外念書。

關鍵字詞

encourage v. 鼓勵　**expat** n. 外派人員（＝ **expatriate**）　**monthly salary** n. 月薪　**make use of** phr. 利用…　**be eager to**-V phr. 渴望…　**speak fluently** phr. 說話流利　**wonder if** phr. 想知道是否…　**get used to** phr. 習慣於…　**be familiar with** phr. 熟悉…

延伸學習

abroad 和 overseas 都可以當副詞，表示「在／到國外」，所以「到海外出差」的英文是 "go abroad/overseas on business"。abroad 只能當副詞用，所以：
（X）I would like to find an abroad job.
（O）I would like to find a job abroad.
另外，abroad 之前雖不能用 in、to 之類的介系詞，但可以用介系詞 from，形成 from abroad（來自海外）的用法，這時 abroad 當名詞，是「異國、海外」的意思。如果要表示「在國內外」可以用 "at home and abroad"。例如：She is famous at home and abroad.（她聞名國內外。）

9. **How do you usually celebrate your birthday? What do you think is the best gift for your birthday?**

你通常如何慶祝你的生日？ 你認為最好的生日禮物是什麼？

答題解說

celebrate 是個英檢初級的單字，相信大部分考生都可以聽得出來，就算一時之間不太確定是哪個字，聽到 birthday 大概也知道是問你「如何過生日」（how to spend your birthday）」吧！每個人對於生日怎麼過的要求都不相同，也許是跟朋友出去一夜狂歡（a night of revelry）、跟家人吃一頓溫馨的晚餐（enjoy a dinner together among a very intimate atmosphere）、跟另一半來個浪漫的約會（have a romantic date with my better half）…等，但也別忘了還有第二個問題喔！生日禮物可以是個具體的東西，也可以是個抽象的狀態，也許是某人答應你的求婚（proposal）之類的事情。如果沒有特別想要什麼禮物，也可以說，只要是某人送的都喜歡，或是只要跟某人在一起，就是最美好的生日，所以這個題目的回答，你也可以特別提到「人」的部分。

回答範例 1

I consider my birthday the most important day of a year, and some of my close friends always remember it. They treat me to lunch or dinner in a fancy restaurant or hold a birthday party for me. We have a lot of fun. As for the birthday gift, I'm not really sure what I want or need. I never ask for a present directly because I think it is impolite. I will be happy with whatever my friends give me, even if it is just a card.

我把我的生日視為一年中最重要的日子，我一些親密的朋友總是記得這一天。他們請我在高檔餐廳吃午餐或晚餐，或者為我舉辦生日派對。 我們玩得很開心。至於生日禮物，我從來不直接向別人要禮物，因為我覺得這樣是不禮貌的。朋友給我任何東西我都會很開心，就算只是一張卡片。

回答範例 2

Basically, I don't think my birthday needs any special arrangement. I'm still single and I don't have a girlfriend. Sometimes my older sister will treat me to very delicious meals, or my father would send me a message of "Happy Birthday to you!" I think that's enough, because at least, there's somebody who always remember my birthday. And I think those are the best birthday gifts for me.

基本上，我覺得我的生日不需要什麼特別的安排。我還是單身，且沒有女朋友。有時候姐姐會請我吃一頓非常美味的餐點，或者爸爸會給我發送「祝你生日快樂！」的訊息，我想這就足夠了，因為至少，有人永遠記得我的生日。我認為這些是給我最好的生日禮物了。

關鍵字詞

treat sb. to sth. phr. 請某人…（吃飯等）　**fancy restaurant** n. 高檔餐廳　**ask for** phr. 要求　**impolite** adj. 不禮貌的　**be happy with** phr. 對…滿意　**arrangement** n. 安排　**single** adj. 單身的

延伸學習

有時候想要用英文祝福對方，卻發現詞不達意，或用字卡卡，不知道如何將中文

的原意更正確傳達嗎？當然，如何在祝福語中表達得體，也要視對象與你之間的關係來做恰當表達，以下這幾種句型搭配，不論是職場或是生活上，都能提升你在傳達祝福的層次！

❶ Wish you good wealth and prosperity!（恭喜發財！）

→這句話不僅過年期間可以派上用場，平時也可以表達「祝福好運到來／有個繁榮興旺的一年！」

❷ May all your wishes come true!（祝你心想事成！）

❸ All the best!（一切順利！）

❹ Wish you good health and happiness everyday.（祝您天天身體健康，幸福滿滿！）→ 這句話也適合用來對長輩說喔！

❺ Don't be afraid of moving forward. It's always good to do the impossible!（繼續前進，不必擔心。勇敢向不可能挑戰吧！）→ 年後也可能遇到轉職或者工作改變的情形，如果你的身邊剛好遇到這樣的人，別忘了替他打氣喔！

10. **Are you afraid of speaking to a foreigner? What did you talk about with him/her last time?**

你害怕和外國人說話嗎？你最近一次和他／她們聊了什麼？

答題解說

第一個是 Yes/No 的問題，只要從 "Yes, I'm (a little) afraid of speaking with a foreigner." 或 "No, I'm (definitely) not afraid of that." 等類似句子開始即可。對於「上一次／最近一次…」的問題，不必刻意去思考時間點，就先想好用 last year（去年），last month（上個月），last week（上個星期）或 a few days ago（幾天前）等特定的時間點來回答。如果真的有跟外國人交談過，可以大概說明談話的內容。不需要一五一十地陳述，只要大概描述一下即可，甚至可以自己編造劇情。如果從來沒跟外國人用英語交談，也不能只說 "I've never spoke to a foreigner." 就結束了，可以接著說，假設有一天遇到外國人你會怎麼做。事實上，台灣有許多外國人很會說中文，有時候你刻意跟他們說英文，如果你程度沒那麼好，他們也會覺得挺麻煩的，所以可能從頭到尾都是用中文交談，類似這樣的情況，也可以加以陳述，或者說希望自己有一天能夠讓外國人與自己用英文侃侃而談之類的話。

回答範例 1

Of course not! I always expect to chat with foreigners. Last week when I was on my way home, a foreigner walked to me and asked me how to get to an MRT station. I said "I'm now going to the MRT station. Please just follow me." Then we chatted about some funny things he encountered in Taiwan. He is from Australia, and he is here on a

第 1 回
第 2 回
第 3 回
第 4 回
第 5 回
第 6 回
第 7 回
第 8 回
第 9 回
第 10 回

student exchange program. We friended each other on LINE, and I guess we'll keep in touch.

當然不會！我一直都期望可以和外國人聊天。上週我在回家的路上時，一個外國人朝著我走來，並問我怎麼去捷運站。我說：「我現在正要去捷運站，請跟我走。」然後我們聊了聊他在台灣遇到的趣事。他來自澳洲，他來這裡參加交換生課程。我們彼此加為 LINE 好友，我想我們會保持聯繫。

回答範例 2

Umm... perhaps... Yes, I'm a bit afraid of speaking with a foreigner, though I have never spoken to one. Actually I hardly meet foreigners, but if I do, I would be too shy to talk with them. Besides, I don't think I speak so well enough in English. What if I misunderstand what they are saying and make a scene? Still, I hope I can be more courageous and confident one day, and make some friends with foreigners.

嗯…也許…是吧，我有點害怕和外國人說話，雖然我從來沒有和一個外國人交談過。其實我很少遇見外國人，即使遇見了，我也會害羞到不敢和他們說話。此外，我認為我的英文說得不夠好。萬一我誤解他們的意思，然後出了個洋相怎麼辦？不過，我還是希望自己有一天能更加勇敢且更有自信，並能多交一些外國朋友。

關鍵字詞

expect to-V phr. 期待…（做某事） **on one's way home** phr. 在某人回家的路上 **chat about** phr. 聊聊… **encounter** v. 遇到 **friend** v. 與…交朋友 **keep in touch** phr. 保持聯絡 **misunderstand** v. 誤會 **make a scene** phr. 出糗 **courageous** adj. 勇敢的 **confident** adj. 有自信的

延伸學習

遇到外國人，想表達在社群軟體（如 FB、LINE）上加對方為好友要怎麼說呢？可別說 "May I add friend with you?" 或是 "May I add you to my LINE?"，這都不是正確的說法喔！正確說法是：「add you on + 社群軟體名稱」，或是「add your + 社群軟體名稱」，例如：

❶ Can I add you on LINE / Facebook?（我可以加你的 LINE / Facebook 嗎？）
❷ Do you mind if I add your LINE / Facebook?
另外還有一種說法是，直接把 friend 當作動詞，表達「加好友」，例如：
Could I friend you on Facebook / LINE?
總之，社群軟體前面要用介系詞 on 喔！

第三部分 看圖敘述

T02P3.mp3

第1回
第2回
第3回
第4回
第5回
第6回
第7回
第8回
第9回
第10回

答題解說

根據題目的提示（什麼地方、在做什麼、為什麼在這地方），再加上自己的判斷與想像來發揮。以下針對提示的部分給您可以用到的字詞建議：

1. 照片裡的人在什麼地.方？

   你可以說 "in a fast food / fancy restaurant"（在一家速食／高檔餐廳內），或是 "in their house"（在他們家中）。但如果只是說「他們在室內」（They are indoors.）之類的，分數會打折扣喔！另外，你可以再補充白天（in the daytime）或晚上的時間。

2. 照片裡的人在做什麼？

   提到「人」的部分時，你可以先提到有多少人，以及他們可能的關係，並稍加描述特徵或其他重點。例如，你可以說 "There are three people chatting at a table."、"The man and the woman might be the parents of the little girl." 以及 "They are enjoying a relaxing afternoon."。

3. 照片裡的人為什麼會在那裡？

   可以從現場的餐桌（dinner table）、飲料（drinks）等判斷他們正在喝下午茶（afternoon tea）。接著你可以更深入說明，這是在一個假日的午後，他們正

在享受一個輕鬆的親子時光。或者如果你認為兩位成人可能是家長與老師的關係，也可以另作描述。

4. 如果尚有時間，請詳細描述圖片中的景物。

例如，從照片中的，你可以繼續補充說，The little girl seems to explain about something and the woman listens to her patiently.。至於照片中男子背對鏡頭，我們看不到他的表情，所以你可以自由發揮，你可以說：I can't see the man's facial expression, but I think he's also listening to the girl patiently.，或是 I think he's also worried about this girl。

回答範例

I guess this picture was taken in a restaurant. There are three people in this picture and they might be enjoying a relaxing afternoon. From what I see, the little girl looks a bit confused, or worried or unhappy. She seems to feel wronged and try to explain about something. The woman smiles and looks patient listening to the little girl's complaint. I can feel that she's the mother of this little girl and she takes her out to talk. She might want to help solve a problem. As for the man, I can't see his facial expression, but I think he's also patiently listening to the girl. He might be the father of the little girl, so both the parents of this little girl are very concerned about their kid. And first, they want to find a good place where the atmosphere is enjoyable. Then they are having drinks and making the girl relaxed, so she could pour out her heart to her parents. Remember, good communication is always a key to solving a difficult problem.

很明顯地，這張照片是在餐廳拍攝的。照片中這三個人可能正在享受輕鬆的下午茶時光。在我看來，小女孩看起來有點茫然，或憂心或不高興。她似乎有些委屈，想要解釋什麼。這位女子微笑著，耐心地聽著小女孩的訴苦。我能感覺到她是這個小女孩的媽媽，她帶她出來聊天。她可能想協助解決問題。至於這名男子，我看不到他的表情，但我想他也很耐心地聽著女孩的話。他可能是小女孩的父親，所以小女孩的父母都很關心他們的孩子。首先，他們想找一個氣氛愉快的好地方。然後他們喝著飲料，讓女孩放鬆下來，這樣她就可以向父母傾訴心聲。請記住，良好的溝通始終是解決難題的關鍵。

關鍵字詞

take a picture phr. 拍張照　**relaxing** adj. 令人放鬆的　**afternoon tea** n. 下午茶　**confused** adj. 感到困惑的　**worried** adj. 憂慮的　**wronged** adj. 受到委屈的　**patient** adj. 耐心地　**complaint** n. 抱怨　**facial expression** n. 面部表情　**be concerned about** phr. 關心　**atmosphere** n. 氣氛　**enjoyable** adj. 愉悅的　**pour out one's heart to sb**. phr. 像某人傾訴　**a key to + Ving** phr. …（做某事）的關鍵

第 1 回
第 2 回
第 3 回
第 4 回
第 5 回
第 6 回
第 7 回
第 8 回
第 9 回
第 10 回

延伸學習

這個大題的結尾，通常也可以用「Remember, 強調的重點」的句，讓整個敘述有一個令人印象深刻的結束。例如，如果遇到圖片意境要強調現代人需要適度休息，結尾可以加上 Remember, taking a break is for accomplishing a longer journey.（要記得，休息是為了走更長遠的路。）

3

GEPT
全民英檢

中級複試
中譯＋解析

Writing | 全民英檢中級寫作能力測驗

第一部分 中譯英

海倫下個月就大學畢業了。她大部分同學們都在準備考研究所，也有一些人正在找工作。另外，有些人準備出國深造，而有些男生準備去當兵，但她卻有別的計畫。海倫打算先到國外打工一年。她不僅能獲得寶貴的工作經驗，還能存到一筆錢。

答題解說

第一句的「大學畢業」可以用 graduate from college/university。因為時間是下個月，可以用未來式、未來進行式，或現在進行式都可以。第二句「準備考研究所」可以寫成 "prepare for the exams of graduate school"，「找工作」則是 "try to look for/hunt a job"，但別寫成 "are finding a job" 了，因為 find 是「（已經）找到了」的意思。第三句「出國深造」可以用 "study abroad" 或 "go abroad to study further" 表示，而「去當兵」則是 "serve in the army" 或是 " do the mandatory military service "。第四句打算（intend）和想要（want）、計畫（plan）的意思差不多，但是 intend 屬於高中的單字，正確運用 intend 會有加分效果，切記主詞 Helen 為第三人稱單數，因此動詞必須用單數。另外，overseas 和 abroad 都是「國外」的意思。到國外念書為 study overseas 或 study abroad。英翻中的其中一個挑戰是，不能從中文的字面意義直接翻譯成英文，「到國外打工一年」可以用 "spend one year working abroad"。最後一句「…不僅…還能…」可以用 not only... but (also) 這個句型，其中「獲得」也可以用 get 或 have，但是 experience（經驗）通常和 gain（取得）搭配，是比較好的表達方式。「寶貴的工作經驗」的表達中，用 valuable 比 precious（珍貴）更適合，因為 precious 比較適合用在形容稀少或難得的事物。save 加上介系詞 up 有「存錢」和「儲蓄」的意思，單純動詞 save 則是「省錢」的意思。

譯文範例

Helen will be graduating from university next month. Most of her classmates are preparing for the exams of graduate school, and some are trying to look for a job. Also, some are going to study abroad, and some guys are going to serve in the army, but she has other plans. Helen intends to spend one year working abroad first. She can not only gain valuable work experience but also save up a fortune.

延伸學習

not only...but also... 中文意思是指「不只…而且…」的意思，而且後面的 also，常常可以省略，這用法很多初學者也都知道了。不過，當 not only...but also... 的句型放在句首時，要特別注意的是：

❶ 句中的動詞，取決於 but also 之後的主詞。例如：Not only I but also Tom is a student.（不只我是個學生，湯姆也是。）

❷ not only 後面的主、動詞需倒裝。例如：Not only did he turn up late, he also forgot his books.（他不但遲到，還忘了帶書。）

第二部分　英文作文

提示

你聽過色彩心理學嗎？其實色彩可以反映出一個人的性格。喜歡什麼顏色，就表示有什麼樣的性格。例如，喜歡黃色的人比較外向；喜歡白色的人比較不接受妥協，且多是完美主義者。你喜歡什麼顏色呢？你覺得自己是什麼個性的人呢？

答題解說

本題主要針對顏色心理學的認知去發揮，當然，如果你不清楚喜歡什麼顏色代表什麼樣的個性，也沒關係。就直接回答喜歡的顏色，然後就當作自我介紹。重點在描述自己的「個性」喔！最後可以再補一句說，「不知道這樣的個性是否呼應色彩心理學呢？（I wonder if such personality traits correspond to color psychology.）」另外，個性有好的和不好的，盡量全面性地去陳述，才會取得較高的分數，千萬別扯太多不相關的（如家中排行、在哪裡工作、學歷…等），離題的話寫再多都會沒分數的。以下就針對人的個性（character / personality trait）提供一些常用的表達。

❶ 好的個性：brave（勇敢的）、broad-minded（寬宏大量的）、calm（冷靜的）、compassionate（有同情心的）、confident（自信的）、considerate（體貼的）、dependable（可靠的）、diligent（勤奮的）、down-to-earth（實際的）、dynamic（充滿活力的）、easy-going（好相處的）、energetic（有活力的）、enthusiastic（熱情的）、fearless（無畏的）、frank（坦然的）、friendly（友善的）、generous（慷慨的）、gentle（溫柔有禮的）、genuine（真誠的）、honest（誠實的）、independent（獨立的）、industrious（勤勞的）……

❷ 不好的個性：timid（怯懦的）、narrow-minded（心胸狹窄的）、impulsive（衝動的）、inconsiderate（不體諒人的）、undependable（不可靠的）、miser（小氣的）……

❸ 除了上述形容個性的形容詞，你還可以這麼說：
  例 1：I am always compassionate and pay more attention to others' feelings.（我總是有同情心，並重視他人的感受。）
  例 2：I'm such a genuine person that I'm well-liked among friends.（我是個相當真誠的人，所以我在朋友群內很受歡迎。）
  例 3：I'm usually resolute in my decision to do anything.（我總是對自己決定做任何事保持堅定的心。）
  例 4：I'm usually thoughtless in my decision to do anything. So I often regret doing something.（我通常不會想太多就做任何事了。所以常常會後悔做了一些事情。）

作文範例

Indeed, I heard of color psychology, but I have no idea what color reveals what kind of personality trait. My favorite color is blue. When I want to buy a cellphone, I chose a sky blue one. Besides, I have many blue jeans and suit jackets. Speaking of what kind of person I belong to, I think I am a very common person. I am normally kind, generous and sympathetic to people, even someone I don't know. I like to help others and will feel satisfied and happy if they fare well because of my help. Of course, I have defects in my character. For example, I am sometimes indecisive when I need to make an important choice. Sometimes I even do not know what I really want. So, does such a personality trait correspond to what the color blue represents?

的確，我聽說過色彩心理學，但我不知道什麼顏色揭示什麼樣的性格特徵。我最喜歡的顏色是藍色。我買手機的時候選了天藍色的。此外，我還有很多藍色牛仔褲和西裝外套。說起我屬於什麼樣的人，我覺得我是一個很普通的人。我通常對人友善、慷慨和富有同情心，即使是對於我不認識的人。我喜歡幫助別人，如果他們因為我的幫助而過得好，我會感到滿足和快樂。當然，我的性格是有缺陷的。例如，當我需要做出重要選擇時，我有時會優柔寡斷。有時我甚至不知道自己真正想要什麼。那麼，這樣的人格特質是否對符合藍色代表的個性呢？

延伸學習

色彩心理學（color psychology）是一門研究色調如何影響人類行為（the study of hues as a determinant of human behavior）的學科。顏色能夠喚起（arouse）人們某些情緒。顏色會影響不明顯的感知（perceptions that are not obvious），例如食物的味道。此外，紅色或橙色的藥丸一般被用作興奮劑（stimulant）。顏色影響個人的程度可能因年齡、性別和文化而不同（How color influences individuals may differ depending on age, gender, and culture.）。例如，異性戀男性認為紅色服裝可以增加對於異性的吸引力（more attractive to the opposite gender），而異性戀女性則認為男性的吸引力與穿何種顏色的衣服無關（irrelevant）。儘管不同文化背景下的顏色偏好（color preference）可能有所不同，但不同性別和種族對顏色的偏好可能相對統一（relatively uniform across gender and race）。

第 1 回
第 2 回
第 3 回
第 4 回
第 5 回
第 6 回
第 7 回
第 8 回
第 9 回
第 10 回

T03P1.mp3

第一部分 朗讀短文

Our boss wanted each of us to take a public-speaking training lesson. Both the management and staff members were asked to decide whether these lessons will be taken during normal working time or outside office hours. According to the result of our recent survey, almost 90% of employees wanted to take the training lesson during the normal working time. No more than 9% of them were willing to sacrifice their after-work hours.

****

In our company, we offer three different programs for employees who have young children. We have a day care center for infants from 3 months to 36 months. We also hire child-care staff to take care of them. In addition, we have a special sensory integration program for these young children. This will help them grow up well and improve the capability of their five senses. If any of you, new comers, need these services, please let me know at once so we can get you an application form.

答題解說

這是一段與上班族有關的小短文，用字遣詞都很平易近人，所以即使你還是學生，應該也都能看得懂。以下標有顏色的單字，請盡可能唸得比較響亮，以下出現「|」的地方，請稍作停頓，試著讓自己融入短文的情境中。最後，請注意字與字之間該連音的部分，像是 each of us、take a、members are、outside office、result of our、after-work hours、take care、help them、if any、of you、at once…。

Our boss wanted | each of us to | take a public-speaking training session. Both the management and staff members were | asked to decide | whether these courses will be taken | during normal working time or outside office hours. According to the result of our recent survey, | almost 90% of employees | wanted to take the training courses | during the normal working time. No more than 9% of them | were willing to sacrifice their after-work hours.

****

In our company, | we offer three different programs for employees | who have young children. We have a day care center for 3-month old infants | to kids of 3 years of age. We also hire child-care staff | to take care of them. In addition, we have a special sensory integration program for these young children. This will help them grow well | and improve the capability of their five senses. If any of you, new comers, need these services, please let me know at once | so we can get you an application form.

短文翻譯

我們的老闆希望我們每個人都要參加公眾演說的訓練課程。管理階層和一般員工都被要求決定這些課程要在正常上班時間還是在上班時間以外去進行。根據我們最近的調查結果，幾乎 90% 的員工都希望在正常上班時間進行訓練課程。只有不到 9% 的人願意犧牲他們下班後的時間。

****

在我們公司，我們為有幼兒的員工提供三種不同的方案。我們為三個月到三十六個月大的嬰幼兒提供一個日間照護中心，我們也聘雇幼保人員來照護他們。此外，我們還為這些年幼的孩子準備專業的感覺統合課程。這將幫助他們健康成長並提高他們的五感能力。如果各位新進人員有任何人需要這些服務，請立刻告知我，好讓我們能提供您申請表。

關鍵字詞

public-speaking adj. 公眾演說的　**session** n. 課程　**management** n. 管理階層
staff member n. 職員　**take a course** phr. 上課　**working time** n. 工作時間
office hour n. 上班時間　**sacrifice** v. 犧牲　**after-work** adj. 下班後的　**day care center** n. 照護中心　**infant** n. 嬰兒　**child-care staff** n. 幼保人員
sensory integration n. 感覺統合　**improve** v. 提升　**capability** n. 能力
five senses n. 五官　**application form** n. 申請表

第二部分 回答問題

T03P2.mp3

1. **Your cousin Mary is a successful Youtuber. Ask her some questions about her job.**

   你的表妹瑪麗是一位成功的 **Youtuber**。問問她一些關於她工作上的問題。

   答題解說

   本題為「問問題」的題型，答題時間 15 秒，所以您必須至少用 3-4 句話來結束這一題。可以從 "I heard that..." 或 "某人 + told me that..." 開始第一句。以下是接下來建議可以用來提問說的話：

   ❶ I'm curious about your income.（我對你的收入很好奇。）/ How could you make a lot of money by making videos?（你如何靠拍影片賺很多錢呢？）→ by 後面要用 V-ing 喔！這裡也可以接 working as a Youtuber 之類的。

   ❷ I'd like to know more about your job...（我想對你的工作有更多的認識…）

   ❸ How do you advertise yourself? Are you busy all the time?（你如何為自己打廣告？你總是很忙嗎？）

   ❹ You work alone or you have a good partner?（你獨自工作，還是你有個好夥伴？）

   回答範例 1

   I heard that you've made a lot of money by making videos. That's fantastic! I'm very curious about your income. How much do you make a month on average over the past year? By the way, how do you advertise yourself?
   我聽說你藉由拍攝影片賺了很多錢。這太妙了！我很好奇你的收入。過去一年來你每個月月平均賺了多少錢？對了，你如何為自己打廣告呢？

   回答範例 2

   Yesterday auntie told me that you work as a part-time Youtuber, and that helps you make more money. Wow! That's cool. I'd like to know more about this job. You work alone or you have a good partner? What do you usually talk about in your videos?
   昨天姑姑告訴我，你兼差做 Youtuber，而且幫助你多賺了不少錢。哇噢！這太酷了。我想更加了解這工作。你一個人做還是有個好夥伴？你通常在你的影片中談論什麼？

   關鍵字詞

   make a video phr. 拍片　**fantastic** adj. 神奇的，美好的　**be curious about** phr. 對…感到好奇　**income** n. 收入　**on average** phr. 平均來說　**advertise** v. 宣

傳，廣告　**alone** adv. 獨自　**partner** n. 夥伴

延伸學習

所謂「成功的 youtuber」即俗稱的「網紅」、「網路名人」，英文通稱為 Internet celebrity。另外還有一種說法叫作 KOL（key opinion leader），中文譯為「關鍵意見領袖」。KOL 指在特定領域或群眾中具有發言權及影響力的人，所以跟一般網紅是有些差異的，他們也會收到許多與其理念相同的網友支持。許多廠牌會與他們所認定符合品牌形象的 KOL 進行合作。另外還有個比較正規的名詞是 influencer（影響者），在歐美國家較常被使用，即在網路上可以具有影響力的人。所以衍生出「-influencer」的後綴字，例如 teenfluencer 是指「具有影響力的青少年」，或者「對青少年具有影響力的人」，而 fitfluencer 是指「健身或健康飲食相關，在網路上有影響力的人」。

2. **Do you think one needs talent for painting? Why or why not?**

你認為繪畫需要天賦嗎？為什麼或為什麼不？

答題解說

本題除了要先回答 Yes/No 之外，主要答題重點是：Why do you think one needs talent for painting? 或是 Why don't you think one needs talent for painting?。這是個見仁見智的問題，因為憑天賦（depend on talents）的反面，就是需要努力（need to pay effort），接著可以進一步說明，有些人確實天生對於某種活動特別行（be inherently good at...），然後再以賽跑、游泳、開車、唱歌…等例子補強自己的論點。如果是認為不需要天賦，可以朝「熟能生巧（Practice makes perfect.）」的方向去寫，只要是很有興趣，願意付出努力和時間（be highly interested and willing to spend time and pay effort）去熟練，都有可能出類拔萃（outstanding），不一定需要天賦。另外，你也可以說，繪畫可以只是一種嗜好、興趣的活動 one of your hobbies or interests，不需要天生就具有這樣的能力。

回答範例 1

No, I don't think you need talent for painting. Just like driving, cooking or swimming, painting can be one of your hobbies. If you're willing to spend time and pay effort to do it, your works of painting can look outstanding, and people might think you have the talent for painting.

不，我不認為繪畫需要天賦。就像開車、烹飪或游泳一樣，繪畫可以成為你的嗜好之一。如果你願意花時間並付出努力去做，你的繪畫作品也可能出類拔萃，也許大家會認為你有繪畫的天賦。

No, I don't think painting requires talent. All you need is to prepare some painting materials, and you can start painting. Even though you've never learned how to paint, you can still paint whatever you like whether you are professional or not.

不，我不認為繪畫需要天賦。你所需要的只是準備繪畫材料，你就可以開始畫畫了。即使你從來沒有學過繪畫的方法，不管你是否專業，你仍然可以畫出任何你喜歡的人事物。

回答範例 3

Yes, I think you need talent for painting or drawing. To paint well, you require certain skills, sources of inspiration, and the abilities to cool down and concentrate on something. If you're a highly talented painter, you probably don't have to spend much time practicing before signing up for a painting contest.

是的，我認為繪畫或素描需要天賦。要畫得好，你必須有一定的技能、靈感來源以及冷靜下來並專注於某事的能力。如果你是一位很有天賦的畫家，你可能不需要花太多時間練習就可以報名參加繪畫比賽了。

關鍵字詞

talent n. 天賦　**hobby** n. 嗜好　**pay effort to**-V phr. 付出努力…（去做某事）**work** n. 作品　**outstanding** adj. 卓越的　**material** n. 材料　**professional** adj. 專業的　**inspiration** n. 靈感　**cool down** phr. 冷靜下來　**concentrate on** phr. 專注於…　**sign up for** phr. 報名參加

延伸學習

說到畫畫，你的記憶庫除了 draw、paint 以外，還有什麼字呢？其實不同的畫法有不同的字喔

❶ draw 這個字非常通用，表示用筆去畫出圖案或形狀，所以畫一張圖可以說 draw a picture，畫一條線可以說 draw a line。

❷ paint 這個字就不是用鉛筆類的材料畫囉，它是指「用顏料上色、著色」，所以它也有「油漆」的意思。例如：paint the wall white（把牆漆成白色）

❸ doodle：不是認真的，而是隨手撇一撇的畫。例如：I doodled on my desk while the teacher was talking.（老師在講話的時候我在我的桌子上亂畫。）

❹ sketch：素描。當你畫的是那種靜物素描、或是寫生的畫，就可以用這個字。

❺ graffiti：塗鴉。指公共場合牆壁上那種大範圍的塗鴉。例如：There is graffiti all around the neighborhood.（在這社區附近到處都有塗鴉。）

3. **Have you ever watched the sunrise or sunset? Where did this experience take place?**

你看過日出或日落嗎？這種體驗是在哪發生的？

答題解說

sunrise 和 sunset 屬於英檢中級單字，如果一時之間聽不出來，總該聽得出 watch 和 sun 吧！如此應該也可以猜出題目要問你什麼。如果真的沒有實際看過，可以說明原因，或者至少在電視或新聞媒體上聽過「新的一年第一道曙光（the new year's first sunrise）」之類的報導或照片吧！接著第二個問題問你 where，記得要說出「在什麼地方」喔！當然，你可以多補充什麼時候，或是和什麼人去看的，並對日出的畫面加以形容。沒看過的話也沒關係，可直接說沒看過，並說明原因，以及未來希望有機會可以有這樣的體驗。

回答範例 1

Yes, I have. Last summer I went to Alishan with my friends. We went watch the sunrise early in the very early morning. Its beauty was really beyond words. Though I had to get up early to enjoy the view, I think it was worth the effort. I was glad I didn't miss it. We took a lot of amazing pictures.

是的，我有看過。去年夏天我跟朋友去了阿里山。我們一大早就去看日出。日出的美簡直無法用文字形容。雖然我為了欣賞此景而必須早起，但我認為努力是值得的。我很高興我沒有錯過日出。我們拍了很多很棒的照片。

回答範例 2

No, I have never watched the sunrise, because I am too lazy to get up so early in very early morning, though I think the sunrise is very beautiful. However, I used to see the sunset. On the last day of last year, I went on a trip to Tamshui with some friends. We sat together at the beach and saw some clouds change colors, and it felt very romantic.

不，我沒看過日出，因為我太懶了，所以沒辦法太早起，雖然我認為日出非常美。不過，我有看過日落。去年的最後一天，我和幾個朋友去淡水玩。我們再沙灘上坐在一起且看到一些雲朵的顏色變換，而且有非常浪漫的感覺。

關鍵字詞

sunrise n. 日出　**sunset** n. 日落　**take place** phr. 發生　**beyond words** phr. 難以言喻　**worth the effort** phr. 值得付出　**amazing** adj. 令人驚奇的　**romantic** adj. 浪漫的

英文裡的「風景」主要有 scenery、view、sight、vision、spectacle，但表達「風景」意思最直接的字是 scenery，和它很像的一個字是 scene：

❶ scene 指某個事件發生的場景，像「犯罪現場」是 crime scene ；抽象名詞是 scenery，意思是「風景，景色」。例如：

The police are searching the crime scene.（警方正在搜查犯罪現場。）

The scenery really was beautiful.（風景真是美。）

❷ spectacle 主要是指「壯觀的風景」，也可以引申為讓人大開眼界或驚嚇的場面。例如：A magnificent spectacle spread itself out before the eyes of the travelers.（映入旅行者們眼廉的是一幅多麼美妙的圖畫呀！）

❸ view 這個字是指從一個特定的視點看到的美景。例如：There's a fine view of the lake from our hotel window.（從我們旅館的窗口可以看到湖的美麗風光。）

❹ sight 和 view 一樣，是眼睛看到的景象。但和 view 不同的是，sight 看到的不一定都是美景，也可能是可怕的景象。例如：

The Great Wall is one of the sights of the world.（長城是世界名勝之一。）

The girl dreaded the sight of snakes.（那女孩害怕看到蛇。）

❺ landscape 裡藏著一個字：land（陸地），原指田園部落，也可以指造景、山水畫、風景畫。例如：From the hill he looked down on the peaceful landscape.（他站在山上眺望下面的寧靜景色。）

4. **Have you ever talked to any kind of animal? If so, what did you say?**

你曾經和任何一種動物說話過嗎？ 如果是，你說了什麼？

答題解說

現在很多人都有養寵物，所以也一定經常和自己的寵物對話，即使你覺得牠不一定聽得懂。那如果你沒有養寵物，也可能接觸過朋友或親友養的寵物，並和牠們有過對話，或者你也可以自己憑空想像，自己遇到一隻狗、貓或鸚鵡時，你會和牠們說什麼。甚至假如你真的沒和接觸過的動物說過任何話，你也可以說 I don't think animals can understand human languages, so I've never tried to converse with them.（我不認為動物能聽懂人類的語言，所以我從未嘗試過與牠們對話。）

回答範例 1

Yes, I often talked to my pet dog. To me, he's just like my kid. I would say to him, "Honey, come here. Here's your lunch box." Before he sleeps at night, I would say,

"Good night, good boy. Have a good dream." Sometimes I believe he understands what I say. I mean it.

是的，我經常和我的寵物狗說話。對我來說，他就像我的孩子一樣。我會對他說，「親愛的，過來這。這是你的午餐便當。」在他晚上睡覺之前，我會說，「晚安，好孩子。祝你有個好夢。」有時候我相信他聽得懂我說的話。我是說真的。

回答範例 2

No, I haven't talked to any animal. Also, I don't keep a pet. Actually, I don't think they can understand what I say, even a single word. However, I believe they can learn about human body languages. For example, if you clap your hands and stretch your both arms in front of your pet dog, it might run into your embrace.

不，我沒有和任何動物交談過。而且，我不養寵物。事實上，我不認為他們聽得懂我說的話，即使只是一個字。不過，我相信他們可以看懂人類的肢體語言。例如，如果你在你的寵物狗面前拍手及伸展雙臂，牠可能會跑到你的懷裡。

關鍵字詞

pet dog n. 寵物狗　**mean it** phr. 說真的　**keep a pet** phr. 養寵物　**single** adj. 單一的　**body language** n. 肢體語言　**clap one's hands** phr. 拍手　**stretch** v. 伸展　**embrace** n. 懷抱

延伸學習

一起來學習幾個和貓狗相關的英文詞彙與慣用語吧！

❶ top dog 與 underdog：top dog 的意思是「贏家，優勝者」或是「有權勢的人」。相反地，underdog 則是「在比賽中不被看好的一方」或是「弱者，弱勢群體」。

❷ copycat 是個負面的字彙，表示缺乏主見的「模仿者，抄襲者」。

❸ All bark and no bite. → bark 的意思是「吠叫」、bite 意思是「咬」，all bark and no bite 的意思是「雷聲大雨點小」，形容喜歡威脅或誇耀卻不會實際做出行動。

❹ Every dog has its day. → 這句話有正面意義，照字面翻譯是「每隻狗都有出頭的一天」，也就是我們所謂的「風水輪流轉。」

5. **Do you get along with your colleagues or classmates? Why or why not?**

你和同事或是同學相處得好嗎？為什麼呢？

答題解說

首先，get along 是「相處融洽，和睦相處」的意思，這個片語一定要知道意

思！那麼 get along with someone 就是「相處得好」，有時候會在 along 後面再加上 well，也是同樣的意思。對於本題的回答，相信一般都會往正面的方向去回答，否則你接下來可能要講一堆抱怨的話了。不過當然，如果真的和周遭的人相處得不好，要如實說明也可以。還有一種答案是比較「中性」的，也就是說，你可以用 "It depends."（看情況。）開頭，接著可以針對和自己合得來，以及合不來的人相處時的差異做說明。

回答範例 1

Yes, I get along well with my colleagues. Since it's hard to avoid interacting with people, I need to learn to get along well with them. Though sometimes I might have argument with my superior, I would calm down and try to communicate patiently. In fact, I always try to respect everyone.

是的，我和同事相處得很好。因為我們很難避免與他人互動，我必須學著與他人相處融洽。雖然有時會和主管有點爭論，但我會靜下心來耐心溝通。事實上，我總是試著尊重每一個人。

回答範例 2

It depends, to tell the truth. I get along not badly with most of my classmates. Honestly, I avoid talking with those often disagree with me. I choose to make friends with people who have something in common with me, such as interests, hobbies or value systems.

說實話，這要看狀況。我和我的大多數同學都相處得還不錯。老實說，我避免與經常和我唱反調的人說話。我選擇和我有共同點的人交朋友，例如興趣、嗜好或價值觀等方面。

關鍵字詞

get along（**well**）**with** phr. 與…（某人）相處融洽　**colleague** n. 同事　**avoid** v. 避免（＋ **Ving**）　**interact with** phr. 與…（某人）互動　**argument** n. 爭論　**superior** n. 上司，主管　**calm down** phr. 冷靜下來　**communicate** v. 溝通　**patiently** adv. 耐性地　**honestly** adv. 老實說　**disagree with** phr. 不同意　**have something in common** phr. 有共同點　**value system** n. 價值觀

延伸學習

「相處融洽」的說法，一般最常見的說法是 get along，後面加上「with 某人」時，表示「與某人相處得好」。另外，get along 還有「進行，過活」的意思，主詞必須是「人」，後面可以接「with + 事物」，表示「進行某項工作或任務。例如：

❶ I got along much better in my new job.（我在新工作上做得還不錯。）

❷ How are you <u>getting along with</u> your schoolwork?（你的學校功課做得如何了？）

6. What if you find something wrong with your friend's clothes or appearance? Would you tell them or not?

如果你發現朋友的穿著或外貌不對勁，你會怎麼辦？ 你告訴他們嗎？

答題解說

What if...? 是很常見的問句型片語，意思是「萬一…怎麼辦？」當我們發現朋友、同學或同事臉臭臭的（pull a long face）、有黑眼圈（dark circles around one's eyes），或是穿著不得體（improperly dressed）…等情況，其實會不會去告訴對方，主要還是看彼此近來的關係（recent relationship），或是當下的心情（in a good/bad mood）等，你也可以說 I tend not to tell them anything like that, because I'm afraid they might be angry with me.（我傾向於不告訴他們這類事情，因為我擔心他們會生我的氣。）

回答範例 1

I think I would tell them about that, because I don't want them to make a fool of themselves in public. They might even be laughed at, ridiculed or cause a bit of scandal. For example, if they have dark circles around their eyes, they look tired. So I'll go further to show more concern with them. Appearance is important both at work and at leisure. It also affects one's impression on you. In brief, I'm used to talking turkey.

我想我會告訴他們，因為我不想看到他們出洋相。他們甚至可能被笑、被嘲弄或引來異樣眼光。 例如，如果他們的眼睛周圍有黑眼圈，他們看起來很疲倦。所以我會更進一步地表現出對他們的更多關注。外表在工作和休閒時都很重要。它也會影響別人對你的印象。簡單說，我習慣有話直說。

回答範例 2

I think I may not tell them about that. Everyone has their own personal aesthetic that sometimes should not be challenged by others. If I do that, they could think I am instructing them something, and this may spoil mutual relationship. For example, people have different tastes in clothes. If I question them, they might be upset and we even have a dispute.

我想我可能不會跟他們說。每個人都有自己的審美觀，有時候不容別人質疑。如果我那麼做，他們可能會覺得我在指導他們什麼事，且可能壞了彼此的關係。比方說，每個人對於服裝的品味不同。如果我質疑它們，他們可能會不高興，甚至我們可能會起爭執。

第1回
第2回
第3回
第4回
第5回
第6回
第7回
第8回
第9回
第10回

appearance n. 外表　**make a fool of** phr. 愚弄…（某人）　**laugh at** phr. 嘲笑　**ridicule** v. 挪揄，戲弄　**cause a bit of scandal** phr. 引來異樣眼光　**dark circle** n. 黑眼圈　**impression on...** phr. 對…的印象　**talk turkey** phr. 有話直說　**aesthetic** n. 審美觀　**challenge** v. 挑戰　**spoil** v. 破壞　**mutual** adj. 相互的　**question** v. 質疑　**dispute** n. 爭吵

延伸學習

在英文裡，有一些關於外表如何的用語，如果中文直譯的話，可能和原本的英文意思完全不同喔！例如：

❶ long face → 這不是「臉長」。long face 是在說一個人愁眉苦臉、像垮下來一樣，板著一張臉就是 pull a long face，動詞可以用 pull 或 wear。

❷ big mouth → 這不是「嘴巴很大」。不過和中文俗稱「大嘴巴 = 保守不住秘密」是一樣的。如果是形容五官特徵的「大嘴巴」，可以用 wide mouth。

❸ gray/grey hair → 這就是俗稱的「白頭髮」，可不是 white hair 喔！例如：I started to turn grey in my mid-forties.（我從 40 多歲開始長白頭髮。）

❹ black eyes → 如果你關心對方怎麼有「黑眼圈」時，可別說 "What's the matter with your black eyes?" 喔！對方會以為「你怎麼說我被揍了」呢！

7. **Do you buy things advertised on the Internet or in the media? Why or why not?**

   您會看到網路或媒體上的廣告而去買東西嗎？為什麼？

答題解說

無論是網路、電子媒體（electronic media）或平面媒體（print media）上，我們經常會看到各式各樣引人注目的廣告，有些人會被廣告吸引（be attracted to certain ads）而去買了東西，但有些人是「貨比三家不吃虧」（Shop around and you won't lose money.），他們會找網路商店比價、看網路評論或詢問朋友的意見。無論如何，本題在構思上算是好發揮的，只是仍要注意避免去使用自己沒把握的字詞、用語。

回答範例 1

Yes, I make purchases because of being attracted to some astonishing ads, but not very often. Sometimes I would ask for advice from family members or friends, because I feel some ads advertised online and on TV are too exaggerated to believe.

是的，我會因為受到一些驚人廣告的吸引而做出購物的行為，不過不會很常。有時我會詢問家人或朋友的意見，因為我覺得有些網路上及電視上的廣告太誇張，

令人難以置信。

第1回 第2回 第3回 第4回 第5回 第6回 第7回 第8回 第9回 第10回

回答範例 2

Actually I'm seldom attracted by any ads or commercials on the Internet or on TV, because I think many of them tend to boast of how good their products are. Besides, I can't touch or try the products I want to purchase, and I don't know whether they are authentic or fake. In short, I prefer to go to a physical store and try to make a bargain.

事實上，我很少被網路或電視上的任何廣告或商業廣告所吸引，因為我認為許多廣告都偏向於吹噓其產品有多好。此外，你沒辦法觸摸到或試用想要購買的產品，也不知道它們是真品還是假貨。總之，我比較喜歡去實體商店看，並且會試著討價還價。

關鍵字詞

advertise v. 打廣告，宣傳　**be attracted to** phr. 被…吸引　**exaggerated** adj. 誇大的　**commercial** n. 商業廣告　**boast of** phr. 吹噓　**authentic** adj. 真實的　**fake** adj. 假冒的　**physical store** n. 實體店　**make a bargain** phr. 討價還價，拿到好價錢

延伸學習

關於「詐騙」，主要有兩個字：**fraud** 和 **scam**。廣義上，兩者算是同義字，不過它們還是有些微的差異，scam 通常規模較小，主要是涉及金錢的詐欺；而 fraud 的範圍更廣，包含金錢、藝術品、身分個資等的偽造。其他相關用詞還有：scammer（詐騙份子）、get scammed、（被騙了）、online fraud（網路詐騙）、fall victim to the scams（成為詐騙受害者）、scam/fraud syndicate（詐騙集團）、gambling and gaming business（博弈產業）、pay ransom（支付贖金）、con（騙局）、a con artist（金光黨騙子）。

8. **Have you ever participated in a competition? Were you satisfied with the outcomes?**

   你參加過任何比賽嗎？你是否滿意比賽結果？

   答題解說

   雖然本題看起來是兩個 Yes/No 的問題，但別忘了答題時間是 30 秒，千萬別答個兩句就停下來了。比賽的項目，不一定要非常正式的（formal/official），你也可以說去籃球場跟幾個不認識的朋友分成幾個隊伍，一起打個三對三的籃球比賽（three-on-three basketball game）之類的。另外，盡量還是想想比較不會說錯的詞彙，像是籃球賽、棒球賽、演講、歌唱、寫作…等，這類比較好講的比賽來

回答。接著對於「是否滿意比賽結果」的回答，除了 Yes/No, ... 之外，你繼續說明當初賽後心情、或（未）得獎的心得，期勉自己未來超越自我或繼續努力等。如果從來沒有參加過任何比賽，也想不出什麼比賽，也可以直接陳述，並說明沒參加過的原因，或未來希望參加什麼樣的比賽。

回答範例 1

Yes, I took part in a speech competition when I was in junior high school. I still remember what I talked about that day. My teacher spent a lot of time training me. I kept repeating the same speech for at least a hundred times. Though I was nervous, I managed to finish it, and I got second place. I was satisfied with the outcome. I hope I can win the first prize in a similar contest in the future.

是的，我在國中時參加過演講比賽。我還記得我那天說了什麼。我的老師花了很多時間訓練我。我一直重複一樣的演說至少一百次。雖然我很緊張，我還是完成了演講，並得到第二名。我對比賽結果很滿意。我希望以後能在類似的比賽中獲得第一名。

回答範例 2

I haven't competed in an official game or contest, but I remember I took part in a puzzle game when I was a student. Maybe that's the only contest I've ever participated in. I need to admit I am a shy person who tends to be nervous, so I don't think I am up to a formal competition. I hope one day I will overcome my fear and have the courage to take part in an official contest.

我沒有參加過正式的比賽或競賽，但我記得我在學生時代參加過一場益智遊戲。也許那是我參加過的唯一一場比賽。我必須承認我是個害羞且容易緊張的人，所以我覺得我無法承受正式的比賽。我希望有一天我能克服恐懼，並能夠有勇氣參加一場正式的比賽。

關鍵字詞

participate in phr. 參加　**competition** n. 比賽，競賽　**be satisfied with** phr. 對…感到滿意　**outcome** n. 結果　**nervous** adj. 緊張的　**manage to-V** phr. 設法做到　**compete** v. 比賽，爭取　**official** adj. 官方的，正式的　**admit** v. 承認　**be up to** phr. 有…的資格　**formal** adj. 正式的　**have the courage to-V** phr. 有…（做某事）的勇氣

延伸學習

英文裡的「比賽」主要有 competition、contest、race 以及 match 四個。competition 通常指「有組織的比賽活動，由參與者試圖擊敗他人而獲勝的比賽

系列」。contest 單純指「看誰在某一方面的能力或特點最優秀的比賽」，或者比的是「誰的能力最強或特點最出色」，尤其是會給優勝者發獎品的比賽。race 是指「由選手爭相最快完成」的競賽，所以比的是「速度」或「時間」；最後是 match，指「在特定體育項目中，由兩人或兩隊相互競爭決出勝負的單一場比賽」，例如，a wrestling match（一場摔跤賽）、a baseball match（一場棒球賽）

9. **What do you think is most important in your life? Why?**

你認為你生命中最重要的是什麼？為什麼？

答題解說

要想出「生命中最重要的」應該不是很困難的事，你可以說錢是最重要的，然後再補上一句諺語「有錢能使鬼推磨（Money talks.）」等，或是某人對你來說是最重要的，或是某物，這可以是具體的東西，也可以是抽象的概念，如快樂（happiness）、愛情（love）、親情（family love）、身體健康（health）…等。或者，你可以說你養的阿狗阿貓，是你唯一的陪伴，也是最重要的，都可以用來陳述與說明。接著你可以拿別的東西來做比較，說明為什麼他是最重要的。但還是提醒一點，用字遣詞上如果沒把握，還是找個適合自己發揮的主題吧！

回答範例 1

Happiness, or spiritual satisfaction, for me, is the most important thing in my life. I think if you always feel happy and satisfied with what you have already had, you won't be troubled in persistent pursuit of something, such as money or fame, which, can only bring you temporary happiness. If you can't get more, you might be depressed or upset for a long period of time. And that may cause another trouble to your work or relationship. Lastly, I'd like to emphasize that, happiness is a matter of choice. It always depends on how you look at things.

快樂，或者說精神上的滿足，對我來說，是我生命中最重要的事情。我想如果你總是對你已經擁有的感到快樂和滿足，你就不會因為不斷追求金錢或名聲等，那些只能帶給你短暫快樂的東西感到苦惱。如果你無法得到更多，你可能有很長一段時間內感到沮喪或心煩意亂。而這可能會給你的工作或人際關係帶來另一個麻煩。最後，我想強調的是，快樂是一種選擇。它永遠取決於你如何看待事物。

回答範例 2

I think money, definitely, is most important in my life, at least at present! I'm already 40 years old and still unmarried. I don't have a girlfriend. In fact, my monthly salary and bank savings can't allow me to get married and start a family. I hope I can win the lottery or make an unexpected fortune in the near future. My parents want to be grandparents soon! So, as an old saying goes, "Money isn't everything, but without money, everything is nothing," I think I need to make more money to live up to my parents' expectation.

當然了，我認金錢，是我生命中最重要的，至少目前如此！我已經 40 歲了，還沒有結婚。我沒有女朋友。事實上，我每個月的薪水和銀行存款都不足以讓我結婚成家。我希望在不久的將來能中樂透或發個意外之財 我的父母想盡快抱孫子！所以，如一句俗話說，「錢不是萬能的，但沒有錢是萬萬不能。」我想我必須賺更多的錢才能不辜負父母的期望。

關鍵字詞

spiritual adj. 精神上的　**satisfaction** n. 滿足（感）　**persistent** adj. 持續的 **in pursuit of** phr. 追求⋯　**fame** n. 名聲　**temporary** adj. 暫時的　**depressed** adj. 沮喪的　**emphasize** v. 強調　**at present** phr. 目前　**start a family** phr. 成家　**win the lottery** phr. 中樂透　**make a fortune** phr. 發財　**live up to one's expectation** phr. 達到某人的期望

延伸學習

每個人心中都有夢想，這夢想或許也是你認為最重要的東西。一起來認識有關夢想和希望的英文名言吧！

❶ Dream big and dare to fail. （敢於夢想並敢於失敗。）

❷ Dreams become reality when we put our minds to it. （如果我們全心全力，夢想將成為事實。）

❸ Too many of us are not living our dreams because we are living our fears. （太多人沒有去實踐他們的夢想，因為他們去實踐恐懼。）

❹ You are never too old to set another goal or to dream a new dream. （你絕不會年長到不能再設一個目標或擁有一個新夢想。）

❺ Never reject an idea, dream or goal because it will be hard work. Success rarely comes without it. （絕不要因為怕辛苦，就拒絕一個想法、夢想或目標，成功很少沒有伴隨辛苦。）

❻ Within our dreams and aspirations we find our opportunities. （在我們的夢想及抱負裡我們找到了機會。）

10. Talk about a trip you took recently. Who do you go with? How was the trip?

談談你最近的一趟旅行。你跟誰一起去的？ 這趟旅行如何？

答題解說

旅行，可以提到的東西很多，你可以用英文的 5W1H 為架構去說，包括自由行或跟團（self-guided tour or group tour）也可以提到。當然，除了題目要求的 who（跟誰去）以及 how（覺得這趟旅行怎麼樣）你必須提到，其他包括時間、地點、旅行的交通工具、住宿（accommodation）、風景、當地的文化…等其他項目，也都可以談談，或者遇到什麼特別的人事物，比如說交了新朋友等，也都是不錯的題材。如果這趟旅行令你非常不愉快（unpleasant），也可以如實陳述，或者說從這趟旅行當中學到什麼寶貴經驗之類的。萬一你最近真的都沒有出去玩，可以說明原因，以及未來希望去旅行的地方等。

回答範例 1

I took a trip to Japan last winter. I went to Hokkaido with my best friend. I have to say that it is the most beautiful place I have ever visited. There are many undisturbed natural environments that always attract many tourists from around the world. Both of us experienced the thrill of skiing down a hill. Besides, we took a cable car and enjoyed breathtaking views. We really had much fun. It's only a pity that time was not enough and there were still many attractions we didn't visit. We agree to go again together next year.

去年冬天我去了日本。我和我最好的朋友去北海道。我必須說，那是我所去過最美麗的地方。那裡有眾多未經人工干擾的自然環境，吸引來自世界各地的遊客到訪。我們倆都體驗了從山上滑雪下來的快感。此外，我們還乘坐了纜車，欣賞了令人嘆為觀止的美景。我們真的玩得很開心。只可惜時間不夠，還有很多景點沒有去。我們說好明年再一起去。

回答範例 2

Frankly, I haven't went on a far-away trip recently. My last trip was too long ago. I can't remember when. I am always busy with my schoolwork and because of the Covid-19 pandemic these days, I dare not go out to take a public transport. Besides, after school I am too tired to go anywhere. If I have the time and money, I would like to take a trip to mainland China. I have long wanted to talk a leisurely walk on the Great Wall and paid a visit to the Shanghai and enjoy the beautiful scene from the Oriental Pearl Tower.

坦白說，我最近都沒有出遠門去旅行。我上次去旅行是很久以前的事了。我不記

第 1 回
第 2 回
第 3 回
第 4 回
第 5 回
第 6 回
第 7 回
第 8 回
第 9 回
第 10 回

得是什麼時候。我總是忙於功課，且最近因為新冠肺炎的疫情，我不敢出門搭乘大眾交通工具。 此外，放學後我累得哪兒也去不了。如果我有時間和金錢，我想去中國大陸旅行。我一直想悠閒地走在長城上，以及去上海逛逛，並在東方明珠上欣賞美景。

關鍵字詞

take a trip to... phr. 來一趟…之旅　**undisturbed** adj. 不受打擾的　**thrill** n. 刺激　**cable car** n. 纜車　**breathtaking** adj. 令人屏息的　**pity** n. 可惜　**attraction** n. 熱門景點　**pandemic** adj.（瘟疫等）大流行　**public transport** n. 大眾運輸

延伸學習

形容「美景」只會用 So beautiful/pretty! 嗎？「食物真好吃」只會講 Yummy!/Delicious 嗎？快來學學以下更有深度的、形容旅遊美好經驗的話吧！

❶ I cherished every visit and every amazing hotel I stayed in left me valuable memories.（我珍惜每一趟旅程，且每我留宿過的每一家飯店都留給我珍貴的回憶。）

❷ I had countless eye-opening experiences through this trip.（從這趟旅程中我十足打開了眼界。）

❸ What a scenic spot that fits "love at first sight."（真是令我「一見鍾情」的景點！）

❹ Shops displaying historic objects line up the hallway.（走道擺滿歷史悠久的古物。）

❺ I was quickly intrigued by all kinds of works of art displayed in different shops.（我很快地被商店裡各式各樣的藝術品所迷住。）

❻ I was totally conquered with the variety of cuisines that it could offer.（我的心完全被它的美食擄獲了。）

❼ From desserts to fancy gourmets, I've never left the area feeling unsatisfied.（從充飢點心到能飽餐一頓的美食，無一是令我不滿意之處。）

第三部分 看圖敘述

T03P3.mp3

第1回
第2回
第3回
第4回
第5回
第6回
第7回
第8回
第9回
第10回

答題解說

要取得高分，不能只說照片中看得到的東西，還必須針對看到的人、事和物做出聯想。。以下針對提示的部分給您可以用到的字詞建議：

1. 照片裡的人在什麼地方？

   你可以說小範圍的 at the airport lounge / waiting room 或是大範圍的 in the departure hall / arrival hall（在機場的候機室／出境大廳內）。但如果只是說「他們在室內」（They are indoors.）之類的，分數會打折扣喔！

2. 照片裡的人在做什麼？

   提到「人」的部分時，你可以先提到一男一女，以及他們可能的關係（情侶、夫妻、同事…等），並稍加描述特徵或其他重點。例如，你可以說 "There are a man and a woman sitting there and having a casual chat."（有一男一女坐在那裡閒聊。）、"The man and the woman might be the colleagues of the same company."（男子與女子可能是同一家公司的同事。）、以及 "They are waiting for their flight"（他們正在等候他們的班機。）

3. 照片裡的人為什麼會在那裡？

   我們可以從照片拍攝地點，以及男子身旁的行李（luggage），很容易判斷照片中的兩人為什麼會在這地方。因此，有「入境（arrival）」和「出境（departure）」兩種可能。當然，也不排除「轉機（transit）」的可能。你可以說 "They are ready to board their flight."（他們準備要登機了。）以及 "They are taking a business trip abroad."（他們將到國外出差。）

4. 如果尚有時間，請詳細描述圖片中的景物。

   例如，從照片中的，你可以繼續補充說，"Both of them are wearing glasses."（他們倆都戴著眼鏡。）或是 "The man is holding a cellphone."（男子手中拿著手機）、"The woman is holding a book."（女子手裡拿著一本書）、"They are chatting happily."（他們愉快地在聊天著。）…等。

回答範例

The first thing that caught my eyes is the baggage beside the man. I think the man and the woman are sitting at the airport lounge. I think they are waiting for their flight, and they are in the departure hall. From what they wear, I guess they must be traveling abroad on business. The man is wearing a suit jacket and the woman is putting on a pair of high heels, which does not look like they are going on a sightseeing tour. From what can be seen in the photo, they look in their thirties, and they are in good spirits. The man is holding a cellphone. Maybe he wants to check out what the weather is like in the country of their destination. The woman is reading a book. I think she's preparing for her assignment she needs to perform the next day. From their pleasant talk I believe they are confident that they can carry out their mission on this business trip.

首先吸引我目光的是這名男子身邊的行李箱。我認為男子和女子坐的地方是機場的候機室。我想他們正在等候他們的班機，而且他們出境大廳。從他們的穿著，我猜他們一定是要到國外出差。男子穿著西裝外套，而女子穿著高跟鞋，他們不太像是要出國觀光的樣子。從照片中可以看出，他們差不多三十多歲，且他們精神很好。男子拿著手機。也許他想查看他們目的地國家的天氣情況。女子正在看書。我認為她正在為第二天需要執行的任務做準備。從他們愉快的談話中，我相信他們有信心在這次差旅中完成他們的任務。

關鍵字詞

catch one's eyes phr. 映入眼簾，吸引某人目光　**baggage** n. 行李　**lounge** n. 休息室　**flight** n. 班機　**departure/arrival hall** n. 出境／入境大廳　**on business** phr. 出差中　**suit jacket** n. 西裝外套　**high heels** n. 高跟鞋　**in good spirits** phr. 精神很好　**destination** n. 目的地　**assignment** n. 任務，作業　**carry out** phr. 執行　**business trip** n. 差旅

說到「行李」，最常看到的就是 suitcase、baggage、luggage，但你知道這三個字有什麼差異嗎？

❶ suitcase 是指「行李箱」，不管有沒有輪子都可以。它是可數名詞，字尾可以直接加 s。例如：My friends lost their suitcases at the train station.（我朋友在火車站遺失了他們的行李箱。）

❷ baggage 是「行李」的通稱，多用於美式英文。不管是 suitcase、carry-on handbag（隨身手提包）、backpack（背包），都可以叫作 baggage。但要注意的是，baggage 是不可數名詞，不會有複數形。如果要表示一件或多件行李，可以說：a piece / … pieces of baggage 或 an item / … items of baggage。例如：Two items of Emily's baggage were stolen in Paris.（Emily 的其中兩件行李在巴黎被偷了。）

❸ luggage 基本上等於 baggage，多用於英式英文。但其實現在沒有很明確區分了。luggage 一樣是不可數名詞，沒有複數形。用法比照上述的 baggage。

第 1 回
第 2 回
第 3 回
第 4 回
第 5 回
第 6 回
第 7 回
第 8 回
第 9 回
第 10 回

4

GEPT 全民英檢

中級複試
中譯＋解析

第一部分 中譯英

有一句話說，「金錢象徵著你對別人的價值。」一個作家有多優秀，看他賣了多少本書，拿了多少版稅。一個畫家有多成功，看他的畫值多少錢。各行各業的成功幾乎都是如此。如果有一個畫家宣稱自己很成功，但他的畫作沒人買單，那只是自我滿足而已。

答題解說

第一句的「有一句話說…」可以用 As a saying goes/There's a saying, "..."。雙引號裡面這句可以把「金錢」當作句子主詞，動詞是「象徵」，受詞是「你對別人的價值」。要注意的是，這裡的「價值」並不是指 value 或是 worth，因為「人」本身不能拿來賣錢（不然就變成人口販運了！）而是指「別人對你這個人的評價（evaluate）」。所以我們在做翻譯時，很多句子都不能「中文直譯」，而是你要稍微思考一下，這個句子要表達的是什麼「概念」。

第二句可以把句意再弄得清楚些：「一個作家有多優秀，就在於…」。所以可以寫成 How excellent a writer is depends on... and...。而這裡的「他賣了多少本書」，你要思考成「他的書有多少本賣出去了」，用被動語態來呈現即可，而不是 how many book he/she has sold out，這樣好像作者自己去擺攤子叫賣一樣，是不符合實際狀況的。其中「版稅」的英文是 royalties。如果你不知道個字，至少 copyright 該知道吧！那麼你可以寫成 the money he/she earned from the copyright of his/her work。

同樣，第三句可以用第二句的句型去呈現：How successful a painter is depends on...。而第四句的「都是如此」就是「被視為這樣的情況」，或是「都被以這樣的標準來看」（...almost be judged by this standard）。另外，「各行各業」是 all walks of life。

最後一句：if a writer... but his works..., that's just...，接著可以用 self-satisfaction 來表示「自我滿足」。至於這裡的「買單」，你可以用 no one pays for...、nobody digs into his (own) pocket for...。總之，記住這段短文一開始就是在談「金錢」。

譯文範例

As a saying goes, "Money symbolizes how you are evaluated by others." How excellent a writer is depends on how many books are sold out and how much royalties he/she earns. How successful a painter is depends on how much his painting works are worth. This is true in terms of success in almost all walks of life. If a painter claims to be successful, but no one pays for his paintings, that is just a kind of self-satisfaction.

延伸學習

value、worth 和 merit 這三個字都有「價值」的意思。value 在表達「價值」的意思時，除了表示事物的「金錢價格」之外，還可以表示「準則、價值觀」；而 worth 則強調「事物自身的價值」，也有「值得」的意思；merit 和其它兩個字相比所指的「價值」是「值得讚揚的優點」，強調正面的肯定。

❶ value 既可以是名詞，也可以作為動詞。作為名詞時，value 包含我們一般人觀念中「用金錢來衡量事物的價值」。例如：The value of the house has been put at no more than 10 million dollars. = The house is valued at no more than 10 million dollars.（這房子的價值被評估為不超過一千萬元。）

❷ worth 作為介系詞時使用的頻率比當名詞使用的頻率要高，通常出現在 be 動詞後面。其中一個常用含義是「值多少錢的」。例如：The house is worth no more than 10 million dollars.（這房子值不到一千萬元。）

worth 另一個常用的含義是「值得、值得去做」的意思。例如：It was a long climb to the top of the mountain, but it was worth it for the view.（雖然需要登很久才能到達山頂，但是能看到那樣的美景，這一切都是值得的。）

❸ merit 的「價值」是指「成就或品質中值得讚揚的優點」，強調得到正面的肯定。例如：This film is praised for its artistic merit.（這部電影因為它的藝術價值受到稱讚。）

第二部分 英文作文

提示

網路商店的商品的價位不必去承受商店租金或店家雇用店員的成本，一般來說都會比實體店面便宜一些。但也容易出現一些交易糾紛。假設你今天在網路上買的東西是防冒品，請寫一封電子郵件向店家抱怨並要求合理補償措施。

答題解說

本題主要針對收到仿冒的網購商品時，該如何向店家反應的問題，寫一封 email 為自己討回公道。信件一開始可以寫 "Dear Sir,"、"To whom it may concern,"（敬啟者）。接著主要內容第一句表明來信的目的，可以寫 "I am writing this email/letter to inform you that..."（我寫這封信的目的是想通知您…）。然後先簡單說明原因，例如：I'm disappointed that...。接著信件主要內容的架構如下：

第 1 回
第 2 回
第 3 回
第 4 回
第 5 回
第 6 回
第 7 回
第 8 回
第 9 回
第 10 回

❶ 說明何時購買了什麼商品，同時可以再補充花了多少錢、付款的方式為何等。比如說「已刷卡（pay by credit card）」、「貨到付款（pay cash on delivery）」等。

❷ 說明收到商品時發現了什麼問題。比方說，「劣質品（product of poor quality）」、「贗品（fake product）」「有使用過的痕跡（show traces of usage）」、「不如預期（not as one expected）」、「不像商品描述那樣的（not look like what the ad describes）⋯」等。

❸ 說明希望店家處理的方式。比方說，「要求退款（request a refund）」、「換貨（exchange）」、「退貨（return）」⋯等。

❹ 信件結尾敬語。一般來說有：Best（regards),、Sincerely（yours),、My best,⋯等。

作文範例

Dear Sir,

I am writing to inform you that the pink blanket I purchased last Monday is of poor quality. I found some traces that show it has been used. Is it a second-hand product? Besides, the color of it is much lighter than that shown in the picture of your ad. I am feeling very disappointed because I've been a loyal customer of your shop for a long time, and I am always confident in your product quality. I also wondered if there was any human error involved. Anyway, I think I need to request a return and refund, or an exchange is also accepted if you really have the quality product as described in your ad.

I hope to receive your reply soon.

Best regards,

Kelly Jordan

先生 您好：

我寫信來通知您，我上週一購買的一條粉紅色毯子品質很差。我有發現一些使用痕跡，這表示它是已經被用過的。這是二手貨嗎？此外，它的顏色比您廣告圖片中呈現的顏色還要淺很多。我感到非常失望，因為我一直是貴店的忠實顧客，且我一直對你們的產品品質充滿信心。我也好奇這是否涉及任何人為疏失。無論如何，我想我必須申請退貨及退款，或者如果您真的有廣告中描述的優質產品，我也可以接受換貨。

我希望盡快收到您的回覆。

敬祝 商祺

凱利・喬丹

第 1 回
第 2 回
第 3 回
第 4 回
第 5 回
第 6 回
第 7 回
第 8 回
第 9 回
第 10 回

延伸學習

「退貨（return）」、「退款（refund）」以及「換貨（exchange）」這三個字都可以當名詞與動詞。請見以下例句及用法：

❶ I want to return this dress; it's a bit smaller for me.（我想退還這件裙子，它有點對我來說太小。）

No returns are allowed on sale merchandise.（特價商品不允許退貨。）

❷ If you don't like the T-shirt, you can exchange it.（你要是不喜歡這件 T 恤，可以換貨。）= ..., you can apply for an exchange of it.

❸ You will receive a full refund if you cancel your booking seven days before your check-in date.（如果您在入住日期前 7 天取消預訂，您可取得全額退款。）

第一部分 朗讀短文

T04P1.mp3

Many health experts have called for further research on "long COVID," because in fact, it occurs in 10 to 20 percent of all cases. As the CECC has said that more than half of the population in Taiwan used to be infected with the virus, the government should also shift some of its attention and resources to understanding, preventing and providing treatment for long COVID.

****

Personal details, such as your address, date of birth, telephone number and bank account information should never be disclosed online unless you use a trusted source. When you're shopping online, it's important to only purchase from web pages that have URLs starting with "HTTPS", which indicates the site is secure. If your detailed information gets into the wrong hands, they can be used for identity theft or fraud.

答題解說

第一篇是與新冠後疫情時代族有關的小短文，其中 COVID 要念成 [ˋkovɪd]，而 CECC（中央流行疫情指揮中心）就直接念字母即可，即使你不知道它代表的是 Central Epidemic Command Center 也沒關係。第二篇則關於安全使用網路。同樣地，HTTPS 直接念字母即可，不過，URLs 中的 URL 直接念字母，但字尾的 –s 還是要發 [z] 的音喔！

以下標有顏色的單字，請盡可能唸得比較響亮，出現「|」的地方，請稍作停頓，試著讓自己融入短文的情境中。最後，請注意字與字之間該連音的部分（以下畫底線），像是 research on、because in、occurs in、percent of all、half of、of its... 等。

Many health experts | have called for further research on "long COVID," | because in fact, | it occurs in 10 to 20 percent of all cases. As the CECC has said that | more than half of the population in Taiwan | used to be infected with the virus, the government should also shift some of its attention and resources | to understanding, preventing and providing treatment for long COVID.

****

Personal details, such as your address, date of birth, telephone number and bank account information | should never be disclosed online unless you use a trusted source. When you're shopping online, it's important to only purchase from web pages that have URLs starting with "HTTPS", which indicates the site is secure. If your detailed information gets into the wrong hands, they can be used for identity theft or fraud.

短文翻譯

許多健康專家呼籲對「長新冠」做進一步的研究，因為事實上，它在所有病例中佔了 10% 到 20% 的比例。根據中央流行疫情指揮中心所述，台灣一半以上的人口曾經感染過此種病毒，政府也應將部分焦點和資源轉移到對長新冠的了解、預防和治療上。

****

個人詳細資料，像是您的地址、出生日期、電話號碼和銀行帳戶資訊切勿在網路上公開，除非使用可信賴的來源。當你在線上購物時，務必僅從 URL 是 HTTPS 開頭的網頁上購買，因為那表示該網站才是安全的。如果你的詳細資訊落入壞人手上，它們可能會被用於身份盜用或詐騙。

關鍵字詞

call for phr. 呼籲，要求　**population** n. 人口　**be infected with** phr. 受到…感染　**virus** n. 病毒　**shift... to...** phr. 將…轉移至…　**treatment** n. 治療　**bank account** n. 銀行帳戶　**disclose** v. 揭露，公開　**trusted** adj. 可信的　**secure** adj. 安全的　**identity theft** n. 身分盜用　**fraud** n. 詐騙

第二部分 回答問題

T04P2.mp3

1. **Do you like to work from home? Why?**

你喜歡在家工作嗎？為什麼？

答題解說

對於「為什麼喜歡或不喜歡在家工作？」的回答，可以從優缺點（advantage and disadvantage）的方向去說。優點的部分，例如：省去通勤的時間與花費（save the commuting expense and time）、更容易兼顧生活與工作（balance between work and family）、僱主能擴大其徵才範圍（The employers can broaden their scope of recruitment.）…等。缺點的部分，像是不適合「自我管理能力不佳的人（not good at self-management）」、生產力降低（less productive）、不容易專心（get distracted easily）、孤獨感（loneliness）、失去與同事的互動（unable to interact with colleagues）…等。

事實上，有些工作可以或適合 WFH，但有些工作根本難以辦到（例如房仲等 sales、工廠作業員等工作）。所以本題的回答，也可以說出自己是做什麼的，如果是沒辦法在家工作的，也可以如實說明，再補充說自己希望或其實也不渴望在家工作。如果是學生的話，一樣根據以上的提示，把焦點放在遠距上課（distance learning）以及遠距教學（distance education）來回答。

回答範例 1

Yes, I like to work from home, because, I can sleep a little more and save the commuting cost and time. Though working alone may make me feel bored and easily distractive sometimes, I think it's a good chance to train me to develop self-management skills.

是的，我喜歡在家工作，因為我可以多睡一點、節省通勤費用和時間。雖然獨自工作有時會讓我感到無聊且容易分心，但我認為這是訓練我培養自我管理能力的好機會。

回答範例 2

No, I don't like to work from home, and in fact, my job doesn't allow me to work from home. I work as a real estate agent. If I need to be confined home to work, it's very difficult for me to locate a potential client. Then I would be trapped in a state of economic difficulty.

不，我不喜歡在家工作，且事實上，我的工作不允許我在家工作。我是一名房屋仲介。如果我必須被限制在家裡工作，我就很難找到潛在客戶。那麼我就會陷入經濟困難的狀態。

關鍵字詞

work from home (WFH) phr. 遠距工作　**commuting** adj. 通勤的　**alone** adv. 獨自地　**bored** adj. 感到無趣的，乏味的　**distractive** adj. 分心的　**self-management** n. 自我管理　**real estate agent** n. 房產仲介　**confine** v. 限制　**potential** adj. 潛在的　**be trapped in** phr. 陷入…之中　**state** n. 狀態

第 1 回

第 2 回

第 3 回

第 4 回

第 5 回

第 6 回

第 7 回

第 8 回

第 9 回

第 10 回

延伸學習

「在家工作」又被稱為「遠距工作」（work from home, WFH / work remotely / telework / telecommute），指的是「原本在公司工作，因為特殊狀況（例如疫情）才在家工作」。所以可別跟 "work at home" 搞混了。"work at home" 是指「原本就在家工作」，像是自由作家（freelancer）這樣的工作。這個概念要先建立起來，答題的方向才不會偏掉。請參考以下例句：

❶ Many tech companies allow their employees to telecommute.（許多科技公司都允許員工們遠距工作。）

❷ David is now telecommuting from his home 2 days a week.（大衛目前一星期有兩天會在家中遠距工作。）

2. **Do you celebrate your birthday every year? Talk about your most unforgettable birthday.**

你每年都會慶祝生日嗎？談談你最難忘的生日。

答題解說

題目中的關鍵字 birthday，相信大部分人都可以聽得出來，celebrate 是初級單字應該也沒問題，就算聽不太懂 unforgettable，至少可以從字首 un-（表示「否定」）和中間的 forget（忘記）推敲出這個字的意思：unforgettable 是「令人難忘的」意思。另外，第一個問題是問你「是不是每年慶祝生日」，如果去年有，前年沒有之類的，那就以 "I don't... every year." 來開頭。

「令人難忘的生日」也許是愉快的，也許是不堪回首的（too painful to recall it），能夠講的東西很多。當然，你也可以說：「我幾乎沒有過生日的習慣。（I almost have no habit of celebrating my own birthday.）」或是「我的生日都是像平常的每一天一樣，平淡地過去了。（I usually let my birthday pass dully...）」

回答範例 1

Yes. I celebrate my birthday every year. I usually hold a birthday party, or go out for fun with some of my best friends. Speaking of my most unforgettable birthday, I remember last year we went to an amazing beach in eastern Taiwan and stayed at the nearest resort for two days. We had a barbecue and played beach volleyballs. We really had fun!

是的。我每年都會慶祝我的生日。我通常會舉辦生日派對，或者和我最好的朋友出去玩。 說到我最難忘的生日，我記得去年我們去了東台灣一處很棒的海灘，並在最近的度假村住了兩天。我們有烤肉以及打沙灘排球。我們真的玩得很開心！

No, not every year. It depends on whether there's someone who remembers my birthday and wants to hold a party for me, or treats me to dinner. My most unforgettable birthday is a Valentine's Day... of about five years ago. That's when my ex-boyfriend treated me to a romantic candle-lit dinner, and he sent me a very expensive ring as the birthday gift.

不，沒有每年都過。那就看有沒有人記得我的生日，且要為我辦個派對，或請我吃飯。 我最難忘的生日是在一個情人節…大約五年前吧。當時我前男友請我吃了一頓浪漫的燭光晚餐的時候，他還送我一個非常昂貴的戒指作為生日禮物。

關鍵字詞

unforgettable adj. 難忘的　**go out for fun** phr. 出去玩　**resort** n. 渡假村
beach volleyball n. 沙灘排球　**treat** v. 請客　**romantic** adj. 浪漫的　**candle**-lit
dinner n. 燭光晚餐

延伸學習

說到慶生活動，有哪些英文的慣用表達可以運用呢？

❶ 辦生日派對（throw a birthday party）：這裡的 throw 不是「丟」，而是「舉行（派對）」的意思。例如：Can you suggest a cozy place where we can throw a birthday party for Kelly?（你可以建議一個溫馨的地方讓我們可以為 Kelly 辦生日派對嗎？）

❷ 點蠟燭（light the candles）：light 當動詞是「點亮」的意思，它的過去式和過去分詞是 lit。例如：Now's the time. Let's light the candles.（就是現在。我們來點蠟燭吧。）

❸ 把蛋糕拿出來（bring out the cake）。例如：I burst into tears when they brought out the cake.（當們拿出蛋糕時我哭了。）

❹ 閉上眼睛（close one's eyes）。例如：Now close your eyes. Don't peek. We've got a surprise for you.（現在閉上眼睛。別偷看。我們有驚喜要給你。）

❺ 許願（make a wish）。例如：All right, everyone, be quiet. The birthday boy is going to make a wish.（好了，大家，安靜一下。壽星要許願了。）

❻ 吹蠟燭（blow out the candles）。「吹蠟燭」其實是「吹熄蠟燭」的意思，所以要用 blow out。例如：Don't forget to make a wish before you blow out the candles.（吹熄蠟燭前別忘了許願。）

3. **Do you work out on a regular basis? Where do you usually do that?**

   你有規律地在做運動嗎？你通常在哪裡做這件事？

答題解說

work out 是「做運動」的意思，專指「體能方面的運動（physical exercise）」，通常是為了保持身材的強健或健美（keep one's body stronger / stay in shape）或身體健康（keep fit / stay healthy）而做，但也有人當作是一項嗜好，其意義接近 exercise。而 on a regular basis（= regularly）是「規律地，定期地」的意思，你可以回答「一週三次」、「每天晚上」…都可以。本題除了要回答運動的地方，為了充實內容，還可以提及「做什麼運動」、一天大概做多久。至於「運動的地方」，像是 gym（健身房）、fitness center（健身中心）、swimming pool（游泳池），或如果是「慢跑」的運動，可以說 "go jogging along nearby streets"（沿著附近街道上慢跑）或是 "running/jogging on the treadmill at home"（在家裡的跑步機上慢跑）…等。

回答範例 1

Yes, I work out on a regular basis. I go to a famous fitness center twice a week. I usually do weight training and jog on the treadmill there. Besides, there are professional trainers who can teach me how to do exercise without getting hurt. After working out, I'd take a shower and relax in the sauna there .

是的，我有定期在做運動。我每星期會去一家知名的健身中心兩次。在那裡我通常會做重量訓練以及使用跑步機慢跑。此外，還有專業的教練可以教我如何運動才不會受傷。運動過後，我會去沖個澡，然後在那裡的桑拿放鬆一下。

回答範例 2

No, I don't work out regularly. Frankly, I'm very busy on weekdays so, on weekends I spend much time lying lazily on the sofa and watching TV, or playing on my cellphone. I'm planning to apply for the membership of a gym and force myself to work out on a regular basis.

不，我沒有定期在做運動。坦白說，我平時很忙，所以週末我有很多的時間都懶洋洋地躺在沙發上看電視或滑手機。我打算加入健身房的會員，並強迫自己規律地運動。

關鍵字詞

work out phr. 做（體能方面的）運動　**on a regular basis** phr. 規律地，定期地
fitness center n. 健身中心　**weight training** n. 重量訓練　**treadmill** n. 跑步機
professional adj. 專業的　**trainer** n. 訓練師　**do exercise** phr. 做運動　**sauna**

n. 桑拿（含烤箱、蒸氣室、三溫暖等設備的地方）　**play on one's cellphone**
phr. 玩／滑手機　**gym** n. 健身房

延伸學習

英文裡的「運動」，最常見的就是 sport 和 exercise（當動詞 = work out），不
過這兩個「運動」在意義上可是大不相同喔！sport 指的是有「競爭性質」的運
動，必須依循相關的規則，通常是各種「球類」運動。而 exercise 指的是為了
強健身體而做的一些運動，並不帶有競賽的性質。例如：

❶ She did a lot of sports at college, such as football, basketball, and hockey.
（她大學時期從事很多運動，像是(足球、籃球球和曲棍球。）

❷ Jogging is my favorite form of exercise.（慢跑是我最喜歡的運動。）

此外，兩者當名詞時，通常固定和一些動詞搭配。例如： play sport、do exercise/
workout。而運動項目常用於 go + Ving 的形式，例如 go jogging、go swimming...
等。

4. **Do you have the habit of saving money? How do you do that?**

　　你有存錢的習慣嗎？你都如何儲蓄呢？

答題解說

題目的 saving money 可以有兩層意義：存錢 and 省錢。原則上兩者也有重疊的
意思，其實省錢也可能是為了要存錢。所以你可以就自己存錢或省錢的「做法」
去發揮。例如，騎單車不坐公車（go... on bicycle, not on bus）、盡可能走路
（try to walk somewhere）、不亂買東西（avoid impulse purchase）、購物前
先列出較急需的物品清單（make a shopping list that only contains items in
urgent need）、以錢滾錢的方式增加自己的儲蓄（increase one's savings by
way of money making money, instead of labor making money）、選擇較經濟實
惠的手機月租費方案（economical monthly plan）…等。要是自己沒有存錢的習
慣，可以說明原因。例如薪水太少（poor salary），每月入不敷出（can't make
both ends meet），沒有多餘的錢可以存。如果還有時間，再補充說未來如果有
多餘的錢，希望自己可以如何理財與儲蓄等。

回答範例 1

Yes, I think money management is important for everyone. I always try to cut back on
my spending. First, I go to work by U-bike. Second, I make a shopping list. Third, I go
online to look for better deals.

是的，我認為金錢的管理對每個人都重要。我總是想辦法節省開銷。首先，我騎
U-bike 去上班。再來，我會列購物清單。第三，我會上網尋找價格更好的價位

回答範例 2

No, I don't have the habit of saving money. That's because my poor monthly salary doesn't allow me to do that. My room rent accounts for 40% of what I earned every month. I hope I can make more money and save some in the near future.

不，我沒有存錢的習慣。那是因為我微薄的月薪不允許我那樣做。我的房租就占了我每月收入的 40%。我希望我能在不久的將來賺更多的錢並能存一些錢。

關鍵字詞

money management n. 理財，資金管理　**cut back on** phr. 削減　**spending** n. 開支，開銷　**make a shopping list** phr. 列出購物清單　**monthly salary** n. 月薪　**room rent** n. 房租　**accounts for** phr. 占了…（多少分量）

延伸學習

提到存錢、儲蓄，一般都會使用 save money，但其實還有許多實用的片語可以運用，如何更準確地用英文表達？以下是幾個常見的片語：

❶ 為了特定目的存錢，可以用 put aside，例如：I'm putting aside 3,000 dollars a month for our overseas trip next year.（我為了明年的出國旅遊每個月存下三千元。）

❷ 也可以用 build up，原本是「建立、增進」的意思，build up savings/wealth 表示「累積存款，增加財富」的意思。例如：You need to build up savings to cover the cost of raising a kid.（你得累積存款來支付養小孩的費用。）

❸ 先將錢存起來，若未來遇到艱困事件可做為救急資金（emergency fund），其實就是「未雨綢繆」的意思。例如：I am always saving for a rainy day.（我總是未雨綢繆。）

5. **Have you ever felt embarrassed in public? What happened?**

你可曾在公眾場合感到尷尬？發生了什麼事呢？

答題解說

題目中的 embarrassed 是「尷尬的，不好意思的」意思，但須注意的是 in public，要問的是「在公眾場合」發生什麼讓你感到「糗大了（make a fool of oneself）」、「看起來愚蠢（look silly）」的事情，比方說，上了公車發現「衣服穿錯面（inside out）」、「褲子拉鍊沒拉（The fly is open.）」、「在電影院看電影時手機響起（The cellphone rang loudly when...）」、「上台領獎時滑了一跤（slip on the way to...）」...之類的。但如果是打錯電話、把訊息傳給錯的人，雖然也會不好意思，但不算公開場合喔！而如果是在 LINE 群組，就算是公開場合了。所以，盡量以自己的經驗來發想，不用提到太過複雜的事情，只要

想可以用 3-4 句答完的事情就可以了。

回答範例 1

Yes, I felt so embarrassed in a night banquet last weekend. I spent much time earlier thinking about what to wear and I decided to put on a dress shirt and a suit coat. But when I walked to the platform and was ready to talk to the audience, I found my shirt was inside out! I saw some can't help laughing.

是的，我上週末在一場夜宴上感到很尷尬。我之前花了很多時間考慮要穿什麼，然後我決定穿上一件看起來優雅的禮服襯衫和西裝外套。但是當我走到講台準備和聽眾講話時，我發現我的襯衫穿反了！且我看到有些人忍不住笑了。

回答範例 2

Yes, Sometimes I send messages to the wrong group on LINE. Yesterday, I made the mistake again. I sent a private photo to a work group, and about an hour later one of my colleagues called to tell me about it. In the photo I was naked on the upper part of my body. That's really embarrassing!

是的，我有時會在 LINE 上將訊息發錯群。昨天，我又犯了這個錯誤。我把一張私密照片發到一個工作群組，大約一個小時後，我的一位同事打電話來告訴我這件事。照片中我的上半身是赤裸的。真是太令人尷尬了！

關鍵字詞

embarrassed adj. 感到尷尬的　**in public** phr. 在公開場合中　**banquet** n. 宴會　**dress shirt** n. 禮服襯衫　**suit coat** n. 西裝外套　**inside-out** adj. 顛倒的，穿反了的　**embarrassing** adj. 令人尷尬的

延伸學習

常見表示「尷尬」的英文 embarrassed 或是 embarrassing。前者是用來形容「人」，所以句子裡「主詞」是人，而後者是形容「事物」，通常以「事物」為主詞。embarrassed/embarrassing 通常是因為「出糗、丟臉、出洋相」而感到尷尬。另外，awaward 也是「尷尬」的意思，但它通常是指因為「不自在的、怪怪的、棘手的」而感到尷尬。例如：

❶ I was so underscore{embarrassed} of myself when I found the fly is open.（當我發現褲子拉鍊沒拉時，我感到很尷尬。）

❷ I felt awkward when I stood together with my ex-boyfriend.（當我和我前男友站在一起時，我感到很尷尬。）

6. What is one aspect of character you're most proud of? Why?

你對自己最自豪的一種個性特質是什麼？為什麼呢？

答題解說

首先，聽懂本題的關鍵字是 character。這個字其實有很多意思，包括「個性」、「角色」、「文字」等，這裡是「個性」的意思，其實本題就是在問你「你覺得自己有什麼個性上的優點？這樣的個性給你帶來什麼好處？」。

一開始可以用「I'm most proud of my + 名詞..., because...」或是「I am a + 形容詞 + person...」開頭。可以把描述個性這部分用名詞或形容詞來呈現。形容詞的話像是 nice、kind、generous、brave、broad-minded…等，名詞的話有 self-confidence、friendliness、sincerity、diligence…等。當然，還是要提醒：這不是在工作面試，盡量用自己有把握的字詞，沒有要你回答自己真正的個性。

接著你可以繼續說明，因為這樣的個性特質，讓自己在工作上獲得上司的信賴、在社交場合受人歡迎，或是面對困難時能夠冷靜沉著，找到適當的解決辦法…等。

回答範例 1

I think I have some aspects of character I'm very proud of. But if you want me to pick one, I'd say I can always think on my feet when I'm faced with various problems. I don't have a stubborn attitude toward everything. Everything will be alright, and there's no big deal even if I fail. This personality trait helps me develop the ability to take the initiative to find solutions to problems, rather than just sit there to wait for someone to help me. That's because now I have the ear of my boss.

我認為我有一些我非常自豪的個性。但如果你要我選一個，我會說我在面對各種問題時總是能夠獨立思考（隨機應變）。我對任何事情都沒有固執的態度。船到橋頭自然直，且失敗也沒什麼大不了的。這種人格特質幫助我培養主動尋找問題解決方案的能力，而不是坐在那裡等著別人來幫助我。這也是我現在深受老闆重用的原因。

回答範例 2

I don't know what strengths I have in my character that I'm proud of. Sometimes I think I am a person of failure. I'm always worried about my grades. If I really have to answer such a question, I might say I'm always friendly to everyone, whether I am offended intentionally or not. Maybe because of this, I'm somewhat popular among my classmates. Some of them would offer to help me with my homework, though my grades still make a little progress.

我不知道我在個性上有什麼優點，以及可以讓我自豪的。有時候我覺得我是一個

失敗的人。我總是擔心我的成績。如果真要我回答這樣的問題，我可能會說我對每個人都是友善的，無論我是否被故意冒犯。也許正因為如此，我在同學中還算有人緣。而其中有些人會主動幫助我的功課，儘管我的成績仍然進步得很少。

關鍵字詞

aspect n. 方面　**character** n. 個性，人物　**be proud of** phr. 對於…感到自豪
think on one's feet phr. 有主見，隨機應變　**be faced with** phr. 面臨…
stubborn adj. 固執的　**attitude** n. 態度　**no big deal** phr. 沒什麼大不了
personality trait n. 個人特質　**take the initiative to-V** phr. 主動…（去做某事）
solution n. 解決辦法　**have the ear of sb**. phr. 受到某人賞識　**strength** n. 優點，力量　**failure** n. 失敗　**offend** v. 冒犯　**intentionally** adv. 故意地
somewhat adv. 有點，可說是　**offer to-V** phr. 自願要…　**make progress** phr. 有進步

延伸學習

在英文裡，要表達「我（很）有進步」要說 I've made (a lot of) improvement/progress.，不能說 I have improvement.，因為進步不能被「擁有」，但可以被「創造」，所以動詞用 make；如果要表示還有進步的「空間」可以用 room 這個字。例如：There's no room for improvement.（沒有進步空間了。）另外，你也可以說 I've improved.，但不能說 I got improved.

類似的概念還有：我有興趣。

I have interest.（X）vs. I am interested.（O）

中文「有興趣」當中有個「有」，所以很多人就直接說成 I have interest.。這是錯誤的，對某個東西有興趣通常用 I'm interested in... 來表達。如果是用 I have an interest.，雖然不能說錯誤，卻可能被誤解意思，因為 interest 有「股份」的意思，例如：He has an interest in the company.（他在這家公司擁有股份。）注意這句可不是「他對這公司有興趣。」喔！

7. **Nothing goes right recently for your friend David. Say something to offer comfort.**

你的朋友大衛近來諸事不順。說點什麼話來安慰他一下吧！

答題解說

題目應該不難理解，要你說些話來安慰一位朋友。關鍵字彙是 comfort，是個英檢中級單字。雖然題目沒有說大衛發生了什麼事，但你也可以自己發想，想像對方發生了什麼「不如意、不順遂、倒楣」之類的事情來安慰對方。可以是在電話中，或彼此坐在咖啡廳中聊天的情境。一開頭可以說 Hello, David. It's me. I heard that you... recently.，或是 How are you lately, David? You look a bit pale...。可以想像的不順事情可能是「考試被當掉（flunked）」、「一直找不到工作（jobless for long）」、「遇到詐騙（trapped in a scam）」、「與另一半感情不睦（not get along well with one's husband/wife）」…等。至於安慰的話，你可以說「別擔心。一切都會是最好的安排。」、「要正向一點，往好處想」…，或者「我會開車載對方出去散散心」之類的。要是覺得自己不是很擅於安慰別人，可以如時說明，然後說自己總是能夠扮演好傾聽的角色，並適時給予以些建議等。

回答範例 1

Hello, David. It's me. I heard that you've had a hard time looking for a job recently. Don't be worried too much. As far as I know, many of my friends are suffering from the same trouble because of the global economic downturn. I suggest that you keep learning and make yourself better at present. Opportunities are reserved for those who are ready. Don't look down on yourself. Just keep going!

你好，大衛。是我。聽說你最近找工作遇到瓶頸。不要太擔心。據我所知，由於全球經濟不景氣，我很多朋友都遭遇到同樣的困擾。我建議你現在繼續學習，並充實自我。機會是留給準備好的人。別看輕自己。繼續加油！

回答範例 2

Hey David, you look in low spirits. Come on. Take it easy! Things don't always work out as you think. I know I'm not good at comforting someone, but can I invite you to a domestic group tour next week? There will be some close friends joining us. Maybe you'll have the opportunity to meet and get acquainted with a new date. Besides, don't always shut yourself home. Just go out to drive away your cares. I think I'm someone you can rely on.

嘿，大衛，你看起來精神不是很好。別這樣。放輕鬆點！人生不如意事十之八九。我知道我不擅長安慰別人，但我可以邀請你下週來參加一個跟團的國內旅遊嗎？會有一些親密的朋友加入我們。也許你會有機會認識新的對象。此外，不要總是把自己關在家裡。出去外面散散心吧。我想我是你可以信賴的人。

關鍵字詞

comfort v. 安慰　**have a hard time + Ving** phr.（做某事）…有困難　**economic downturn** n. 經濟不景氣　**make oneself better** phr. 充實自我　**look down on** phr. 看不起　**in low spirits** phr. 精神萎靡　**get acquainted with** phr. 認識…　**new date** n. 新的（約會）對象　**shut yourself home** phr. 把自己關在家　**drive away** phr. 驅趕　**rely on** phr. 依靠

延伸學習

每個人都難免碰到一些不如意、令人沮喪的事情,這時候好朋友的安慰就很重要了,以下提供可以用英文來安慰別人的話:

❶ I feel sorry to hear that. Is there anything I can help you with?(我很遺憾聽到那件事。有任何我幫你的嗎?)

❷ I'm just a phone call away if you ever need me.(需要我的話,隨時打給我。)

❸ Stop being so hard on yourself.(別太苛責自己。)

❹ I'm always here with you.(我永遠支持你。)

❺ Oh, that's nothing. I've been through worse.(喔,那沒什麼。我還有經歷過更糟的。)

8. **How much do your three meals cost you a day? What do you usually eat?**

你一天花多少錢吃飯呢?你都吃些什麼呢?

答題解說

雖然本題看起來是要回答「多少錢」以及「吃什麼」,但別忘了答題時間是 30 秒,千萬別簡單答個兩三句就停下來了。每個人一天三餐的花費(the cost of three meals)都不一樣,你不一定要回答一個精確的數字,也可以說一個數字的範圍,例如 NT$250-300 之類的。有些人與家人同住(live with parents/ family),可能早餐、晚餐都吃家裡(eat in),有些人也許「三餐老是在外(always eat out)」,可以如實回答或自己編故事都行。現在叫外送(order food delivery)也很普遍,也是個答題的方向,或是選擇比較簡單的、自己有把握的字詞來回答。像是 bread(麵包)、toast(吐司)、hamburger(漢堡)、sandwich(三明治)、soybean milk(豆漿)、French fries(薯條)…等。

最後,別忘了題目中的 three meals 喔!也就是說,題目要你回答早餐、中餐、晚餐通常吃什麼。要是時間不夠回答,你可以直接 skip 掉一兩餐,說自己通常不吃早/晚餐之類的。又或者,你可以說「沒有固定吃什麼(have no regular meals)」,然後再舉例可能吃火鍋(hot pot)、炒麵(fried noodles)、泡麵(instant noodles)、炒飯(fried rice),要是不確定「排骨飯(rice with pork ribs)」、「雞腿飯(rice with drumstick)」…怎麼說的話,就別太為難自己去冒險了。

回答範例 1

It costs me about three to four hundred dollars for my meals a day. I rent a house and I always eat out, or order food delivery. I usually have two slices of grilled toast plus a bowl of corn soup for my breakfast. At noon, I order a boxed meal. For dinner, I have no regular meals. Sometimes I skip it if I do not feel too hungry, and sometimes I may only eat a piece of chicken steak.

我一天三餐大約花 300-400 元。我在外租房子，總是在外面吃飯，或者叫外送。我早餐通常吃兩片烤吐司加一碗玉米湯。中午時，我會訂便當。晚餐的話，我沒有吃固定的餐點。有時不覺得太餓就不吃了，有時可能只吃一塊雞排。

回答範例 2

I spend about one hundred dollars a day only for lunch, because I live with my parents. My mother prepares breakfast for me, which usually includes a sandwich plus a fried egg, and a glass of soybean milk. At noon, I usually go out for lunch with some of my colleagues. I like to eat fried noodles or fried rice plus a piece of chicken steak. As for dinner, I skip it because I'm trying to lose weight now.

我每天只花一百元吃午餐，因為我和父母同住。媽媽會給我準備早餐，通常是一個三明治加一個荷包蛋，還有一杯豆漿。中午時，我通常和幾個同事一起出去吃午飯。我喜歡吃炒麵或炒飯加一塊雞排。至於晚餐，我通常不吃，因為我正努力在減重。

關鍵字詞

eat out phr. 外食　**order delivery** phr. 叫外送　**corn soup** n. 玉米（濃）湯　**boxed meal** n. 便當　**fried egg** n. 荷包蛋　**soybean milk** n. 豆漿　**go out for lunch** phr. 外出吃午餐　**fried noodles** n. 炒麵　**fried rice** n. 炒飯　**chicken steak** n. 雞排　**skip** v. 略過　**lose weight** phr. 減重

延伸學習

如果要說「中餐／晚餐吃便當」的話，千萬別說成 eat a lunch/dinner box 了，這像是要把便當盒吞下肚子裡去了，而要說 have a boxed meal for lunch/dinner。同樣，「吃麥當勞」也別說成 eat MacDonald 了，可以說 go to MacDonald to grab something to eat... 等。另外，常見的一些餐點名稱有：

❶ 肉類：beef（牛）、chicken（雞）、lamb（羊）、salmon（鮭魚）

❷ 蛋類：boiled egg（水煮蛋）、tea egg (= egg boiled with tea bags)（茶葉蛋）、fried egg（荷包蛋）、braised egg（滷蛋）

❸ 配餐類：(French) fries（薯條）、sweet potato（地瓜）、hash brown（薯餅）

❹ 麵類：pasta / spaghetti（義大利麵）、sliced noodles（刀削麵）、beef noodles（牛肉麵）、cold noodles（涼麵）、ramen（拉麵）

9. **What drives you mad most? What would you do at that moment?**

什麼事情是讓你最抓狂的？在那時候你會做什麼？

答題解說

題目中的 drive you mad 是「讓你發瘋／抓狂／生氣」的意思，也就是問你「最讓你受不了」的事情是什麼。開頭第一句，你可以簡單說 I would be very angry when/if... 或是 It drives me crazy/mad/nuts when/if... 。而會令人抓狂的事，比方說，入睡時被吵醒（awakened when I fall asleep / be waked up by noises）——也許是公司午休時，有人手機大聲響起，或是「真心換絕情（My sincerity was unfeeling to...）」（也許是被好朋友欺騙等）、盡心盡力仍被嫌棄（I am given the cold shoulder after I try hard...）、有人插隊（cut in line）…等。接著可以用過去的經驗來說明發生的事情。至於第二個問題「會做什麼」，就看個人當下習慣性的反應，有些人雖然生氣，但是會忍住（hold back），不想滋事（avoid causing trouble），有些人可能會直接找對方討公道（claim justice with sb.）。可以找自己容易發揮的表達用語，不一定要確實回答。

回答範例 1

It would drive me crazy when my sleep is interrupted, and if this happens during lunch break, I can't take a good rest and I would feel very sleepy at work in the afternoon. Yesterday when I needed to catch a nap at noon, and when the whole office was quiet, a colleague's cellphone rang loudly! I was irritated and later I told my boss about that, and then he sent an email to all employees to announce that cellphones should be set to mute during office hours.

當我的睡眠被打斷時，我會抓狂且如果發生在午休時間，我就不能好好休息，下午上班時我會很睏。昨天中午我要睡午覺，且整間辦公室都很安靜時，一位同事的手機突然大聲地響了起來！我很生氣了，且後來我把這件事告訴了老闆，然後他給所有員工發了一封郵件，宣布上班時間手機要調成靜音。

回答範例 2

There are indeed things I can't stand, especially when someone cuts in line. Yesterday morning I took a U-bike to an MRT station as usual. There were so many passengers standing in line for the train to arrive. When the train bound for my destination was pulling into the station, I saw two young guys run into the carriage from nowhere. Then I shouted loudly to them, "Don't cut in line." This didn't stop them, and the next day I asked the station crew to pay more attention to that.

確實有些事情是我無法忍受的，尤其是遇到有人插隊時。昨天早上，我像往常一樣騎著 U-bike 到捷運站。當時有很多乘客排隊等待。當前往我目的地的列車進

站時，我看到兩個不知從哪冒出的小伙子往車廂裡跑進去。然後我大聲對他們喊，「不要插隊。」這並沒有阻止他們，第二天我請站務人員要多注意這樣的事。

關鍵字詞

drive sb. mad phr. 使某人抓狂　**lunch break** n. 午休時間　**take a good rest** phr. 好好休息　**catch a nap** phr. 小睡片刻　**irritate** v. 激怒　**mute** n. 靜音　**office hours** n. 上班時間　**stand** v. 忍受　**cut in line** phr. 插隊　**be bound for** phr. 預計前往…　**pull** v.（車）行駛　**carriage** n. 車廂　**nowhere** n. 不知名的地方　**station crew** n. 站務人員

延伸學習

當你要表達「我快氣死了！」，只會說 I'm very angry. 嗎？來學學以下更多表達憤怒的說法吧！

❶ choke with rage（氣得說不出話）→ choke 有噎住、阻塞的意思，所以 choke with rage 就是指氣到都得內傷，氣得都說不出話來了。

❷ get hot under the collar（氣得臉紅脖子粗）→ collar 是「衣領」的意思，領子下面很熱？意思就是太生氣了，整個身體都發熱，氣得臉紅脖子粗。

❸ foam at the mouth（火冒三丈）→ foam 是「泡沫」的意思，foam at the mouth 嘴包裡都是泡泡，意指你真的很生氣，氣得口吐白沫。

❹ hit the ceiling（氣得發火）→ 直接翻譯的話就是「撞到了天花板」。形容一個人太生氣了，暴跳如雷，像卡通那樣氣得都飛起來撞上天花板了。

❺ fly into a rage（暴怒）→ rage 比 anger 的「生氣」指數更高，可以說「氣瘋了」，所以 fly into a rage 非常簡單明瞭意思。

10. Have you ever lent money to anyone? Then what happened?

你曾經借錢給任何人嗎？然後如何呢？

答題解說

這是個很好理解的題目，且「借錢給別人後發生的事情」可以陳述的內容也很多。但有時候題目簡單不一定可以拿到好的分數，因為你可能答個兩三句就不知道要再說什麼了。對於第二個問題，回答的內容可能是對方有借有還（return what you borrowed on time）、借了之後搞失蹤、人間蒸發（be ghosted by... after that）或傳訊息卻已讀不回（have/has read but not yet texted me back / leave me on read）、答應何時還卻又藉故一延再延（repeatedly put it off with one excuse and another）…等。然後你可以針對這樣的結果，說說自己的感言或因應之道。如果自己從來沒被借錢過，或是沒借錢給別人過，也可以說一下原

因。比方說，朋友、親友間不要有金錢的往來（avoid having financial dealings with friends or relatives）會比較不傷感情等（no hard feelings）。又或者自己從來沒借錢給別人，但有跟別人借過錢，也可以用來回答本題喔！只是要提醒：要掌握住 lend 和 borrow 的差異。

回答範例 1

Yes. One of my past classmates borrowed some money from me several times. For the first and second times, he borrowed NT$5000 respectively and kept his promise and returned me the money on time. But for the third time, I lent him NT$20,000, and he broke his promise and tried to avoid my contact. I think I'm ghosted by him because he doesn't answer my phone calls and leave me on read after I text him. I just wonder what happened to him. If he's really in trouble now, I won't force him to give the money back to me soon.

是的。有一位以前的同學跟我借了幾次錢。第一次和第二次，他借 5000 元，並且他信守承諾，按時還給我。但第三次他跟我借兩萬元，且他食言了，還逃避我的聯繫。我想他是搞失蹤了，因為他不接我的電話，且在我傳訊息給他後，他已讀不回。我只是想知道他發生什麼事了。如果他現在真的有麻煩，我不會逼他要盡快把錢還我。

回答範例 2

No, I've never lent money to anyone, including any of my close family members. I think it's better to avoid financial dealings with friends, colleagues and even family members. You know, money can easily ruin a relationship. I cherish both friendship and family harmony. Besides, I'm not good at asking for money back. And to tell the truth, I can hardly make both ends meet every month. How could I have extra money to help others?

不，我從來沒有借錢給任何人，包括我任何親密的家人。我認為最好避免與朋友、同事甚至家人有金錢上的往來。你知道，金錢容易毀掉一段關係。我珍惜友誼和家庭的和睦。此外，我也不擅長把錢要回來。而且說實話，我每個月都入不敷出。我怎可能有多餘的錢去幫助別人呢？

關鍵字詞

for the first time phr. 第一次時　**keep/break one's promise** phr. 信守／違背承諾　**on time** phr. 準時　**avoid** v. 避免，逃避　**contact** n. 聯繫，接觸　**leave sb. on read** phr. 對某人已讀不回　**text** v. 傳訊息給…（某人）　**in trouble** phr. 陷入困境　**financial dealings** n. 金錢往來　**ruin** v. 毀壞　**cherish** v. 珍惜　**harmony** n. 和諧　**make both ends meet** phr. 收支平衡

延伸學習

money money money！生活中許多環節都跟「錢」有關，你知道多少與錢有關的英文慣用語、片語或用法嗎？

❶ 俗話說 Money talks. / Money can make the mare go around.（有錢的就是老大。／有錢能使鬼推磨。）

❷ make a killing（賺飽飽／賺很大）

❸ be loaded（很有錢）

❹ (sth.) cost an arm and a leg（某物很貴）

❺ pinch penny 精打細算

❻ Money doesn't grow on tress.（錢難賺。）

第 1 回
第 2 回
第 3 回
第 4 回
第 5 回
第 6 回
第 7 回
第 8 回
第 9 回
第 10 回

T04P3.mp3

答題解說

首先，從圖片本身去判斷其主題，然後就以下 3 點提示陳述自己要說的內容。若對於圖片中的人事物相關英文沒有太大把握的話，試著用代名詞或簡單字彙去表達。

1. 照片裡的人在什麼地方？

   你可以說 at the beach（在海邊）或是 on the beach（在沙灘上），請注意這裡 at 和 on 的區別喔！。如果只是說「他們在室外」（They are outdoors.）之類的，分數會打折扣喔！

2. 照片裡的人在做什麼？

   提到「人」的部分時，你可以先提有多少人（There are five...），以及他們可能的關係（三代同堂 extended family），並稍加描述特徵或其他重點。例如，你可以說 "There are an old couple and a young couple, and a little girl, whose parents might be the young couple." 以及 "The old couple might be the little girl's grandparents."。接著要描述的是「正在做什麼」。可能用到的英文有 "sing some songs"、"clap their hands"、"clap and cheer"…等。

3. 照片裡的人為什麼會在那裡？

我們可以從照片拍攝地點，以及當中人物的行為、動作來判斷他們為什麼會來這地方。例如，你可以說 "They are here on (summer) vacation."、"They take a vacation here."、"on a tour"、"take a trip abroad"...等。

4. 如果尚有時間，請詳細描述圖片中的景物。

例如，從照片中的，你可以繼續補充說，"They are having a picnic on the beach."、"There are some food and wine on the desk."、"They are enjoying family happiness."…等。

第 1 回　第 2 回　第 3 回　第 4 回　第 5 回　第 6 回　第 7 回　第 8 回　第 9 回　第 10 回

回答範例

It is quite obvious that this picture was taken at the beach. There are five people in the picture including four adults and a little girl. It is noted that there are a young couple and an old couple. The young may be the parents of the little girl, and the old are her grandparents. Besides, the little girl standing beside the old couple is, I guess, singing a song or telling the adults how well she performs at school, and both the young and old adults are clapping their hands and cheering for the girl's performance. I think the extended family members came to a resort and had a picnic on the beach, because I can see two folding chairs, a short bench and a desk where there are delicious food and drinks. Besides, from what they wear I'm sure it was summer, and the warm sunlight was shining on them. To enjoy the fun of family union at the beach is not a bad idea.

很明顯地，這張照片是在海邊拍攝的。照片中有五個人，包括四個大人和一個小女孩。值得注意的是，有一對年輕夫婦和一對老夫婦。年輕夫婦可能是小女孩的父母，老夫婦的可能是她的爺爺和奶奶。另外，我想站在老夫婦身邊的小女孩正在唱歌，或是在告訴大人們她在學校表現得很棒，所以長輩們都在為這小女孩的表現拍手及歡呼。我想這個三代同堂的家人們來到一個度假村，然後在沙灘上野餐，因為我可以看到兩張折疊椅、一張矮小的長椅和一張桌子，桌上有美味的食物和飲料。此外，從他們的穿著來看，我確定當時應該是夏天，溫暖的陽光照在他們身上。在海邊享受合家歡樂真不失為一個好主意。

關鍵字詞

at the beach phr. 在海邊　**on the beach** phr. 在沙灘上　**adult** n. 成人　**perform** v. 表現，表演　**clap one's hands** phr. 拍手，鼓掌　**cheer for sb.** phr. 為某人喝采／歡呼　**extended family** n. 大家庭　**sunlight** n. 陽光　**shine** v. 照耀　**family union** n. 家庭聚會

延伸學習

許多人去海邊，都不是真正想進到水中玩水或游泳，而是喜歡在沙灘上愜意的休息。這時候可能會用到以下幾個片語：

at the beach（在海邊）

on the beach（在沙/海灘上）

in the shade（在陰涼處）

以上的介系詞 in/on/at 在使用上都要特別注意，因為英文和中文往往都不是可以直譯的。像在這裡 at the beach 是廣泛指「在海邊（範圍包括海水和沙灘）」從事任何活動，而 on the beach 就是具體地指位置「在沙灘上」。例如：

I'm at the beach. 我在海邊（玩）。

I'm on the beach. 我（踩在）沙灘上。

享受日光浴的英文就是 sunbathing，有時候也會選擇在沙灘上鋪上沙灘巾 beach towel，躺在上面曬太陽。而曬太陽時為了防止曬黑（suntan）一定會擦非常足夠的防曬乳（sunscreen）。長時間曝曬在陽光下一定要記得多多補充水份，否則就容易中暑（heat stroke）喔！

5

GEPT
全民英檢

中級複試
中譯＋解析

第一部分 中譯英

一般對於單身或結婚的選擇有著各種優缺點的爭論。這個爭議性話題最常被討論的是陪伴、責任和生活方式這三方面。在過去，很少人會否認「婚姻是人生必經之路」的說法。而如今，這句老話已受到許多不婚族的挑戰。他們認為婚姻，甚至有無自己的後代，都只是一種人生的選擇。

答題解說

第一句可以用「There be + 主詞」的句型來陳述。主詞是「爭論」（debates/disputes），後面接介系詞 about（對於…）再接「單身或結婚選擇的優缺點」這個名詞詞組。「優缺點」可以用 advantages and disadvantages 或是 pros and cons。第二句的主詞當然就是「這個爭議性話題」，可以用 this controversial issue，而「最常被討論的是…這三方面」可以解讀為「最常被以…的觀點討論」，可以用 in terms of（就…而言）。第三句的架構是「很少人（few people）+ 會否認（would deny）+ …的說法（that...）」，「必經之路」可以用 the road one must take 或是 the only way one must go 來表示。第四句的主詞是「這句老話（this old saying）」，動詞是「已受到挑戰（has been challenged）」，後面接 by 後再接名詞「許多不婚族（many people among the Never-Marry group）」。關於「不婚族」或「獨身主義者」的英文說法，比較正式的是 celibate(s) 或 bachelorist(s)，如果沒把握寫得正確，只要用「釋義」的方式來表達即可，你也可以寫 those who have decided not to get married for their lifetime。最後一句則用 They think/believe 或 They hold the view that 開頭，that 子句內的主詞可以用「婚姻，甚至連帶著有後代」或是「婚姻以及有後代」，注意前者要用單數動詞，後者因為主詞有兩個東西（getting married and even having offspring of their own），所以要用複數動詞。請注意 offspring 是不可數名詞，不要寫成 their offsprings 了，你可以用最簡單的 their kids/children 來表示也可以。「一種人生的選擇」可以用 a（kind of）choice in your life 或是 one of the choices in your life。

譯文範例

There are generally debates over the advantages and disadvantages about the choice of being single or being married. This controversial issue is most commonly discussed in terms of three most commonly aspects: companionship, responsibilities, and lifestyle. In the past, few people would deny that "Getting married is the road one must take in life". But today, this old saying has been challenged by many people among the Never-Marry group. They hold the view that marriage, even along with having offspring of their own, is just a one of the choices in your life.

延伸學習

除了 advantage 和 disadvantage 以外，還有哪些表達「優缺點」或「利弊」的英文呢？

❶ benefit(s) and drawback(s)（優點和缺點，好處和壞處）。例如：The best way to determine which lady is right for you is to analyze the benefits and drawbacks of each.（要決定哪個女孩最適合你，就是分析每一位的優缺點。）

❷ positive aspect(s) and negative aspect(s)（好處和壞處，積極面與消極面）。例如：What are the positive aspects and negative aspects of being a "slasher"?（成為「斜槓族」有什麼好處和壞處？）

❸ pros and cons（利與弊）。例如：We need to look at the pros and cons of this newly-introduced system.（我們要看的是這個新引進系統的利與弊。）

❹ plus point(s) and minus point(s)（好的一面與壞的一面）例如：What are the plus points and minus points of getting married with a trust fund baby?（嫁給一個富二代有什麼好壞處？）

❺ upside and downside（優缺點）例如：Let's analyze the upside and downside of their proposal first.（我們先分析一下他們提案的優缺點吧。）

第二部分 英文作文

提示

無論是小孩子、青少年或是成人，朋友在每個人的生活中都是相當重要的。有句話說「近朱者赤，近墨者黑（If you live with a lame person you will learn to limp.）」學習如何結交好的朋友，並遠離不好的朋友，也是一門重要的人生課題。請提出自己對於「朋友」的看法。

答題解說

對於「朋友」的看法，可能依每個人當下的處境（circumstances）或人生階段（a certain period of lifetime），會有不同的感受。所謂「人無法離群索居。（One cannot live alone and forsake the society.）」當一個小朋友離開父母去上學時，如果在學校與其他學生相處不好（not get along well），完全沒有要好的同學，相信也會過得不快樂，甚至會發生一些事情。從學生時代到離開校園，

115

踏入社會就業（enter the workplace），幾乎每個人生的階段都離不開「社交、群體生活（social life, life in the community）」。當然，還是會有一些習慣於獨來獨往（be accustomed to being a lone wolf）的人，他們也不見得會過得不快樂，或者有些人因為曾經被朋友欺騙、背叛（be cheated or betrayed），而最終選擇不信任「友情（friendship）」。等到人生的中後半段，有了自己的家庭、另一半、孩子時，生活重心（one's focus of life）都在這些人身上，對於朋友，很多人也會更加「隨緣（leave it to fate/destiny）」，而到了退休後（after one's retirement）的老年生活，也許健康對他們來說才是最重要的（What matters most is health.），友情這東西自然已變成可有可無。

另外，有些人覺得，朋友貴在精不在多（What counts is the quality, not the quantity.）。談得來的，一兩位就夠了，如果真的沒有一個，也無所謂，對自己好一點就好了。

以上，提供一些寫作的方向，可以再加些自己的經驗，例如什麼時候曾經有過一個很要好朋友，感謝對方的資助，或是曾經被朋友騙了多少錢，現在人也不見了…等等，都可以作為補充陳述的內容。

作文範例

As an old saying goes, "A friend in need is a friend indeed." In terms of friendship, I always hold the view that, what counts is the quality, instead of the quantity. Good friends share their happiness and joy with us. They will be happy for us when we achieve our goals and vice versa. They enrich our knowledge and mind. When we have a hard time, good friends will stay with us and encourage us to look at the bright side of life. And they will try their best to give us good advice. On the other hand, bad friends may lead us to get addicted to drugs or become violent. When you fall into a bad habit, it's very difficult to fall out of it. So we need to carefully choose friends.

古語有云：患難見真情。就友誼來說，我始終認為「貴在精不在多。」好的朋友會與我們分享他們的幸福和快樂。當我們實現目標時，他們會為我們感到高興，反之亦然。他們豐富了我們的知識和思想。當我們遇到困難時，好朋友會陪伴在我們身邊，鼓勵我們看人生的光明面。他們會盡力給我們好的建議。但另一方面，壞朋友可能會帶領我們去吸毒或變得有暴力傾向。當你養成一個壞習慣時，就很難戒掉。所以我們需要慎重選擇朋友。

延伸學習

俗話說：「在家靠父母，出外靠朋友。（At home one depends on his parents; abroad, he needs the help of his friends.）」朋友是一生中不可或缺的角色。以下就來看看有那些深得人心的友誼金句吧！

❶ A true friend is known in the day of adversity.（疾風知勁草，患難見真情。）

❷ A friend is one who believes in you when you have ceased to believe in yourself.（朋友是當你自己都不相信你自己時，他依然相信著你。）

❸ A friend is someone who understands your past, believes in your future, and accepts you just the way you are.（真正的朋友願意去理解你的過去，相信你的未來，並接受你現在的樣子。）

❹ A friend without faults will never be found.（沒有缺點的朋友是永遠找不到的。）

❺ A single hand that wipes tears during failures is much better than countless hands that come together to clap on success.（失敗時有人伸出一隻手來為你擦淚，會好過成功時無數人伸手為你鼓掌。）

❻ A strong friendship doesn't need daily conversation or being together.（堅固的友情不需要每天對話或見面，只要情誼存心中，好友永不離。）

第1回
第2回
第3回
第4回
第5回
第6回
第7回
第8回
第9回
第10回

T05P1.mp3

第一部分 朗讀短文

Life is short and sometimes in a messy and ever-changing world. Precious things can easily become lost. Frequently, circumstances out of our control cause loss, and our own choices may cause us to lose the things that mean the most. Each of us has different needs and priorities in life, but we share one thing in common: the absence of certain things in our lives can make us feel that our lives are incomplete.

****

Many of us take it for granted that we live safely, until something life-changing happens because our health is at risk. With good health, anything is possible. Without it, you can feel hopeless and helpless for the future. To be healthy means to take care of your emotion, body and soul. Don't be ignorant of what your body is telling you. Eat healthy and exercise daily to minimize preventable illnesses and the stress that may be keeping you from enjoying life.

答題解說

這兩篇分別關於「人生無常」與「身體健康」的小短文，其中 priority [praɪˋɔrətɪ] 屬於英檢中高級單字，如果不會的話也不彷先學起來吧！而也是中高級的 minimize 是 minimum（[ˋmɪnəməm]，最小化）的衍生字，只要注意字尾的 [-maɪz] 發音即可。另外，有幾個屬於英檢中級的字彙。像是 messy [ˋmɛsɪ]、frequently [ˋfrikwəntlɪ]、circumstances [ˋsɝkəmˌstænsɪs]、incomplete [ˌɪnkəmˋplit]、ignorant [ˋɪgnərənt] 以及 preventable [prɪˋvɛntəbl]，也必須注意自己的發音是否正確。另外，第一篇的動詞 lose [luz] 以及名詞 loss [lɔs] 當中字母 o 的發音是不一樣的，第二篇的 hopeless 以及 helpless 的字尾 –less 發 [lɪs] 的音，請特別注意。

以下標有顏色的單字，請盡可能唸得比較響亮，出現「|」的地方，請稍作停頓，試著讓自己融入短文的情境中。最後，也請注意字與字之間該連音（包括「消音」」）的部分（以下畫底線），像是 Life is short、out of our、absence of、take it、is at、what your... 等。最後，要提醒一點：朗讀短文時，並不是每一個可以連音的部分都要發連音。例如第一篇的 "circumstances out of..." 當中的 circumstances 與 out 就不一定要連音，因為我們畢竟不是母語人士，連音不見得會連得漂亮，而且朗讀短文的部分不但有足夠的時間唸完，而且該念清楚的地方絕對不能馬虎。但也不能「每個字的每個音」都念得很清楚。例如 take care，不要念成 [tek-kɛr]。

Life is short and sometimes in a messy │ and ever-changing world. Precious things can easily become lost. Frequently, │ circumstances out of our control cause loss, │ and our own choices may cause us to lose the things that mean the most. Each of us has different needs and priorities in life, │ but we share one thing in common: │ the absence of certain things in our lives │ can make us feel that │ our lives are incomplete.

****

Many of us take it for granted that │ we live safely, │ until something life-changing happens │ because our health is at risk. With good health, │ anything is possible. Without it, │ you can feel hopeless and helpless for the future. To stay healthy means to take care of your emotion, body and soul. Don't be ignorant of │ what your body is telling you. Eat healthy and exercise daily │ to minimize preventable illnesses and the stress │ that may be keeping you from enjoying life.

短文翻譯

人生苦短，且有時候生命處於一個雜亂無章、瞬息萬變的世界中。珍貴的東西很容易丟失。往往，我們的失去是來自我們無法控制的狀況，而我們自己的選擇又可能使我們失去最重要的東西。我們每個人生命中都有不同的需求和最要緊的事，但我們有一個共同點：生活中缺少了什麼，會讓我們感到自己的生命是不完整的。

****

我們許多人會認為能好好活著是理所當然的，直到改變生活的事情發生了，因為我們的健康處於危險之中。有了健康，一切都有可能。沒了健康，你會對未來感到絕望和無助。身體健康意味著照顧好你的情緒、身體和靈魂。不要忽視你的身體在告訴你什麼。吃得健康以及每天運動，將可預防的疾病，以及可能讓你無法享受生活的壓力降至最低吧。

關鍵字詞

messy adj. 凌亂的　**ever-changing** adj. 瞬息萬變的　**every now and then** phr. 有時，偶爾　**circumstance** n. 狀況，環境　**out of one's control** phr. 不在某人控制中的　**priority** n. 優先事項　**share... in common** phr. 有共同的…　**absence** n. 不存在　**incomplete** adj. 不完整的　**take it for granted that...** phr. 將…視為理所當然　**at risk** phr. 有風險，處於危險中　**be ignorant of** phr. 對於…無知　**minimize** v. 將…最小化　**preventable** adj. 可避免的　**illness** n. 疾病　**stress** n. 壓力　**keep sb. from –ing** phr. 讓某人無法…（做某事）

第二部分 回答問題

T05P2.mp3

1. **Have you ever been to a night market? What food or drink do you like best there?**

   你去過夜市嗎？你最喜歡那裡的什麼食物或飲料？

答題解說

題目第一句的 "Have you ever been to...?" 是「你曾經去過…嗎？」的意思。關鍵字詞 night market 是「夜市」。而第二個問題 "What food or drink..." 告訴你，可以回答一種自己最愛的夜市美食或是飲料即可，如果沒有把握，不必說太多食物的英文名稱，說錯了反而扣分。可以自己先想好什麼食物你有把握不會說錯。像是比較簡單的 stinky tofu（臭豆腐）、fried chicken（炸雞）、sweet potato（地瓜）、sweet potato balls（地瓜球）、hot pot（火鍋）、milk tea（奶茶）、bubble tea（泡沫紅茶）...等。如果對於 pig's blood cake（豬血糕）、oyster omelet（蚵仔煎）、intestine vermicelli（大腸麵線）, scallion pancakes（蔥油餅）、pork sausage sandwiched in a sticky rice（大腸包小腸）…這些食物沒把握說得正確的話，就千萬別冒險喔！

那麼，在簡單回答完兩個問題時，還能再說什麼呢？針對第一個問題，你可以再補充為什麼喜歡去這種地方、通常跟什麼人去，或者雖然有去過，但並不是很喜歡去，原因為何…等。針對第二個問題，你可以補充說這種食物或飲料讓你回想起什麼感覺，或者某個攤商是個美女、帥哥之類的。如果從來沒去過夜市，也可以大略說明一下原因。

第 1 回
第 2 回
第 3 回
第 4 回
第 5 回
第 6 回
第 7 回
第 8 回
第 9 回
第 10 回

回答範例 **1**

Yes, I go to night markets very often, especially on weekends or holidays. I think the night market is a good place where I can feel relaxed and enjoy the fun of seeking delicious food or drinks. I like many kinds of food, especially fried chicken and stinky tofu most. Besides, I don't mind standing in a long line.

是的，我經常去夜市，尤其是在週末或假日。我覺得夜市是一個放鬆身心，享受尋找美食或飲料樂趣的好地方。我喜歡的食物有很多種，尤其是炸雞和臭豆腐。此外，我不介意去排很長的隊。

回答範例 **2**

Of course, I used to go there, though I don't like night markets much. Night markets are normally crowed, especially on holidays or on weekends, which makes me feel like a fish out of water. However, I like a night market's pearl milk tea, which reminds me of the good old days when I was still a university student.

當然，我去過，雖然我不太喜歡夜市。夜市通常很擁擠，尤其是在假期或週末，這讓我感到渾身不自在。儘管如此，我喜歡某夜市的珍珠奶茶，它讓我想起我大學時代的美好時光。

關鍵字詞

night market n. 夜市　**fried chicken** n. 炸雞　**stinky tofu** n. 臭豆腐　**crowed** adj. 擁擠的　**feel like a fish out of water** phr. 感到渾身不自在　**pearl milk tea** n. 珍珠奶茶　**remind sb. of sth.** phr. 使某人想起某事

延伸學習

跟外國朋友聊天時，想要介紹美食、小吃英文給對方卻詞窮嗎？以下繼續為您補充一些常見的美食英文。

Taiwanese salt crispy chicken（鹽酥雞）、fried chicken cutlet（炸雞排）、pork belly bun/gua bao（刈包）、Taiwanese oden（甜不辣）、giant meat dumplings（肉圓）、scallion pancake（蔥油餅）、pepper cake（胡椒餅）、meat-based geng noodle（肉羹麵）、pan-fried bun（水煎包）、grilled sausage（烤香腸）、grilled squid（烤魷魚）、century egg tofu（皮蛋豆腐）、coffin bread（棺材板）、pork ball soup（貢丸湯）、fish ball soup（魚丸湯）、rib stewed in medicinal herbs（藥燉排骨）、sesame oil chicken soup（麻油雞）、shaved ice（刨冰／剉冰）、roasted sweet potato（烤地瓜）、tofu pudding（豆花）、hot grass jelly（燒仙草）、taro balls（芋圓）、egg pancake（雞蛋糕）

另外，如何形容食物有多好吃呢？你可以用以下的形容詞：

delicious / tasty / yummy / flavorful（美味的，可口的）、mouth-watering（令人垂涎的）。如果很難吃的話，你可以用 yucky / dreadful / disgusting / horrible（糟糕的，令人厭惡的）、stale（不新鮮的，走味的）、inedible（不能吃的）如果要形容食物的「口味」、「口感」等，你可以用 sour（酸酸的）、sweet（甜的）、bitter（苦的）、spicy / hot（辣的）、salty（鹹的）、crispy（酥脆的）、plain / tasteless（沒味道的）、strong（重口味的）、greasy（油膩的）、juicy（多汁的）、tender（軟嫩的）、chewy（有嚼勁的）、fluffy（鬆軟的）、smoky（煙燻的）

2. **Do you often complain? Talk about your experience.**

   你經常發牢騷嗎？談談你的經驗。

   答題解說

   第一個問題是個 Yes/No 的回答，但也不一定是「非黑即白」的問題。你也可以回答說 "Sometimes I do, but most of the time I can always hold back."（有時候我會，但大部分時候我都能忍住。）第二個問題「談談你的經驗」，就是要你敘述過去生活中發生了什麼事讓你抱怨的，如果還有時間，可以再補充說明你如何因應或面對那件事情。

   對學生而言，抱怨功課太多、考試太多；上班族可能工作太多、太累或是上下班大塞車…等，都可以是抱怨的原因。當然，你也可以說自己從來不抱怨，秉持著「一切都是上天最好的安排」的心態，只要存好心、做好事、說好話也可以。或者自己很少抱怨事情，但身旁的某某人經常抱怨東抱怨西的，大小事都要抱怨之類的說法，也都可以拿來發揮喔！

   回答範例 1

   Yes, I do. I often complain we need to take too many exams, and I really have too little time to prepare for them. For example, I have three English tests and four math ones next week, and the mid-term exam is coming next month. Sometimes I just feel tired and helpless for those tests.

   是的，我會發牢騷。我經常抱怨我們有太多的考試，而我真的沒有足夠的時間來準備。比如說，我下週要考三次英文考試以及和四次數學考試，而下個月就要期中考試了。有時我只是對那些考試感到疲倦和無助。

   回答範例 2

   I'm not the one who likes to complain. I always try to hold back from making complaints and to find a solution to each problem. For example, I am often overloaded with work, but I'll communicate patiently with my boss about that. He is always willing to make a proper adjustment for my assignments.

我不是那種喜歡發牢騷的人。我總是盡量克制自己不去抱怨，並為每個問題找到解決方案。比如我經常有超過負荷的工作量，但我會耐心地和老闆溝通。他總是願意為我的任務做適當的調整。

第 1 回
第 2 回
第 3 回
第 4 回
第 5 回
第 6 回
第 7 回
第 8 回
第 9 回
第 10 回

關鍵字詞

prepare for phr. 準備… **mid-term** adj. 期中的 **hold back from** phr. 抑制（免於…） **complaint** n. 抱怨（的事情） **solution** n. 解決辦法 **be overloaded with** phr. 過度承受… **patiently** adv. 耐心地 **proper** adj. 適當的 **adjustment** n. 調整 **assignment** n. 任務

延伸學習

人生不如意十之八九，職場上難免遇到工作量暴增（overloaded with work）、同事太雷（such a spoilsport）或其它不順心（against one's will）、讓你感到委屈（feel wronged）的事情。其實適時地抱怨、發洩並非壞事，甚至可以讓心情舒緩（relief）許多，也可以調整好心情再出發。以下字詞也可以用來抱怨工作上的事情，而且可以讓你的英文表達更上一層樓喔！

❶ pull rank（on someone）拿職位壓人

rank 當名詞，有「排名、名次」的意思，職場上總會遇到喜歡拿職位壓人的主管，認為自己的位階高，便可以對下屬頤指氣使，這時候你就可以用 pull rank on somone 來抱怨上司。例如：My supervisor always pulls rank on me; I'm so sick of it!（我的上司總是拿職位壓我，我真的是受夠了。）

❷ micromanager 管東管西的人

字首 micro- 有「微的」意思，後面加上動詞 manage 是「微管理」的意思，其實就如透過顯微鏡在檢視一個人的所有舉動，也就衍生用來描述一個人喜歡管東管西。例如：Ben is such a micromanager. He micromanages all the outgoing emails by his staff, which is very stressful for everyone.（Ben 是這麼一個愛管東管西的人，他監視所有下屬寄出的電子郵件內容，讓每個人都備感壓力。）

❸ dirty work 吃力不討好的事

dirty 大家都知道是「骯髒的」意思，在職場上，我們對於吃力不討好的事情，會用 dirty work 來表示。例如：He's always passing his dirty work to the interns at work. That's unacceptable.（他總是叫實習生做吃力不討好的工作，這很不合理。）

3. **What is your life goal now? How will you achieve it?**

   你現在的人生目標是什麼？你會如何達成呢？

   答題解說

   人生因為有目標而顯得有意義！每個人當下的目標肯定都不一樣，比如說，你想成為什麼人、想做什麼事或成就什麼結果，都是可以答題的方向。具體的目標可能是「希望在幾歲前擁有多少財富（然後就可以退休了）」（hope to have a wealth of... before I retire）、「希望去環遊世界，不用擔心生活」（go traveling around the world and have no worries about money），或者「找到談得來、合得來的另一半（find the better half that is mutually matched）」。一般來說，具體的人生目標可能與財富金錢、事業發展、家庭生活、學習成長、人際關係以及休閒娛樂有關。當然，也許有些人本不知道自己要什麼，有些人也許覺得「平安就是福（Peace and safety is the root of happiness.）」、「過得快樂就是人生的目標（To live happily is the life goal.）」。接著可以大略想要達成此目標的動機為何。

   至於「如何達成」的第二個部分，你可以說「努力工作賺錢」、「學習待人接物（treat people with respect），讓自己成為一個更好的人」、「鍛鍊強健的體魄」（work out to be physically strong）…等。

   回答範例 1

   My life goal at present is to have my own house. I have a girlfriend and we have been together for almost five years. We plan to get married within 2 years, but I still rent a house now. I'm working hard and plan to work part-time to earn more. Besides, I'll ask my parents for additional housing funds.

   我目前的人生目標是擁有自己的房子。我有一個女朋友，且我們在一起快五年了。我們計劃在 2 年內結婚，但我現在還在租房子。我努力工作並打算再兼差多賺一些錢。此外，我會要求我父母提供額外的購物資金。

   回答範例 2

   Frankly speaking, I have no idea what my life goal is. I have a steady job and income. I'm single, but I don't want to get married and have kids. I don't have any real estate, but I think it's OK. If I need to tell you what my goal is, I'd say peace and happiness are forever my goal of life.

   坦白說，我不知道我的人生目標是什麼。我有一份穩定的工作和收入。我單身，但我不打算結婚生子。我沒有任何房地產，但我認為沒關係。如果我必須告訴你我的目標是什麼，我會說平安與幸福是我永遠的人生目標。

第 1 回
第 2 回
第 3 回
第 4 回
第 5 回
第 6 回
第 7 回
第 8 回
第 9 回
第 10 回

關鍵字詞

additional adj. 額外的，更多的　**housing fund** n. 購屋資金　**frankly** adv. 坦白地　**steady** adj. 穩定的　**single** adj. 單身的　**real estate** n. 房地產　**house loan** n. 房貸

延伸學習

aim、goal、objective、target 都有「目標」的意思，但其著重的點以及用法都有一些差異。

❶ aim 是「瞄準」、「旨在」、「對準」，所以有「目標」的意思。例如：She outlined the company's aims and prospects in her speech.（她在演說中大致說明了公司的目標與願景。）

❷ goal 在足球場上有「射門，進球得分」的意思，也引伸出「目標，目的」的解釋。例句：You should set goals for yourself at the beginning of each school year.（您應該在每個學年開始時為自己設定目標。）

❸ objective 當形容詞有「客觀的」意思，代表的是一種「總體的目標」，常用於商用英語中。例如：The principal objective of the department is to identify market opportunities.（本部門主要目標是確認市場上的機會。）

❹ target 原指射箭、射飛鏢的「標靶」，因此也被引伸為「（要針對的、攻擊的）目標」。例如：The kidnappers carefully selected their targets.（綁匪精心挑選了他們的目標。）

4. **Do you keep a pet? Why or why not?**

   你有養寵物嗎？為什麼要，或為什麼不要養呢？

   答題解說

keep a pet 是「養寵物」的意思，keep 可以用 have/get/foster/raise/bring up 等動詞取代，但無論如何，pet 這個名詞，你一定要聽得出來，否則會答非所問了。以現在的流行用語就叫「毛小孩」，特別指 pet dog（寵物狗）或 pet cat（寵物貓在目前這個生育率走下坡的年代，加上通貨膨脹（inflation）、物價上漲（price hike）趨勢以及低薪的環境（low-income environment），許多家庭寧可不生小孩，而改養阿貓阿狗來增添生活樂趣（spice up one's life）或多一個陪伴（companion）。此外，養寵物也可以讓你多了一些社交的機會（more opportunities of social interaction）。許多人養貓養狗幾乎就是當作自己的小孩般的寵愛（dote on），甚至付出比對人類還要無微不至的照顧（take so much care of）。這樣的現象與趨勢，就可以用來作養寵物者的答題方向。那麼，不養寵物的人可以怎麼說呢？比方說，因為在外租屋，而房東不准、怕咬傷家裡或鄰

居的小孩、準備出國工作／念書、會在家亂大小便、寵物壽命短…等。

回答範例 1

Yes, I have had a French bulldog for more than seven years, and I named him Ice Cream. I rent a house and live alone, so I considered him one of my family members. He's always listening quietly to my complaints about everything. After having talked to him, I feel better. That's why I want to keep a pet.

是的，我養了一隻法國鬥牛犬七年多了，我給它取名叫「冰淇淋」。我在外租屋且一個人住，所以我把他當成我的家人之一。他總是靜靜地傾聽我的所有抱怨。和他傾訴過後，我感覺好多了。這就是我想養寵物的原因。

回答範例 2

No, I don't keep a pet, though I used to consider raising one. I have two kids and they always make a mess around the house. Sometimes I need to spend a lot of time tidying up everywhere. I'm afraid I won't have time taking care of a pet dog or pet cat, because I'm constantly busy with work.

不，我不養寵物，雖然我曾經考慮過要養。我有兩個孩子，他們總是把房子弄得一團糟。有時我得花很多時間四處清理。我恐怕我沒有時間照顧寵物阿狗阿貓，因為我一直忙於工作。

關鍵字詞

keep a pet phr. 養寵物　　**name** v. 取名　　**consider** v. 視…為…　　**complaint** v. 抱怨（的話）　　**raise** v. 扶養，飼養　　**make a mess** phr. 弄得一團亂　　**tidy up** phr. 整理，清理　　**be busy with** phr. 忙於…

延伸學習

飼養寵物讓我們多了很多社交的機會，但是當我們遇到老外時，如何跟他們開啟有關寵物的話題呢？首先，以常見的狗貓品種（breed）說，有「貴賓狗（Poodle）」、「柴犬（Shiba Inu）」、「吉娃娃（Chihuahua）」、「米格魯（Beagle）」、「巴吉度（Hush Puppy）」、「鬥牛犬（Bulldog）」、「臘腸狗（Sausage Dog）」、「杜賓狗（Doberman Pinscher）」、「牧羊犬（Shepherd dog）」、「波斯貓（Persian Cat）」、「暹邏貓（Siamese Cat）」、「孟加拉貓（Bengal Cat）」、「孟買貓（Bombay Cat）」、「俄羅斯藍貓（Russian Blue Cat）」等。

就寵物用品來說，有「項圈（collar）」、「牽繩（leash）」、「防暴衝背帶（harness）」、「自動飲水器（water feeder）」、「貓砂（cat litter）」...等。而飼料方面最簡單的是「寵物飼料（dry pet food）」、「寵物罐頭（canned pet food）」…等。

5. Do you like to be a leader? What does leadership mean to you?

你喜歡成為領導人嗎？你對於領導能力有何看法？

答題解說

其實這是個職場面試經常會被問到的問題，因為你的回答會展露出你是什麼樣個性的人。不過因為現在是面對英檢考試，你不必為了真實回答而冒險去說一些自己沒有把握的字詞或表達用語。而對於這裡第二個問題，首先你要了解 leadership 代表什麼。它的涵義包括「領導特質，領袖身分，領導地位」。假設你是希望自己成為一個領導人的話，可以針對「如何成為領導人」或是「領導能力要具備那些特質（What does leadership need?）」來回答。像是「給予團隊成員適當的權力（authorize your team members or subordinates to be on their appropriate duties）」、「有效的溝通能力（effective communicative skills）」、「展現高超的情緒智商（display superb EQ）」、「擁有解決問題的能力（be capable of solving problems）」、「尊重他人的意見（pay respect to others' opinions）」…等。

如果你的回答是 No, I don't want to be a leader. 呢？可以針對「為什麼不喜歡當領導人」這個方向，去陳述自己對於 leadership 的看法，比較普遍的說法可能是，「本身個性內向害羞（introverted & shy），不喜歡面對人群（dislike standing in the presence of a crowd）」、「領導人的責任重大，很有壓力（Leadership brings responsibilities and powerful stress.）」…等。

回答範例 1

Yes, I like to be a leader and I frequently act as a leader during different periods of my life. When I was a junior high school student, I was elected the class leader. Now I am the supervisor of a department. I think being a leader can help me develop effective communicative skills and the ability to solve problems.

是的，我喜歡當領導人，而且在我生命中的不同時期，我經常擔任領導人。國中時我就被選為班長。而現在我是一個部門的主管。我認為成為領導者可以幫助我培養有效的溝通技能以及解決問題的能力。

回答範例 2

No, I don't like to be a leader, because I have a bit dislike of taking care of others, excluding my family members, of course. And I think I don't inherently have the capability of dealing with so many problems among people. I just want to do my own jobs well. In short, I like to live a simple life.

不，我不喜歡當領導人，因為我不是很喜歡處理別人的事，當然，我的家人除外。而且我認為我天生沒有能力處理人與人之間那麼多的問題。我只想做好自己

第 1 回
第 2 回
第 3 回
第 4 回
第 5 回
第 6 回
第 7 回
第 8 回
第 9 回
第 10 回

的份內工作。總之，我喜歡過單純的生活。

關鍵字詞

supervisor n. 主管，監督者　**communicative skill** n. 溝通技巧　**exclude** v. 將…排除　**inherently** adv. 天生地　**do one's own jobs** phr. 做好份內工作　**simple** adj. 單純的

延伸學習

leadership 這個名詞是從動詞 lead 衍生而來：lead（帶領，引導）→ leader（帶領人，領導人）→ leadership（領導特質，領袖身分，領導地位）。常見用法如下：

❶ 後面搭配介系詞 of。例如，He failed to win the leadership of the party.（他無法拿下該黨的黨主席位置。）

❷ 前面常搭配介系詞 under：under sb's leadership。例如，They invaded the Roman Empire under the leadership of Alaric I.（他們在阿拉里克一世的領導下入侵了羅馬帝國。）

❸ 與其他名詞形成複合名詞：a leadership struggle/contest/challenge。例如，The leadership struggle in the party will grow more intense in the future.（未來，黨內的領導階層鬥爭將更加激烈。）

6. **What do you think about yourself? What kind of person gets along well with you?**

你對自己有什麼看法？什麼樣的人會跟你合得來呢？

答題解說

第一個問題問你覺得「對自己有什麼看法」，似乎是個很模糊的問題，當下可能不知道要回答什麼。要回答「什麼樣個性的人」、「對自己有什麼期許」還是「覺得自己有什麼優缺點」？但其實以全民英檢這道題來說，如果同一題問了你兩個問題，那這兩個問題肯定是相關的，所以請務必要從這個方向去判斷題目要你回答什麼。既然第二個問題問你覺得「什麼樣的人會跟你合得來」，那麼第一個問題就是要請你回答「自己是什麼樣（個性）的人」。

一開始你可以說，It's hard to say, but others say that I am a...（我說不上來，不過別人都說我是…）來開頭，接著可以帶入自己的工作，或其他與自己性格有因果關係的事項。你可以先想好一些簡單的用詞，比方說 friendly（友善的）、confident（有自信的）、humble（謙虛的）、have a sense of justice（有正義感）、have a heart of gold（心地善良）、be grateful for everything（對一切抱著感恩的心）…等，盡可能避免負面觀感的字詞，像是 lazy（懶惰的）、selfish

（自私的）、have a disposition of violence（有暴力傾向）…等。而第二個問題等於是根據第一個問題的回答來說明，所以請務必注意兩者間的合理性與邏輯性。雖然跟自己合得來的人不見得是一樣個性的人，但你一樣可以根據回答第一個問題時所想好的、與個性有關的字詞來回答。比方說，因為自己是內向的（introverted）人、害羞的人，覺得跟比較外向（extroverted/outgoing）、直言不諱的（straight from the shoulder）人會比較合得來。或者你可以說，自己是個很隨和的（easy-going）人，跟什麼樣個性的人都可以相處得來。

回答範例 1

I think I am an easy-going and outgoing person. I like to go out to meet people and talk with them about anything. As a matter of fact, that's why I choose to be a salesperson. I work as a real estate agent and I'm happy that I can see people from all walks of life, and I can even learn something from chatting with them. As for what kind of person I can get along with, I think there's nobody that's hard to get along with for me.

我想我是一個隨和且外向的人。我喜歡出去外面見到人，並和他們聊任何事情。事實上，這就是我選擇成為業務人員的原因。我是一名房仲，我很高興能遇見各行各業的人，甚至可以從與他們的聊天當中學到一些東西。至於我能和什麼樣的人相處得來，我覺得對我來說沒有難以相處的人。

回答範例 2

It's hard to say what kind of person I am, but most of the time, I'm somewhat popular with my classmates. When there's someone who needs my help, for example, with homework or class notes, I'll proceed without hesitation, as long as that's within my capabilities. Of course, there's someone I dislike, especially those who are full of themselves and always take others' help for granted. I'm helpful, but that doesn't mean I'm obliged to help, so I think I'll stay far away from such classmates.

很難說我是個什麼樣的人，但大多數時候，我在同學中是有點受歡迎的。當有人需要我幫忙時，例如回家作業或上課筆記，我都義無反顧，只要是在我的能力範圍內。當然，也有我不喜歡的人，尤其是那些自以為是，總是把別人的幫助當成理所當然的人。我樂於助人，但這並不代表我有義務幫忙，所以我想我會遠離這樣的同學。

關鍵字詞

get along phr. 相處　**easy-going** adj. 隨遇而安的　**outgoing** adj. 外向的　**from all walks of life** phr. 來自各行業　**as for** phr. 至於…　**class note** n.上課筆記 **without hesitation** phr. 果斷地，毫不猶豫地　**within one's capabilities** phr. 在某人能力範圍內　**be full of oneself** phr. 自以為是　**take... for granted** phr.

視⋯為理所當然　**helpful** adj. 樂於助人的　**be obliged to-V** phr. 有義務⋯（做某事）　**stay far away from** phr. 遠離⋯

延伸學習

在談話過程中，為了了解對方的想法，我們經常會用 What do you think? 與 How do you think? 來表達「你覺得呢？」但這話都可以用嗎？兩者沒有差別嗎？如果有人問你：These are my ideas. How do you think?（以上是我的想法。你們覺得怎麼樣？）

其實這是個標準的「中式英文」。因為這樣問的話，意思就變成「你怎麼想的？」、「你用什麼方式來思考的？」所以正確說法是：These are my ideas. What do you think?。又比方說，跟好友去逛街，試穿完鞋子後想問朋友的看法，可以說：I love this pair of shoes! What do you think?（我喜歡這雙鞋！你覺得呢？）這時對方可能會說：It looks great on you. Buy it!（你穿起來超好看。買下去吧！）

7. **Do you prefer certain brands when you make purchases? Why or why not?**

   當你買東西時，會偏好特定品牌嗎？為什麼？

   答題解說

「特定品牌（certain brand）」是有些消費者在做出購買決定（make a purchasing decision）時的考量之一。如果你的回答是肯定的，可以直接說 Yes, I prefer certain brands when I buy things, because...。接著就舉例說明買什麼東西會選特定、知名或高檔品牌。比方說，智慧型手機（smartphone），會選 Apple/iPhone、Samsung...等，買包包一定要買 LV、衣服的話會選 Nike、Gucci、Chanel⋯等，鞋子一定要穿 Adidas、FILA⋯。至於選擇特定品牌的原因，有時候也很難解釋什麼，你也可以說，「使用某個品牌久了有感情，不會想換」也可以喔！

如果你答案是否定的，就得先想好「偏好的因素」是什麼？比方說，主要會考量「預算／價格（in consideration of <u>one's budget</u>/ <u>the prices</u>）」、「正在促銷／打折（whether <u>it is on sale</u> / <u>there's a discount</u>）」、「時下流行（in fashion）」⋯等。不過，還有一種答案是：It depends.。也就是說，要看買什麼東西。如果是手機，有人就是習慣用 Android 或 iOS 系統的，如果是車子，有人開 Toyota、Nissan、或 Volvo...等廠牌的習慣了，每次換車都是在同個品牌換，但衣服的話，也許就是「便宜、耐穿（cheap and durable）」就好。

回答範例 1

Hmmm... I think it depends. Different purchases have different considerations. If I want to buy a new smartphone, I will choose Apple's iPhone, because it offers the safer and stable iOS system and it is more value-maintaining. But if I want to buy a new pair of leather shoes, price will be my prior consideration. I would go online to pick a good deal, because it is easier to compare product prices of the brand or the same style.

嗯⋯我想這要看買什麼。買不同的東西會有不同的考量。如果我想買支新的智慧型手機，我會選擇蘋果的 iPhone，因為它提供了更安全且穩定的 iOS 系統，也更保值。但如果我想買一雙新皮鞋，價格會是我的首要的考量。我會上網挑選優惠價格的，因為上網可以更容易比較同品牌或同款式的產品價格。

回答範例 2

Yes, brand is normally a major consideration when I make purchases. In fact, many products have their own brands, which can promise you that the products you buy are not parallel or fake goods. I have used Samsung cellphones for many years and I always choose to buy Honda cars. But it's actually a bit hard to explain why I choose certain brands. Maybe you can say I have great feelings for them, or I'm just accustomed to using these products of certain brands.

是的，品牌通常是我購買時的主要考慮因素。事實上，很多產品都有自己的品牌，而品牌可以保證你沒有買到水貨或假貨。我用三星手機很多年了，且我總是選擇買本田的車子。但為什麼選擇某些品牌其實是有點難解釋的。也許你可以說我對它們有感情，或者我只是習慣使用某些品牌的產品。

關鍵字詞

make purchases phr. 購物　**consideration** n. 考量（因素）　**value-maintaining** adj. 保值的　**leather shoes** n. 皮鞋　**parallel goods** n. 水貨　**fake** adj. 仿冒的　**have a feeling for** phr. 對⋯有感情　**be accustomed to -ing** phr. 習慣於⋯

延伸學習

當你到實體店面去購物時，有時候當下還無法立即決定買或不買時，你可能會說「我考慮一下。」也許你可以說 I'll think about it.。在多數老外的耳裡，這句話給人感覺是「拒絕的藉口」，如果是到店裡走馬看花，服務人員想推銷東西，但你不想買，直接說 No... 似乎不太禮貌，所以很多人會委婉地說 I'll think about it.，而一般店員也都能習以為常，聽到這句話，就會明白意思而離開了。

I'll think about it. 也常常出現在父母和孩子的對話，或女孩拒絕男孩約會邀請時候也會用。例如：

❶ Son：Dad, can I get an iPad?（兒子：爸，我可以買一台 iPad 嗎？）

Dad：I won't get it for you now but I'll think about it.（父親：現在不行，但我會考慮。）→ 已委婉拒絕，並非日後真的要買

❷ Guy：Hey, I kinda like you, will you go out with me?（男：我很喜歡妳，可以和我約會嗎？）

Girl：I'll think about it.（女：我再想想。）→ 已委婉拒絕，並非還想給對方機會

8. Do you have any health problems? How do you solve these problems?

你有任何健康上的問題嗎？你如何解決這些問題呢？

答題解說

health problem 是「健康上的問題」。大部分人多多少少都有一些身體上的大小毛病，也許是「過胖（overweight）」、「過敏（allergy）」、「背痛（backache）」、「口臭（bad breath）」…等，但請注意這裡是問你比較長期性（long-term / chronic）、經常性的（frequent）健康問題，也可以提到特定時節、條件或狀況時才會發生。而針對第一個問題的回答，你可以說出一些疾病的名稱，像是 diabetes（糖尿病）、high/low blood pressure（高／低血壓）、heart disease（心臟病）、sleeplessness / insomnia（失眠）、asthma / short of breath（氣喘）...等。如果一時之間說不出這些名詞，也可以直接敘述「狀況」，像是天氣一變冷就會鼻子過敏、打噴嚏（sneeze）、容易感冒等。接著你可以補充一下不舒服的狀況、這個健康問題多久了、可能的原因為何等。

至於如何解決問題的回答，你可以說有定期吃藥（take medicine on a regular basis）、規律運動（work out regularly）、定期吃保健食品（health supplements）…等。但注意「吃藥」的「吃」，千萬別說成 eat 了。當然如果你不知道如何解決，或是覺得也無所謂，反正只要還能呼吸、活得好好的就可以了，也可以如實說明。沒有標準的答案，也沒有要你誠實回答，重點還是說自己有把握說得正確的話喔！

回答範例 1

Yes, I have some health-related problems, and what upsets me most is the difficulty of falling asleep soon. This problem has bothered me for years. Sometimes I feel very tired but when I lie on the bed and close my eyes, I keep awake for at least two hours before falling asleep. Maybe that's because I am always pressured from work and have too many worries. I'll try taking sleeping pills though I know that's not a good solution in the long run.

是的，我有一些健康上的問題，而最讓我煩惱的是難以很快入睡。這個問題困擾

了我很多年了。有時我覺得很累，但當我躺在床上閉上眼睛時，我至少要醒著兩個小時才會入睡。也許那是因為我總是工作壓力大及有太多顧慮。我會嘗試吃安眠藥，但我知道長遠來看這不是一個好的解決方案。

第 1 回
第 2 回
第 3 回
第 4 回
第 5 回
第 6 回
第 7 回
第 8 回
第 9 回
第 10 回

回答範例 2

I don't think I have any too serious health problems, except that I am overweight. I am 160 centimeters in height and 80 kilograms in weight. I'm interested in many kinds of food and drinks, such as salt crispy chicken and fried chicken steak, and pearl milk tea. I eat and drink them almost three times a week. I know overweight can cause some diseases such as diabetes, heart disease and high blood pressure. OK, I'll definitely try my best to take my appetite under control.

我不認為我有任何太嚴重的健康問題，除了過胖之外。我身高 160 公分，體重 80 公斤。我對很多食物和飲料都很感興趣，比如鹹酥雞和炸雞排，還有珍珠奶茶。我幾乎每週都會吃或喝個 3 次。我知道過重會導致一些疾病，例如糖尿病、心臟病和高血壓。好吧，我一定會盡量控制住我的食慾的。

關鍵字詞

upset v. 使煩惱　**bother** v. 使困擾　**awake** adj. 清醒的　**pressure** v. 使感受到壓力　**sleeping pill** n. 安眠藥　**in the long run** phr. 到最後，最終　**overweight** adj. 過重的　**disease** n. 疾病　**diabetes** n. 糖尿病　**heart disease** n. 心臟病　**high blood pressure** n. 高血壓　**appetite** n. 口腹之慾　**take... under control** phr. 將…控制住

延伸學習

你都如何維持一個健康的生活型態（healthy lifestyle）呢？以下教你一些與「健康飲食」有關的用語：

❶ go on a diet：當你要開始執行健康飲食計畫時，可以說 I'm starting a diet. 或 I'm going on a diet.。如果你不想要吃不在自己飲食計畫中的不健康食物，可以說 I need to stick to my diet.。

❷ cutting carbs：低醣（碳水化合物）飲食是指吃少一點的碳水化合物（糖和澱粉）。

❸ staying hydrated：保持水分，是指在一天之中飲用大量的液體（像是水或果汁等等）。例如：It's important that you stay hydrated when you are exercising.

❹ following a meal plan：執行用餐計畫，就像 go on a diet 一樣，一個 meal plan 是指你只吃某種特定食物。通常這是由專業的營養師設計，或者可以請你的健身教練幫你設計。

❺ get your daily dose of vitamins：每日維他命攝取量。dose（劑量）這個字是用來談論藥物，是一個很小的特定量。你也可以使用這個字來討論維他命。

9. **What do think about school uniforms? Do you think middle school students must wear them to school?**

你對學校制服有什麼看法？你認為中學生必須穿制服去上學嗎？

答題解說

幾乎所有國高中的學校都會規定學生上學要穿著制服（wear uniforms to school）。站在校方的觀點（From the point of view...），學生穿上學校精心設計的（well-designed）制服，代表的是這個學校的形象之一（present an image of...），也認為才有學生的樣子。但很多學生對於制服有所抱怨，比方說認為制服太醜，或認為學校管太多（too much rules）。站在學生的觀點，很多人希望可以穿著自己喜歡的衣服來到學校上課，且若是可以穿上自己或家人替他們買的新衣服，就會特別高興，上課時自然也會跟著開心起來（feel more delighted when they're in class）。

對於第二題的回答，也不一定只有「必須」或「不必」兩種答案，你也可以有彈性的（flexible）觀點，比方說可以建議一個星期的星期三或星期五，可以允許學生穿便服（casual clothes）上課。或者轉移到社會上的工作來說，許多行業也都要穿制服上班，像是警察（policeman）、郵差（mailman）、銀行行員（banker）…等，所以穿制服上學其實沒什麼好爭議的（controversial）。其實無論是學生或上班族，穿制服上學或上班都是很正常的要求，只是對於年紀較小的學生族群，因為各方面還在發育、成長的階段（during a period of physical and mental growth），理應給予更多的自由空間。

以上，提供一些回答的建議，類似這種爭議性的問題，可以依照自己的看法選邊站（take sides），不管支持或反對（pros or cons）都可以盡情發揮。

回答範例 1

I don't disagree on the rule that students wear uniforms to school. The school uniforms represent a kind of team spirit and a sense of identity. As for the uniform style, it is better to be decided, for example, through a questionnaire or a voting activity, by all students in the school. I know many students like to wear what they like to school, so I would suggest that they be allowed to do so on one of the weekdays. Maybe such a flexible rule would be accepted by more students, parents and school staff.

我不反對學生穿制服上學的規定。制服代表一種團隊精神與認同感。至於制服的樣式，最好由全校學生共同決定，例如透過問卷調查或投票活動。我知道很多學生喜歡穿自己喜歡的衣服去學校，所以我建議可以允許他們在平日的某一天穿。

也許這樣一個彈性的規則會被更多的學生、家長和學校職員所接受。

回答範例 2

I always consider it reasonable for middle school students to wear uniforms to school. You don't have to waste too much time thinking about what to wear to school today. Besides, school uniforms help students develop a sense of belonging. What's more, if there are strangers or offenders stealing into the campus, they will be recognized at once, and the school authorities can have immediate response. This makes a school and its students safer.

我一直認為中學生穿制服上學是合理的。你不必浪費太多時間思考今天要穿什麼衣服去上學。此外,制服有助於培養學生的歸屬感。再者,如果有陌生人或歹徒潛入校園,他們會在第一時間就被認出,且校方可即時作出反應。這讓學校及其學生更加安全。

關鍵字詞

agree/disagree on phr. 同意／不同意…　**represent** v. 代表　**team spirit** n. 團隊精神　**sense of identity** n. 認同感　**flexible** adj. 彈性的,靈活的　**reasonable** phr. 有理由的,合理的　**sense of belonging** n. 歸屬感　**offender** n. 歹徒,侵犯者　**steal into** phr. 偷偷溜進…　**recognize** v. 認出　**at once** phr. 立刻　**school authorities** n. 校方,學校當局　**immediate** adj. 立即的　**response** n. 回應

延伸學習

談到「穿著」,俗話說「人要衣裝、佛要金裝。」職場上的成功人士也需要合適的服裝為自己加分。當你要向別人提供穿搭上的建議時,可以這麼說:

❶ Be sure to dress up more.(務必要穿得更正式些。):dress up 是「盛裝打扮」的意思,你也可以說 Put on your best clothes.(穿上你最稱頭的服裝)。

❷ Your wardrobe needs to be complementary to your build.(你的服裝必須合你的身形。):wardrobe 是指一個人穿上的「整體服裝」,包含衣服、褲子、鞋子甚至帽子等。而 build 當名詞表示「體格、體型」

❸ Pick a signature item.(挑選一樣具代表性的配件。):有了基本款後,挑選一樣能凸顯個人特色的配件,可以是 bow tie(領結)或是 brooch(胸針)等。

10. **Have you ever been deceived? Talk about your experience.**

你曾經被騙過嗎?談談你的經驗。

第 1 回
第 2 回
第 3 回
第 4 回
第 5 回
第 6 回
第 7 回
第 8 回
第 9 回
第 10 回

首先，deceive 這個英檢中級的單字一定要聽得出來，否則你會愣在那邊不知所措了！另外，deceive 可不包括善意謊言（white lie）的欺騙喔！被惡意欺騙的經驗相信很多人都有過，無論是被騙錢、騙感情可以作為經驗之談，而被騙的結果也可能很嚴重或是覺得「算了，沒關係」，都可以拿來陳述。重點還是要掌握住自己不會語塞或說錯話、用錯字詞。本題主要針對「被騙的經驗」去陳述，若不知道從何說起，你可以用 5W1H 的觀點（不一定要全部都談到）來架構你的內容。首先，何時被騙，然後被誰騙、在什麼情況或場合被騙，對方用什麼方法騙你，以及事後你如何因應或從這起事件中你學到了什麼。

如果你真的未曾被騙過什麼，可以說明原因，比方說，自己一直都是個小心謹慎的（cautious/meticulous）人，或本來就不容易相信別人或是電視、網路上的廣告。

回答範例 1

Of course, and I'll never forget about how I was deceived into paying NT$4,990 for a piece of trash last year. An ad caught my eyes on the Internet and I clicked on the photo to see what's there. It showed a smartphone whose screen is foldable, and whose functions almost rival those of the Samsung Flip series, according to the ad. I bought it without hesitation. But when I received the product on delivery, I found it was just a gamepad that cost only several hundred at best. What's worse, I wasn't able to contact the seller.

當然，我永遠不會忘記去年我是如何被騙去花 4990 元買了個垃圾。網路上一個廣告引起我的注意，於是我點擊照片，想一探究竟。根據廣告內容，它是一款螢幕可折疊的智慧手機，其功能幾乎可以媲美三星 Flip 系列的手機。我毫不遲疑地買下了它。但是當我收到貨時，發現它只是一個遊戲手柄，最多也就幾百塊。更糟糕的是，我無法聯繫到賣家了。

回答範例 2

To tell the truth, to deceive me is not that easy because I'm a person who always walk on eggs. Besides, I've heard of too many news reports on online fraud or other forms of deception. I receive cellphone messages about favorable loans or investments almost every day. Some investment messages tell me that I can make a fortune by only investing a little money. I'm sick of those trash messages and do nothing but delete them right away.

老實說，要騙我可沒那麼容易，因為我是一個總是如履薄冰的人。此外，我聽說過太多關於網絡欺詐或其他詐騙形式的新聞報導。我幾乎每天都會收到有關優惠貸款或投資的手機短訊。有些投資訊息告訴我，只要投入一點錢，就能發大財。

我受夠了那些垃圾短訊，我只會立刻刪除掉，不會做任何事情。

關鍵字詞

deceive sb. into -ing phr. 騙某人去做某事　**catch one's eyes** phr. 吸引某人目光　**click on** phr. 點擊，按下…（網路連結等）　**foldable** adj. 可折疊的　**rival** v. 可與…較勁，可媲美…　**without hesitation** phr. 不遲疑地　**on delivery** phr. 到貨時　**walk on eggs** phr. 如履薄冰，戰戰兢兢　**fraud** n. 詐欺　**deception** n. 欺騙　**favorable** adj. 優惠的　**make a fortune** phr. 賺大錢　**be sick of** phr. 厭倦了…　**do nothing but** phr. 除了…不做任何事情

延伸學習

deceive 這個動詞是由字首 de- 和字根 -ceive-（take、hold 的意思）構成，所以 receive 就是「收到」的意思！而字首換成 de-（＝ away）時，可以想像成「讓你拿不到（你要的東西）」，就可以理解為「欺騙」的意思。不過，另外兩個比較不常見的字 conceive 和 perceive 又和「拿」、「取」，有什麼關係呢？其實，在英文裡，take 很常被用在「理解」的意思上。例如：Oh please! Don't took me wrong again!（噢，拜託！別又誤會我了！）

conceive 是由 con（加強語氣）＋ ceive（理解）構成，自然而然就有「認為」的意思，而 perceive 則是 per（＝ all）＋ ceive（理解）組成，「全知的狀態」就好像是「發現、發覺」了什麼。

第三部分 看圖敘述

T05P3.mp3

雖然題目有提示你從四個點去回答問題，但如果每個點你只能回答一句話，這樣的內容是絕對不夠的。所以請先從圖片本身去掌握這張照片的主題，然後根據 where、who、why、what...等架構來充實你的內容。若對於圖片中的人事物相關英文沒有太大把握的話，試著用代名詞或自己有把握說得正確的詞彙來表達。

1. 照片裡的人在什麼地方？

   你可以說 in the office（在辦公室裡）或是 at a meeting room（在會議室）。如果只是說「他們在室內」（They are indoors.）之類的，分數會打折扣喔！

2. 照片裡的人在做什麼？

   提到「人」的部分時，你可以先提有多少人（There are a man and a woman...），以及他們可能的關係（the interviewer and the interviewee），並稍加描述特徵或其他重點。例如，你可以說 "The man and the woman are sitting in the office." 以及 "They are having a talk, which I guess is very formal because both of their dresses look formal."。

3. 照片裡的人為什麼會在那裡？

   我們可以從照片拍攝地點，以及當中人物的行為、動作來判斷他們為什麼會來這地方。例如，你可以說 "The man is holding a paper that looks like a resume, and the woman is answering the man's questions." 以及 "From this point of view I can be sure that they are having a job interview."...等。

4. 如果尚有時間，請詳細描述圖片中的景物。

   例如，從照片中的，你可以繼續補充說，「I suppose the lady is the interviewee and the man the interviewer, who might be a supervisor or manager of the company.」、「There is a computer behind the lady, so I think they are at a meeting room of the man's company.」以及「The lady looks confident, so I think she will be accepted by the company.」…等。

From what I can see, this picture was taken in a meeting room or in an office because there is a computer behind the woman, who is in very formal dress. Besides, the man is also wearing a formal shirt though I can only see his back. What also caught my eye is the paper that the man is holding, and that looks like someone's resume, because I can see a small headshot at the upper-right corner of the paper. I think the man and the woman in this photo are having an interview and the man, whom I think is the interviewer and a supervisor or a manager of one of the company's department, is carefully checking out the woman's resume, and coming up with some questions that the woman, the interviewee, needs to answer. I don't know whether the man is satisfied with the woman's educational background and work experiences, but from the smile on the face of the woman, I think she is confident about her seniority and competence in certain field, and the company will ultimately accept the woman's applications.

就我所看到的，這張照片是在會議室或辦公室拍攝的，因為這位穿著非常正式的女士身後有一台電腦。此外，雖然我只能看到這名男子的背影，但他也穿著一件正式的襯衫。同樣映入我眼簾的是男子手裡拿著的那張紙，且看起來像是某人的履歷，因為我可以看到這張的右上角有一個小小的大頭照。我想照片中的男女正在進行面試，我認為這名男子是面試官，也是該公司某部門的主管或經理，他正仔細查看女子的履歷，並提出一些這名女子 —求職者— 必須回答的問題。我不知道男子對女子的學歷經歷是否滿意，但看到女方臉上的笑容，我覺得她對自己在某領域的資歷和能力很有信心，我想該公司最終會錄取這位女士。

關鍵字詞

meeting room n. 會議室　**in formal dress** phr. 穿著正式的　**headshot** n. 大頭照　**upper-right** adj. 右上角的　**interviewer** n. 面試官　**interviewee** n. 面試者　**supervisor** n. 主管　**come up with** phr. 提出　**seniority** n. 資深　**competence** n. 能力　**ultimately** adv. 最終　**accept** v. 錄取，接受　**application** n. 求職，申請

延伸學習

你只會用 wear 來「穿」衣服嗎？以下補充三種與「服裝穿著」有關的介系詞用法：

❶ 人 + in + 衣物／顏色

Mary will go to the party in a red hat and a purple dress.
Mary 會戴一頂紅色帽子並穿著紫色洋裝去參加這場派對。

❷ 衣物／飾品 + on + 人

The shoes on my feet were given by my brother as a birthday gift.
我腳上穿的鞋子是我哥送我的生日禮物。

❸ 人 + with + 配件／飾品

The young lady with the scarf is my girlfriend.
戴圍巾的那位年輕女子是我的女友。

GEPT 全民英檢

中級複試
中譯＋解析

第一部分 中譯英

台灣的交通擁擠是眾所皆知的大問題。在許多城市，道路常常擁擠不堪，特別是在上下班時間和週末假期，交通堵塞更是難以避免。加上車輛與行人互爭道路空間，交通事故也時有所聞。此外，台灣的公共運輸系統雖然完善，但仍難以負荷高峰時刻的客流量。

答題解說

第一句的可以用 It is widely known that 的句型來陳述。在 that 子句中，主詞是「台灣的交通壅擠」（Taiwan's traffic congestion），動詞是 is，後接主詞補語 a major problem。第二句的主詞是「道路（roads）」，「擁擠不堪」可以用 be overcrowded 來表示，後面的「特別是在…」可以用 especially during... 表示，其中「上下班時間」就是所謂的「尖峰時間」，用 rush / peak hours 即可，而「交通堵塞更是難以避免」這部分可以用一個分詞構句 "making...inevitable" 來呈現，「交通堵塞」是 traffic bottlenecks。第三句的「加上…」應視為「此外，因為…」，所以可以用 Additionally, due to... 表示。「車輛與行人互爭道路空間」可以用 the competition between vehicles and pedestrians for road space 表示。「時有所聞」就是「經常發生」的意思，可以用 occur frequently 表示。最後一句是「雖然…但…」的句型，但千萬不要讓 (al)though 和 but 同時出現了！「公共運輸系統」是 public transportation system，「完善」可以用 well-developed 表示，「難以負荷」可以用 struggle to handle... 表示，而「客流量」可以用 the volume of passengers 表示。

譯文範例

It is widely known that Taiwan's traffic congestion is a major problem. In many cities, roads are often overcrowded, especially during rush hours and on weekends, making traffic bottlenecks inevitable. Additionally, due to the competition between vehicles and pedestrians for road space, traffic accidents occur frequently. Furthermore, although Taiwan's public transportation system is well-developed, it still struggles to handle the high volume of passengers during peak hours.

延伸學習

traffic congestion 和 traffic jam 都是指「交通阻塞」，通常表示道路上車輛太多或事故等原因造成的堵塞等狀況。而 heavy traffic 指的是道路上車輛密度高，交

通繁忙的狀況。另外有一個字是 gridlock，它是指交通網絡完全陷入僵局，無法前進或後退的狀況，也就是俗稱的「紫爆」。其他像是 bottleneck 是指「交通瓶頸」，通常是道路狹窄或路口設計不良等原因造成的交通擁擠。

第 1 回
第 2 回
第 3 回
第 4 回
第 5 回
第 6 回
第 7 回
第 8 回
第 9 回
第 10 回

第二部分 英文作文

提示

社群媒體扮演著極為重要的角色。有些人認為社群媒體對我們的溝通技巧和建立有意義關係的能力有負面影響。你同意還或是不同意這樣的說法？請舉例說明並佐證來支持自己的立場。

答題解說

所謂「社群媒體」就是 social media，它提供一個方便的平台（platform），讓人們可以與世界上任何地方的人進行交流和互動（interaction）。而本題則針對其負面影響的部分，來問你同不同意。但回答本題的方式，你可以有三種方式來回答：同意、不同意、看情況（有好有壞）。比方說，社群媒體為企業和品牌提供了一個廣泛的、低成本的市場宣傳途徑（a broad, cost-effective market platform for businesses），可以讓他們輕鬆接觸到大量的目標顧客（reach a large audience of target consumers），但社群媒體可能會侵犯個人隱私（invade individuals' privacy），因為用戶的個人資訊可能會被盜用或被未經授權的第三方（unauthorized third parties）收集和使用。此外，社群媒體提供便利的方式讓人們進行線上活動，如線上會議、視訊聊天、線上購物（online activities such as virtual meetings, video chats, online shopping）等，而社群媒體上也有許多虛假的資訊，這些資訊可能會對用戶造成誤導和損害（mislead users and cause harm）。

作文範例

In my opinion, I believe that social media can have both positive and negative effects, depending on how we use it. I think social media provides a platform for us to connect with people from all around the world and can be an excellent tool for building relationships. For example, I have friends whom I met through Facebook or Twitter, and these friendships have become an important part of my life. However, some people may rely too heavily on social media to communicate, which can lead to a gradual lack of face-to-face communication skills. Additionally, it can create a false sense of intimacy, where we feel as if we know someone well even though we have never actually met them in person.

在我看來，我認為社群媒體可以帶來正面與負面的影響，但這取決於我們如何使用。我想社群媒體為我們提供了一個與世界各地人們聯繫的平台，它可以是建立關係的絕佳工具。例如，我透過 Facebook 或 Twitter 認識一些朋友，這些友誼已成為我生活中重要的一部分。然而，有些人可能過於依賴社交媒體來溝通，這將造成人們漸漸失去面對面交流的技巧。此外，它會產生一種虛假的親密感，讓我們覺得我們很了解某人，即使我們從未親自見過他們。

延伸學習

social media 經常和一些名詞搭配，形成時下的流行詞彙。例如 social media platform 是「社群媒體平台」，像是 Facebook、Twitter、Instagram、LinkedIn 等。social media influencer 是「社群媒體網紅」，指那些在社群媒體上擁有大量追隨者的人，通常被用於行銷或推廣產品和服務。social media marketing 是「社群媒體行銷」，指使用社群媒體平台進行推廣、宣傳和銷售產品和服務的活動。social media campaign 是「社群媒體活動」，指在社群媒體平台上進行的宣傳、推廣和宣傳活動。social media engagement 是「社群媒體互動」，指在社群媒體上與其他用戶互動的活動，例如分享、點贊、留言和回覆等。social media analytics 是「社群媒體分析」，指使用數據分析工具來分析社群媒體活動和效果的活動。social media listening 是「社群媒體聆聽」，指監聽社群媒體上的對話和評論來了解用戶對品牌和產品的看法和反應。social media strategy 是「社群媒體策略」，指企業或品牌在社群媒體平台上制定的目標、戰略和計劃。

第一部分 朗讀短文

T06P1.mp3

Everyone knows it's important to bear a positive and optimistic attitude toward life, though life doesn't always turn out the way we expected. We are not able to avoid frustrating results. Optimism means you treat people and things around you with an open-minded, tolerant, and accepting attitude. Even if you are getting into trouble, you can have the willpower to adjust your mood. For optimistic people, it's not that there are no troubles in his life, but that they are able to turn obstacles into motivation.

****

In our daily life, we are always tempted by various things. Once you become famous, you may not let go of fame; when you become rich, you may not give up seeking wealth; if you have a lover, you won't let him or her go even when they want to. When you are running your own business, you don't want to let it go bankrupt. The more you have, the more you want.

答題解說

這兩篇分別關於「樂觀面對人生」與「追求慾望」的小短文，其中 optimistic [ˌɑptəˋmɪstɪk] 以及 optimism [ˋɑptəmɪsəm] 的發音要特別注意。前者重音在後面，後者重音在前面。另外，有幾個屬於英檢中級的字彙，像是 tolerant [ˋtɑlərənt]、obstacle [ˋɑbstək!]、motivation [ˌmotəˋveʃən]、bankrupt [ˋbæŋkrʌpt] 等，也必須注意自己的發音是否正確。第一篇的 open-minded 以及第二篇的 tempted 字尾 –d 的發音都是 [ɪd]，而不是 [d]。

以下標有顏色的單字，請盡可能唸得比較響亮，以及出現「|」的地方，請稍作停頓，試著讓自己融入短文的情境中。最後，也要注意字與字之間該連音（含「消音」）的部分（以下畫底線），像是 knows it's、optimistic attitude、around you、adjust your、not that、troubles in、Once you、let go、give up... 等，其中 around you 的第一個字尾音 [d]，和第二個字開頭音 [j] 連音時，[j] 要

145

發類似 [dʒ] 的音,而 adjust your 的第一個字尾音 [t],和第二個字開頭音 [j] 連音時,[t] 要發類似 [tʃ] 的音。而 not that、let go 這兩個連音組合中,第一個字的尾音 [t] 都要「消音」(不唸出聲)。

Everyone knows it's important │ to bear a positive and optimistic attitude toward life, │ though life doesn't always turn out the way │ we expected. We are not able to avoid frustrating results. Optimism means you treat people and things around you │ with an open-minded, tolerant, and accepting attitude. Even if you are getting into trouble, │ you can have the willpower to adjust your mood. For optimistic people, │ it's not that there are no troubles in their life, │ but that they are able to turning obstacles into motivation.

****

In our daily life, │ we are always tempted by various things. Once you become famous, │ you may not let go of fame; │ when you become rich, │ you may not give up seeking wealth; │ if you have a lover, │ you won't let him or her go │ even when they want to. When you are running your own business, │ you don't want to let it go bankrupt. The more you have, │ the more you want.

短文翻譯

每個人都知道對生活抱持正面及樂觀的態度很重要,儘管生活並非總是如我們所願。我們無法避免令人沮喪的結果。樂觀是指你以豁達、寬容、接納的態度處理身邊的人和事物。即使你遇到麻煩,你也可以用意志力來調整你的心情。對於樂觀的人來說,他的生活並不是沒有煩惱,而是能夠化障礙為動力。

****

在我們日常生活中,我們總是受到各種各樣事物的誘惑。一旦成名了,就可能放不下名聲;當你變得富有時,你可能不會放棄追求財富;如果你有愛人,你不會想讓他們離開,即使他們想走。當你有自己的事業時,您不會想讓它倒閉。你擁有的越多,你想要的就越多。

關鍵字詞

bear... attitude phr. 抱持…態度　**positive** adj. 正面的,積極的　**optimistic** adj. 樂觀的　**turn out the way one expected** phr.(事情的)結果如預期　**frustrating** adj. 令人挫折的　**optimism** n. 樂觀(態度)　**open-minded** adj. 心胸開放的　**tolerant** adj. 容忍的　**accepting** adj. 接受的　**get into trouble** phr.

陷入困境　**willpower** n. 意志力　**adjust** v. 調整　**turn... into...** phr. 將⋯變成⋯
obstacle n. 障礙　**motivation** n. 激勵　**tempt** v. 引誘。煽動　**fame** n. 名聲
run one' own business phr. 有自己的事業　**go bankrupt** phr. 破產

第 1 回
第 2 回
第 3 回
第 4 回
第 5 回
第 6 回
第 7 回
第 8 回
第 9 回
第 10 回

第二部分 回答問題

T06P2.mp3

1. **How did you spend your pocket money when you were still a child?**

   當你還是個小孩時，你都把零用錢花在哪裡？

   答題解說

   首先你要知道 pocket money 是「零用錢」的意思，它是指「父母定期給小孩子的錢」，當然也包括過年時的壓歲錢（lucky money / New Year's money）。不過要注意的是，過年時拿到的紅包，英文是 red envelop/packet，它僅指「紅色的紙袋」，可不包括「錢」喔！所以不要再問別人 "How much red envelop do you get?" 這種中式英文了！正確說法是 "How much (money) do you get in your red envelopes?"。

   另外，請注意本題要問的是 when you were still a child 你如何使用零用錢，請將年齡範圍設想為國中（14 歲）之前，且記得動詞要用過去式喔！至於零用錢的用途，基本上不是「存起來（save/deposit it for...）」，就是「花掉（spend it on...）」。但回答的時間有 15 秒，你不能只講一句話，所以你可以針對以上兩個方向再去延伸，例如通常什麼時候會拿到（多少）零用錢、是誰告訴你要存起來、存錢的目的為何、曾經很想要什麼東西而忍住不花錢，先把錢存起來之類的。

   也許有些貧困家庭人小孩通常沒有多餘的（extra）零用錢可以額外花用，父母只有給搭車、吃飯的錢（the money for commuting and lunch/dinner），也可以如實說明。如果還有時間，可以再補充一些感謝父母或誰曾經給你零用錢，或是期盼自己未來如何教導孩子規劃零用錢用途等。

   回答範例 1

   I remember when I was a young kid, I got two to three thousand dollars in my red envelopes during the Lunar Chinese New Year. My mother told me that I should not waste the money on useless or trivial things. Consequently, when I graduated from elementary school, I already had a deposit of more than twenty thousand dollars.

   我記得小時候過年時，我可以拿到二至三千元的紅包。我母親告訴我，不要把錢浪費在無用或瑣碎的東西上。因此，在我小學畢業時，我已經有超過兩萬元的存款了。

When I was the first grader of the elementary school, if my memory serves me right, my father gave me NT$500 a week, which included my commuting fees. So I didn't have extra money for anything else except a cold drink or something.

當我小學一年級的時候，我沒記錯的話，父親每個星期給我 500 元，其中包括我的通勤費。所以除了買個冷飲之類的什麼的，我沒有多餘的錢買別的東西。

關鍵字詞

pocket money n. 零用錢　**lucky money** n. 壓歲錢　**red envelope** n. 紅包
Lunar Chinese New Year n. 農曆新年　**waste money on...** phr. 把錢浪費在⋯
trivial adj. 瑣碎的　**elementary school** n. 小學　**deposit** n. 存款　**first grader** n. 一年級　**if my memory serves me right** phr. 如果沒記錯的話　**commuting fee** n. 通勤費

延伸學習

「紅包」的英文就是 red envelope，也有 red packet 這種說法。envelope 本來是「信封」，而 packet 則是「小包裝，小袋子」的意思，所以 red envelope 和 red packet 就所謂的「紅包」！另外，在紅包裡裝錢的用意是要祝福收到的人在新的一年，或是未來婚姻生活中，或是一個重要的人生轉類點之後，能夠平安吉祥、好運連連、事事順利，所以放在裡面的錢，也稱之為 lucky money。不過，New Year's money 也可以指「壓歲錢」，但當然不能用來指參加婚宴時，包給新人的「禮金（cash gift）」了。以下列舉關於 red envelope 的用法：

❶ How do you prepare red envelopes?（你紅包會怎麼包？）
❷ How much money should I give in the red envelope?（我紅包該包多少？）
　→ 可以回答：Little things mean a lot.（禮輕情意重。）

2. **What's the most precious thing you've ever lost? What happened then?**

　你遺失過最貴重的東西是什麼？後來呢？

答題解說

首先，對於題目中 precious 這個形容詞的認知，要有正確的概念。它不一定是用來指金錢衡量的東西，可以指珠寶（jewelry）、鑽戒（ring）、百萬名車（luxury car），也可以指「國中時暗戀的女生寫給我的卡片（a card...by a girl I had a crush on when I was a... student）」⋯等具體的東西，你也可以說是婚姻（marriage）、健康（health）、青春歲月（youth）、時間（time）、快樂（happiness）⋯等抽象的東西，如果都沒有的話，你可以說「某人」對你來說（曾）是最珍貴的，而你已經失去他／她了⋯等等。

第二個問題的回答，你可以針對如何遺失、失去後的感覺、心情或是做過什麼事要去找回來，以及找不回來的遺憾（regret / remorse），或是有找回來且未來將更加珍惜（will cherish it more in the future）等。

回答範例 1

The most precious thing I've ever lost is a portable storage device on which I saved many files of precious photos. I was so careless that I dropped it to the ground and I couldn't see anything on it later. I tried every way to retrieve the files but failed because it was seriously damaged.

我遺失過最珍貴的東西是一顆行動硬碟，裡面有我儲存的很多珍貴照片。我太粗心了，不小心掉在地上，後來裡面的東西我都看不到了。我試過各種方法要回復檔案，但都失敗了，因為它已嚴重損壞了。

回答範例 2

Hmmm... Not until I need to lie on the bed of a hospital and couldn't go anywhere, did I find I lost my precious thing: freedom. Last year I was severely injured in a traffic accident. During five months of hospitalization, I learned a bitter experience and decided never to ride a motorcycle again.

嗯……直到我必須躺在醫院的病床上，哪裡也不能去時，我才發現我失去了我最寶貴的東西：自由。去年我在一場交通事故中傷勢嚴重。在住院的五個月裡，我痛定思痛，並決定再也不騎摩托車了。

關鍵字詞

precious adj. 珍貴的　**portable storage device** n. 行動儲存裝置　**first love** n. 初戀　**try every way to-V** phr. 用盡一切方法…　**retrieve** v. 找回，回復　**seriously damaged** phr. 嚴重損壞　**lie on** phr. 躺在…上面　**severely injured** phr. 傷勢嚴重　**learn a bitter experience** phr. 痛定思痛

延伸學習

說到「貴重的，針貴的」，除了 precious 這個字（由 price 衍生而來），常見的還有 valuable（由 value 衍生而來），兩者都可以用來表示「金錢價值」以及「重要性」。但如果要表達「不貴重的」或是「沒有價值的」，可以用 valueless 或是 worthless。例如：

❶ The antique turned out to be a valueless replica.（這件古董被發現是一文不值的複製品。）

❷ The company's shares are now virtually worthless.（這家公司的股票實際上已經毫無價值了。）

第 1 回
第 2 回
第 3 回
第 4 回
第 5 回
第 6 回
第 7 回
第 8 回
第 9 回
第 10 回

另外，很多人會誤解 invaluable 和 priceless，以為是「沒有價值的」意思，其實兩者都是「無價的，極為珍貴的」意思，且其「珍貴指數」可是超越 valuable 和 precious 喔！

3. **How can you help your company become better in the future?**

你如何幫助公司未來變得更好？

答題解說

how 開頭的問句當然就是問你「方法」、「如何做」，而本題可以理解為「做些什麼」可以幫助公司。不過本題也是個開放性的問題，你可以往其他方向陳述，例如，也許你覺得現實生活中，公司變得更好，也不一定會回饋給員工（give positive feedback on employees），或者只回饋給特定員工，所以只要獨善其身（mind one's own business）就好…之類的回答也沒關係！另外，本題也是某些工作面試場合會被問到的問題。對於上班族而言，不外是「做好自己的份內工作（do one's job well）」、「努力達成公司／老闆設定的目標（reach the goal set by the company/boss）」、「透過團隊建立的活動培養同事們的合作精神（develop employees' spirit of cooperation by way of team building）」…等。如果你目前還是學生，或是待業中的社會人士，或者你從未想過「如何幫助公司」這類問題，也可以如實說明，你可以說「希望貢獻自己目前所學給我未來的公司（contribute what I have learned in school to my future companies）」，或是「努力習得一技之長，希望幫未來的公司賺大錢（try to be skilled at something and help make a good fortune for my future companies）」。

回答範例 1

As a member of a marketing team, I'll try to reach the goal set by the company. If I have time after getting off work, then I'll go to some vocational training center to learn some skills more helpful for my job. If the company can make a good fortune, I think every employee will also benefit.

身為行銷團隊一員，我會努力去達到公司設定的目標。如果我下班後有時間，我會去某個職業培訓中心去學些對我工作有助益的技能。如果公司能發大財，我想每一位員工也都會受益。

回答範例 2

I'm still a university student, and I've never thought about such a question, though I'm working part-time at a MacDonald restaurant now. I think I'll just do my job well and avoid making mistakes, which is perhaps the best for a company.

我還是個大學生，且從來沒有想過這樣的問題，儘管我現在有在麥當勞打工。我想我會做好我的工作，避免犯錯，或許這對一家公司來說可能是最好的了。

關鍵字詞

reach a goal phr. 達成目標　**get off work** phr. 下班　**vocational** adj. 職業的
make a good fortune phr. 賺大錢　**benefit** v. 獲益，受益　**do one's job** phr. 做
自己的事

延伸學習

在一家公司上班，最基本的是做好自己的份內工作，若有餘力，可以增強自己的技能或幫助其他同事，也都是值得鼓勵的。以下來學學老闆最喜歡的員工態度，相關英文如何表達：

❶ I'll do my job well and look around for, create or ask for more real work.（我會做好份內事而且主動尋找、創造或要求更多實際的工作。）

I'll tie up the loose ends of my assignments. I won't wait to be reminded, particularly by a supervisor.（我會對於份內的工作有始有終，不會等到別人提醒，特別是讓主管提醒更不應該。）

❸ I won't take problems to the boss. If I lack the authority, I'll come prepared with solutions when I broach the problem, even if the boss may not use my solutions. I will be a problem solver instead of a problem collector.（我不會別把問題丟給老闆。如果我沒有權限，在向老闆報告以前我也會預想解決方案，即使老闆可能不會採納我的方案。我會試解決問題，而不是收集問題的人。）

❹ I won't stop with getting approval. When I need some special work to be done, and if the other person doesn't follow through, I'll make things go on in a proper way.（我不會因為等著批准而停下來。當我需要完成某些特殊工作，且如果別人不配合，我也會讓事情適當地繼續進行。）

4. **What subject do you like most at school? What do you like about it?**

你在學校時最喜歡什麼科目？你喜歡它哪一點？

答題解說

首先，讓自己複習一下有各科的英文怎麼說：英文（English）、數學（Math）、國文（Mandarin Chinese）、歷史（History）、地理（Geography）、物理（Physics）、生物（Biology）、自然（Natural Science）、社會（Social Studies）、化學（Chemistry）、健康教育（Health）、體育（Physical education / PE）、工藝（Crafts）、家政（Home

Economics）、音樂（Music）…等，但如果沒把握說得正確，還是挑個 English 或 Math 這種簡單的單字吧！答題時間 15 秒，不要多花時間去思考「我究竟最喜歡哪一科」這種問題喔！

第二個問題等同於 Why do you like this subject?，每個科目有它的特性和目的，這部分你只要講個兩句話就可以了。如果覺得還要去想科目的特質太麻煩，可以開玩笑說，學生時期喜歡化學，因為化學老師長得很帥／很漂亮／說話幽默（humorous）。或是正經一點說，喜歡英文，因為它是國際的語言（an international language），不只考試要考，以後工作、生活中都會用到…等。

回答範例 1

Of course, PE is my favorite subject, when I was a junior high school student. Maybe that's because I didn't like to always sit upright in class. I just liked to move, jump and run. Besides, I remember the PE teacher looked very handsome, so I always looked forward to attending this class.

當然，體育是我國中時最喜歡的科目。也許那是因為我不喜歡在課堂上總是正襟危坐。我只是喜歡移動、跳躍和奔跑。另外，我記得體育老師長得很帥，所以我一直很期待上這門課。

回答範例 2

Among so many subjects at school, I like English most, because it is an international language. What's more, I can read many messages when I play online games, which is one of my favorite hobbies now.

在學校那麼多科目中，我最喜歡英文了，因為它是一種國際語言。更重要的是，我在玩網絡遊戲時可以閱讀很多消息，這是我現在最喜歡的嗜好之一。

關鍵字詞

upright adv. 直挺挺地　**in class** phr. phr. 在課堂上　**look forward to** phr. 期待　**attend sb's class** phr. 上某人的課　**play online games** phr. 玩線上遊戲

延伸學習

class、course、lesson 這三個字意思都非常接近，本身都有「課」的意思，你知道它們用法上的差異嗎？

❶ class 是指「課、課堂」，比方說，如果你要講：我要去上課了，可以說 I'm going to a class.，或者「我昨天沒去上有氧課。」可以說 I missed my aerobic class yesterday.

另外，class 還有「班級」的意思。例如：Which class are you in this year?（今年你在哪個班？）

❷ course 是指「課程」，通常是指期間比較久、針對某個主題有一系列的課程。例如：I took a course in creative writing.（我上過創意寫作課程。）

❸ lesson 是指「一堂／節課」的意思。例如：
He gives Japanese lessons.（他教日文課。）
You should teach him a lesson.（你該給他上一課。）
I learned a lesson.（我學到了一課／一個教訓。）

5. **Talk about your experience of being helped.**

談談你被人幫助的經驗。

答題解說

首先，注意這是 15 秒還是 30 秒的回答時間，才能夠給個比較完整的答案。再者，務必聽懂題目句尾的 being helped，回答時不要往「我如何幫助他人」的方向去了！請你談經驗的這類題型（Talk about your experience of...）其實就是要你簡單說個小故事。可以用 5W1H 的概念來思考，但因為時間有限，你只要提到誰（who）在什麼時候（when）幫過你什麼事情（what）就可以了，還有時間的話可以補充自己獲得幫忙的感受（feelings）、如何回報對方，或是希望自己未來有機會回報對方之類的敘述。

要是一時之間想不到什麼經驗可以分享，也別花太多時間去思考，因為答題時間很短。其實日常生活中，大家多多少少都會受到周圍人的一點小幫助，從「別人讓路給你過」、「有人幫你把掉在地上的東西撿起來」、「幫你提袋子」、「幫你指路怎麼走」…，到「幫你關門／關窗戶／買便當」等，都是「受人幫助」的例子喔！

回答範例 1

Yesterday when I was on the bus home, I couldn't find my wallet! The bus was about to pull over at my stop. I helplessly said sorry to the bus driver, when a passenger threw some coins into the coin box, and said to me, "It's OK. I'll pay." Then he disappeared into the crowd shortly.

昨天我在搭公車回家的路上，我找不到我的皮包！公車就要停靠我要下車的站了。我無助地對公車司機說抱歉，就在這時，一名乘客往投幣箱中丟了一些硬幣，且對我說「沒關係，我來付。」然後他很快地消失在人群中了。

回答範例 2

When I was new at my company, my supervisor helped me a lot. She taught me many things and even some good tips to get along with the colleagues. I really appreciate her considerate care about me, though she had retired last August.

我剛到公司時，我的主管幫了我很多。她教我很多東西，甚至還有一些與同事相處的技巧。我很感謝她對我的體貼關懷，雖然她已於去年八月退休了。

關鍵字詞

on the bus home phr. 在搭公車回家途中　　**pull over** phr. 停車，（車輛）停靠
stop n. 站　　**helplessly** adv. 無助地　　**coin box** n. 投幣箱　　**disappear** v. 消失
shortly adv. 不久，很快地　　**be new at...** phr. 剛來到…　　**supervisor** n. 主管
considerate adj. 善體人意的

延伸學習

在英文裡，表示「幫助」的動詞，一般都會先想到用 help，另外還有一個字，assist，相較於 help 是比較正式，或常用於書寫、書信等正式場合。例如：

❶ assist sb. with/in + 名詞：I have a lot of work to do and I don't have enough time. Could you assist me with it?（我有很多工作要做，但我時間不夠，你能幫我嗎？）

❷ assist sb. in + 動名詞（V-ing）：Several top landscape designers assisted in building up the garden.（幾位頂級的景觀設計師協助打造這座花園。）

❸ assist sb. to-V：The scheme can assist you to find a better job.（這項計畫可以幫助你找到一個更好的工作。）

❹ assist +sb./sth.：Eventually she agreed to assist the investigation.（最後她同意協助調查。）

6. **What are some ways you try to stay healthy?**

   你嘗試過用哪些方法來保持健康呢？

   答題解說

   保持健康的方式很多，基本上應綜合考量飲食、運動、壓力管理、睡眠、檢查和良好的生活習慣…等。以下提供一些答題方向的建議：

   ◆ 健康飲食（healthy eating）：保持均衡的膳食（balanced diet），攝取足夠的營養素，避免過度攝入糖分、飽和脂肪和鹽分。

   ◆ 規律運動（regular exercise）：每週進行適當的（moderate）有氧運動，如跑步、游泳、騎自行車等。

   ◆ 壓力管理（stress management）：學習有效應對壓力的方法，如冥想、呼吸練習和瑜伽（meditation, breathing exercises, and yoga）等，有助於降低身體緊張和壓力，促進身心健康。

   ◆ 睡眠充足（sufficient sleep）：每晚睡眠 7-8 小時，有助於恢復體力、提高免疫力和增強注意力和記憶力（restore physical energy, enhance immune function, and improve attention and memory）。

◆ 定期體檢（regular check-ups）：定期進行身體檢查，包括視力、聽力、血壓、血糖…等，有助於早期發現和預防健康問題（help detect and prevent health issues early on）。

回答範例 1

To stay healthy, I try to eat a balanced diet with plenty of fruits and vegetables. I also make sure to exercise regularly by going to the gym or taking a yoga class. Additionally, I prioritize getting enough sleep and staying hydrated by drinking plenty of water throughout the day. It is also important to practice good hygiene, such as washing hands frequently and avoiding close contact with people who are sick.

為了保持健康，我試著均衡飲食，並多吃水果和蔬菜。我還上健身房或上瑜伽課，以確保規律運動的執行。此外，我會將充足的睡眠列為第一要務，且一整天會喝大量的水來保持水分的充足。保持良好的衛生習慣也很重要，例如經常洗手和避免與病人密切接觸。

回答範例 2

There are a few things I do to stay healthy. First, I try to limit my intake of processed and junk food and opt for natural foods instead. I also enjoy going for long walks or hikes to get some fresh air and exercise. Besides, after I sit at my desk throughout the day, I make sure to stretch and move my body. Lastly, I receive regular check-ups that help detect and prevent health issues early on.

我會做些事情來維持健康。首先，我會盡量少吃加工食品和垃圾食物，且選擇天然食品。我也喜歡長距離散步或遠足，呼吸新鮮空氣並鍛煉身體。此外，當我一整天坐在辦公桌前工作之後，我一定會讓我的身體伸展並活動一下。 最後，我接受定期檢查，這有助於及早發現以及預防健康上的問題。

關鍵字詞

balanced diet n. 均衡飲食　　**plenty of** phr. 大量的　　**make sure to-V** phr. 一定會…　　**prioritize** v. 將…視為第一要務　　**hydrated** adj. 含水的　　**hygiene** n. 衛生　　**intake** n. 攝取　　**processed food** n. 加工食品　　**junk food** n. 垃圾食物　　**opt for** phr. 選擇　　**check-up** n. 檢查　　**detect** v. 偵測　　**early on** phr. 在初期

延伸學習

healthy 和 healthful 都是 health 衍生的形容詞，用來描述人體或動物的健康狀態、食品或飲料的營養價值等，但它們在用法上有些微妙的不同。一般情況下，healthy 用於描述人或動物的身體狀態或行為，例如：She is healthy and active.

（她身體健康且活力充沛。）而 healthful 則多用於描述食品或飲料的營養價值和對身體健康的影響，例如：Eating a healthful diet is important for maintaining good health.（吃得健康對於保持身體健康很重要。）需要注意的是，在某些情況下，兩字可以交替使用，並且兩者的意思非常相似。因此，使用哪個字通常取決於語境和個人的偏好。

7. **If tomorrow were the end of the world, what would you do?**

   如果明天是世界末日，你會做什麼？

   答題解說

   像這種「假設狀況」的問題就是讓你盡量發揮自己的想像力，只要扣著題目本身，並注意用字遣詞無誤即可。你也可以發揮一點幽默感，比方說「準備下輩子會用到的東西（prepare for the daily necessities for my next life）」…之類的。另外，因為本題的回答時間是 30 秒，所以答完「要做什麼」之後，可以說明一下為什麼選擇做那件事情。你可以朝著「自己最在意或關注的人事物」這樣的方向去陳述，比方說：I'll spend every minute and even every second with my lover(s) because...（我會每一分，甚至每一秒都跟我的情人在起，因為…），或者 I just want to sleep and wait for the "Armageddon" to come...（我只想睡覺並等著「末日」的到來…）。你也可以直接挑戰這個問題說：What an absurd question! That's totally impossible...（這什麼荒謬的問題！那是完全不可能的…），或者稱讚這是個好問題：I think this is a good question that reminds us of the importance of seizing the day...（我想這是個好問題，它提醒了我們「把握今朝」的重要性…）。

   回答範例 1

   I think I would go on a crazy trip with my lovers. I'd request that we stay at a deluxe hotel with a breathtaking lake view. Besides, we would go to eat what's most delicious at a night market or in a fancy restaurant, because, at that moment, you don't need to save money. As a matter of fact, this is a good question, because it implies that anybody can be dead tomorrow, and we need to learn to "seize the day."
   我想我會和我愛的人一起來一趟瘋狂的旅行。我會要求我們住在一間有壯麗湖景的豪華飯店。此外，我們會去夜市或高級餐廳吃最好吃的東西，因為，在那時候，你不必再省錢了。事實上，這是個好問題，因為它暗示著任何人明天都可能死去，我們要學會「活在當下」。

   回答範例 2

   What? That's impossible! The plot of "The End of World" exists only in a movie theater, I think. I have a happy family, I work hard and I work out very often to stay healthy. I hope I can have a lifespan of more than 100 years. Even if life is indeed full of uncertainties, that doesn't mean you have the excuse to only care about today and needn't take tomorrow or the future into consideration.

什麼？那是不可能的事！我想，「世界末日」的情節只存在於電影院。我有一個幸福的家庭、我努力工作，且我經常運動以保持健康。我希望我可以活超過 100 歲。即使生命的確充滿了不確定性，但這並不意味著你有藉口只在乎今日而不必考慮明天或未來。

request v. 要求　**deluxe** adj. 豪華的　**breathtaking** adj. 令人屏息的　**imply** v. 暗指　**seize the day** phr. 把握今朝　**plot** n. 劇情　**work out** phr. 運動，鍛鍊　**lifespan** n. 壽命　**uncertainty** n. 不確定性　**take...into consideration** phr. 將…納入考量

The End of the World 是一首著名的老歌歌名，不過，在英文裡要表達「世界末日」時，至少還有 Armageddon、apocalypse 跟 doomsday 三個字。the Apocalypse 是新約聖經中的《啟示錄》，而 Armageddon 是裡面提及的一個詞，被翻譯為「末日審判」或「世界末日」。而 apocalypse 在現代英語中有「啟示」和「世界末日」的雙重意思。在今日，apocalypse 在很多語境下已經脫去了原有的宗教、寓言色彩，而單純地表示某種毀滅性的大災難。比如 environmental apocalypse（環境災難）和 post-apocalyptic world（劫後世界）。

另外，doomsday 是個與宗教無關、表示「世界末日」的單字。英文裡有個片語 till/until doomsday（直到世界末日）。例如：You can wait till doomsday to be a president of this country.（你要當這國家的總統就等到世界末日吧！）

8. **What do you think about same-sex marriage? Do you support it? Why or why not?**

   你對於同婚有何看法？你支持嗎？為什麼？

關於「同性戀」的英文，一般來說辨識度最高的單字就是 gay，所以 same-sex 在乍聽之下，若不夠專注，有些考生可能一時腦袋空白。但即使如此，總該聽得出 marriage 這個單字吧！再從第二個問題 Do you support it? 就可以猜出題目要問你是不是支持某種婚姻。那麼你當然會想到是問「同性婚姻」了。

第 1 回　第 2 回　第 3 回　第 4 回　第 5 回　第 6 回　第 7 回　第 8 回　第 9 回　第 10 回

157

首先，對於第一個問題，可以先用一句話帶過去。例如：To me, same-sex marriage symbolizes the protection of one of human rights.（對我來說，同性婚姻象徵著一種人權的保障。）或是 I think same-sex marriage is nothing more than a joke / a violation against normal human behavior.（我認為同性婚姻只不過是個笑話／違反正常行為。）…之類的說法。

「支不支持同婚」當然是個見仁見智的問題，但主要還是要針對支持或反對的「理由」來陳述。支持的理由，例如，可以說「每個人都有追求幸福的權利」，反對的話可以朝著「對於下一代的影響」這個方向去說明。

回答範例 1

I don't think same-sex marriage should be different from "traditional marriage," because everybody has the right of getting married. Besides, I don't think marriage should be defined as the union between one man and one woman. The tendency that you love a man, or you love a woman, is by no means to be changed. Even if gay people have no legal rights to get married, you still can't stop them from loving each other, right? So basically I take the side of supporting same-sex marriage.

我認為同性婚姻與「傳統婚姻」不該有區別，因為每個人都有結婚的權利。此外，我認為婚姻不應該被定義為一男一女的結合。無論你愛的是男人或女人，都是無法改變的傾向。即使同性戀者沒有結婚的合法權利，你仍然不能阻止他們彼此相愛，對吧？所以基本上我站在支持同性婚姻的一邊。

回答範例 2

I think same-sex marriage is immoral and unnatural, and I need to say sorry that I don't support it, because, to me, one of the important functions of marriage is to produce babies. But same-sex couples can't produce babies on their own. Even if they can adopt one, how could the adopted child, if he or she isn't homosexual, face others' peculiar look at them because of their same-sex parents?

我認為同性婚姻是不道德且不自然的，且我必須說聲抱歉，我不支持，因為，對我來說，婚姻的一項重要功能就是生小孩。但同性伴侶無法自己生育。即使可以領養，但被領養的孩子如果不是同性戀，又要如何面對別人對於自己同性雙親的異樣眼光呢？

關鍵字詞

same-sex adj. 同性的　**traditional** adj. 傳統的　**union** n. 結合　**by no means** phr. 絕非　**legal** adj. 合法的　**take the side of** phr. 選…邊站　**immoral** adj. 不道德的　**unnatural** adj. 不自然的　**adopt** v. 領養　**peculiar look** n. 異樣眼光

延伸學習

marriage 雖然是個英檢初級單字，但與它相關的、實用的慣用語，卻是中高級以上的程度喔！比方說，「我和約翰是姻親上的關係。」可以說：I am related to John by marriage.。by marriage 的字面意思是「藉由婚姻」，所以像 mother-in-law、brother-in-law... 這類單字，也都可解讀為 be related to... by marriage。另外，古代有所謂「媒妁之言的婚姻」，英文就是 arranged marriage。而台灣一度很盛行的「假結婚、真賣淫」情形，就是透過一種所謂「形式婚姻」，英文叫作 marriage of convenience，也就是基於特定目的而與另一人進行婚禮或法律上的結婚手續，但實際上只是名義上的夫妻身份，而無實質的關係。最後，marriage 有「緊密結合」的意思。例如：I love this song because there is perfect marriage of lyrics and melody.（我喜歡這首歌是因為其歌詞與旋律有緊密的結合。）

9. **Are you in favor of owning or renting a house? Why?**

   你贊成擁有一間房子還是租房子呢？為什麼？

答題解說

題目中的 in favor of 是「贊成，支持」的意思，即使你一時恍惚聽不出來，總該聽得出 "owning or renting a house" 吧！一般而言，買房還是租屋取決於個人的經濟情況（depend on your personal financial situation）。想擁有自己的房子，可以就其優點做說明，像是「擁有房產資產，可以隨著時間增值（appreciate over time）」、「擁有固定居住地點（have a permanent residence），可以長期穩定生活（provide stability for the long term）」或是「可以將房屋變成出租收入（turn your house into another source of income）或抵押貸款」。
至於傾向於租屋不買房者，可提出租物的優點及買房的缺點。像是「租金相對較低，負擔較輕（more affordable and less stressful for your life），可擁有較好的生活品質」、「買房必須承擔高額的預付款以及尾款（it requires a significant amount of money upfront for the down payment and closing costs）」、「額外的日常開支，例如財產稅、維修費和房屋保險（additional ongoing expenses such as property taxes, maintenance, and the house's insurance）」…等。

回答範例 1

I'm in favor of owning my own house. First and foremost, it gives me a sense of stability and security. I can decorate and renovate as pleased without worrying about landlords or lease agreements. Additionally, owning a home can be a long-term investment. Over time, the value of my home may increase, providing me with a substantial financial asset. Finally, owning my own home can also give me a sense of pride and accomplishment.

我贊成擁有自己的房子。首先,它給我一種穩定感和安全感。我可以隨心所欲地裝修和翻新,而不用擔心房東或租賃協議。此外,有房子可以成為一種長期投資。隨著時間過去,我的房價可能會增漲,進而給我一筆可觀的資產。最後,擁有自己的家也能讓我感到自豪和成就感。

回答範例 2

I think renting a house is more suitable for me. Unlike buying a home, renting allows for greater flexibility in terms of location and lifestyle. It also provides a more affordable option for those who are unable to have the immediate money to purchase a house. Additionally, renting a house often includes maintenance and repair services. Renting an apartment allows me to have a better, stress-free quality of life due to less financial burdens.

我覺得租房子更適合我。租屋不同於買房,租屋在居住地點和生活方式上有更大的彈性。 它還為那些手頭上沒有購屋資金者,提供更實惠的選擇。此外,租房通常附帶維護和維修服務。由於金錢的負擔較少,租房子可以讓我擁有更佳、無壓力的生活品質。

關鍵字詞

in favor of phr. 贊成,偏好　**first and foremost** phr. 首先　**stability** n. 穩定性
security n. 安全感　**decorate** v. 裝飾　**renovate** v. 翻修　**landlord** n. 房東
lease agreement n. 租賃協議　**investment** n. 投資　**substantial** adj. 實質的
accomplishment n. 成就　**flexibility** n. 靈活性　**affordable** adj. 可負擔的
immediate money n. 可立即運用的資金　**maintenance** n. 維護　**stress-free**
adj. 無壓力的

延伸學習

在英文裡,rent 這個字看似簡單,但日常生活中運用範圍很廣,使用也相當頻繁,特別是在房地產租賃、汽車租賃等場合,可以當名詞,也可以當動詞,表達「出租」、「租來」或「租用的物品」。例如:

❶ 當名詞,表示「租金,房租」。例如:The rent for this apartment is $1000 per month. (這公寓房子的租金每月一千美元。)

❷ 當名詞,表示「租用的東西」。例如:I need to return the rent on this car tomorrow. (我明天得去繳這輛車的租金。)

❸ 當動詞,表示「租用,租借」。例如:I'm going to rent a car for the weekend. (我要去租輛周末要用的車。)

❹ 當動詞，表示「出租，出借」。例如：They decided to rent out their spare room to a tenant.（他們決定把那間閒置的房間出租給一名房客。）

10. **Your cousin Peter is always forgetful. Give him some advice.**

你的堂弟彼得總是忘東忘西的。給他一些建議吧。

答題解說

對於一個老是健忘的（forgetful）人，我們可以從幾個方面來給予建議：
1. 工具提醒：用手機或隨身小筆記本（pocket notebook）等工具，設置提醒事項（reminder）的時間。
2. 記憶技巧：比方說，利用已知事物之關性。像是記憶單字（memorize vocabulary）的話，可以用字根歸納（induction of roots）、發音記憶（memorize words by pronunciation）等方式。
3. 學習傾聽（learn to listen）：人若容易分心或不專注（easily distracted or unfocused），那麼記憶力通常會下降，因此建議他們在與他人交談或閱讀時盡可能集中注意力（try the best to pay attention when talking with others or reading）。
4. 保持身體健康（stay healthy）：健康對於大腦的正常運作（normal functioning of the brain）非常重要。保持健康的飲食習慣，適度運動，充足的睡眠（maintain a healthy diet, exercise moderately, and get enough sleep）等。
5. 請求協助（seek help）：若記憶的問題影響了正常生活，建議他們尋求醫生或專業人士的幫助。

回答範例 1

Peter, why are you always so forgetful? I suggest you create reminders on your cellphone, use a pocket notebook, and practice memory techniques. It's also important for you to pay attention and stay focused during conversations or when reading. Maintaining a healthy lifestyle with a balanced diet, exercise, and sufficient sleep can also help. If forgetfulness affects your daily life, you should seek professional help.
彼得，你為什麼老是那麼健忘？我建議你在手機上設置提醒事項、使用口袋型筆記本，並練習記憶技巧。在談話或閱讀時集中注意力對你來說也是很重要的。均衡飲食、運動和充足的睡眠來保持健康的生活方式也是有幫助的。但如果你的健忘影響了你的日常生活，你應該尋求專業的幫助。

回答範例 2

Hello, Peter. I heard that you have a bad memory. I think I can give you some useful advice. First, you can write things down in a notebook or a to-do list. Second, spare some time to practice memory techniques. You can repeat silently what you're going to do a few times whenever you take a walk, ride a bike or drive a car, which will definitely help store it in memory.

哈囉，彼得。聽說你記性不太好。我想我可以給你一些有用的建議。首先，你可以將事情記在筆記本或待辦事項的清單中。其次，撥出一些時間練習記憶技巧。你可以在每次走路、騎腳踏車或開車時，將自己要做的事情默念幾遍，這肯定有助於記憶。

關鍵字詞

reminder n. 提醒事項　**pocket notebook** n. 口袋型筆記本　**stay focused** phr. 保持專注　**maintain** v. 維持　**balanced** adj. 均衡的　**sufficient** adj. 充足的　**forgetfulness** n. 健忘　**have a bad memory** phr. 記性差　**to-do list** n. 代辦清單　**spare time to-V** phr. 撥出時間…（去做某事）　**in memory** phr. 在記憶中

延伸學習

advise 和 advice 長得很像，但它們的用法與含義是完全不同的。advise 是個動詞，表示「給予建議或指導」，常用於「advise sb. to-V」的用語中。例如：

I advise you to study hard for your exams.（我建議你努力用功作備考試。）

The doctor advised me to quit smoking.（醫生建議我戒菸。）

advice 是個名詞，表示「建議、意見或指導」，它是個不可數名詞，所以沒有 two advices 或 many advices 的說法。例如：

Thank you for your advice.（謝謝你的建議。）

Let me give you some advice.（我給你一些建議吧！）

I took his advice and left.（我接受了他的建議而離開了。）

Can you give me some advice on how to improve my writing skills?（你能給我一些如何提高寫作技巧的建議嗎？）

第三部分 看圖敘述

答題解說

雖然題目有提示你從四個點去回答問題，但如果每個點你只能回答一句話，這樣的內容是絕對不夠的。所以請先從圖片本身去掌握這張照片的主題，然後根據 where、who、why、what...等架構來充實你的內容。若對於圖片中的人事物相關英文沒有太大把握的話，試著用代名詞或自己有把握說得正確的詞彙來表達。

1. 照片裡的人在什麼地方？

   你可以說 in a restaurant / diner / café / bistro（在一家餐廳／餐館／咖啡廳／小酒館）。如果只是說「他們在室內」（They are indoors.）之類的，分數會打折扣喔！

2. 照片裡的人在做什麼？

   提到「人」的部分時，你可以先提有多少人（There are three men and two women...），以及他們可能的身份或關係。比方說，The man wearing a cook's uniform may be the chef of this restaurant...或是 There is a chef and four guests...，或是 A bald man and the other two ladies sit at the same table...，接著繼續說明他們正在抱怨食物有問題以及這位 chef 試著在解釋些什麼。

3. 照片裡的人為什麼會在那裡？

　　我們可以從照片拍攝地點，以及當中人物的行為、動作來判斷他們為什麼會來這地方。例如，你可以說 The guests in this restaurant may have a business dinner.，或是 They might be here to have a business talk.。

4. 如果尚有時間，請詳細描述圖片中的景物。

　　例如，從照片中的，你可以繼續補充說，"I suppose the man is complaining about his pizza which may turn sour or what..."、"They also have delicious drinks on the table"、"Besides, there is a man drinking alone, and I think he's here to think about something important..."…等。

回答範例

I'm pretty sure that this picture was taken in a bistro because, what caught my eye first is the liquor cabinet. There are a bald man and two ladies sitting at the same table, and a man sitting alone at another table. They might be here to relax a bit and have a good chat after a long day of tedious work. The guests are having a meal of pizza and a couple of drinks. The man who wears a cook's uniform should be the one of the chefs of this restaurant. It is obvious that the bald man wearing a suit is complaining about his pizza to the chef. I guess the pizza may turn sour or smell weird, and from the chef's gesture I think he is trying to explain that there's nothing wrong with the food. I'm afraid they might have a serious fight later. Sitting close the liquor cabinet is also a bald man, and he wears in a more casual way. I think he's here to enjoy being alone for a while.

我很確定這張照片是在一家小酒館裡拍的，因為首先映入我眼簾的是酒櫃。同桌坐著一名光頭男子與兩位小姐，另一桌則坐著一名男子。經過一整天的繁瑣工作後，他們可能來這裡放鬆一下並好好聊天。客人們正在享用披薩和一些飲料。至於那位穿著廚師制服的男子，應該定就是這家餐廳的廚師之一。顯然，那位穿著西裝的光頭男是在向這名廚師抱怨他的披薩。我想這披薩可能是變酸了或有怪怪的味道，從廚師的手勢來看我認為他試圖解釋食物沒有問題。恐怕他們等一下會大吵一架。坐在酒櫃旁邊的也是一名光頭男子，且他的穿著比較休閒。我認為他來這裡是為了享受獨處一段時間。

關鍵字詞

bistro n. 小酒館　**liquor cabinet** n. 酒櫃　**bald** adj. 禿頭的　**tedious** adj. 使人厭煩的　**chef** n. 廚師　**sour** adj. 臭酸的　**weird** adj. 怪怪的　**gesture** n. 手勢　**casual** adj. 休閒的，隨意的

無論是求學期間參加活動，或是出社會後需要因應不同場合，都需要搭配相對應的穿著，這種「為了因應場合的穿搭」，我們稱為 dress code。以下介紹幾種常見的 dress code 風格，搭配實用英文單字。

❶ casual：休閒風格。可以稱為 casual wear 或 leisure wear，casual 與 leisure 都有「休閒的、閒暇的」意思，因此重點是穿得舒適，不必配合特定場合而穿的衣服。例如 jeans、T-shirts、sweaters、sneakers。

❷ smart casual：時髦俐落的風格。smart 意指「俐落的、時髦的」，並不是「聰明的」！這種穿著適合與友人的聚會，或是比較沒那麼正式的工作場合。例如 fashionable tops / shirts（時尚的上衣）、collared tops / shirts（有領的上衣）

❸ business casual：莊重、適合辦公室的穿著。 smart casual 再更正式一些，而且更適合商業場合，例如會議、商務聚餐等。例如 blazers（西裝外套）、collared tops / shirts（有領上衣）、khaki pants（卡其褲）

❹ business attire / wear：正裝，就是辦公、商業場所適合穿的服裝了。例如 suit and tie（西裝打領帶）、white collar shirts（白色有領上衣）

❺ formal black tie：隆重、適合正式宴會與典禮的服裝。例如 black tuxedo / suit（黑色燕尾服 / 西裝）、black tie / bow tie（黑色領帶 / 蝴蝶領結）、floor-length gown（長及觸地的禮服）

MEMO

7

GEPT 全民英檢

中級複試
中譯＋解析

第一部分 中譯英

道歉是一門藝術，需要有真心誠意和細緻的技巧。首先，道歉要明確承認自己的錯誤並且展現慚愧之情。其次，多注意對方的感受，並尋求彌補辦法。最後，要付諸實際行動，展現改變的意志。道歉不僅是改正錯誤，更是重建信任的機會。

答題解說

第一句可以用動名詞 making an apology 當主詞。而「需要有真心誠意和細緻的技巧」這部分可以用一個形容詞子句 "that requires..." 來呈現，修飾其先行詞「一門藝術」。「真心誠意和細緻的技巧」有多種表達方式，可以用 sincerity and finesse/fine skills 表示。第二句至第四句都是以一個帶動句子的連接性副詞開始，分別是 Firstly, ... Secondly, ... 以及 Lastly, ...。第二句「道歉要…並且…」可以用 to apologize, it is crucial to... 的結構表達。第三句「多注意…並尋求…」可以用一個祈使句帶著分詞構句來呈現："care much about... while seeking ways to..." 來表示。「對方的感受」是 the feelings of the person you apologize to。請記住，「向某人道歉」，要用到介系詞 to。第四句的「付諸實際行動」可以用一個諺語「坐而言不如起而行」來表達更為貼切，也就是 actions speak louder than words，「展現改變的意志」可以用 demonstrating your willingness to change 來表示。最後一句可以用 not only/just... but also... 的句型結尾。可以用 correcting a mistake 來表達「改正錯誤」，以及 rebuild trust 來表達「重建信任」。

譯文範例

Making an apology is a kind of art that requires sincerity and finesse. Firstly, to apologize, it is crucial to explicitly admit your own mistakes and express genuine remorse. Secondly, care much about the feelings of the person you apologize to while seeking ways to make amends. Lastly, actions speak louder than words. Demonstrating your willingness to change is essential. Apologizing is not just about correcting a mistake, but also an opportunity to rebuild trust.

延伸學習

apologize 是個動詞，表示道歉或表達歉意。例如：He apologized for his mistake and promised to make it right.（他因為自己的錯誤道歉，並承諾改正。）

apology 是個名詞，指的是一種口頭或書面形式的表達歉意和承認錯誤的話語或行為。例如：She made a sincere apology to her friend for being late.（她為自己的遲到向朋友真誠地道歉。）

apologetic 是個形容詞，表示感到慚愧或對自己的行為感到遺憾。例如：She had an apologetic tone when she realized her mistake.（當她意識到自己的錯誤時，她的口氣顯得有些歉意。）

在道歉時，可以使用 apologize 或 make an apology 這兩種方式。例如：I want to apologize for my behavior yesterday. 或 I want to make an apology for my behavior yesterday.

第二部分 英文作文

提示

無論你是學生或上班族，或許有過在外租屋的經驗，但一般來說，租屋前自己最好先做些功課，到時候才不會遇到太多問題。你認為租房子時，應該注意那些事情，請發表你的看法。

答題解說

租房子時應該注意的事情很多，一般來說，可以從以下幾個面向來陳述：

◆ 簽約（signing a lease agreement）：在簽約前應該仔細閱讀租賃合約，了解其中的條款和細節（terms and conditions），確保自己知道自己的權益和義務（rights and obligations）。如果有任何疑問，應該及時向房東或房屋中介詢問（the landlord or the rental agency）。

◆ 設施（facility）：在租房前應該仔細檢查房間的設施（inspect the facilities and amenities carefully），確認有沒有缺陷或損壞（defects or damages）。如果有問題，應該及時向房東反映並要求修復或更換（ask for repairs or replacements）。

◆ 鄰居問題（neighbor problems）：在租房時應該尊重鄰居（be respectful of one's neighbors），避免發出過度噪音和造成紛擾（making excessive noise or causing any disturbance）。如果有任何糾紛或問題，應該儘早與鄰居溝通解決。

◆ 安全問題：在租房時應該保持警覺（stay vigilant），注意周圍環境和安全狀況，特別是在夜間。如果發現任何安全問題，應立即通知房東或當地警察（notify the landlord or the local police）。

First of all, when going to look around the house I want to rent and its surroundings, I must carefully inspect the facilities and amenities in the house, and ensure that everything is in good condition. If there are any defects or damages, I will report them immediately to the landlord and ask for repairs or replacements. Before signing a lease agreement, I would carefully read and understand the terms and conditions of the contract to ensure that I am aware of my own rights and obligations. Last, I would pay attention to my safety and security especially at night or in unfamiliar surroundings. If I notice any safety concerns, I will notify the landlord or the local police.

首先,當我要去看看我想租的房子及其四周為環境時,我一定會仔細查看房間的設施,並確認一切是否狀況良好。若有任何缺陷或損壞,我會該及時向房東反映並要求修復或更換。在簽訂租賃合約之前,我會仔細閱讀並了解合約中的條款和細節,以確保自己知道自己的權利和義務。最後,我會注意我的安全狀況,特別是在夜間或不熟悉的環境中。如果我有發現任何安全上的疑慮,我會通知房東或當地警察。

延伸學習

出國遊學或打工度假正夯!想要在國外生活,首先必須解決租屋問題。以下為您補充一些租屋的相關英文:

deposit(押金)、sign a lease(簽租約)、rent(房租)、tenant(房客)、utilities(水電、瓦斯)、landlord(房東)、studio(套房)、room to share(雅房分租)、single room(單人房)、double room(雙人房)、apartment(公寓)、house(獨棟房子)、available(有空位)、included(包含)、parking(停車場)、furniture(家具)、roommate(室友)、housemate(同公寓室友)

第 1 回
第 2 回
第 3 回
第 4 回
第 5 回
第 6 回
第 7 回
第 8 回
第 9 回
第 10 回

Speaking | 全民英檢中級口說能力測驗

第一部分 朗讀短文

T07P1.mp3

The internet is constantly evolving, with new terms emerging that reflect the changing digital landscape. Some recent additions include "doxxing" referring to the act of publicly exposing someone's personal information online, "deepfake" meaning the use of AI to create realistic fake videos, and "cancel culture" which describes the phenomenon of people being publicly blamed and excluded for controversial views or actions. As the internet continues to shape our lives, we can expect more new terms that reflect its impact on society.

****

Living in a dormitory can offer several advantages. Firstly, it allows students to be in close proximity to their academic environment, which can enhance their educational experience. Secondly, dorms provide a sense of community and facilitate the formation of new friendships. Additionally, living in a dorm can provide students with access to resources such as on-site advice and study groups. Finally, dorm living can also be cost-effective, as room and board costs are usually much lower than those of renting off-campus apartments.

答題解說

這兩篇分別關於「網路新詞彙」與「住校的好處」的小短文,第一篇有幾個屬於英檢中級的字彙,像是 evolving [ɪˋvɑlvɪŋ]、landscape [ˋlændˏskep]、phenomenon [fəˋnɑməˏnɑn]、emerge[ɪˋmɝdʒ] 等,請注意自己的發音是否正確。另外,第一篇短文提到的術語需要注意其發音:doxxing 中的 xx 要發 [k] 的音,而不是像 fox 中的 x 發 [ks] 的音;deepfake 就是 deep 和 fake 結合成的,只要發各自的 [dip] 和 [fek] 連在一起即可;而 culture 的 cu 發 [kʌ],與 cute 的 cu 不同。而短文中有一些「詞組」必須連在一起念(中間不可停頓),例如 constantly evolving、publicly exposed…等。最後,由於第一篇短文主要是介紹新的網絡術語,因此在朗讀時應注意強調這些詞彙的發音,才能讓聽者更加理解

文章的主題。

第二篇的 dormitory 字尾 –tory，就像 factory 一樣，應唸成 [trɪ]。在英文朗讀中，適當使用連接詞和停頓可以幫助表達文章的邏輯結構和強調重點。例如，在這段短文中，Firstly 和 Secondly 就是連接性副詞，用來引導及說明不同的優點。同時，在每個優點之間，要有適當的停頓，以幫助聽眾理解內容。此外，語調和節奏也很重要，因為它們可以幫助傳達文章的情感和重點。例如，在這段文章中，Living in a dormitory can offer several advantages. 這句話，Living 這個字的語調就要提高一些，以突顯重點。類似情況顯示於以下標有顏色的單字，請盡可能唸得比較響亮，以及出現「|」的地方，請稍作停頓，試著讓自己融入短文的情境中。最後，也請注意字與字之間該連音（含「消音」）的部分（以下畫底線），像是 act of、use of、views or、impact on、provide a、sense of、such as、cost-effective…等。

The internet is constantly evolving, | with new terms emerging that reflect the changing digital landscape. Some recent additions include "doxxing" | referring to the act of publicly exposing someone's personal information online, | "deepfake" meaning the use of AI | to create realistic fake videos, | and "cancel culture" | which describes the phenomenon of people being publicly blamed and excluded | for controversial views or actions. As the internet continues to shape our lives, | we can expect new terms to emerge | that reflect its impact on society.

****

Living in a dormitory | can offer several advantages. Firstly, | it allows students to be in close proximity | to their academic environment, | which can enhance their educational experience. Secondly, dorms provide a sense of community | and facilitate the formation of new friendships. Additionally, | living in a dorm can provide students with access to resources | such as on-site advice and study groups. Finally, | dorm living can also be cost-effective, | as room and board costs are usually much lower | than those of renting off-campus apartments.

短文翻譯

網路世界不斷進化，而隨之冒出的新詞彙也反映出這個不斷變化的數位景觀。近年來常見的新名詞包括「doxxing」，指的是公開曝光某人的個人資訊；「deepfake」則是使用人工智慧製作逼真的假影片；「cancel culture」描述的是

因為具爭議性的言論或行為而遭到公眾譴責和排斥的現象。隨著網路持續形塑著我們的生活，我們可以預期新的詞彙會出現，並反映出網路對社會的影響。

****

住在學校宿舍有許多好處。首先，它讓學生們更接近他們的學術環境，這可以提升他們的教育體驗。其次，宿舍提供社群意識並促進新友誼的形成。此外，住在宿舍可以為學生提供現場諮詢和學習小組等資源。最後，宿舍生活也具有成本效益，因為食宿花費通常遠低於在校外租房子的費用。

關鍵字詞

constantly adv. 經常地　**evolve** v. 演進　**reflect** v. 反映　**digital** adj. 數位的　**landscape** n. 景觀，樣貌　**addition** n. 增添　**expose** v. 暴露　**realistic** adj. 寫實的，實際的　**fake** adj. 仿冒的　**phenomenon** n. 現象　**exclude** v. 排除　**emerge** v. 出現　**proximity** n. 近距離　**academic** adj. 學術的　**enhance** v. 提升　**facilitate** v. 促進　**on-site** adj. 現場的　**cost-effective** adj. 具成本效益的，省錢的　**board** n. 膳食
off-campus adj. 校外的

第二部分 回答問題

T07P2.mp3

1. **What website do you visit most frequently? Why?**

   您最常上哪個網站？為什麼？

   答題解說

   每個人每天都離不開網際網路，無論是工作、休閒、通勤或等待之餘，而且上網的工具，除了電腦，就是智慧型手機，因此針對本題的回答，你可以在腦海中先浮現一些一般人最常造訪的網站（或手機 APP）。像是 Google、YouTube、Facebook、Wikipedia…或是一些購物網站，以及新聞媒體。
   接著，你要針對自己「最常」造訪的網站說明，其實你可以解讀為「最愛的網站」。比方說，Google 是全球最大的搜索引擎（one of the largest search engines）之一，大家通常用它來搜索各種資訊，也可以解決問題、學習新知識、瞭解新聞、查詢產品評價（solve problems, learn new things, stay up-to-date with news, check product reviews）等。YouTube 是全球最大的影音分享平台（video-sharing platform），許多人會上來消磨時間，觀看各種影片，如音樂、新聞、紀錄片、教育等。Facebook 是全球最大的社交網站（social

networking site）之一，人們可在上面與朋友聊天、與朋友和家人保持聯繫、分享照片和影片、參加社群（share photos and videos, join communities）、線上聊天室上交朋友等。Wikipedia 是一個全球性的維基百科（global wiki-based encyclopedia），可在上面查詢各種知識和資訊。另外，很多人會上網購物，因為網路購物可以方便快速地購買商品（it is convenient and fast to purchase products online），也可以比較不同商品的價格和評價。最後，與很多人的工作有關，許多人需要上網工作或學習，例如在網路會議上開視訊會議（video conference），或進行遠距工作或線上課程學習（take online courses）。這種趨勢在 COVID-19 疫情期間更加明顯。

回答範例 1

The website I pay most visits to is Facebook. As a marketing supervisor, I use Facebook to promote our products and services, connect with customers, and build our brands. Privately I share messages, photos, videos, links, games, and more with friends.
我最常上的網站是 Facebook。身為行銷主管的我，會使用 Facebook 來推廣我們的產品和服務、與客戶建立聯繫關係並打造我們的品牌。而私底下我會與朋友分享訊息、照片、影片、連結、遊戲等。

回答範例 2

I usually visit the website of Youtube on my computer, or just use my smartphone to enjoy its various features. I can watch a wide variety of videos, such as music videos, movie trailers, video clips related to tutorials, as well as useful equipment operation.
我通常會用電腦去上 Youtube 網站，或者用手機來享受它的各種功能。我可以觀賞各種影片，例如音樂視頻、課程相關短片，以及有用的設備操作等小影片。

關鍵字詞

pay visit to phr. 造訪⋯　**marketing supervisor** n. 行銷主管　**promote** v. 推動，促銷　**connect with** phr. 與⋯聯繫（或互動）　**feature** n. 功能，特色　**a wide variety of** phr. 各種各樣的　**video clip** n. 短影片，剪輯過的短視頻　**tutorial** n. 輔導課　**equipment operation** n. 設備操作

延伸學習

對於英文學習者來說，「上網搜尋」是個很好的學習方式，因為現代網際網路是一個豐富的資訊來源（rich source of information）。以下提供幾個技巧：

❶ 使用適當的關鍵字（appropriate keyword）。比方說，如果要找有關狗狗飼養的資訊，可以輸入 "how to raise a dog"。

❷ 使用適當的搜索引擎（appropriate search engine）：目前有許多不同的搜索引擎可供使用，例如 Google、Bing 和 Yahoo 等。不同的搜索引擎可能會提

供不同的搜尋結果。因此，選擇適當的搜索引擎非常重要。通常來說，Google 是最受歡迎的搜索引擎之一，因此，如果您不確定使用哪一個搜索引擎，建議您從 Google 開始。

❸ 瀏覽多個網站（Browse multiple websites）：開始瀏覽搜索結果時，不要只看第一個或前幾個結果（Don't just look at the first or top few results.）。相反，建議您瀏覽多個網站以獲取更全面的資訊（get a more comprehensive understanding of the information）。同時，不要忘記檢查網站的可信度和資訊的準確性（the credibility of the website and the accuracy of the information）。

2. **What's the most expensive gift you've ever received? Talk about your experience.**

你曾收過最貴的禮物是什麼？談談你的經驗。

答題解說

首先，對於「禮物」的觀點要有「有形（tangible）」與「無形（intangible）」的區分概念，這樣你在回答本題時，就不用真的去回想自己收到過什麼貴重的禮物了。接著你可以陳述的是收到這樣的禮物時，是在什麼樣的場合或情況下。也許是生日的時候，也許是個特別的紀念日（anniversary）。最後再些微補充收到禮物之後的「感受」。通常最貴重的禮物可能是來自親人、朋友或伴侶，感受到的是愛與關懷（love and care from a loved one, friend or partner）。另外，有些人會認為最貴重的禮物是時間。當有人願意花時間陪伴你、聆聽你的故事和分享他們的生活（when there's someone willing to spend time with you, listen to your stories, and share his/her life with you）時，這是一種非常珍貴的禮物。總之，最貴重的禮物可能無法以價格來衡量（priceless）。

回答範例 1

The most expensive gift I've ever got were some pieces of jewelry. Last year when my husband and I were celebrating our 20th wedding anniversary at a fancy restaurant, he told me to close my eyes and took out that gift before I open my eyes. Wow! I was so excited that I gave him a deep kiss.

我收到過的最昂貴的禮物是幾件珠寶。去年我和丈夫在一家高檔餐廳慶祝結婚 20 週年時，他請我閉上眼睛，然後在我睜開眼睛之前他拿出了那份禮物。哇！我激動地給了他一個深深的吻。

回答範例 2

I seldom get any physical gift from anybody, even on my birthdays, but I think I have already had the most expensive gift in my life. That is, the endless love given by my father. He's not rich and makes a little money, but he always takes good care of me. I'm very thankful for what he has done to me.

我很少收到任何人給的實體禮物，即使是在我生日那天，但我想我已經有了我生命中最昂貴的禮物。那就是父親給予我的無盡的愛。他並不富有，他賺的錢不多，但他總是很照顧我。我非常感謝他對我所做的一切。

關鍵字詞

jewelry n. 珠寶，首飾　**celebrate** v. 慶祝　**anniversary** n. 周年紀念日
physical adj. 實體的　**endless love** n. 無盡的愛　**make a little money** phr. 賺的錢不多　**take good care of** phr. 把…照顧得很好　**be thankful for** phr. 感謝…

延伸學習

提到「孝順」，很多人都會翻成 filial piety，filial 是父母跟孩子的關係， piety 是「崇敬、敬畏」。這樣的翻譯雖然正確，但這是一個很學術的單字，除非是很喜歡研究亞洲文化或是喜歡儒家思想的外國人，不然在口語中很少會聽到 filial piety。

另外，「孝順」這是中國人東方文化思想中的一個詞，西方國家不太會用到這個字。但如果要把「孝順父母」用英文來解釋呢？其實就是「尊重、尊敬、感謝父母」。以這個層面來說，可以翻成：

Respecting your parents

Honoring your parents

Being thankful for what your parents have done for you.

但如果把「孝」這個字往更深一點的層面探討，對華人來說，「孝」是你對你父母的一種義務，是你對他們的一種天經地義的責任，甚至可以說是你欠父母的一種債。所以如果想說「孝」這個字，建議可以用 Chinese parental respect。雖然不是直接的翻譯，但可以讓外國人比較懂孝順的含義與感覺，而且對方會領悟到不只是 parental respect 那麼簡單，加了一個 Chinese，外國人就會懂這是一種文化的概念，它有更深澳的含義。

3. **What is your favorite holiday? Why do you like it?**

你最喜歡的節日是什麼？為什麼喜歡它？

答題解說

在台灣，人們喜歡過的節日有很多，比方說，中秋節（Mid-Autumn Festival）、農曆新年（Lunar New Year）、端午節（Dragon Boat Festival）、國慶日（National Day）、情人節（Valentine's Day）…等。至於為什麼喜歡這些節日

的回答，可以先針對節日本身的特色說明，再加上自己對於這些節日的感受。以中秋節來說，人們會吃月餅、賞月、和家人團聚（eat moon cakes, admire the full moon, and reunite with one's families）。此外，中秋節也有烤肉、舞獅（enjoy the view of the moon）、吃月餅（eat moon cakes）等活動，讓人們感受到節日的氣氛。而農曆年是台灣最重要的傳統節日，通常在 1 月或 2 月初慶祝。這個節日有很多習俗，如貼春聯、掃年貨、吃團年飯、放鞭炮（pasting Spring Festival couplets, buying New Year's goods, having family reunion dinner, and setting off firecrackers）等。在端午節時，人們會吃粽子、賽龍舟（eat rice dumplings, compete in dragon boat races），以此來慶祝這個重要的節日。另外，以上三個節日即是所謂「三節」，許多公司都會發放禮金或獎金給員工，相信也會是多數人喜歡這些節日的原因之一。至於情人節，它是一個全球性的節日，通常在 2 月 14 日慶祝。在這個節日裡，人們會送花、送巧克力、寫情書（send flowers, chocolates, and love letters），以此來表達對另一半的愛意。在台灣，這個節日也非常受歡迎，很多人會特別為此準備禮物和浪漫的約會（prepare special gifts and romantic dates）。

回答範例 1

I love Chinese New Year the best, because it is a time for our family reunion. Some of my family members and relatives return from different parts of the world to have a meal together! Besides, I can get red envelopes, watch lion dances, play firecrackers and eat special foods.

我最喜歡農曆新年，因為這是我們全家團圓的日子。我的一些家人和親戚從世界各地趕回來一起吃一頓飯！此外，我還可以發紅包、看舞獅、放鞭炮、吃特色食品。

回答範例 2

My favorite holiday is New Year's Day, because it is a time for a fresh start and making resolutions. I always take the time to look back at the previous year and evaluate my accomplishments, failures, and lessons learned. I think this self-reflection can help me gain aspirations for the coming year.

我最喜歡的假期是元旦，因為這是重新開始和下決心的時候。我總會花點時間來回顧過去的一年，評估一下我的成就、失敗和學到的教訓。我認為這種自我反省可以幫助我對於新的一年得到啟發。

關鍵字詞

family reunion n. 家庭聚會　**relative** n. 親戚　**red envelope** n. 紅包　**lion dance** n. 舞獅　**firecracker** n. 鞭炮　**fresh start** n. 新的開始　**resolution** n. 決

意 **evaluate** v. 評估　**accomplishment** n. 成就　**self-reflection** n. 自省
aspiration n. 願望

延伸學習

It is（high）time... 是個常見的句型，後面常跟著不定詞（to-V）。它用來表示某事件或行動應該馬上進行（或已經過了應該去做的時間），亦即某種狀況已經達到需要採取行動的地步。例如，It is time to start the meeting. 表示，開會時間到了。

另外，it is time 和 it is high time 都可以用來表示某件事情應該進行了，但 it is high time 更強調事情的急迫性以及若未採取行動造成的負面影響。例如，It is high time you started studying for the exam. 表示你應該早就開始準備考試了，因為現在離考試日期已經很近了。

4. **Have you ever taken other classes after school? Why?**

   你可曾在放學後去上別的課程嗎？為什麼？

   答題解說

本題雖然針對學生族群提問，但如果您已是出社會多年的上班族，可以回想一下當初自己當學生時的情況。一般來說，放學後的各種課程分為補習課程（tutoring classes）、語言課程（language classes）、體育課程（sports classes）、藝術課程（art classes）、STEM（科學、技術、工程和數學）課程…等。

以補習而言，你可以說需要補習來提高自己在學校的成績，以期在考試中表現更好（improve one's grades in school or perform better in exams）。去上語言課程的話，可能是為了提高本身的英語或其他語言能力，有助於自己在未來的學習和職業生涯中更成功（be more successful in one's future academic and professional careers）。體育類的話，像是籃球、足球、游泳等，有助於學生保持健康，增強體能和協作能力（stay fit, develop one's physical abilities, and learn teamwork）。

如果從來沒有在放學後去參加過什麼課程，也可以如實說明，並補充為什麼不會想去參加那些課程的原因。

回答範例 1

Yes, I remember when I was still a senior high school student, I took a Japanese-language class near my home. In order to better understand the messages and information in the online games, I needed to learn Japanese.

是的，我記得還是高中生的時候，我在我家附近上日語課。為了更加了解網絡遊

戲中的訊息和資訊，我必須學日語。

第 1 回
第 2 回
第 3 回
第 4 回
第 5 回
第 6 回
第 7 回
第 8 回
第 9 回
第 10 回

回答範例 2

No, I've never taken any class after school. After a long tiring day of school courses, I just wanted to go home and lie on the sofa watching TV. But now, I admit I should learn more when I was still young. If I had additional skills, I wouldn't work as a deliveryman now!

不，我從來沒有在放學後去上過什麼課。在經過一整天累人的學校課程後，我只想回家躺在沙發上看電視。但是現在，我承認我錯了。我應該在我還年輕的時候多學習。如果我有額外的技能，我現在就不會做送貨員了！

關鍵字詞

take a... class phr. 上…課程　**tiring** adj. 累人的　**admit** v. 承認　**additional** adj. 更多的，額外的　**deliveryman** n. 送貨員

延伸學習

學生課後的課程（after-school class），常見的有：

❶ 補習班：通常會在放學後提供各類科目（a variety of subjects）的輔導課程，例如數學、英文、物理、化學等。補習班的目的是幫助學生提高學業成績，並且在學習上更有自信心（improve the academic performance and gain more confidence in studies）。

❷ 興趣班（enrichment classes）：興趣班是學生可以參加的課後課程之一，例如繪畫、音樂、舞蹈、籃球等。這些課程可以讓學生在放學後放鬆自己，發展自己的興趣和才能，並且可以交到新朋友（develop one's talents while making new friends）。

❸ 社團活動（club activities）：例如學生會、音樂社、戲劇社、攝影社（student council, music clubs, drama clubs, photography clubs）等。這些課程可以讓學生發展自己的興趣和才能，並且可以學習團隊合作和領導能力（develop one's interests and skills while learning teamwork and leadership abilities）。

❹ 家教（private lessons）：通常由一位或多位老師上門進行一對一的教學（one-on-one lessons）。這些課程可以提供學生個人化的輔導以及量身訂做的課程（offer students personalized attention and a tailored curriculum），並且可以提高學生的學業成績。

5. **Are you satisfied with your salary now? How much do you think is ideal for you?**

你滿意你現在的薪水嗎？你認為多少對你來說是理想的？

答題解說

相信大部分對於自己的薪水都不會是滿意的！但針對本題回答完 Yes/No 以及「滿意的數字」之後，還能說什麼呢？你可以針對自己每個月的固定支出，說明為什麼需要這樣的數字，以及期望有更多的錢來做些什麼。當然，你也可以說除了金錢以外，你更重視工作的哪個部分，舉一反三，讓自己回答的內容更有深度。像是希望能夠在自己擅長或感興趣的領域中工作（work in one's area of expertise or interest），並且有機會學習新的技能和知識（have opportunities to learn new skills and knowledge），挑戰自己。或是希望能夠在一個舒適、安全、友好、積極向上的工作環境中工作（a comfortable, safe, friendly, and positive working environment），與同事之間有良好的互動和合作（interaction and collaboration）…等。

如果你現在還沒出社會工作賺錢，可以說明未來希望的薪資是多少，或者希望自己幾歲之前能有有多少的財富來達成什麼願望等。

回答範例 1

I don't think most people would be satisfied with their salary. To me, the more, the better, of course. However, I also value job security, work-life balance, and opportunities for career advancement over just a high salary.

我認為大多數人不會對自己的薪水感到滿意。對我來說，當然是越多越好。 然而，相對於較高的薪水，我也更看重工作安全、工作與生活的平衡以及職業發展機會。

回答範例 2

Since I am still a student now, I don't work for any company. But to me, in the future, I hope I can make at least NT$50,000 a month before I am 30, and in the long run, maybe before 35, a yearly income of NT$1,000,000 would be ideal for me. I'll work hard to achieve this goal.

因為我現在還是個學生，所以我沒有在任何一家公司工作。但對我來說，未來我希望在 30 歲之前每個月能至少有新台幣 5 萬的收入，而長遠來說，或許 35 歲之前，希望年收入可達 100 萬元，這對我來說是最理想的。我會努力實現這個目標。

第 1 回

第 2 回

第 3 回

第 4 回

第 5 回

第 6 回

第 7 回

第 8 回

第 9 回

第 10 回

關鍵字詞

be satisfied with phr. 對…感到滿意　**job security** n. 工作安全　**work-life balance** n. 工作與生活的平衡　**advancement** n. 進展　**work for** phr. 在…（某公司）工作　**in the long run** phr. 長遠來看　**yearly income** n. 年收入　**ideal** adj. 理想的

延伸學習

「the+ 比較級, the + 比較級」的句型是一種用來比較兩個事物的方式，強調兩者之間的關係，通常用於形容詞和副詞的比較。例如，"The more you practice, the better you get."（你練習得越多，你就會變得更好。）或者 "The earlier you arrive, the better seat you will get."（你越早到，你座位就越好。）

在以上例子中，第一個比較級（more、earlier）與第二個比較級（better）分別闡明了兩個事物之間的相對關係，也就是說，這個句型將比較重點放在了兩者之間的關係上。此外，這個句型也可以用於比較兩個相反的情況。例如，"The harder you try, the less likely you are to fail."（你越努力，失敗的可能性就越小）。總之，「the+ 比較級, the + 比較級」的句型可以幫助我們更清晰地表達事物之間的相對關係，讓我們的比較更具體、更有力。

6. **How many work hours per day do you think is reasonable? What do you think about overtime work?**

   你認為一天工作幾個小時是合理的？你對加班有何看法？

   答題解說

   在台灣，一般來說每天的工作時數是 8 小時，不含午休時間，因此對於「合理的每日工作時數」可以根據法令的規範的回答即可。至於「加班」的看法，，一般上班族的看法可能褒貶不一（have mixed opinions about...）。有些人認為加班是為了完成工作而必要的。因此，他們可能會視加班為工作的一部分，並且不太會對此抱怨或抗議（see overtime as a regular part of their job and not complain or protest about it）。有些人認為加班是負面的，因為它意味著他們必須花更多的時間在工作上，而無法享受自己的生活（spend more time working and cannot enjoy their personal life）。這些人可能會對加班感到不滿。而有些人認為加班可以帶來額外的收入（view overtime as an opportunity to earn extra income），因此他們可能會樂於加班。這些人可能會在需要賺取更多錢時選擇加班。還有些人會認為加班是因為公司管理不善，導致工作時間無法合理分配（overtime is caused by poor management within the company, which results in an unreasonable allocation of work hours）。這些人可能會批評公司的管理

方式，並呼籲改善工作環境。

According to relevant labor laws in Taiwan, the standard work hours per week in Taiwan are 40 hours, and the maximum work hours per day are 8 hours, which I think is reasonable. I don't agree to work overtime, even if I can make more money. Besides, I need to take care of my young kids after work, so I won't choose to work for a company that needs their employees to work overtime often.

根據台灣相關的勞工法案，台灣每星期的標準工作時間是 40 小時，每天最多工作時間是 8 小時，我覺得這是合理的。我不同意加班，即使我可以賺更多的錢。另外，下班後我還要照顧年幼的孩子，所以我不會選擇在一個需要員工經常加班的公司工作。

In my opinion, how many work hours per day or per week is reasonable depends on the individual's work environment, job responsibilities, and personal circumstances. Besides, factors such as age, health, and family responsibilities can also affect what is defined as reasonable work hours for an individual. As for overtime work, I think it's also up to the individual and their employers to negotiate a work schedule that is both reasonable and meets the needs of the job.

在我看來，每天或每週工作多少小時是合理的，取決於個人的工作環境、工作職責和個人狀況。此外，年齡、健康和家庭責任等因素也會影響個人認定的合理工作時間。至於加班，我認為還是要個人和雇主協商一個合理又能滿足工作需要的工作時程。

relevant adj. 相關的　**work hours** n. 工作時數　**reasonable** adj. 合理的　**overtime** adv. 加班　**in one's opinion** phr. 就某人看來　**factor** n. 因素　**up to** prep. 由…（某人）決定　**individual** n. 個人　**meet the needs of...** phr. 符合…的需求

在英文裡，有一些從 work 衍生而來的名詞，在工作職場上也非常實用喔！

workforce：工作人員，指一個公司或組織的所有員工。

workload：工作量，指一個人或一個團隊在一段時間內需要完成的工作量。

workspace：工作空間，指一個人在工作時使用的空間，通常是指辦公室、工作臺或工作區域。

workaholic：工作狂，指一個人對工作非常狂熱，可能會犧牲休閒和家庭時間以

第 1 回

第 2 回

第 3 回

第 4 回

第 5 回

第 6 回

第 7 回

第 8 回

第 9 回

第 10 回

工作為優先。

workday：工作日，指在一個工作週期中被視為正常工作日的日期。

workweek：工作週，指一個工作週期中的一週時間，通常從周一開始。

workplace：工作場所，指一個人在工作時所在的地方，可以是辦公室、工廠或其他工作場所。

workstation：工作站，指一個人在工作時使用的電腦或工作區域，通常包括桌子、椅子和電腦。

7. **What is something you are proud of that you can do by yourself? Why?**

有什麼事情是你可以自己做而讓你感到自豪的？ 為什麼？

答題解說

一般來說，人們可能會對自己可以獨立完成的一系列事情感到自豪。比方說，

❶ 完成困難的任務（accomplishing a difficult task）：完成複雜的專案計畫、解決具有挑戰性的問題或掌握新技能（finishing a complex project, solving a challenging problem, or mastering a new skill）都需要付出艱苦的努力，能夠完成這些工作可以讓人們對自己的能力和毅力感到自豪。

❷ 獨立自主（being independent）：能夠自我照顧、做出決定並承擔責任，不依賴他人（Being able to take care of oneself, make decisions, and handle responsibilities without relying on others）可以成為許多人自豪的來源。這可以給他們帶來自信和自給自足的感覺。

❸ 克服障礙（overcoming obstacles）：克服重大障礙，例如身體或精神健康問題、財務困難或個人挫折的人（overcome significant obstacles, such as physical or mental health challenges, financial difficulties, or personal setbacks）可能會對自己在逆境中的韌性和決心感到自豪。

❹ 創造（creating something）：寫作一本書、畫一幅畫或製作一件家具等，從無到有地創造出某物（creating something from scratch）可以是一種深刻的滿足感。看到自己的創造力和努力的具體成果也可以成為自豪的來源。

❺ 幫助他人：志願服務可以讓人們對自己能夠對世界產生正面的影響（make a positive impact on the world）感到自豪。幫助他人還可以為生命中提供目的和意義。

回答範例 1

I started and built a successful business from scratch five years ago. Starting a business can be a challenging task that requires a lot of hard work, dedication, and risk-taking. I need to face significant challenges in the early stages, such as securing funding, developing a product or service, building a customer base, and competing in a crowded market. So, I'm so proud of this achievement and I hope my company will be in operation forever.

我在五年前白手起家,創建了一家成功的企業。創業可能是一項具挑戰性的任務,它需要很多的努力、執著和冒險。在早期的階段我就必須面對著重大的挑戰,例如取得資金、開發產品或服務、建立顧客群,並於擁擠的市場中與人競爭。所以,對於這項成就,我感到非常自豪,我希望我的公司能夠永續經營。

回答範例 2

Being able to take care of myself, make decisions, and handle responsibilities without relying on others can be a source of pride for me. I moved out of my parents' home to live on my own last year. Then I worked part-time and paid for my own tuition fees. Besides, I made my own decisions about how to spend my time and money. I think this is something I am proud of.

能夠在不依賴他人的情況下,照顧自己、做出決定及處理責任,這些都是讓我感到自豪的來源。去年我搬出父母的家自食其力。然後我兼差工作並支付自己的學費。此外,我自己決定如何花費我的時間和金錢。我覺得這是我引以為傲的事情。

關鍵字詞

from scratch phr. 從頭開始地　**hard work** n. 辛勞,努力　**dedication** n. 奉獻,執著　**significant** adj. 重大的,大量的　**secure** v. 取得　**customer base** n. 顧客群　**in operation** phr. 營運中　**rely on** phr. 依賴⋯　**live on one's own** phr. 自食其力　**tuition fee** n. 學費

延伸學習

scratch 可以作動詞或名詞使用。當動詞時表示「刮、搔、抓、挖」等意思,通常用於描述用手或尖銳物體的動作。例如:The cat scratched the sofa.(貓抓壞了沙發。)

當名詞時表示「刮痕、抓痕或搔癢」等意思,例如:There's a scratch on my phone screen.(我手機屏幕上有一道刮痕。)

scratch 也常見於以下慣用語:

❶ start from scratch:從頭開始,重新開始。

❷ scratch the surface:只是表面,沒有深入了解或處理問題。

8. How do you manage your time? Do you have any secrets to managing it effectively?

你如何管理你的時間？你有任何有效時間管理的秘訣嗎？

答題解說

提到「管理時間（time management）」，每個人的方法可能不盡相同，一般常見的時間管理技巧可能是「設定明確的目標（set specific goals）」，目標明確才能規劃時程。另外是「設定目標完成的時間表（create a schedule）」或「待辦事項列表（to-do list）」以便追縱進度（follow-ups）、不會忘記需要完成的任務及更有針對性、更有效地分配時間並控制工作量。

總之，時間管理的秘訣是在有效管理時間的同時保持靈活性（flexibility）。在對自己的時間表進行規劃的同時，但也要考慮到可能出現的突發情況（unexpected circumstances）。同時，給自己留些時間放鬆和休息（relax and take breaks）也很重要。最後，保持積極的態度和樂觀的心態（bear a positive and optimistic attitude），對於處理時間和任務時，保持高度的效率相當重要喔！

回答範例 1

I usually make decisions on which tasks should be carried out based on their importance and urgency. This helps me focus on the most important things first and I'll try my best to complete them on time. Besides, I would say no to the tasks that don't align with my goals or are not a priority. By doing so, I can avoid spending too much time on trivial things and thus manage time effectively.

我通常會根據工作的重要性和緊迫性來決定現在應做哪些事情。這有助於我先關注最重要的事情，且我會盡全力按時完成。此外，我會拒絕那些與我的目標不符或不是優先事項的任務。如此一來，可以讓我避免花太多時間在瑣事上，並可有效地管理時間。

回答範例 2

First of all, I'll set time-bound goals that are relevant and achievable for myself. Second, I think I will need to concentrate on and keep track of how things proceed. I admit that sometimes I will be distracted by cellphone messages, social media, or emails from electronic devices while working. I'll try to stay focused so that I can complete my tasks efficiently.

首先，我會為自己設定相關且可實現的目標，並訂出一個時間限制。其次，我認為我必須專注並追蹤事情的進展情況。我承認有時我在工作上會被手機訊息、社交媒體或電子設備的電子郵件等分散了注意力。我會努力保持專注，以便有效地完成任務。

第 1 回
第 2 回
第 3 回
第 4 回
第 5 回
第 6 回
第 7 回
第 8 回
第 9 回
第 10 回

關鍵字詞

make a decision on phr. 對於…做出決定　**urgency** n. 急迫性　**try one's best to-V** phr. 盡最大努力…　**on time** phr. 準時地　**align with** phr. 與…一致　**priority** n. 第一要務　**trivial** adj. 瑣碎的　**effectively** adv. 有效地　**time-bound** adj. 有時間限制的　**relevant** adj. 相關的　**achievable** adj. 可達成的　**focus / concentrate on** phr. 專注於…　**keep track of** phr. 追蹤，記錄　**distract** v. 使分心　**efficiently** adv. 有效率地

延伸學習

schedule 這個字動、名詞同形，當名詞時意思是「規劃表」、「行程表」，當動詞時是「規劃，安排…的時程」的意思，前面若是加上字首 re- 時，變成 reschedule，意指「重新規劃」。例如：

❶ The project is on schedule.（這個專案照計畫進行。）

❷ The flight's schedule has changed.（班機的時間表已更改。）

❸ We need to schedule a meeting for next week.（我們必須安排下週的會議。）

❹ I have scheduled some time in the afternoon to work on my presentation.（我安排了下午一些時間來製作我的講演文稿。）

9. **Do you pay by credit card when shopping online? Why or why not?**

你在網購時會使用信用卡付款嗎？為什麼？

答題解說

基本上本題就是要你針對「線上購物使用信用卡支付」的優缺點來做說明。一般來說，「便利性」是它最大的優點，因為幾乎所有的網路商家都接受信用卡支付（accepted by most online merchants）。此外，如果線上購物出現問題，例如收到了有瑕疵或錯誤的商品（defective or incorrect item），您可以向信用卡公司提出異議，他們將與商家合作解決問題。再者，許多信用卡公司提供現金回饋、積分或里程獎勵計畫，每筆交易可以獲得一定的獎勵（allow you to earn cash back, points, or miles for every purchase you make），長期累積可以省下不少費用。

至於缺點的部分，主要是「安全性」的問題（security risks）。網路交易有被盜用卡號的風險（carry a risk of fraud and identity theft），如果卡號被盜取可能會導致經濟損失。另外，使用信用卡消費時，很容易忽略自己的購買能力和預算，過度消費（overspending）可能會導致負債問題。

回答範例 1

I usually make online purchases by debit cards, instead of credit cards. I don't want to borrow money to buy anything, and credit cards can be risky. It might lead to debt and interest charges if the balance is not paid off in full each month. The advantage of using my funds available won't allow me to spend more than I have in my bank account. Besides, I can also be rewarded bonus points by using debit cards.

我通常在網購時會用簽帳卡，而不用信用卡。我不想借錢買東西，且信用卡可能有風險。如果每月未全額還清餘額，會導致債務和利息費用。有多少錢就用多少錢，這樣的好處是，不會讓我花費超過我銀行存款的資金。此外，使用簽帳卡還可以讓我累積獎勵金。

回答範例 2

Yes, I usually make online purchases by credit cards. Many credit card companies offer reward programs that allow you to earn cash back, points, or miles for every purchase you make, which can add up to significant savings over time. Lastly, Using a credit card responsibly and paying off the balance in full each month can help you build a positive credit history, which can be helpful if you need to borrow money in the future, such as for a mortgage or car loan.

是的，我通常使用借信用進行網購。許多信用卡公司都有提供獎勵方案，讓你每次購物都能賺取現金回饋、積分或搭機的里程優惠，而時間久了，可以讓你節省不少費用。最後，以負責任的態度使用信用卡，並每月結清所欠之餘額，可以幫你建立良好的信用記錄，如果未來你需要借錢（例如房貸或車貸），這會很有幫助。

關鍵字詞

debit card n. 簽帳卡　**risky** adj. 有風險的　**lead to** phr. 導致，造成　**balance** n. 餘額　**pay off... in full** phr. 結清，全額支付　**bonus point** n. 紅利點數　**add up to** phr. 加總為…　**credit history** n. 信用紀錄　**mortgage** n. 質押

延伸學習

一般來說，信用卡的種類包括「普通卡」（classic card）、「金卡」（preferred/gold card）、「白金卡」（platinum card）、「商務卡／公司卡」（corporate card）、「聯名卡」（co-branded card）、「附卡」（supplementary card）。以「付款方式」（payment method）而言，我們通常稱為「刷卡」。例如：I'd like to pay by credit card.，如果不確定店家是否接受信用卡付款時，你可以詢問 Do you take/accept credit cards?（你們接受信用卡嗎？）。如果濫用信用卡的話，很容易導致 debt（負債），「卡債」就叫作

credit card debt，如果要表示自己身上背了很多卡債，我們會用介係詞 in 來表示，如 be in credit card debt「背了卡債」。如果要表示「繳清，償還」卡債，我們會使用 pay 或者 clear 這兩個動詞，如 clear my credit card debt 就是「繳清我的卡債」的意思。

當你收到一張新的信用卡時，需要先進行開通才能開始使用，這個過程我們稱為開卡。在英文的說法裡，我們不說 open，而會使用動詞 activate（啟用，啟動）來表示，因此 activate a credit card 就是「開通信用卡」的意思。

10. **If you need not go to school, or go to work anymore, would you enjoy it and what would you do?**

如果你不再需要上學或去上班，你會喜歡嗎？你會做什麼呢？

答題解說

雖然本題對於大部分人來說，是幾乎不可能發生，且從來不會去想到的事情。但如果可以真的不需要去上班或上課了，大部分人可能會喜歡更多自由的時間，可以用於追求自己的興趣愛好、培養自己的技能或者放鬆自己（to pursue hobbies, develop new skills, or just relax）。這樣的自由時間可以讓他們有更多的機會去做那些平常因為忙碌而無法做的事情。

有些人可能會選擇參加課程、研討會或工作坊，以提高自己的技能或掌握新的知識（take courses, attend webinars, or workshops to improve their skills or learn something new）。此外，你也可以說，可能會選擇旅遊、戶外運動、社交活動或者自己的創意項目（go traveling, do exercise, socialize with friends and family, or work on personal projects）。不過，可能也會有人認為，如果不必去上班或上課了，生活會頓時失去重心（lose one's balance in life），甚至過得沒有意義。

回答範例 1

I need to say loudly, "Yes, I do! I'll enjoy it." I've worked for over twenty years and I have constantly felt burnout and tired at work. So if I had no obligations or responsibilities that require me to attend work, I would pursue the hobbies and interests that I enjoy, such as reading, writing, playing music, making art, cooking, or exercising. Besides, I would also travel, or pursue further things I am passionate about.

我必須大聲說：「是的，我要！我會喜歡的！」我工作了二十多年，一直覺得工作很累很累。因此，如果我沒有要去工作的義務或責任了，我會追求我喜歡的愛好和興趣，例如閱讀、寫作、演奏音樂、藝術創作、烹飪或鍛鍊。此外，我也會去旅行，或繼續追求我所熱衷的事情。

第 1 回
第 2 回
第 3 回
第 4 回
第 5 回
第 6 回
第 7 回
第 8 回
第 9 回
第 10 回

回答範例 2

Actually, I've never thought of such a question... but if I didn't need to go to work, I might feel bored and unfulfilled, or even purposeless because, work often provides me with a sense of community and social interaction. If I stopped working, I would feel isolated and lonely. Besides, I would feel powerless, which can lead to a loss of motivation and a lack of direction in my life.

其實,我從沒有想過這樣的問題…但如果我不必去上班了,我可能會感到無聊和沒有成就感,甚至沒有目的,因為工作經常給我的是一種社群感和社交上的互動。如果我不再工作了,我會感到孤立和孤獨。此外,我會感到無力,這會導致我的生活失去動力和方向。

關鍵字詞

burnout adj. 工作倦怠的　**obligation** n. 義務　**responsibility** n. 責任
passionate adj. 熱情的　**unfulfilled adj** 沒有成就感的　**purposeless** adj. 沒有目的的　**interaction** n. 互動　**isolated** adj. 孤立的　**powerless** adj. 無力的
motivation n. 動機,動力

延伸學習

「職業倦怠」又稱為「工作倦怠」,英文是 burnout,它的原意為「燒盡」,也可以在前面加上 job 或 occupational(職業上的)等字。職業倦怠涵蓋心理、精神上的衰竭(mental/spiritual exhaustion)、沮喪(depression)以及憤世忌俗(cynism)等層面,任一症狀都可能降低工作效率(efficiency)。

有研究指出,職業倦怠的發生率與工作投入的程度(job engagement)有關。當一個人愈投入工作,就表示他愈將生活重心放在工作上(focus one's life on work),導致情緒常受工作影響。這類型的人極重視工作,往往會設定許多想要實踐的目標(set many goals to be desired)。然而面對實踐目標的渴望跟動力可能會與現實能力不足的落差感產生衝突,導致無法承受這樣的矛盾感而陷入負面迴圈(negative loop),產生對工作的倦怠跟厭倦。

答題解說

雖然題目有 提示 你從四個點去回答問題，但如果每個點你只能回答一句話，這樣的內容是絕對不夠的。所以請先從圖片本身去掌握這張照片的主題，然後根據 where、who、why、what...等架構來充實你的內容。若對於圖片中的人事物相關英文沒有太大把握的話，試著用代名詞或自己有把握說得正確的詞彙來表達。

1. 照片裡的人在什麼地方？

   你可以說 in a park（在公園裡）或是 on the grass of a park（在公園的草地上）。如果只是說「他們在室外」（They are outdoors.）之類的，分數可會打折扣喔！

2. 照片裡的人在做什麼？

   提到「人」的部分時，你可以先提有多少人（There are five people...），以及他們可能的關係。比方說，There is a teacher/conductor and four old students sitting on the green.，They might be good neighbors or friends living in the nearby neighborhood/community.，接著繼續說明他們正在進行晨操（do morning exercise），或是做體操。

3. 照片裡的人為什麼會在那裡？

   我們可以從照片拍攝地點，以及當中人物的行為、動作來判斷他們為什麼會

來這地方。例如，你可以說 These old men and women follow their conductor's movements。以及 They are stretching their arms upward...。 From these movements they do, I guess they are here to do morning exercise, because the importance of health can't be overemphasized. Besides, making friends or socializing may be another purpose of gathering here.

4. 如果尚有時間，請詳細描述圖片中的景物。

例如，從照片中的，你可以繼續補充說，I guess they must enjoy what they are doing...、There are many trees standing tall in the park and they help keep off the sunlight, so I think doing activities in this park is a great enjoyment.…等。

回答範例

This is a great park, just like many other parks I've ever seen. There are five people sitting on their yoga mats on the grass. They may be friendly neighbors living in the same community. One of them is the teacher, or conductor, who is leading the other four old gentlemen and old ladies to do morning exercise – they are stretching their arms upward. I think the park is a great place for people to do outdoor exercise or for kids to play sports. Besides, there are many trees standing tall in the park and they help keep off the sunlight, so I think doing exercise in this park is a great enjoyment. For old people, the park is also a place where they can gather and socialize with friends. In short, visitors can take a walk, go jogging, go cycling, have a picnic, and play sports there. Also, they can enjoy bird-watching, wildlife viewing, and exploring natural environments.

這是一個很棒的公園，就像我見過的其他許多公園一樣。有五個人用瑜伽墊坐在草地上。他們可能是住在同一個社區的好鄰居。其中一位是老師，或者說是帶動者，她帶領著另外四位老先生和老太太做早操 — 他們正在做往上伸展雙臂的動作。我認為公園是人們進行戶外運動或孩子們運動的好地方。此外，公園裡有許多高聳的樹木，可以遮擋陽光，所以我覺得在這個公園運動是一種享受。對於老年人來說，公園也是他們與朋友聚會和社交的地方。總之，遊客們可以這裡散步、慢跑、騎自行車、野餐、運動等。此外，他們還可以享受觀鳥、觀賞野生動物和探索自然環境的樂趣。

關鍵字詞

yoga mat n. 瑜伽墊　**conductor** n. 指揮者，帶動者　**morning exercise** n. 晨操　**stretch** v. 伸展　**upward** adv. 向上　**keep off** phr. 阻擋　**socialize with** phr. 與…交際　**bird-watching** n. 賞鳥　**wildlife** n. 野生動物　**explore** v. 探索

第 1 回
第 2 回
第 3 回
第 4 回
第 5 回
第 6 回
第 7 回
第 8 回
第 9 回
第 10 回

在英文文法中，動名詞（gerund）、現在分詞（present participle）、以及現在進行式（present progressive）都具有「動詞-ing」的外觀，在文法中我們給他們一個名稱，叫作「動狀詞」。它們在句中所扮演的角色以及功能是不一樣的：

❶ 動名詞（gerund）：動名詞是一種「具有動作意味的名詞」，所以當然具有名詞的功能及扮演名詞的角色（主詞、受詞等）。常以-ing 結尾。例如：Playing football is my favorite hobby.（踢足球是我的最愛嗜好。）→ 在這句中，"playing" 是動名詞作主詞。

❷ 現在分詞（present participle）：現在分詞通常作為形容詞，少部分作副詞。例如：The running water is very refreshing.（流動的水很清涼。）→ 在這句中，running 是現在分詞，用來修飾 water，形容詞用法。又比方說：The weather is scorching hot in the southern part of this country.（該國南部的天氣極為炎熱。）→ 在這句中，scorching 當副詞，修飾形容詞 hot。

❸ 現在進行式（present progressive）：「現在進行式」是由 be 動詞加上現在分詞組成的動詞時態，用來表示正在進行中的動作。例如：I am studying English now.（我現在正在學英語。）→ 在這句中，am studying 是現在進行式，用來表示現在正在進行的動作。

8

GEPT 全民英檢

中級複試
中譯＋解析

第一部分 中譯英

英文單字並不需要死記硬背，可以運用各種技巧幫助自己更有效地學習。例如，可以使用單字卡、聯想法、背誦歌曲歌詞等方法，增加單字的印象深度。同時，每天多閱讀英文文章以及聽英語音檔，也有助於強化單字的記憶。

答題解說

首先，要確定每一個句子的意思和結構。第一句可以看成「你不必以『死記硬背』的方式來學習英文字彙，並且…」，所以主詞可以用 You，接著是 don't have to learn 的動詞部位，其受詞是 English vocabulary，「以…方式」可以用 by + Ving 來表示，這裡可以用 by repeating words many times（以多次重複字彙的方式）來表達「死記硬背」。接著第一個句子的的二個對等子句可以看成「你可以善加利用『可以幫助自己更有效學習的各種技巧』」，所以受詞是 various techniques that can help you learn more effectively。第二句的結構是 You can use + 單字卡、聯想法、背誦歌曲歌詞 + to increase +「單字的印象度」。「單字卡、聯想法、背誦歌曲歌詞」可以用 flashcards, association, memorization of song lyrics 表示。「單字的印象深度」可以用 the depth of impression of the words 表示。第三句可以用動名詞當主詞：reading English articles and listening to English audio files every day（每天多閱讀英文文章以及聽英語音檔），動詞是 can help（有助於），受詞是 strengthen your memory of the vocabulary（強化單字的記憶）。

總之，請記住，務必先架構出一個句子的主詞、動詞…等基本元素，然後再確認翻譯句子的流暢性和易讀性。為了讓英文句子更流暢和易讀，可以適當地調整單字或字詞的順序。最後，再次檢查英文句子的文法和拼寫是否正確。

譯文範例

You don't have to learn English vocabulary by repeating words many times, and you can take advantages of various techniques that can help you learn more effectively. For example, you can use flashcards, association, memorizing song lyrics to increase the depth of impression of the words. Meanwhile, reading English articles and listening to English audio files every day can help strengthen your memory of the vocabulary.

延伸學習

「死記硬背」有一個英文的說法是 rote learning。rote 意思是「機械性的背

誦」。例如：You should not learn vocabulary by rote.（你不該死記硬背英文單字。）這種學習方式通常被視為缺乏創造力和批判性思維（lack of creativity and critical thinking），因為它只是單純地背誦和重複所學的知識（Simply recite and repeat what you have learned）。然而，對於某些學科和技能來說，死記硬背是必要的。例如，在學習語言時，掌握文法和詞彙需要反覆練習和背誦（Mastering grammar and vocabulary requires repeated practice and memorization）。同樣地，在學習樂器時，熟練的技巧需要透過不斷的、反覆的練習來達到（Proficient skill is achieved through constant, repeated practice.）。因此，與其說不應死記硬背，不如說在掌握技巧之後，應多花時間反覆練習（After you have mastered some technique, spend more time practicing it over and over again.），並與批判性思維和創造性學習相結合，以建立更深入和全面的知識和技能（Build deeper and comprehensive knowledge and skills.）。

第二部分 英文作文

提示

保持良好身材也可以保持身體的健康、加強心理層面的健康並提高自信心。此外，良好的身體狀態可以使人更有活力和耐力，進而更有意願參與各種活動，提升生活品質。你認為保持良好身材的方法有哪些呢？

答題解說

一般來說，保持良好身材（keep oneself in good shape）可以從幾個面向來陳述：

◆ 健康的飲食習慣（healthy eating）：選擇食物時要多吃蔬果、全穀物和蛋白質（...rich in fruits, vegetables, lean protein, and whole grains），盡量避免高糖、高脂肪和加工食品（high-sugar, high-fat, and processed foods）。

◆ 規律運動（regular exercise）：每週至少進行 150 分鐘的有氧運動（aerobic exercise），例如慢跑、游泳或騎自行車。此外，也可以進行重量訓練（weight training），以增加肌肉量和代謝率（increases muscle mass and metabolic rate）。

◆ 睡眠充足（sufficient sleep）：保持足夠的睡眠時間有助於身體的恢復和新陳代謝（help with body recovery and metabolism），並且有助於控制體重。

◆ 壓力管理（managing stress）：長期的壓力可能會導致體重增加和其他健康問題，可以學習冥想、瑜伽或深呼吸練習（meditation, yoga, or deep breathing exercises）等壓力管理技巧，幫助管理壓力並促進良好體態

（promote good shape）。

◆ 減少坐著的時間（reducing the time of being seated）：長時間坐著對身體健康不利，應該盡量避免長時間坐著，並且要多站起來活動一下（avoid sitting for a long time and stand up to move around）。

Keeping in good shape is essential for leading a healthy and fulfilling life. Here are some of my ways to stay in good shape. Firstly, regular exercise is key. It not only helps to keep the body fit but also has numerous mental health benefits. Secondly, having a balanced diet that includes plenty of fruits, vegetables, and whole grains is crucial for providing the body with essential nutrients. Thirdly, getting enough rest and sleep is important to allow the body to recover and regenerate. Lastly, avoiding harmful habits such as smoking and excessive alcohol consumption can help to keep the body in good shape. By incorporating these habits into one's daily routine, it is possible to maintain a healthy and active lifestyle.

保持良好的體態對於擁有健康和充實的生活相當重要。以下是我的一些保持良好身材的方法。首先，規律運動是主要關鍵。它不僅有助於保持身體健康，而且對心理健康也有許多好處。再來是均衡飲食，包括大量水果、蔬菜和全穀物，對於為身體提供必需的營養，是相當重要的。第三，充足的休息和睡眠對於身體恢復和恢復活力很重要。最後，避免吸煙和過度飲酒等不良習慣也有助於保持體態的健康。只要將這些習慣融入日常生活中，就可以維持健康和積極正面的生活型態。

延伸學習

身材的好壞，是許多人相當在意的問題，因此在形容別人的身材時，用字務必要小心謹慎，別只會用 thin、fat 喔！

slim：指的是瘦長型的身材，通常是指身體線條柔美，體型瘦削。

lean：指的是身材偏瘦，但肌肉纖瘦，較為緊實。

petite：指的是身材嬌小玲瓏，尤其是指女性身材。

curvy：指的是身材曲線優美，尤其是指女性有較豐滿的胸部和臀部。

athletic：指的是身材健美有力，肌肉緊實而不失柔韌。

stocky：指的是身材矮壯而粗壯，肌肉發達。

plump：指的是身材豐滿且稍微圓潤，通常是指肥胖的程度較輕微。

stout：指的是身材肥胖，但是較為結實，肌肉量較大。

obese：指的是身材極度肥胖，體重明顯超出正常範圍。

T08P1.mp3

第1回
第2回
第3回
第4回
第5回
第6回
第7回
第8回
第9回
第10回

第一部分 朗讀短文

News media plays a vital role in shaping public opinion. It provides a platform for reporting on current events and issues, enabling people to stay up-to-date. However, in recent times, the media has gradually become biased to reporting and tried to incite hatred. They have also created a flood of misleading information. Despite these challenges, news media remains a crucial part of our society, and it is important for journalists to maintain their integrity and uphold moral reporting standards.

****

Sports are regarded as part of our lives, whether we're playing them or watching them. They promote physical fitness and provide us with a healthy outlet for our competitive instincts. From football and basketball to tennis and swimming, they not only teach us important life skills such as teamwork, discipline, and dedication but also bring people from different cultures and backgrounds together. Whether you're a professional athlete or just a weekend warrior, sports can enrich your life in countless ways.

答題解說

這兩篇分別關於「新聞媒體」與「運動」的小短文。第一篇有幾個關鍵字彙,像是 vital [`vaɪt!]、current [`kɜ·ənt]、biased [`baɪəst]、incite [ɪn`saɪt]、hatred [`hetrɪd] 等,請注意自己的發音是否正確。另外,第一篇短文的 media 的 me 發 [mi],而不是 [mɛ] 的音,另外像是 gradually 當中的 du 是雙子音 [dj],要發接近 [dʒju] 的音,以及 Despite 中的 sp,要發接近 [sb] 的音。適當的節奏和速度是朗讀的重要元素。不要急促地朗讀,也不要太慢,要根據文章的內容和情感選擇適當的速度和節奏。

第二篇的 whether we're playing them or watching them 這部分,請注意「一氣呵成」讓語句的自然流暢,避免出現不當的斷句(請勿在 or 的位置停頓)或卡

頓的情況。另外，請注意音量和音調的變化，以使文章更生動有趣。在闡述文章的核心觀點和情感時，像是" teamwork, discipline, and dedication..." 可以加強每一個字的音量和音調，以突出重點。類似情況顯示於以下標有顏色的單字，請盡可能唸得比較響亮，以及出現「|」的地方，請稍作停頓，試著讓自己融入短文的情境中。最後，也請注意字與字之間該連音（含「消音」）的部分（以下畫底線），像是 plays a、provides a、events and、biased to、flood of、regarded as、part of our、events and、flood of、regarded as、part of our⋯等。

News media plays a vital role | in shaping public opinion. It provides a platform | for reporting on current events and issues, | enabling people to stay up-to-date. However, | in recent times, the media has gradually become biased to reporting | and tried to incite hatred. They have also created a flood of misleading information. Despite these challenges, | news media remains a crucial part of our society, | and it is important for journalists | to maintain their integrity | and uphold moral reporting standards.

****

Sports are regarded as part of our lives, | whether we're playing them or watching them. They promote physical fitness and provide us with a healthy outlet | for our competitive instincts. From football and basketball | to tennis and swimming, they not only teach us important life skills | such as teamwork, discipline, and dedication | but also bring people from different cultures and backgrounds together. Whether you're a professional athlete | or just a weekend warrior, sports can enrich your life in countless ways.

短文翻譯

新聞媒體在形塑輿論這方面扮演著重要的角色。它提供了一個平台來報導即時的事件與問題，讓個人能夠及時掌握最新資訊。然而，近來，這些媒體對於報導越來越偏頗且試圖煽動仇恨。它們也創造誤導性消息的湧入。儘管存在這些挑戰，新聞媒體仍然是我們社會中不可或缺的一部分，但重要的是，記者們要保持自己的正直和遵守職業道德標準。

****

運動被視為我們生活的一部分，不論是你是參與其中還是當個觀眾。運動可以促進身體健康，並為我們與人競爭的本能提供一個健康的出口。從足球、籃球到網球和游泳，它們不僅教導我們重要的生活技能，如團隊合作、紀律和奉獻精神，

還能讓不同文化和背景的人們聚在一起。無論你是職業運動員還是週末戰士，運動都可以在許多方面豐富你的生活。

關鍵字詞

public opinion n. 輿論　**stay up-to-date** phr. 隨時掌握最新消息　**be biased to** phr. 對有偏見　**incite** v. 激起，煽動　**hatred** n. 仇恨　**a flood of** phr. 一大片的⋯　**misleading** adj. 誤導的　**integrity** n. 正值　**uphold** v. 維持　**moral** adj. 道德的　**be regarded as** phr. 被視為⋯　**physical fitness** n. 身體健康　**competitive** adj. 有競爭力的　**instinct** n. 本能　**teamwork** n. 團隊精神　**discipline** n. 紀律　**dedication** n. 奉獻精神　**weekend warrior** n. 週末戰士（非專業的，只有在放假時才去玩比賽的運動員）　**countless** adj. 無數的

T08P2.mp3

第二部分 回答問題

1. Do you hope to have many friends? Why?

你希望有很多朋友嗎？ 為什麼？

答題解說

對於是否希望擁有很多朋友，不同的人可能有不同的看法。有些人喜歡擁有許多社交關係，因為他們享受社交活動和交朋友的樂趣（enjoy the fun of socializing with people and making friends），而且也可以擴大自己的社交網絡。另外一些人則偏好較少的交友圈子，可能會選擇與一些重要的人建立深刻的關係（prefer a smaller group of friends; choose to establish deeper relationships with a select few important people）。

「擁有很多朋友」的好處也許可以增加社交能力、擴大社交圈（have a larger social circle）以及不同的朋友可以帶來不同的觀點和見解（bring diverse perspectives and viewpoints），這有助於人們開拓視野（broaden one's horizon）和理解世界。但如果不希望擁有很多朋友，可以提出，維護眾多朋友之間的關係需要耗費大量的時間和精力（Maintaining relationships with many friends requires a significant amount of time and energy.）。或者，擁有太多朋友時，可能沒有足夠的時間和精力去與每個人建立深刻的關係，可能導致交往變得表面化（superficial interactions）。此外，擁有很多朋友時，我們可能會感到社交壓力，需要參加許多社交活動和應酬（feel social pressure to attend many social events and gatherings），可能感到疲憊和煩惱等。

Yes, I hope so, and I indeed have many friends. In my opinions, interacting with more people can help me enhance and strengthen my social abilities. Besides, different friends can bring diverse perspectives and viewpoints and broaden my horizons and understanding of the world.

是的,我希望如此,而且我的確有很多朋友。我的看法是,與更多人交往可以幫助我提升及強化我的社交能力。此外,不同的朋友可以帶來不同的視角和觀點,以及開拓視野及了解這個世界。

回答範例 2

No, I don't want to have too many friends. I think maintaining relationships with many friends consumes a significant amount of time and energy. Besides, I won't have time and energy to establish deep relationships with each individual, which may make our friendship look superficial.

不,我並不想擁有太多朋友。我認為跟很多朋友維持關係會消耗大量的時間和精力。另外,我也沒有時間和精力去和每個人建立深厚的關係,這樣可能會讓我們的友誼顯得很膚淺。

關鍵字詞

enhance v. 提升　**strengthen** v. 強化,加強　**diverse** adj. adj. 多樣化的
perspective n. 看法,展望　**viewpoint** n. 見解,觀點　**horizon** n. 視野
maintain v. 維持　**superficial** adj. 表面的,膚淺的

延伸學習

說到「朋友」,你只想到 friend 嗎?其實與「朋友」有關的英文有多種說法。像是 acquaintance,就是所謂的「點頭之交」,就是互相會在 facebook 按讚,見到面會打招呼,但從來不會講超過五句話。這種人可以被歸類為「認識的人」。至於 friend 就是俗稱的「普通朋友」。但若在 friend 前面加上 close 或 good,表示親暱程度增加、可以聊很多事的好朋友類型。再來是「知己」,英文裡有 confidante 這個字來表達。有一種人,超懂你的心。開心的時候,他陪你笑,難過的時候,他陪你哭,分手的時候可以跟你一起痛罵前任,不用多說什麼就可以理解你,這種朋友就叫作 confidante。

另外,bff = best friend forever,每次跟好友們聚會、拍照打卡,都不忘要標記 #bff!buddy 通常為男生之間的暱稱,而 bestie 通常用於女生之間,就是俗稱的「閨密」囉!

bosom friend 就是「知心好友」。bosom 是胸襟、胸懷的意思。放在心上的人,當然就是好朋友囉!

childhood sweetheart 就是「青梅竹馬」，這種認識超過十年的好朋友從小玩在一起、念書一起、連彼此的婚禮都不會缺席的朋友！

pen pal 是「筆友」，在以前通訊軟體尚未發達的時候，很多人會寫信來交友！現在這種靠文字傳達心意的東西，不知道是否還存在呢？

最後還有一種叫作「酒肉朋友」：fair-weather friend。fair weather 是好天氣的意思。只有好天氣時才存在的朋友，想必就是有福同享，有難不同當囉！有些人就是平常玩在一起，當你發生困難時卻第一個落跑？這種人就是「酒肉朋友」無誤！

2. **What's your best childhood memory? Talk about your experience.**

你最美好的童年記憶是什麼？談談你的經歷。

答題解說

每個人的童年經歷都是獨特的，因此最美好的回憶也因人而異（vary from person to person）。一般來說，大家最有感的童年記憶可能是與朋友或兄弟姐妹（friends and siblings）玩耍的美好回憶，無論是建造堡壘、玩桌遊還是在外面奔跑（building forts, playing board games, or just running around outside），或者和家人一起度假（going on vacation with family）、旅行、慶祝節日等，都可以創造出許多珍貴的回憶和經歷，且可持續一輩子（cherished memories and experiences that can last a lifetime）。另外，童年是學習的時光，許多人經常有發現新事物的美好回憶（have fond memories of discovering new things），無論是學習閱讀、騎自行車還是與父母一起做飯等，都可以提出來說明。

回答範例 1

Let me think... one of my favorite childhood pleasures was having much time exploring the woods behind my house. I loved discovering new trails, building forts, and listening to the sounds of nature. It was a simple pleasure that brought me great joy and a sense of freedom.

讓我想想…我最愛的童年樂趣之一就是有很多時間在探索我家後面的樹林。我喜歡探索新的路徑、建造堡壘和聆聽大自然的聲音。這是一種簡單的快樂，給我帶來了極大的快樂和自由感。

回答範例 2

As a child, I loved spending time with my grandmother in our garden. She would teach me about different flowers and plants, and we would spend hours planting and tending to them. I enjoyed the fresh air and the satisfaction of seeing our hard work grow into something beautiful.

小時候，我喜歡和奶奶一起在我們的花園裡度過的時光。她會教我認識不同的花卉和植物，我們會花幾個小時種植和照料它們。我享受著新鮮的空氣，也享受著看到我們的辛勤工作變成美好事物的滿足感。

關鍵字詞

pleasure n. 樂趣　**explore** v. 探索　**woods** n. 森林，樹林　**trail** n. 路徑　**fort** n. 堡壘　**simple pleasure** n. 簡單的樂趣　**tend** v. 照顧　**satisfaction** n. 滿足感

延伸學習

英文裡，從 child 衍生出來單字也不少，像 childhood（童年）、childcare（兒童照護）…等就是。另外還有 child labor（童工）、childproof（防護兒童的、兒童不易受傷的）、child-minder（保姆）、child-friendly（適合兒童的，友善兒童的）、child support（照顧費。撫養費）。請見以下例句：

❶ Many countries have laws against child labor.（許多國家都有禁止童工的法律。）

❷ The new medicine bottle has a childproof cap.（新的藥瓶有一個防護兒童的蓋子。）

❸ She hired a child-minder to take care of her children while she was at work.（她僱了一位保姆，在她上班時照顧她的孩子。）

❹ The restaurant has a child-friendly menu with lots of options for kids.（這家餐廳有一份適合兒童的菜單，提供很多孩子喜歡的選擇。）

❺ After the divorce, he had to pay child support for his two children.（離婚後，他得支付兩個孩子的撫養費。）

3. **Do you think a college degree is important to get a good job? Why?**

   你認為大學的學位對於找份好工作重要嗎？為什麼？

   答題解說

   大部分人都會認為，大學畢業對於找工作是基本且是必要的。雖然大學生滿街跑，不同等級的大學，在企業主的眼裡自然也有不同的評價考量，但或許也有人不視其為必要的，他們認為大學學歷的重要性可能取決於不同的產業、具體職位和個人狀況（depend on different industries, specific jobs, and the individual's personal circumstances）。

   對於本題來說，如果你是認同的，可以針對這樣的原因進行陳述：一般來說，擁有大學學位的人比沒有學位的人賺更多的錢；大學學位可以提供一定的工作穩定性和保障（provide a level of job security and stability），這對於沒有學位的人

來說可能不可得；大學教育通常會為學生提供在職場中有用的寶貴技能和知識（valuable skills and knowledge that are useful in the job market）。但如果你是不認同的，你可以這麼說：有些工作和產業可能不需要大學學位（Some jobs and industries may not require a college degree.），像是廚師、修車師傅…等。另外，大學教育可能很昂貴，有些人可能因財務限制而選擇不進修（may opt not to pursue it due to financial constraints）。

回答範例 1

Yes, I think a college degree is crucial to get a good job, because generally, those with a college degree earn more than those without one. Besides, a college degree can provide a level of job security and stability that may not be available to those without a degree.
是的，我認為大學學位對於找到一份好工作是重要的，因為一般來說，擁有大學學位的人比沒有大學學位的人收入會高一點。此外，大學學位可以提供一定程度的工作保障和穩定性，這是沒有學位的人可能無法獲得的。

回答範例 2

No, I don't think a college degree can guarantee a good job because, in some cases, work experience and skills acquired on certain jobs may be more important than a degree. Besides, those who want to start their own businesses may not require a college degree to be successful.
不，我不認為大學學位能保證找到一份好工作，因為在某些情況下，工作經驗和工作中獲得的技能可能比學位更重要。此外，想要創業的人可能不需要大學學位就可以成功。

關鍵字詞

college degree n. 大學學位　**job security** n. 工作保障　**stability** n. 穩定性　**guarantee** v. 保證　**work experience** n. 工作經驗　**acquire** v. 取得　**start one's own business** phr. 自行創業

延伸學習

大家較熟悉的學士學位用法為 bachelor's degree、undergraduate degree、college degree，完成學士學位的人也可以稱作 bachelor。如果是指還在就讀大學的學生，則可以用 undergraduate student / college student。
碩士學位可以稱為 master's degree，而完成碩士學位的人則可以稱為 master，指正在就讀碩士的學生，可以說 master's student。如果是指已經完成碩士課程，但尚未交出論文，則可以稱作 master's candidate。
博士學位可稱作 doctor's degree、doctoral degree、doctorate degree，正在攻

第 1 回
第 2 回
第 3 回
第 4 回
第 5 回
第 6 回
第 7 回
第 8 回
第 9 回
第 10 回

讀博士的學生則可以稱為 doctor 或是 PhD student。跟碩士一樣，如果是指已經完成博士課程，但還未交出論文的人，稱作 PhD candidate 或是 doctoral candidate，意思為博士候選人。

4. **What do you think are some characteristics of a good teacher?**

   你認為一位好老師應具備哪些特點？

   答題解說

   首先，characteristic 是個英檢中級的單字，聽不出來可能就答非所問了！一般來說，一位好老師的特質不外乎是知識豐富（knowledgeable）、對學生及教學充滿熱情（passionate）、有耐心（patient）、溝通能力強（communicative ability）、具有創意思維（creativity）、教學有靈活性（flexibility）、有同理心（empathy），能夠理解學生的觀點（understand students' perspectives）等。接著你可以針對這些特點稍微補充說明。比方說，對於「知識豐富」，可以說明好老師應該對所教授的學科有深刻的了解，能夠以清晰易懂的方式傳達知識給學生（have a deep understanding of the subjects they are teaching and be able to convey that knowledge in a way that is clear and understandable for students）；對於「充滿熱情」，可以說明好老師應該對教學充滿熱情，渴望幫助學生學習和成長（should be passionate about teaching and have a desire to help students learn and grow）等。

   回答範例 1

   I think a good teacher should be patient and understanding, particularly when students are struggling with a concept or skill. Besides, they should be able to communicate effectively with students, both in terms of conveying information and listening to and understanding students' needs.
   我認為一位好老師應應該有耐心和理解力，特別是當學生在理解概念或技能方面遇到困難時。此外，他們應該要能夠有效地與學生溝通，無論是傳達信息還是傾聽和理解學生的需求。

   回答範例 2

   From my point of view, a good teacher should be able to adapt to different teaching styles and adjust their approach to meet the needs of individual students or groups. Of course, a good teacher should be committed to staying up to date with new research and educational practices to continually improve their teaching skills.
   在我看來，一位好的老師應該能夠適應不同的教學風格，調整自己的方法以滿足個別學生或群體的需求。當然，好的老師應致力於與時俱進，了解新的研究和教

育實踐，不斷提高自己的教學技能。

關鍵字詞

struggle with phr. 在…（方面）遇到困難　**concept** n. 觀念　**communicate effectively with** phr. 與…有效溝通　**in terms of** phr. 從…的觀點　**convey** v. 傳達　**adapt to** phr. 適應…　**adjust** v. 調整　**approach** n. 方法　**be committed to-Ving** phr. 致力於…

延伸學習

小時候我們就被教導要尊師重道，看到老師一定要喊「老師好」，但 teacher，就英文來說其實是個職業，外國人不會用 Teacher Lee、Teacher David 來稱呼老師，就像老師也不會叫學生 Student Tina、Student Judy 一樣。稱呼老師時，男性用 Mr. 加上「姓」，女性用用 Ms.（未婚或不知道是否已婚）或 Mrs.（已婚）加上姓。但如果是大學教授，無論性別，可以用 Professor 或 Doctor 稱呼。

同樣地，到國外講英語的國家中，去到餐廳裡要叫服務員時，也別喊 waiter/waitress！了！因為這是很不禮貌的稱呼。在餐廳要叫服務生，一般是舉手讓人看到，但不要擺手（別人會以為你在打招呼），要喊的話，可以用 Excuse me. 或是 Hello! 來吸引服務生的注意，可以沒有稱謂。例如：Excuse me, could you please clean the table?（服務員，請清理桌面！）

5. **What are you most worried about now? How will you solve it?**

你現在最大的煩惱是什麼？你會如何解決它呢？

答題解說

無論你是上班族還是學生，每個人多多少少都會有一些煩惱，而本題還是側重在 how to solve your biggest worry。一般來說，人的煩惱可分為幾個面向：人際關係、工作、健康、金錢、自我價值（interpersonal relationships, work, health, money, self-esteem）。人際關係方面，比方說許多人會在與家人、朋友、同事、伴侶等人的相處中遇到煩惱，例如衝突、矛盾、沒有共識（conflicts, disagreements, and a lack of understanding）等。健康方面的問題可能會給人帶來焦慮和壓力（feel anxious and stressed），例如疾病、身體不適、體重控制（illness, physical discomfort, and weight management）等。最常見的可能就是缺錢了，財務困難、債務、投資風險（financial difficulties, debt, investment risks）等問題也可能會使人感到煩惱。

至於如何解決的回答，以健康方面而言，你可以說，保持健康的生活方式可以預防許多健康問題，例如健康飲食、適當運動（healthy diet, appropriate exercise）等。金錢方面，可以說學習理財知識，建立穩健的財務基礎（building a sound financial foundation），可以減少財務風險和財務困難（reduce financial risks and difficulties）。

回答範例 1

My biggest worry may be the same as that of many people: lack of money. I want to have my own house and I need some money for the down payment. I think I'll try to communicate with my parents and ask them to help me with it.

我最大的煩惱可能和很多人一樣：缺錢。我想擁有自己的房子，而我需要一些錢來支付自備款。我想我會試著和我的父母溝通，請他們幫助我。

回答範例 2

What I'm now most worried about is that I don't have a girlfriend. Maybe that's because I'm too heavy and feel insecure about my appearance. I think I need to learn to accept my weakness and rebuild self-confidence and self-esteem.

我現在最煩惱的是我沒有女朋友。也許那是因為我太胖了，我對自己的外表沒有安全感。我想我必須學會接受自己的弱點，重建自信和自尊。

關鍵字詞

be worried about phr. 對於…感到憂心　**down payment** n. 頭期款，自備款 **heavy** adj.（體重）重的，胖的　**feel insecure about** phr. 對…感到自卑 **appearance** n. 外表　**weakness** n. 弱點　**self-confidence** n. 自信　**self-esteem** n. 自尊

延伸學習

以下提供幾個向外國朋友訴說自己的煩惱時可以說的話：

❶ I'm feeling really stressed out lately and I don't know how to deal with it.（我最近壓力很大，不知道怎麼處理。）

❷ I'm going through a tough time right now and I don't have someone to talk to.（我現在很苦，沒有人可以傾訴。）

❸ I'm feeling overwhelmed and I don't know where to turn.（我感到不知所措，不知該何去何從。）

❹ I'm really struggling with... and I need some advice or support.（我真的不知如何處理…我需要一些建議或支持。）

❺ I'm having a hard time coping with... and I need some help.（我很難應付……我需要一些幫助。）

❻ I'm feeling really lonely and isolated and I need some company.（我感到非常孤獨和孤立，我需要有人陪伴。）

6. **How much do you pay for recreation every month? Do you think that's too much?**

你每個月花多少錢在娛樂花費上？你覺得太多了嗎？

答題解說

recreation 是個英檢中級的單字，相當於 entertainment，所以如果聽不出來，或聽成 creation（創造）之類的意思，答題內容可能會偏掉喔！因為本題要你回答 30 秒的時間，你可能必須提到像是看電影、國內外旅行（travel at home or abroad）、朋友聚會用餐、加入健身中心房或運動課程（participating in fitness classes, gym memberships）、打高爾夫球…等娛樂花費。對於花費在娛樂上的金額是否太多，則因人而異。但如果你覺得太多了，可以再補充說明什麼呢？你可以說希望將資金用於其他事情，如儲蓄或投資（allocate my funds towards other priorities, such as savings or investments），或者會試著尋找更多經濟實惠的活動或娛樂方式（looking for more affordable ways to engage in recreational activities）。如果覺得這樣的花費是合理的，也可以說娛樂對生活品質很重要（entertainment is an important aspect of the quality of my life）之類的話。

回答範例 1

It costs me NT$4,000~5000 a month for entertainment, and most of the money is spent on playing golf. I don't think it is not reasonable. My monthly salary is about NT$80,000 and that only accounts for 6% of it. Besides, I think recreation is important for the quality of my life. In other words, allocating a portion of my income towards leisure activities helps me stay motivated and productive in my professional life.

我每個月的娛樂費用在 4000~5000 台幣之間，而大部分錢都花在了打高爾夫球上。我不認為這是不合理的。我的月薪大約是新台幣八萬元，那只佔了百分之六。此外，我認為娛樂對我的生活品質很重要。換句話說，將我收入的一部分用於休閒活動有助於我在職業生涯中保持積極性和生產力。

回答範例 2

I spend about NT$2,000 per month on recreation. Sometimes I'll eat out at restaurants with friends and sometimes I go traveling with them. I think this money is just too much for my monthly recreation. While I enjoy spending time with friends and exploring new places, I believe that finding a balance between leisure activities and my managing expenses is important for achieving financial stability and my long-term goals.

我每個月在娛樂上的花費大約是新台幣 2,000 元。有時我會和朋友去餐廳吃飯，有時我會和朋友一起去旅行。我認為這個花費對我每月的娛樂活動來說太多了。

雖然我喜歡與朋友共度時光和探索新的地方，但我相信在休閒活動和管理開支之間找到平衡對於實現財務穩定和我的長期目標是很重要的。

關鍵字詞

recreation n. 娛樂，消遣　**entertainment** n. 娛樂活動　**reasonable** adj. 合理的　**account for** phr. 佔了…（百分比）　**allocate** v. 提撥，撥出　**motivated** adj. 有積極性的　**productive** adj. 有生產力的　**explore** v. 探索　**balance** n. 平衡　**achieve** v. 達到　**long-term goal** n. 長遠目標

延伸學習

recreation 是休閒的活動。所以，recreation 本身就是 activity 的一種，可以認 recreation = leisure activity。recreation 在學術上被譯「遊憩活動」。當然，你也可以說 recreation activity。遊憩活動就是 了製造 enjoyment、amusement、pleasure，就是 了「好玩（fun）」。

entertainment 是能引起參與者的興趣，並使他們感到快樂的活動。所以，entertainment 本身也是 activity，可以解釋「娛樂活動」。

amusement 是在娛樂活動體驗中產生的快樂狀態，它和 enjoyment，happiness 和 pleasure 基本上意思相同，都是表達一種快樂狀態，可以解釋「快樂、娛樂、遊樂」。比如，amusement park（遊樂園）。

簡單說，我們可以用下面一句話能區別以上各個單字：

在你的 leisure time 裡，你可以參與一些 leisure activities，比如積極參與 recreation，或參加一些 entertainment，這樣你就會保持 amusement。

7. **What kind of drinks do you like best? Why do you like it?**

你最喜歡喝什麼飲料？你為什麼喜歡它？

答題解說

常見的飲料類型有：水、咖啡、茶、汽水（不含酒精飲料）、酒精飲料、果汁、運動飲料（water, coffee, tea, soft drinks, alcoholic beverages, fruit juice, sports drinks）等。至於喜歡喝這些飲料的原因，可能與個人偏好、文化背景和個人經驗（individual preferences, cultural backgrounds, and personal experiences）有關。

如果你只喜歡喝白開水（plain/boiled water）的話，可以說水是人類生存所必需的飲料，也非常清爽（a necessity for human survival and also very refreshing），因此是全世界最受歡迎的飲料之一。如果是咖啡的話，你可以說喜歡咖啡因含量，可以提高能量水平和改善注意力（boost energy levels and improve mental focus），也喜歡它的濃郁、豐富的口味（its rich, bold flavor），尤其是黑咖啡、拿鐵咖啡（black coffee, latte coffee）…等。如果喜歡的是茶類的話，可以說它有許多健康益處，如抗氧化劑和鎮靜效果（health benefits, such as antioxidants, and its calming effect）等。還有很多人最喜歡果汁，可以說喜歡它的天然甜味和清爽口感（natural sweetness and refreshing taste），同時也是維生素和礦物質的良好來源（a good source of vitamins and minerals）。

最後如果還有時間，可以補充一些注意事項，代表自己對於飲料的攝取（intake / consumption）有健康概念。

回答範例 1

I like sports drinks most, especially when and after I do physical exercise. They can replenish electrolytes lost through sweat and help prevent a dangerous lack of water in my body. In addition, sports drinks often contain some elements that can provide energy during prolonged exercise. However, I need to emphasize that sports drinks should be consumed in moderation, as excessive intake can lead to unnecessary sugar and calorie consumption.

我最喜歡喝運動飲料，尤其是在運動當中及運動後。它們可以補充因出汗而流失的電解質，並有助於防止我體內出現危險的缺水情況。此外，運動飲料中往往含有一些可以在長時間運動時提供能量的元素。不過，我必須強調的是，運動飲料要適量飲用，過量攝入會導致不必要的糖分和熱量消耗。

回答範例 2

Coffee is my favorite drinks. I enjoy latte coffee for its flavor and aroma. Besides, its caffeine content can help boost energy levels and improve mental focus at work. In spite of this, I want to note that excessive consumption of caffeine can lead to negative side effects such as anxiety, insomnia, and increased heart rate. Though individual tolerance to caffeine can vary, it's best to listen to your body and adjust your consumption accordingly.

咖啡是我最愛的飲料。我喜歡拿鐵咖啡的味道和香氣。此外，它的咖啡因含量有助於提高能量水平並改善工作中的精神集中度。儘管如此，我還是要指出，過量攝入咖啡因會帶來負面影響，例如焦慮、失眠和心率加快。儘管每個人對咖啡因的耐受度不同，但最好傾聽自己身體的聲音並相應地調整攝取量。

關鍵字詞

replenish v. 補足　**electrolyte** n. 電解質　**prolonged** adj. 長時間的　**moderation** n. 適量　**excessive** adj. 過度的　**intake** n. 攝取　**consumption** n. 消耗　**flavor** n. 風味　**aroma** n. 香味　**caffeine content** n. 咖啡因含量

mental focus n. 精神專注　**side effect** n. 副作用　**anxiety** n. 焦慮　**insomnia** n. 失眠　**increased heart rate** n. 心率加快　**tolerance** n. 耐受度

延伸學習

要形容食物或飲料等的特殊口感或風味（taste or flavor），以下都是一些很好用的形容詞，不要再只會說 yummy 或 special 了喔！

buttery（有奶油風味的）、citrusy（有柑橘味的）、fruity（有水果味的）、creamy（口感滑順的）、crispy（酥脆的）、nutty（有堅果風味的）、savory（有鹹香辣滋味的）、tangy（有強烈或特殊味道的）、gamy（有野味的）、succulent（多汁的）、moist（濕潤的）、juicy（多汁的）、tender（軟嫩的）、mellow（水果成熟多汁的；酒很香醇的）

例如：This Thai dish has a very tangy taste.（這泰式料理的味道非常強烈且特別。）

8. **Do you often stay home on rainy holidays? Why?**

你通常放假遇到下雨天時，會待在家裡嗎？為什麼？

答題解說

「放假遇到下雨」的時候，待在家裡還是外出遊玩，一般取決於個人喜好和情況。如果你是選擇待在家裡，可以說喜歡自己家裡的舒適（prefer the comfort of my own home），特別是當天氣不好時。此外，還可以放鬆、有溫暖的感覺，避免外面潮濕和寒冷的麻煩（relax, stay warm, and avoid the hassle of getting wet or cold outside）。

如果還是想出去玩的話，可以說說雨天外出遊玩的好處，像是在雨天中探索新的地方或嘗試新的冒險活動（enjoy the thrill of exploring new places or trying new adventurous activities），會有新鮮感且可以避開人潮。另外，下雨時其實也還有室內活動可供選擇，如博物館、電影院或室內運動設施（there are indoor activities available, such as museums, movie theaters, or indoor sports facilities）。

回答範例 1

I prefer to stay home on rainy holidays because I can relax, stay warm, and avoid the hassle of getting wet or cold outside. Besides, rainy weather can make driving or walking outside more hazardous. Staying home can avoid potential accidents. Also, I can engage in some indoor activities, such as reading a book, watching movies, or trying out a new recipe. It can be a perfect day to relax and recharge before returning to regular routines.

在雨天的假日時我較喜歡待在家裡，因為我可以放鬆一下、享受溫暖且可避免在外面弄濕或受涼的麻煩。此外，雨天駕車或在外面走路更有危險性。待在家裡可以避免可能的意外。我還可以從事一些室內活動，例如讀書、看電影或試試新的食譜。在回復正常工作之前，這可能是放鬆和充電的完美一天。

第 1 回
第 2 回
第 3 回
第 4 回
第 5 回
第 6 回
第 7 回
第 8 回
第 9 回
第 10 回

回答範例 2

During holidays, I don't like to stay home, even when it's raining or the weather is not so good. I can enjoy the thrill of exploring new places or trying new activities such as watching surging waves at the seashore. It's a perfect opportunity to connect with nature and appreciate its beauty, leaving behind the hustle and bustle of daily life. Besides, taking a break from routine and enjoying the simple pleasures in life can bring a sense of relaxation.

我平常假日時就不喜歡待在家裡，就算是下雨或者天氣不好時。我可以享受探索新的地方或嘗試新活動的快感，例如在海邊觀看洶湧的海浪。這是與大自然連結並欣賞其美麗的絕好機會，也可以將日常生活的喧囂拋在腦後。此外，從平日的工作抽身休息一下，享受生活中簡單的樂趣，可以帶來放鬆的感覺。

關鍵字詞

prefer v. 偏好，較喜歡　**hassle** n. 麻煩，困難　**hazardous** adj. 危險的　**engage in** phr. 從事⋯　**recharge** v. 充電　**regular routines** n. 日常作息　**thrill** n. 刺激感　**surging** adj. 澎湃的　**leave... behind** phr. 將⋯拋在腦後　**hustle and bustle** n. 喧囂擾攘，熙熙攘攘　**relaxation** n. 放鬆

延伸學習

在許多社交場合中，「天氣」一直都是個很夯的話題。就算是比較正式的場合，像是商務會議，天氣也是一個很適合閒聊的話題。常見用來形容天氣的形容詞有：

cold / cool（冷／涼爽）
sunny / rainy（晴天／雨天）
clear / cloudy（晴朗的／多雲的）
dry / humid（乾燥／潮濕）
foggy / misty（有霧的／朦朧的）
gusty / windy（陣風／有風的）
thunder / lightning（打雷／閃電）

另外，blue skies 是象徵好天氣的用法。例如：There's nothing but blue skies outside.（外面晴空萬里。）而 boiling 和 freezing 這兩個 -ing 結尾的副詞，可以用來形容天氣的冷熱。例如：boiling hot（酷熱的，熱斃了）、freezing cold（冷死人了，冰冷的）。

9. **What's the proverb you like most? What does it inspire in you?**

你最喜歡的諺語是什麼？它給了你什麼啟示？

答題解說

proverb 是「諺語」，inspire 是「啟發」，都是中級程度的單字。對於自己最喜歡的諺語，如果真的講不出，或沒有把握可以講得正確，就不要冒險去說，別跟分數過意不去喔！可以找些簡單的來發揮就好了。例如 Practice makes perfect. （熟能生巧。）、Actions speak louder than words. （坐而言不如起而行。）、More haste, less speed. （欲速則不達。）、To see is to believe. （眼見為憑。）…等。接著你可以稍微說明一下自己喜歡的諺語意思，然後舉個生活中或經歷過的例子補充說明。例如，「熟能生巧」是只要勤加練習，就能熟練掌握某項技能（lead to mastery）。它激勵自己要持之以恆地學習和訓練自己（motivate myself to persevere in learning and self-training）。「坐而言不如起而行」用來期勉自己說的話和做的事要一致（what you do should be consistent with what you say），並激勵自己要言行一致（walk your talk），實踐承諾（put one's words into practice）。

回答範例 1

I like the proverb best: "Failure teaches success." It inspires me to believe that, failure is a necessary step towards achieving success. Every time when I fail, I'll think I get an opportunity to reflect on what goes wrong. I'll adjust my approach, and try again. Every failure is, for me, a chance to learn and grow, and ultimately, to succeed. So, why not embrace failure as a teacher, or use it to our advantage in our pursuit of success?
我最喜歡這句諺語：「失敗為成功之母。」它給我的啟示是，我相信失敗是邁向成功必要的一步。每次我失敗時，我會認為這讓有機會反省哪裡出了問題。我會調整我的方法，然後再試一次。 對我來說，每一次失敗都是學習和成長，以及最終獲得成功的機會。那麼，何不將失敗當作是一位老師來擁抱它，或者以它作為追求成功的過程中的利用價值呢？

回答範例 2

As an old proverb goes, "Rome was not built in a day," great things take time and effort. And yes, I like this old saying most. It inspires me to believe that any goals worth achieving require hard work and patience. Besides, the proverb reminds me to be patient and persistent, and not to be discouraged by setbacks. The road to success is rarely easy, but if we stay committed and work hard, we can achieve great things.
正如一句古老的諺語所說，「羅馬不是一天造成的」，偉大的事情需要時間和努力。是的，我最喜歡這句老話。它給我的啟發是，任何值得去達成的目標都需要

努力和耐心。此外，這句諺語提醒我要有耐心、堅持，不要因挫折而氣餒。通往成功的道路從來都不是一帆風順的，但如果我們保持堅定不移與努力，我們就能有偉大的成就。

關鍵字詞

proverb n. 諺語　**inspire sth. in sb.** phr. 給了某人…啟示／啟發　**reflect on** phr. 反省，反思…　**go wrong** phr. 出差錯　**adjust** v. 調整　**approach** n. 方法　**to one's advantage** phr. 對某人有利　**in pursuit of** phr. 追求…　**hard work** n. 辛勤，努力　**patience** n. 耐性　**persistent** adj. 堅持的　**discourage** v. 使挫敗　**setback** n. 挫折　**committed** adj. 堅定不移的

延伸學習

無論是中文或英文的寫作，諺語、名言（saying）或格言（motto）都是增添文章豐富度的利器，而且你可以從解釋這句諺語再充實一些內容。以下是一些常見、常聽到的英文諺語：

Never put off till tomorrow what may be done today.（今日事，今日畢。）
Empty vessels make the most sound.（滿瓶不響半瓶響叮噹。）
Let bygones be bygones.（既往不究。）
Man proposes, God disposes.（謀事在人，成事在天。）
Beauty is only skin-deep.（人不可貌相。）
Great oaks from little acorns grow.（萬丈高樓平地起。）
A contented mind is a perpetual feast.（知足常樂。）
As you sow, so shall you reap.（種豆得豆，種瓜得瓜。）
A young idler, an old beggar.（少壯不努力，老大徒傷悲。）
Look before you leap.（三思而後行。）
Even Homer sometimes nods.（智者千慮必有一失。）
Experience is the mother of wisdom.（不經一事，不長一智。）

10. **If you have the ability to foresee something bad that's going to happen to your friend, would you tell them? Why or why not?**

如果你有能力預見到你的朋友將要發生的壞事，你會告訴他們嗎？為什麼或為什麼不？

答題解說

這其實是個很有趣且有深度的問題（an interesting and in-depth question）。雖然大部分人沒有預知未來的能力，但你一樣可以發揮想像力來回答。一般來說，不是每一位預言家每一次的預言都是準確的（accurate），所以你一開頭可以

213

說，假設我的預知能力非常準確，或是我對自己的預言很有信心（if I am confident in my own prophecy），我認為說出來應該會有幫助，可以讓對方做出相應的準備（it may be helpful to inform this friend so that he/she can take necessary precautions）。但假如我對自己的預知能力不是很有信心，那麼說出來可能會造成對方不必要的恐慌和混亂（may cause unnecessary panic and confusion）。另外，如果說了也無法改變結果，那麼說出來可能會帶來不必要的痛苦和焦慮（if it is unavoidable or unchangeable, sharing the prediction may cause unnecessary pain and suffering）。

回答範例 1

What an interesting question! If I were capable of foreseeing a friend's upcoming disaster, and if I were very confident in my own foretelling ability, I would definitely let him or her know, because I believe it is my moral responsibility as a friend to offer support and assistance. Even if my friend may not believe in my prediction, it is still important for me to express my concern and make sure they are aware of the potential risks.

多麼有趣的問題啊！如果我有能力預見到朋友即將發生的災難，且如果我對自己的預言能力非常有信心，我一定會讓他或她知道，因為我認為提供支持和幫助是我作為朋友的道義責任。即使我的朋友可能不相信我的預言，向對方表達我的擔憂並確保他們意識到潛在的風險，對我來說仍然很重要。

回答範例 2

I won't tell a friend about what will happen to them, whether it is something good or bad, because I believe everyone has the right to their own experiences and to live their life without feeling like they are being constantly watched or judged. Moreover, if the news is about something negative, it may create unnecessary worry or anxiety. Instead, I will offer my support and be there for them if and when they need me, no matter what the future holds.

我不會告訴朋友他們會發生什麼事，無論是好是壞，因為我認為每個人都有權利掌握自己的經歷並過自己的生活，而不必覺得自己一直被監視或評判。此外，如果這消息是負面的，可能會造成不必要的擔憂或焦慮。相反地，不管未來會發生什麼事情，當他們需要我，我都會提供支持並與他們同在。

關鍵字詞

foresee v. 預見　**upcoming** adj. 即將到來的　**be confident in** phr. 對⋯有信心　**foretell** v. 預先告知　**assistance** n. 協助　**prediction** n. 預測　**express one's concern** phr. 表達某人的關切　**be aware of** phr. 知道，了解⋯　**potential** adj.

潛在的，可能的　**live one's life** phr. 過某人自己的生活　**worry** n. 擔憂
anxiety n. 焦慮

延伸學習

fore- 是個表示「（在...）之前」，常出現在英語單字中。以下是這個階段常見
的一些單字及其用法：

❶ foreground（前景）：指圖像或景觀中最接近觀察者的部分。例如：The
trees in the foreground of the painting are beautifully detailed.（這幅畫前景
中的樹木描繪得相當精緻且優美。）

❷ forehead（額頭）：指臉部上方的平坦部分。例如：She had a large
forehead and a sharp nose.（她的額頭很大，鼻子很尖。）

❸ forefather（祖先）：指一個人的先輩或祖先。例如：My forefathers came
from Ireland.（我的祖先來自愛爾蘭。）

❹ forecast（預報）：指預測未來天氣、經濟趨勢等方面的報告。例如：The
weather forecast for tomorrow calls for rain.（明天的天氣預報說有雨。）

❺ forewarn（預先警告）：指提前警告或告知。例如：I want to forewarn you
that the meeting may be postponed.（我想預先警告你，會議可能會延期。）

第三部分 看圖敘述

雖然題目有提示你從四個點去回答問題，但如果每個點你只能回答一句話，這樣的內容是絕對不夠的。所以請先從圖片本身去掌握這張照片的主題，然後根據 where、who、why、what... 等架構來充實你的內容。若對於圖片中的人事物相關英文沒有太大把握的話，試著用代名詞或自己有把握說得正確的詞彙來表達。

1. 照片裡的人在什麼地方？

   你可以說 in the living room（在客廳裡）。如果只是說「他們在室內」（They are indoors.）之類的，分數可會打折扣喔！

2. 照片裡的人在做什麼？

   提到「人」的部分時，你可以先提有多少人（There are three persons...），以及他們可能的關係。比方說，The man and the woman could be a couple, and the little girl their daughter...，接著繼續說明他們正在做的事：They are sitting on the sofa... The father is using a laptop computer, the mother is using her smartphone, and the little girl is surfing the Internet on a tablet.

3. 照片裡的人為什麼會在那裡？

   我們可以從照片拍攝地點，以及當中人物的行為、動作來判斷他們為什麼會來這地方。例如，你可以先說明可能的時間：It could be off work time in the evening, and the family members are busy with their respective tasks...，或者可以再更詳細一點說：The father is still working on his project his boss assigned him, while the mother is watching a movie on her cellphone...。

4. 如果尚有時間，請詳細描述圖片中的景物。

   你可以從這張照片給人的一個感覺著手，例如，你可以繼續補充說：In the picture, I saw these family members are engrossed in their electronic devices, with each member seemingly lost in their own world. Despite being in the same space, there is no interaction or conversation taking place between them.

The people in the picture are sitting on the sofa in the living room. There are the father, the mother and their daughter. I can see the three family members are busy using their respective electronic devices. The father is typing away on his laptop, maybe catching up on work emails or browsing the internet. The mother is scrolling through her phone, perhaps checking the news or social media. The daughter is engrossed in her tablet, playing a game or watching a video. As I observe the family before me, the scene is a common sight in many households today. It is a reflection of our times that technology has become such an integral part of our lives that even when we are together, we are often not fully present with each other. I can't help but wonder how much we are missing out on by not engaging with each other. I want to say that the bonds we form with our loved ones are what truly matter in life.

照片中的人們正坐在客廳的沙發上。有父親、母親和他們的女兒。我可以看到三個家庭成員正忙著使用各自的電子設備。父親在他的筆電上不停地打字，也許是處理工作上的電子郵件或上網。這位母親正在看她的手機，也許是在查看新聞或社交媒體。女兒全神貫注於她的平板電腦，玩遊戲或看影片。當我觀察眼前的家庭時，這種場景在今天的許多家庭中都是司空見慣的景象。科技已經成為我們生活中不可或缺的一部分，這反映了我們這個時代，即使我們在一起，也常常無法完全相處。我不禁想知道，如果不相互交流，我們會錯過多少東西。我想說的是，我們與所愛之人建立的關係才是生活中真正重要的。

關鍵字詞

respective adj. 各自的　**electronic device** n. 電子設備　**type away** phr. 不停地打字　**laptop** n. 筆電　**catch up on** phr. 趕著做⋯　**scroll through** phr. 滾動瀏覽⋯　**be engrossed in** phr. 沉浸於⋯　**tablet** n. 平板　**reflection** n. 反映　**integral** adj. 整體的，不可缺的　**present** adj. 存在的　**miss out on** phr. 錯失⋯　**engage with** phr. 與⋯交流　**bond** n. 關係

延伸學習

常見的 3C 設備包括電腦（computer）、手機（mobile phone）、智慧型手機（smartphone）、平板電腦（tablet）、相機（camera）、音響（audio equipment）、電視（television）等。除了了解這些名詞的英文之外，與使用這些設備時會用到相關英文也要記住喔！例如：

❶ computer: operate a computer, troubleshoot a computer, upgrade a computer（操作電腦，將電腦故障排除，將電腦升級）

❷ mobile phone: make/receive a phone call, send/receive a text message, check email/social media, take a photo/video, download/install apps（撥打／接聽電話、發送／接收文字訊息、查看電子郵件／社交媒體、拍照／拍攝影片、下載／安裝應用程式）

❸ tablet: browse the web, watch movies/videos, read books/magazines, play games, take notes（瀏覽網頁、看電影／影片、閱讀書籍／雜誌、玩遊戲、記筆記）

❹ camera: take a photo/picture, shoot a video/film, capture an image, zoom in/out, adjust focus（拍照、拍攝影片／影集、捕捉影像、放大／縮小、調整焦距）

❺ audio equipment: listen to music, play/pause/rewind/forward a song, adjust volume/bass/treble, connect to bluetooth/wireless, etc.（聽音樂，播放／暫停／快退／快進一首歌曲，調整音量／低音／高音，連接藍牙／無線等。）

❻ television: watch TV/movies, change channels, adjust volume/brightness/contrast, stream content, connect to HDMI/USB（看電視／電影，切換頻道，調整音量／亮度／對比度、串流內容、連接至 HDMI／USB）

9

GEPT
全民英檢

中級複試
中譯＋解析

第一部分 中譯英

當與他人發生爭執時,很重要的是保持冷靜與沉著。不要讓情緒控制你的行為,因為這可能會讓事情變得更糟糕。在辯論中,要尊重對方的觀點,不要打斷他們的發言,而是先讓對方說完。當你有自己的觀點時,務必清晰地表達出來,但要注意措辭,不要使用攻擊性的言語。

答題解說

首先,要確定每一個句子的意思和結構。第一句可以用 When you..., it is very important that... 的「副詞子句 + 主要子句」結構來表示。「與他人發生爭執」是 have a dispute with others。「保持」可以用 keep 或 stay,記得後面要接形容詞,而非名詞喔!第二句的句型結構是以一個祈使句開頭,再接一個副詞子句:Don't let..., because/as...。「讓事情變得更糟糕」可以用 worsen the situation 表示。第三句「在辯論中,要尊重…,不要打斷…」同樣可以用祈使句來表現,但務必在兩個祈使句之間加上對等連接詞 and 喔!接著「而是…」可以用一個新的句子,或是以分號(;)區隔前面的句子,在「; instead/Instead, ...」之後同樣可以用一個祈使句,「讓對方說完」可以用 let the other person finish first 表示。最後一句比較長,可以用「When you..., 祈使句 1 + 祈使句 2 + and 祈使句 3」的結構呈現。「有自己的觀點」可以說 have your own opinion,「清晰地表達出來」是 express it clearly,「注意措辭」可以用表示 be attentive to your wording,「攻擊性的言語」是 offensive language。注意這裡的 language 是指一種「語言風格」,應視為不可數名詞,不可加 s,如果 language 是可數名詞,它指的是「不同國家的語言」。

譯文範例

When you have a dispute with others, it is very important that you stay calm and composed. Don't let your emotions take control of your actions, as this can worsen the situation. During a debate, show respect for the other party's point of view, and do not interrupt their speech; instead, let the other person finish first. When you have your own opinion, be sure to express it clearly, be attentive to your wording and don't use offensive language.

延伸學習

說到「爭執,爭吵」,大家應該都學過 quarrel、argument、dispute、debate、

fight 這幾個名詞吧！那麼它們在意義與用法上，有什麼不同呢？

❶ argument 可以是負面的「爭論、爭吵」，也可以是「論點、理由」的意思。例如：have a big argument with sb.（與某人大吵一架）、a persuasive argument（有說服力的論點）

❷ dispute 和 argument 其實意思很接近，硬要說差別的話，可以看成「（激烈程度較高的）爭論、爭吵」，但它更常用於複合名詞中，例如勞資爭議（labor dispute）、國土糾紛（land dispute）、合約糾紛（contract dispute）...等正式用語中。例如：settle the dispute over the contracts（解決合約方面的爭議）

❸ quarrel 可以是「無理取鬧、情緒性的吵架」，不像 argument 爭吵時有點「邏輯性」、雙方有各自的立場。例如：I don't want to get involved in my parents' quarrel again.（我不想再度捲入我爸媽的爭吵中。）

❹ fight 原指肢體衝突的「打架」、拳打腳踢的「戰鬥」，但在口語中也常用來表示「爭論，爭吵」。例如：Their fights are always about money.（他們的爭吵總是跟錢有關。）

❺ debate 主要是指一種正式的「辯論會」或「辯論賽」，通常就是雙方準備很多資料來進行爭論或討論。例如：presidential debate（總統大選辯論會）、have several debates about this policy（就這項政策進行多次辯論）。

第二部分 英文作文

提示

為了讓民眾能夠更有效地與國際接軌，並增進國家的國際競爭力與文化多樣性，政府近年來著手推動「雙語國家政策」，而「全英語授課（English as a medium of instruction, EMI）」就是這項政策的一環。請以此為題，說明你是否贊成全英語授課及理由。

答題解說

贊成或反對「全英語授課」，當然要從它的優缺點來起筆。首先，優點的部分，你可以說學生在全英語的課堂環境中（in an EMI environment），需要用英語進行聆聽、閱讀、寫作、口語表達等各方面的學習，進一步提升了學生的英語能力（Listen, read, write, express orally in English, thus helping them improve their proficiency in English）。你還可以再進一步說明，全英語授課的課程通常會引入外國教授、跨國企業的案例等國際元素（introduce such international elements as foreign professors and cases of multinational companies），讓學生接觸到更多來自不同文化背景的知識和觀點，培養了學生的國際化視野

（Make students exposed to more knowledge and viewpoints from different cultural backgrounds, and cultivate their international vision）。至於缺點的部分，主要可能是英語程度不足的學生會受到影響（It could be a barrier for students who do not have a strong command of English），還會造成學業成績不佳、挫折感和心理壓力（It may lead to poor academic performance, frustration and psychological stress.），對學習成效產生負面影響（can have a negative impact on their effectiveness in learning）。此外，對於英文程度較低以及非英文系學生來說，閱讀和理解英文教材、學術論文和報告的成本較高（It may cost a lot to read and understand learning materials, academic papers and reports.），需要進行翻譯和理解的過程，耗費了更多時間和精力（You need to additionally run the process of translation before understanding, which consumes more time and effort.）。

作文範例

Regarding the "English as a medium of instruction（EMI）" policy, some people believe that it can improve the English proficiency of Taiwan's students and increase their international competitiveness. In addition, this policy can also facilitate international exchange and communication, thereby enhancing Taiwan's international status. However, personally I'm opposed to this policy. This may affect students' learning effectiveness because English is not their mother tongue. Furthermore, teaching in English may also cause psychological burden, as students have to learn in an unfamiliar language environment. In short, I think the effectiveness of this policy requires time to evaluate to determine whether it has achieved the expected results. During this process, the government needs to closely monitor students' learning conditions, and adjust policies according to actual situations.

關於「全英語上課」政策，有些人認為它可以提升台灣學生的英語能力，並增加他們的國際競爭力。此外，這項政策促進國際間的交流與溝通，進而提升台灣的國際地位。然而，我個人反對這項政策。這可能影響學生的學習成效，因為英文不是他們的母語。再者，用英語上課可能帶來心理負擔，因為學生必須在不熟悉的語言環境下學習。簡言之，我認為這項政策的的成效需要時間來評估，以確定它是否已達成一個預期效果。在這個過程中，政府需要密切關注學生的學習狀況，並根據實際情況調整政策。

延伸學習

無論未來全英文上課成效如何，它似乎就是個國際趨勢且勢在必行。現在就先把以下列舉的最基本、最常說的實用例句學起來吧！

開始上課時的開場白，通常會告訴學生今天要學習的主題或內容，這時候老師可

會說 Good morning/afternoon, class. Today we will be discussing...。當開始上課或使用網路工具時，老師會確認學生的視聽設備是否正常，可能會問 Can everyone see/hear me okay?；如果老師想讓學生有機會提出問題，可能會說 Does anyone have any questions so far?；在討論完一個主題後，老師會引導學生進入下一個主題，可能會說 Let's move on to the next point/topic.；如果學生或老師的發音不清楚時，可以要求對方重複一次，可以說 Could you repeat that, please?；當需要進行小組討論或小組作業時，引導學生分組時，老師可能會說 Let's break into small groups.；當需要學生閱讀特定的教材或內容時，指示學生翻閱至某頁面或章節時，會說 Please turn to page/section/chapter X.；在課程結束前，總結學生今天學到的主要內容，老師會說 Let me summarize what we've covered today.；當老師對學生指示作業繳交的時間時可能會說 Please submit your assignment by... (date/time).；最後，在課程結束前，老師通常會表達對學生專注聆聽或參與的感謝和讚賞，他們會說 Thank you for your attention/participation today.。

第 1 回
第 2 回
第 3 回
第 4 回
第 5 回
第 6 回
第 7 回
第 8 回
第 9 回
第 10 回

第一部分 朗讀短文

T09P1.mp3

Making a good impression is crucial, whether it's during a job interview, a first date, or when you meet someone new. It is also important to be confident, friendly, and genuine. Dressing appropriately for certain occasions, using good posture, and maintaining eye contact are also key factors. Additionally, showing interest in the other person by actively listening and asking thoughtful questions can make a big impact. Remember to be yourself and stay positive, as a positive attitude can be infectious and help leave a lasting impression.

****

Painting is a form of visual art that involves applying color to a surface, such as canvas, paper, or wood. It expresses ideas or emotions through the use of different colors and techniques. Paintings convey a sense of mood or atmosphere. Artists throughout history have used painting as a means of communicating, documenting historical events, and expressing their creativity. Today, painting continues to be a popular form of artistic expression and a valued part of many cultures around the world.

答題解說

這兩篇分別關於「如何給人好印象」以及「繪畫藝術」的小短文。第一篇有幾個關鍵字彙，像是 impression [ɪm`prɛʃən]、genuine [`dʒɛnjʊɪn]、appropriately [ə`proprɪˌetlɪ]、eye contact [`aɪ `kɑntækt]，以及 infectious [ɪn`fɛkʃəs] 等，請注意自己的發音是否正確。另外，第一篇短文的第一句中 crucial 的 cru 發 [kru]，而不是 [krʌ] 的音，另外像是 posture 當中的 t 不是 [t] 的音，而是要發 [tʃ] 的音，以及 the other 中的 the，要發 [ði] 的音，而非 [ðə]，因為 the 後面的 other 是以母音 [ʌ] 開頭。適當的節奏和速度是朗讀的重要元素。不要急促地朗讀，也不要太慢，要根據文章的內容和情感選擇適當的速度和節奏。
第二篇的 a means of communicating, documenting historical events, and

expressing their creativity 這部分，請注意「一氣呵成」讓語句的自然流暢，避免出現不當的斷句或卡頓的情況。另外，請注意音量和音調的變化，以使文章更生動有趣。在闡述文章的核心觀點和情感時，像是 "canvas, paper, or wood" 可以加強每一個字的音量和音調，以突出重點。類似情況顯示於以下標有顏色的單字，請盡可能唸得比較響亮，以及出現「|」的地方，請稍作停頓，試著讓自己融入短文的情境中。最後，也請注意字與字之間該連音（含「消音」）的部分（以下畫底線），像是 first date、

It is、important to、good posture、contact are、interest in、make a…等。

Making a good impression is crucial, | whether it's during a job interview, | a first date, | or when you meet someone new. It is also important to be confident, | friendly, | and genuine. Dressing appropriately for certain occasions, | using good posture, | and maintaining eye contact are also key factors. Additionally, | showing interest in the other person | by actively listening and asking thoughtful questions | can make a big impact. Remember to be yourself and stay positive, | as a positive attitude can be infectious and help leave a lasting impression.

****

Painting is a form of visual art that involves applying color to a surface, | such as canvas, paper, or wood. It expresses ideas or emotions | through the use of different colors and techniques. Paintings convey a sense of mood or atmosphere. Artists throughout history | have used painting as a means of communicating, | documenting historical events, | and expressing their creativity. Today, | painting continues to be a popular form of artistic expression and | a valued part of many cultures around the world.

短文翻譯

給人留下好的印象是很重要的事，無論是在面試、第一次約會還是認識新朋友時。還有保持自信、友善和真誠也很重要。特定場合中穿著適當、良好的姿勢和保持眼神的接觸也是關鍵因素。此外，積極傾聽，展現對於他人的興趣，並提出有思考性的問題也可以產生重大影響。記得做自己並保持積極態度，因為積極的態度可以感染他人，也有助於留下深刻的印象。

****

繪畫是一種視覺藝術形式，包括將色彩塗在一個表面上，如帆布、紙張或木材。它藉由不同顏色與技術的使用，來表達思想或情感。繪畫作品傳達出一種情感或

氛圍。歷史上的藝術家以繪畫作為一種傳達訊息、記錄歷史事件以及表達其創造力的手段。如今，繪畫仍然是一種受歡迎的藝術表達形式，是世界許多文化的重要部分。

關鍵字詞

genuine adj. 真實的　**appropriately** adv. 適當地　**eye contact** n. 眼神接觸／交流　**factor** n. 因素　**thoughtful** adj. 思慮周到的　**infectious** adj. 有傳染力的　**lasting** adj. 持續的　**visual** adj. 視覺上的　**involve** v. 包含　**apply... to...** phr. 將…運用於…　**canvas** n. 帆布　**convey** v. 傳達　**atmosphere** n. 氛圍　**means** n. 手段，工具　**document** v. 記載　**artistic** adj. 藝術的　**expression** n. 表達

第二部分 回答問題

T09P2.mp3

1. What's your definition of success? What do you think you have done successfully in the past?

你對成功的定義是什麼？你認為自己過去做過什麼成功的事情？

答題解說

題目中 definition of success 就是「成功的定義」，每個人對於「何謂成功」或「什麼樣的人是成功的」應該都有不同的看法。是賺大錢（make a fortune）、有名氣（rise to fame），還是獲得眾人敬仰（publicly respectable）、有著高高在上的聲望（high reputation）呢？其實你可以這麼說：在達到自己目標的過程中感到快樂和滿足，就是成功（feeling happy and fulfilled in the process of achieving one's goals）。比方說，有一個美滿的家庭，與配偶幸福美滿、子女成就卓越、家庭和諧（a happy marriage, children's outstanding achievements, and harmonious family life）等；或者擁有穩定的收入和財富（have a stable income and wealth），有房、有車或俗話說的「五子登科」等。接著，你要具體說明過去的「成功案例」。比方說，原本一直考不及格的科目，後來經過努力用功後，考了 70 或 80 分，或者成功地登上玉山峰頂（climb to the summit of Mt. Jade）等。

回答範例 1

I think success means to maintain a healthy lifestyle and mental state. I used to get sick and was hospitalized for a few months, which made me realize the importance of health. Now, I make it a rule to exercise and eat healthy, and I haven't been sick for a long time.

我認為成功是指保持健康的生活方式和精神狀態。我曾經生病而住院幾個月，這讓我意識到健康的重要性。現在，我養成運動和健康飲食的習慣，且我很久沒有生病了。

回答範例 2

In my opinion, success means to have a successful career. Several years ago, I used to be very worried about my future career. But now, I am running my own business and have a decent pay. Only if you try your best, I think, can you achieve your success.

在我看來，成功就是事業有成。幾年前，我曾經非常擔心我未來的職業。但是現在，我在經營自己的公司並擁有不錯的收入。我認為，只有盡自己最大努力才能獲得成功。

關鍵字詞

maintain v. 維持　**lifestyle** n. 生活型態　**hospitalize** v. 就醫，住院　**make it a rule to** phr. 規律地…（做某事）　**future career** n. 未來職業　**run one's own business** phr. 自營事業　**decent pay** n. 優渥的薪資　**achieve one's success** phr. 獲得成功

延伸學習

❶ success 是個名詞。例如：Success and happiness are two different things. Some people have achieved a lot, but they still aren't happy.（成功跟快樂是兩件不同的事情。有些人成就很高，但他們仍然不開心。）

❷ succeed 是個動詞，當及物動詞的話，表示「繼承」，當不及物動詞的話，表示「成功」，所以要接受詞的話，就需搭配介系詞 in。例如：After years of treatment, he finally succeeded in conquering cancer.（在多年的治療過後，他終於成功戰勝癌症。）

❸ successful 是個形容詞，表示「成功的，有成就的」，例如：Bill Gates is considered to be a successful entrepreneur, and his hard work has really inspired me.（比爾·蓋茲被視為一位成功的企業家，而他的努力真的很激勵我。）

❹ successive 也是個形容詞，因為衍生自 succeed，所以它也有兩個截然不同的意思：連續的，繼承的。例如：We've had five successive murders these three months, and everyone in town is scared and anxious.（我們這三個月已經有連續五起謀殺案了，鎮上每一個人都既害怕又焦慮。）

2. **What's your favorite season? What do you like to do during that season?**

你最喜歡哪個季節？你在那個季節時喜歡做什麼？

答題解說

春夏秋冬四季的英文分別是 spring、summer、fall/autumn、winter，記住它們搭配的介系詞是 in，前面不加 the 喔！每個人基於個人喜好、嗜好以及所在地區的氣候因素，在四季當中會有不同的喜愛活動。例如，在春季，很多人喜歡參加戶外活動，如徒步旅行、騎自行車、園藝和野餐（engage in outdoor activities like hiking, biking, gardening, and picnicking）；在夏季，人們通常喜歡去海灘、游泳、露營和烤肉（enjoy going to the beach, swimming, camping, and having barbeques）；秋天時，很多人喜歡徒步旅行、蘋果採摘、南瓜雕刻和參加秋季節日（hiking, apple picking, pumpkin carving, and attending fall festivals）；在某些國家，冬季當然是滑雪、滑板、溜冰和堆雪人（enjoy skiing, snowboarding, ice-skating, and building snowmen）的季節。

回答範例 1

I like spring most because it's a season of new beginnings and renewal. The fresh green buds on the trees, the vibrant blooms of flowers, and the longer, warmer days all bring a sense of hope and rejuvenation. Plus, it's the perfect time to enjoy outdoor activities and spend time in nature.
我最喜歡春天，因為它是一個新的開始以及復甦的季節。 樹上鮮嫩的綠芽、生機勃勃的鮮花盛開，以及更長、更溫暖的日子，都帶來了希望和復興的感覺。此外，這是享受戶外活動和親近大自然的最佳時機。

回答範例 2

I like autumn most because of its cozy atmosphere. The changing leaves, fresh air, and warm colors create a beautiful scene of calming surroundings. It's also a time for reflection and gratitude as we gather with loved ones and celebrate the harvest season.
我最喜歡秋天，因為它舒適的氛圍。變幻的樹葉、清新的空氣、溫暖的色彩創造出一幅寧靜祥和的美麗景象。它也是一個反省和感恩的時刻，與此同時，我們與親人相聚並慶祝這個收穫的季節。

關鍵字詞

renewal n. 更新，重新開始　**bud** n. 芽　**vibrant** adj. 律動的　**bloom** n. 開花　**rejuvenation** n. 回春，恢復活力　**cozy** adj. 溫馨的　**atmosphere** n. 氣氛　**reflection** n. 反省　**gratitude** n. 感恩之心

第 1 回

第 2 回

第 3 回

第 4 回

第 5 回

第 6 回

第 7 回

第 8 回

第 9 回

第 10 回

延伸學習

spring 有好幾個意思，除了當「春天」之外，還有「泉水」、「彈簧」的意思。冬天時，很多人喜歡去泡「溫泉（hot spring）」，夏天時則是「冷泉（cold spring）」。

summer 一般情況下，只有「夏天」的意思，「暑假」的英文是 summer vacation。而「夏令營」則是 summer camp。「秋天」有 fall 和 winter 兩種說法。fall 本來有「掉落」的意思，而秋天時會看到很多落葉，因此 fall 有秋天之意。 autumn 是個比較正式和文學化的字，它來自拉丁文的 autumnus，表示「收穫的季節」。winter 是以 win（贏）開頭的，想像過年時大家總是想多「贏」一點，也可以聯想贏得在冬季所需的勇氣和毅力，進一步體驗和享受這個季節的美好。

3. **Do you like to work for your current company? Why?**

   你喜歡在現在的公司工作嗎？為什麼？

答題解說

喜歡或不喜歡在一家公司工作的原因，通常與薪資福利、工作環境、職業發展以及公司文化（salary and benefits, working environment, career development, company culture）等因素有關。可以朝這幾個面向去說明。

如果你現在還是個學生，如何回答這問題呢？除了如實說明之外，你可以說明未來希望在什麼樣的公司工作。比方說，希望能夠在一個開放、有創造力、鼓勵多樣性和尊重個人差異的公司工作（a company with an open, creative, diverse, and respectful culture），因為這樣的公司通常會提供支持創新和發展的機會，並且關注員工的福利和生活平衡（employee welfare and work-life balance）。

回答範例 1

Yes, I have enjoyed working for my current company because of the supportive work environment, challenging yet fulfilling tasks, and opportunities for career growth. The company values its employees and encourages a healthy work-life balance, which has helped me stay motivated and dedicated to my job.

是的，我很喜歡我現在公司的工作，因為這裡有支持性的工作環境、具有挑戰性且令人滿意的任務以及職業發展機會。公司重視員工並鼓勵健康的工作與生活平衡，這有助於我在工作上保持積極和專注的態度。

回答範例 2

No, I don't want to work for my current company anymore, because I feel undervalued and unappreciated for my contributions. The lack of growth opportunities have made me realize that it's time for a change. I want to seek new challenges that align with my career goals and aspirations.

不，我不想在我現在的公司工作了，因為我覺得自己的貢獻被低估且不被賞識。缺乏成長的機會，也讓我意識到是時候換工作了。我想找尋符合我職業目標和抱負的新挑戰。

關鍵字詞

supportive adj. 支持性的　**fulfilling** adj. 實現自我的　**motivated** adj. 積極進取的　**be dedicated to** phr. 專注於⋯　**undervalued** adj. 被低估的　**unappreciated** adj. 不被賞識的　**contribution** n. 貢獻　**align with** phr. 符合⋯　**aspiration** n. 抱負

延伸學習

work 當動詞時，可以運用於很多層面，不是只有在日常工作上喔！除了表示「工作、從事某職業」之外，以下是一些常見的用法：

❶（機器等的）運作、運轉：The machine works perfectly.

❷ 努力去做某事。例如：I need to work harder to improve my skills.

❸ 後面接 out，表示打造出，擬出。例如：
We need to work out a solution to this problem.
I need to work out my schedule for next week.

❹（努力等）產生效果、產生影響。例如：Her efforts finally worked and she got the promotion.

❺ 後面接 on，表示「進行整修，著手處理」。例如：
The car needs to be worked on by a mechanic.
She's working on a new novel.

4. **What do you think are some characteristics of a good employee?**

你認為一位好的員工應具備哪些特點？

答題解說

題目中的 employee 要聽清楚，千萬別聽成 employer 了！一般來說，好的員工不外乎能夠準時到達工作場所，高效地完成工作任務並達成工作期限（show up to work on time, complete their tasks efficiently and effectively, and meet deadlines），對自己的工作負責，願意承擔額外的責任（take ownership of one's work and be willing to take on additional responsibilities），積極尋找解決問題的方案（be proactive in finding solutions to problems）。另外，能夠適應變化的情況和環境（adapt to changing situations and environments）、願意

學習新技能（be willing to learn new skills）、承擔新的任務（take on new tasks）也是相當重要的。

回答範例 1

I think a good employee should have strong communication skills, both in written and verbal forms. They can effectively convey their ideas and thoughts to others and listen actively to feedback. Besides, they should work well with others and be team players.
我認為一個好的員工應該具有強大的溝通技巧，無論是書面上或口頭上的表達。他們能夠有效地傳達自己的想法和觀點，並積極聆聽回饋意見。此外，他們應該要善於與他人合作，並且當一個團隊中的合作者。

回答範例 2

The characteristics that make a good employee, in my opinion, include reliability and responsibility. A good employee should be dependable and complete his or her tasks efficiently and effectively, and meet deadlines. They should also take ownership of their work and be accountable for their actions.
在我看來，成為一位好的員工應具備的特質包括可靠性與責任感。一位好的員工應該要能被信賴且有效率地完成工作任務並於期限內完成工作。他們還要對自己的工作，並為自己的行為負責。

關鍵字詞

communication skill n. 溝通技巧 **effectively** adv. 有效地 **convey... to...** phr. 傳達…給… **feedback** n. 回饋意見 **work well with** phr. 與…好好合作 **reliability** n. 可靠性 **responsibility** n. 責任感 **dependable** adj. 可信賴的 **efficiently** adv. 有效率地 **meet deadlines** phr. 期限內完成工作 **take ownership of** phr. 對自己的工作負責 **be accountable for** phr. 為…負責

延伸學習

employer 和 employee 都是衍生自動詞 employ、與「人」有關的名詞。另外一個表示「員工」的名詞是 staff，一般譯為「工作人員」，但不管是否領薪，只要是「工作中的人員」，都可以稱 staff，所以 volunteer（義工）也算是 staff 喔。不過要注意的是，staff 指的是「全體員工」，是個集合名詞，所以沒有複數，要表示「一位員工」的話，可以說 a staff member 或是 a staffer。在面試中，你可以問對方 Are you a staff member here?（你是這裡的員工嗎？）」，以確認對方的身份。而如果要詢問一家公司的員工規模，可以說 What's the size of your staff?（貴公司有多少員工？）

第 1 回
第 2 回
第 3 回
第 4 回
第 5 回
第 6 回
第 7 回
第 8 回
第 9 回
第 10 回

5. **Would you buy something second-hand? Why or why not?**

你會買二手的東西嗎？為什麼會或為什麼不會？

答題解說

second-hand 就是 used（被用過的），像是「中古車」，通常被譯為 a used car，而「中古屋」可以用 used、second-hand 或是 pre-owned 來表示。一般來說，是否會買「二手商品」，可能與「商品本身」有關，其原因不外乎是價格較低，對於經濟拮据的人來說是一個重要因素（a significant factor for people on a tight budget）。此外，某些商品雖然是被用過的，但其品質可能不輸給相同的新商品，尤其對於一些設計用來持久使用的物品（be made to last），房子、車子或一些家具即屬之。還有一些人喜歡復古或古董物品的獨特性和歷史背景（unique character and history of vintage or antique items）。這些物品往往難以或無法在新物品中找到，使得二手是唯一的選擇（difficult or impossible to find new, making second-hand the only option）。

至於不會購買二手商品的原因，可能與「衛生問題（hygiene concerns）」、「未知的歷史（unknown history）」、「風格或潮流（style or trend）」、「保修或保證（warranty or guarantee）」等因素有關。比方說，像衣服或寢具這樣的物品（items such as clothing or bedding），一般人不會去跳蚤市場（flea market）買別人用過的。此外，二手物品，往往沒有辦法知道物品的完整歷史，包括它的使用、維護或保養情況（how it was used, maintained, or cared for），例如機車或汽車，能不能買到優質中古車（a used quality vehicle）有時候看運氣。

回答範例 1

I think it depends. If I want to buy a car, I would choose a used one because for me, it's just a means of transport. But if I want to change my cellphone, I'll definitely get a newer model that usually has better features and performance compared to my current phone.

我認為不一定。如果我想買部車，我會選擇二手車，因為對我來說，它只是一種代步工具而已。但如果我想換手機，我肯定會買一個更新的款式，它通常比我現在的手機有更好的功能和性能。

回答範例 2

I have never bought something second-hand because I don't like to use anything having been used by others. The main reason is that it's not easy to know the full history of the item, including how it was used, maintained, or cared for. However, I understand that buying used items is good to save money.

我從不買二手的東西，因為我不喜歡用別人用過的東西。主要原因是不容易知道這個物品的完整歷史，包括它過去如何被使用、維護或保養。不過，我明白買二手貨可以省錢。

關鍵字詞

second-hand adj. 二手的　**used adj.** 使用過的　**means of transport** n. 代步工具　**feature** n. 功能　**performance** n. 表現　**compared to** phr. 相較於…　**item** n. 項目　**maintain** v. 維護　**save money** phr. 省錢

延伸學習

在台灣，我們通常說舊東西是二手的，所以會說「二手衣、二手商店」。但其實在美國，很少會聽到當地母語人士說 second-hand shop 或是 second-hand books。他們通常用 used（用過的）來形容我們所謂的「二手貨」，譬如 used clothes、used books、used car。一般大概只有提到「二手菸」時，會說 second-hand smoke。至於賣舊東西的二手店，美國當地的說法是 consignment store，表示東西「托賣或買斷」，或是 thrift shop，表示東西大多是人家捐贈的。另外，如果要形容只用過幾次，狀況良好，可以說 gently used，像有些手機之類的電子商品網站上，會看到 normal wear and tear（正常磨損）的字眼。

6. **How long have you known your best friend? How did you meet each other?**

   你和你最要好的朋友認識多久了？你們是怎麼認識的？

   答題解說

   第一個問題，可以用「for + 一段時間」來回答。例如 I have known my best friend for more than ten years.，而針對「怎麼認識的」回答，一般來說可能與「共同的興趣和活動（shared interests and activities）」、「學校或工作（at school or at work）」、「透過彼此間共同的朋友（mutual friends）」、「偶然相遇（by chance）」、「在網路上認識（meet online）」等有關。你可以說，彼此因為在同一個球隊、同個讀書俱樂部或一個音樂團體（meet someone through a sports team, a book club, or a music group）認識；或者在高中時期學校或同一家公司工作中認識，因為在共同的環境中有大量時間相處而產生緊密的聯繫（spending a lot of time together in a shared environment, which leads to strong bonds）；或者透過共同認識的人或朋友（through mutual acquaintances or friends），在一次聚會或社交活動中相互介紹認識的（be introduced to each other at a party or during a social event）；或者在一家咖啡廳或在某天搭公車時，與原本陌生的這位朋友人攀談而認識（striking up a

conversation with a stranger at a coffee shop or on public transportation）等。
最後，有時間的話可以再補充彼此現在的聯繫狀況。

回答範例 1

I have known my best friend, David, for more than 20 years. As for how we met each other, I remember that we joined the same book club during our school days. We had a shared passion for reading and often discussed our favorite books together. Over the years, our friendship has grown stronger, and we have been through many ups and downs together. David is not just a friend to me, but a family member.

我認識我最好的朋友大衛已經有 20 多年了。至於我們是怎麼認識的，我記得我們在學生時代加入了同一個讀書會。我們對閱讀有著共同的熱情，且經常一起討論我們最喜歡的書。多年來，我們的友誼越來越深，且我們一起經歷了許多風風雨雨。大衛不僅是我的朋友；他也是一位家庭成員。

回答範例 2

Helen is one of my colleagues when I first entered the workforce 20 years ago. And yes, she's my best friend now though we have been working for different companies. Helen and I still make it a point to stay in touch and catch up with each other regularly. Our friendship has stood the test of time and distance, and I am grateful for her constant support and encouragement throughout the years.

海倫是我 20 年前剛進入職場時的一位同事。是的，她現在是我最要好的朋友，儘管我們已經在不同的公司服務了。海倫和我仍然堅持保持聯繫並定期互相交流。我們的友誼經得起時間和距離的考驗，我感謝她多年來一直給我的支持和鼓勵。

關鍵字詞

book club n. 讀書會　**during one's school days** phr. 在學生時代　**have a passion for** phr. 熱衷於⋯，對⋯有熱情　**ups and downs** n. 起起落落，風風雨雨　**enter the workforce** phr. 進入職場　**make it a point to-V** phr. 務必／堅持要⋯　**catch up with each other** phr. 互相交流　**constant** adj. 經常的

延伸學習

我們中文常講的「出社會」、「踏入社會」，你會用到 society 嗎？如果是，那就糗大了喔！因為對老外來說，我們生下來就在社會上了！事實上，中文所謂的「出社會」或「踏入社會」，切確一點說是「進入職場」或是「開始工作」，英文正確說法是 enter the workforce 或 start working，而不是 enter the society。workforce 本來是「勞動力」、「勞動人口」的意思。例如：Our company's workforce exceeds 2,000 people.（我們公司的員工超過兩千人。）

另外，所謂「社會新鮮人」可別說成 social freshman 了。freshman 本指「大學一年級學生」，但社會新鮮人是大學剛畢業的人，和大一新生無關。「剛畢業的人」英文可以用 new graduate 或 fresh graduate。graduate 也可以簡單說成 grad。在美國，大學生還沒取得文憑之前，都叫作 undergraduate，也就是我們的 college/university student，而研究所就是 graduate school。

7. **If you could visit a world-renowned attraction right now, where would it be? Why?**

   如果你現在可以去一個世界知名的景點，那會是哪裡？為什麼？

   答題解說

   本題關鍵字彙 attraction 本來是「吸引」的意思，經常在很多地方被引申為「景點」，因此 world-renowned attraction 就是「世界知名景點」。所以本題並不是要你回答想要去紐約、倫敦、巴黎，還是哪個國家或地方，而是像紐約的自由女神像（Statue of Liberty in New York）、倫敦的大笨鐘（Big Ben in London）、巴黎的艾菲爾鐵塔（Eiffel Tower in Paris）、埃及的金字塔（The Pyramids in Egypt）、中國的萬里長城（The Great Wall in China）…等。盡量找自己有把握說得正確的景點名稱，如果真的都沒把握說得正確，你也可以針對一個知名建築物，用 the very famous... 的描述方式來講。比方說：the famous windmill in Netherlands、the very famous tower in Paris/France... 等。

   接著再補充這個景點有什麼特別之處。例如，埃及的金字塔代表著古埃及文明的輝煌和驕傲，具有豐富的歷史和文化遺產價值（It represents the glory and pride of ancient Egyptian civilization and have significant historical and cultural value）；美國亞利桑那州的大峽谷的巨大的規模和多彩的岩層構成令人驚歎的景色，令人流連忘返（Its massive scale and colorful rock formations make it a truly unique and awe-inspiring sight.）…等。

   回答範例 1

   I hope I could take a leisurely walk with some of my best friends along the Great Wall in China, which has a rich history that spans thousands of years. We can not only explore this ancient marvel, but also spend quality time together while enjoying the stunning views of the surrounding landscape. With its unique blend of natural and cultural attractions, a visit to the Great Wall will truly be an unforgettable experience that is sure to create lasting memories.

   我希望我能和幾個最好的朋友悠閒地漫步在有著數千年悠久歷史的中國萬里長城

第 1 回
第 2 回
第 3 回
第 4 回
第 5 回
第 6 回
第 7 回
第 8 回
第 9 回
第 10 回

上。我們不但可以探索這個古老的奇蹟，還可以欣賞周圍的美景、共度美好的時光。因為有著它自然與文化景點獨特的結合，遊覽長城將真正成為一次難忘的經歷，也一定會留下永恆的回憶。

If I could visit a world-renowned attraction right now, my first choice would be the Pyramids in Egypt. I believe visiting the Pyramids will be a truly awe-inspiring experience, allowing me to immerse myself in a rich and fascinating cultural heritage that has fascinated people for centuries. From exploring the intricate interiors of the pyramids to admiring the majestic Sphinx and the ancient temples nearby, a trip to the Pyramids is sure to be an unforgettable adventure.

如果我現在可以前往一個世界知名景點，我的首選會是埃及的金字塔。我相信參觀金字塔將會是一次真正令人驚嘆的體驗，我將會沉浸在一個豐富而迷人、讓人著迷了數千年的文化遺產中。從探索金字塔錯綜複雜的內部結構，到欣賞雄偉的人面獅身像，以及附近古老的寺廟，金字塔之旅一定會是一次難忘的冒險。

關鍵字詞

attraction n. 景點　**leisurely** adj. 悠閒的　**span** v. 跨越　**marvel** n. 奇蹟　**spend quality time together** phr. 共度美好時光　**stunning** adj. 絕美的　**landscape** n. 景觀　**blend** n. 融合　**unforgettable** adj. 令人難忘的　**lasting** adj. 持久的　**pyramid** n. 金字塔　**awe-inspiring** adj. 令人驚嘆的　**immerse oneself in** phr. 沉浸在…　**fascinating** adj. 迷人的　**heritage** n. 遺產　**intricate** adj. 錯綜複雜的　**interior** n. 內部　**majestic** adj. 雄偉的　**Sphinx** n. 人面獅身像

延伸學習

有人問你旅途如何，且用滿心期盼的眼神想聽你分享，而你心裡有滿滿的感動，卻也只能回答 So beautiful! 然後尷尬地傻笑嗎？快把以下的詞彙學起來，把美景形容得更美，讓你珍貴的旅行經驗聽起來更加鮮活動人吧！

❶ stunning：是 stun(v.)（暈倒）+ 重複短母音後的子音字母字尾 n +ing ，合起來的意思就是「美到令人暈倒的」。記下這個要點，我們就可以理解很多同樣結構的形容詞，例如：amazing（令人感到驚奇的）、charming（迷人的）、dazzling（令人目眩神迷的）

❷ breath-taking：breath(n.)（呼吸）+ taking（原形為 take，取走），合起來字面上的意思是「被取走呼吸的」，也就是「美到令人忘了呼吸的」。同樣結構的形容詞，例如：eye-opening（令人大開眼界的）、awe-inspiring（令人敬畏的）。

❸ 以下這些形容詞都可以讓你發表讚嘆美景時使用：
magnificent（華麗的，雄偉的，宏偉的）、spectacular（壯觀的，引人入勝的）、epic（如史詩般的，經典的，極好的）、fantastic（奇妙的，美妙到，讓人難以置信的，奇異的）、grand（壯觀的，雄偉的，顯赫的，盛大豪華的）、glamorous（充滿魅力的，迷人的）、gorgeous（美麗的，燦爛的，華麗的）、picturesque（如畫一般的，生動的，獨特的）

8. **Do you use the services of online banking? Why or why not?**

你使用網路銀行的服務嗎？為什麼或為什麼不？

答題解說

online banking 是「網路銀行業務」，也可以說成 Internet banking、web banking。一般最常被使用的網銀服務包括轉賬、餘額查詢、信用卡付款、申請貸款、電子對帳單（funds transfer, balance inquiry, credit card payments, loan application, electronic statements）⋯等。至於為什麼要使用這些網銀服務的回答，可以針對其「便利性」、「快捷」等特色來說明。例如，餘額查詢讓用戶可以隨時查看其帳戶餘額，包括儲蓄帳戶、支票帳戶、信用卡帳戶（allow users to check their account balances, including savings accounts, checking accounts, credit card accounts）等；最常被使用的當然就是「轉帳（funds transfer）」了，因為你可以不用跑去 ATM 進行操作。而且如果是「薪轉帳戶（payroll transfer account）」的話，有些銀行會提供每月數次的免手續費（no handling fee）優惠。同樣地，如果想要跟銀行申請貸款，你也不一定要跑到銀行臨櫃去抽號碼牌（no need to go to the bank counter to draw a number plate）然後等老半天才能辦理，直接在該銀行網站上就有相關的管道可以辦理且迅速獲得批准（apply for loans online and receive approval quickly）。

如果你從來沒用過任何網銀服務，或不喜歡使用這樣的服務，可以說明你會更喜歡傳統的銀行服務，或是你對網路安全方面持有擔憂（prefer traditional banking services, or have concerns about internet security）。或者可以說，現今的網路科技越來越發達，大多數的網銀平台都有著高度的安全性和便利性（most online banking platforms have a high level of security and convenience），自己會試著使用網銀服務，或許會是個值得嘗試的選擇。

回答範例 1

Yes, I often use the online services of funds transfer and credit card payments. It's a convenient and fast way to manage my finances, especially when I don't have the time to go to the bank or make payments in person. It's particularly useful when I need to send money to friends or family who live far away, or when I need to make an urgent

第 1 回
第 2 回
第 3 回
第 4 回
第 5 回
第 6 回
第 7 回
第 8 回
第 9 回
第 10 回

payment for a bill. However, I always make sure to use secure websites or apps to protect my personal information.

是的，我經常使用網銀服務的轉帳和信用卡付款功能。這是一種方便且快速的財務管理方式，尤其是當我沒有時間去銀行或親自付款時。當我必須匯款給住很遠的朋友或家人時，或必須臨時支付賬單時，它特別有用。不過，我一定會使用安全的網站或 APP，來保護我的個資。

回答範例 2

No, I've never accessed any online banking services. Actually I'm a bit concerned about Internet security. With so many reports of hacking and data breaches, it's hard to trust that my personal and financial information will be safe online. I prefer to visit local banks in person and complete transactions with a teller. I know it may not be as convenient as online banking, but it gives me peace of mind and that my information is less vulnerable to cyber attacks.

不，我從未使用過任何網路銀行服務。其實我對網路安全是有點擔憂的。近年來，有許多有關駭客和資料外洩的報導，讓我很難相信我的個人和財務資訊在網路上是安全的。我更喜歡親自到當地銀行，與櫃員完成交易。我知道這可能沒有網路銀行那麼便利，但這讓我更放心，因為我知道我的資訊不容易成為網路攻擊的目標。

關鍵字詞

fund transfer n. 轉帳　**finance** n. 財務　**make a payment** phr. 付帳，付款　**in person** phr. 親自　**secure** adj. 安全的　**protect** v. 保護　**access** v. 處理，存取　**be concerned about** phr. 關切…　**security** n. 安全性　**hacking** n. 駭客　**data breach** n. 資料外洩　**transaction** n. 交易　**teller** n. 出納，櫃員　**peace of mind** n. 放心　**be vulnerable to** phr. 易受…侵害的　**cyber attack** n. 網路攻擊

延伸學習

account 這個字有著廣泛的應用，其中一個常見的用法是指一個人或組織的「銀行帳戶」。例如：I want to open an account.（我想要開戶。）如果是「活期帳戶」的話，就是 current account，而「定存帳戶」則是 fixed deposit account。account 這個字除了可以指銀行的戶頭之外，也可以是各種網站、APP 的會員「帳號」，這時「新建帳號」就是 create an account。除了銀行帳戶和網站帳號，account 這個字還有其他的運用場景。例如，在商業會計中，account 意味著將資產、負債和收入等事項記錄下來的過程。在這種情況下，account 常常被翻譯為「帳目」。另外，account 也可以被用來表示一個人或事物的描述或敘述。例如：The newspaper gave an account of the crime.（這份報紙有這起犯

罪案件的報導。）此外，account 還可以當動詞，後面接 for，表示「解釋，說明」。例如：Can you account for your absence yesterday?（你能解釋昨天的缺席嗎？）

9. **What's the most expensive thing you've ever bought? Why did you buy that?**

你買過最貴的東西是什麼？你為什麼要買？

答題解說

一般來說，昂貴的東西不外乎是房子、車子、珠寶（jewelry）、黃金（gold）、手錶或是高端電子產品（high-end electronics）以及精品包（designer handbag）等。很多人購買豪華汽車是為了展示其社會地位、品味和成功（to show off their social status, taste, and success）。買珠寶、黃金通常是以作為禮物、紀念品或展示個人品味和風格的方式（be purchased as gifts, mementos, or as a way to showcase personal taste and style），也可能是一種保值的投資（a value-preserved investment）；電子產品像是智慧型手機、平板電腦、筆記型電腦和電視等，高價位的通常有最先進的技術和設計（latest technology and design），並且可以提供更好的使用體驗（offer a better user experience）。

回答範例 1

The most expensive thing I've ever bought is a smartphone, the iPhone 14 Pro 256G. At first, I was hesitant to spend so much money on an electronic device that would eventually become outdated. But at last, I decided to invest in the latest model to ensure that I would have the best possible experience with my device. While it was a hefty purchase to me, I have no regrets because I can show off my social status, taste, and style.

我買過的最貴的東西是 iPhone 14 Pro 256G 這款智慧型手機。一開始時，我很猶豫要不要花這麼多錢買一部最終會過時的電子設備。但最後，我決定把錢投入這款最新的型號，以確保我能獲得最佳的設備體驗。雖然這對我來說是大手筆的購買，但我並不後悔，因為我可以炫耀我的社會地位、品味和風格。

回答範例 2

Last year on our 10th wedding anniversary, I bought a gold necklace for my wife, and that's the most expensive thing I've ever bought. It was a stunning piece of jewelry, and I knew it would be something she could treasure for years to come. Seeing the look on her face when she opened the box made every penny worth it. It was a small token of my love and appreciation for all that she has done for our family and our marriage.

第 1 回
第 2 回
第 3 回
第 4 回
第 5 回
第 6 回
第 7 回
第 8 回
第 9 回
第 10 回

去年在我們結婚 10 週年的日子，我買了一條金項鍊給我太太，那是我買過最貴的東西了。這是一件令人驚嘆的珠寶，我知道這將是她可以珍藏多年的東西。看著她打開盒子時臉上的表情，每一分錢都值得了。對於她為我們的家庭和婚姻所做的一切，這代表著我的愛與感激。

關鍵字詞

hesitant adj. 猶豫的　**electronic device** n. 電子設備　**eventually** adv. 最終　**outdated** adj. 過時的　**hefty** adj. 大手筆的購買　**show off** phr. 炫耀　**social status** n. 社會地位　**wedding anniversary** n. 結婚週年　**gold necklace** n. 金項鍊　**stunning** adj. 令人驚嘆的　**jewelry** n. 珠寶　**treasure** v. 珍藏　**penny** n. 一分錢　**token** n. 代表，象徵　**appreciation** n. 感激

延伸學習

日常生活會話中，總避免不了談到「錢」。當你要和別人說某個東西「很貴」時，除了 expensive，還可以怎麼說？

❶ 某物 + cost an arm and a leg → an arm and a leg 表示要砍掉「一隻手臂和一條腿」的代價，引申為「一大筆錢」的意思。

❷ 人 + pay through nose → 在中世紀的英國，如果一個人沒有繳稅，那麼他的鼻子就會被用刀刺穿一個洞以示懲罰。這正是 pay through the nose for something，「透過鼻子來支付」這個說法的由來，爾後被引申為「花一大筆錢；支付高出合理範圍的費用」。

❸ 某物 + be 動詞 + daylight robbery → 此典故源自古代英國「窗戶稅」，其含意是，對生活裡面必不可少的成分 — 如陽光和空氣 — 徵稅。所以就用 daylight robbery 來形容「敲竹槓，漫天要價」。

❹ 某物 + break the bank → 這可不是「搶銀行」的意思喔！它是指把自己財庫裡的錢都花掉，就是「花太多錢」的意思。

❺ 人 + pay top dollar → top 是「最高的」，dollar 在這裡是「價錢」，字面意思是「付出最高的價錢」，應該很好理解了！

10. **Your colleague Peter is frequently late for work. Please give him some suggestions.**

你的同事彼得上班經常遲到。請給他一些建議。

答題解說

首先，你腦海裡可以先整理一些一般人會習慣性遲到的原因，可能有「缺乏時間管理的概念（unconscious of time management）」、「缺乏自我管理能力（lack of self-management）」、「長期以來的習慣（long-standing habit）」、「交通問題（transportation issues）」、「沒有足夠的動力（lack of motivation）」…等。然後你可以假設已經知道 Peter 經常遲到的原因，大略提一下之後，再給予實質的建議。比方說，對於習慣性遲到的人，可以建議對方每天早上固定時間起床，每晚睡前確認好隔天要帶去的物品（get up at a regular time every morning, and check the items you will bring the next day before going to bed every night）等，以幫助自己養成準時到達的好習慣；或者提早出門（leave earlier than usual），以因應任何意料之外的延誤（in response to any unexpected delays），例如交通問題或其他不可預見的情況（other unforeseen circumstances）。最後，可以再告知對方遲到對於公司、同事和自己的形象都會造成負面影響（have negative impact on the image of the company, colleagues and yourself），因此要及時改善。

回答範例 1

Hi Peter, you were late again this morning! Let me tell you what you should do. First, it's important to think about why you are consistently late. What's something that is beyond your control, such as transportation issues, or is it a matter of poor time management? Once you've identified the root cause, you can start taking steps to address it. You may need to leave earlier, or set reminders to help you stay on track.

嗨，彼得，你今天早上又遲到了！我來告訴你應該怎麼做吧。首先，你要去思考一下為什麼總是遲到。有什麼事情是你無法控制的，比如交通問題，或者是時間管理不善的問題？一旦你確認根本原因，就可開始設法解決。你可能必須提早出門，或設定提醒來幫助保持在正確的生活軌道上。

回答範例 2

Peter, I heard that you have been late for work four times this week. I think you should make an effort to arrive on time. Being punctual shows respect for your colleagues and the company. Being late can affect your chances of career advancement. Consider setting your alarm earlier, preparing your clothes the night before, and leaving earlier to avoid traffic jam. Being on time demonstrates your commitment to the job and sets a positive tone for the rest of the day.

彼得，我聽說你這星期上班已經遲到四次了。我認為你應該努力準時到達公司了。守時展現出你對同事和公司的尊重。遲到會影響你的職業發展機會。考慮將鬧鐘的設定時間提前，在前一天晚上準備好衣服，並提早出門以避開塞車。準時，意味著你對工作的承諾，並為接下來一天的時間立定一個積極的步調。

關鍵字詞

consistently adv. 經常地　　**beyond one's control** phr. 某人無法掌控的　　**poor**

time management n. 時間管理不善　**identify** v. 確認　**root cause** n. 根本原因
take steps to-V phr. 設法，採取步驟…　**address** v. 解決　**reminder** n. 提醒
stay on track phr. 維持在正軌上　**on time** phr. 準時　**punctual** adj. 守時的
show respect for phr. 對…展現尊重　**career advancement** n. 職業發展
demonstrate v. 展示出　**commitment** n. 承諾

延伸學習

late 雖然是個簡單的英文單字，不過衍生出來的 lately、latest、latter 卻有著完全不同的意義：

❶ late 當「遲到的」解釋時，通常用於主詞補語，而不擺在「人」的名詞前修飾。比方說，「總是遲到的大衛」，不可以說 always late David，正確是 David who is always late。又例如：He arrived late for the meeting.（他開會遲到了。）late 放在「人」前面修飾時，通常表示「已故的」。

❷ lately 是個副詞，表示「最近」。例如：I haven't been sleeping well lately.（我最近睡眠不好。）

　latest 是個最高級的形容詞，表示「最近的，最新的」。例如：Have you seen the latest episode of that TV show?（你看過那個電視節目的最新一集嗎？）

❹ latter 可以當形容詞和代名詞，表示在提到的兩件事物中的後者，例如：John and Sarah both applied for the job, but only the latter was hired.（約翰和莎拉都申請了這份工作，但只有後者被錄用了。）

第三部分 看圖敘述

T09P3.mp3

第 1 回

第 2 回

第 3 回

第 4 回

第 5 回

第 6 回

第 7 回

第 8 回

第 9 回

第 10 回

答題解說

雖然題目有提示你從四個點去回答問題，但如果每個點你只能回答一句話，這樣的內容是絕對不夠的。所以請先從圖片本身去掌握這張照片的主題，然後根據where、who、why、what...等架構來充實你的內容。若對於圖片中的人事物相關英文沒有太大把握的話，試著用代名詞或自己有把握說得正確的詞彙來表達。

1. 照片裡的人在什麼地方？

　　你可以說 in a hospital（在醫院）或是 in a clinic（在診所）。如果只是說「他們在室內」（They are indoors.）之類的，分數可會打折扣喔！

2. 照片裡的人在做什麼？

　　提到「人」的部分時，你可以先提有多少人（There are three persons...），以及他們可能的身分或關係。比方說，The woman is a doctor and the man is the kid's father. He takes her kid/son to see a doctor because....，然後繼續說明他們正在做的事：The doctor leans in closely to listen to the kid's breathing and feel for any signs of discomfort...

3. 照片裡的人為什麼會在那裡？

　　我們可以從照片拍攝地點，以及當中人物的行為、動作來判斷他們為什麼會來這地方。例如，你可以先說明可能的原因：The little child probably caught a cold or just feel uncomfortable for some unknown reason...，或者可以再提到：The father of the child is smiling, and it seems that he is confident that the doctor will treat his kid well.。

4. 如果尚有時間，請詳細描述圖片中的景物。

　　你可以從這張照片給人的一個感覺著手，例如，你可以繼續補充說：From the interaction between the doctor, the kid and the father, I can feel that human connection in healthcare is very important.，或者 It's heartening to see that even in a clinical setting, the doctor has taken the time to connect with her patient on a personal level...。

回答範例

The people in the picture are in a clinic. The little child is probably sitting on his father's lap in front of the woman, who is the doctor and is making a diagnosis of the kid. Maybe the kid is catching a cold or feeling uncomfortable for some unknown reason. The doctor gives a warm and kind smile at the kid and she leans in closely to listen to his breathing and feel for any signs of discomfort. Besides, the father of the child is smiling too. It seems to me that he is confident that the doctor will treat his kid well. From the interaction among the doctor, the kid and the father in the picture, I think human interaction in healthcare is very important. In a world where technology and automation are rapidly transforming the field, it's easy to forget that the most critical aspect of medicine is the relationship between a patient and their healthcare provider. Such connection should be valued and nurtured in the medical profession.

照片中的人在診所裡。在這名女子的面前，小孩子可能正坐在他父親的膝上，女子是個醫生，正在為孩子進行診斷。也許孩子感冒，或因為某種原因感到不舒服。醫生對孩子露出溫暖親切的微笑，她往前靠近並仔細聆聽他的呼吸，感受他是否有任何不適的跡象。此外，孩子的父親也微笑著。在我看來，他有信心醫生會將他的孩子治療好。從照片中醫生、孩子和父親之間的互動來看，我認為醫療照護這方面人與人的互動非常重要。當科技和自動化正迅速改變這個領域的同時，人們很容易忘記醫療這方面最重要的東西是，病患與其醫療保健提供者之間的關係。這種聯繫關係在醫療的專業領域中應該受到重視與培養。

關鍵字詞

clinic n. 診所　**lap** n.（人坐著時）腰以下到膝為止的大腿部　**diagnosis** n. 診斷　**uncomfortable** adj. 不舒服的　**lean in** phr. 往裡面靠　**discomfort** n. 不舒適　**treat** v. 治療　**interaction** n. 互動　**healthcare** n. 健康照護　**automation** n. 自動化　**transform** v. 轉型　**critical** adj. 重要的　**nurture** v. 培養　**profession** n. 專業

延伸學習

當我們生病了，會說「去看醫生」，一般會用 go see a doctor 來表示，而中文說的「去醫院」，就不一定是因為生病、受傷之類的事情，也可能是去看朋友、辦手續、健檢等。但有些人會說 I'm going to hospital. 來表示「我要去醫院。」就像 go to school（去上學）、go to church（去做禮拜）、go to prison（入獄）這類型的用法。其實 go to hospital 這聽在外國人耳裡，是一件很嚴重的事，是生病，而且可能是開刀、住院之類較嚴重的生病。school、church、prison 都不只是一個「地方」，而是到這個地方從事特定活動，所以這些地方前面都不加冠詞。如果是感冒、過敏這類輕微的小病，只會說 go to a doctor、see a doctor，而不會說 go to (the) hospital。另外，一般英式英語用法，直接用 go to hospital，而美式英語則用 go to the hospital。而如果我們說某人 in hospital，並不是指他人在醫院，而是指他住院了。

10

GEPT 全民英檢

中級複試

中譯＋解析

第一部分 中譯英

尊重他人是建立良好人際關係的重要基礎。我們應該學會欣賞他人的價值觀、文化背景和生活方式，且避免評論或批評他人的行為或選擇。在日常生活中，我們可以從小事做起，如不打擾他人、不侵犯他人的私人空間，也不以言語或肢體進對他人進行威脅或攻擊。只有從自己做起，才能營造出和諧的社會環境。

答題解說

首先，要確定每一個句子的意思和結構。第一句可以用「尊重他人」當主詞，也就是 Respect for others，「基礎」是 foundation，後面用介系詞 for 來引導一個後位修飾的形容詞片語，「建立良好人際關係的」可以用 for building good interpersonal relationships 表示。第二句可以用一個「合句」，也就是「對等子句 1 + and + 對等子句 2」的結構來呈現。共同主詞是「我們」，對等子句 1 的動詞是「學會欣賞」（learn to appreciate），其受詞是「他人的價值觀、文化背景和生活方式」（the values, cultural backgrounds, and lifestyles of others），而對等子句 2 的動詞是「避免」（avoid），其受詞為「評論或批評他人的行為或選擇」（judging or criticizing their behavior or choices）。第三句用一個修飾全句的副詞片語開頭，也就是 In daily life, ...。接著「我們可以從……做起，如……」可以用 we can start with... such as... and ... 來表示。其中「打擾」、「侵犯」、「私人空間」、「以言語或肢體」、「威脅或攻擊」的英文分別是 disturb、invade、personal space、with words or actions、threaten or attack。請記得 such as 是個介系詞，後面要接名詞或動名詞。最後一句「只有…才能…」可以用 Only by... can we... 這樣的倒裝句型來呈現。「從自己做起」是 starting with ourselves，「和諧的社會環境」可以用 harmonious social environment 表示。

譯文範例

Respect for others is an essential foundation for building good interpersonal relationships. We should learn to appreciate the values, cultural backgrounds, and lifestyles of others, and avoid judging or criticizing their behavior or choices. In daily life, we can start with small things, such as not disturbing others, not invading their personal space, and not threatening or attacking others with words or actions. Only by starting with ourselves can we create a harmonious social environment.

延伸學習

「倒裝句」是將一般肯定句或陳述句的主詞與動詞順序顛倒的文法結構，它能夠增強句子的表現力及語氣，使其更有文學性和表現力。其目的通常是為了突出或強調句中的某些部分。例如：Not only was he tired, but he was also hungry.（不僅累了，而且還餓了。）→ 這個句子屬於「完全倒裝句」，因為是 Not 開頭，所以是強調「否定」，也就是「不只是…，還有…」這個句型。另外，Little did he know that he was being watched."（他根本不知道自己被人監視了。）→ 這個句子以否定詞 Little 開頭，也對於「否定」的意味加強語氣。

基本來說，要強調哪個部位，就把哪個部位當作句子開頭，然後主詞與動詞要做倒裝，像是 In the garden were some beautiful flowers.（花園裡有些美麗的花。）以及 In the woods ran a deer.（森林中奔跑著一隻鹿。）→ 就是強調「在這個地方」有什麼。

最後，有一些副詞擺在句首，也必須倒裝。例如 here、there、only 等。例如：

❶ Here comes the bus.（公車來了）

❷ There is a book on the table.（桌子上有一本書。）→ 請注意：there be 的句型中，主詞是 be 動詞後面的名詞，不是 There 喔！也就是說，There be... 其實就是倒裝句型的一種！

❸ Only by working hard can you achieve success.（只有努力工作才能獲得成功。）

第二部分 英文作文

提示

近年來，人工智慧（AI）與和機器人學習技術發展迅速，而大家也開始有所關切：AI 未來是否會影響自己的工作機會，或是對於自己生活上會產生什麼影響。請寫一篇短文論述你對這項技術的了解。

答題解說

AI（Artificial Intelligence）技術的發展其實已經不是這一兩年的事，且「人工智慧」也早已是大家熟悉的名詞。因此對於本篇英文作文的撰寫，應該不至於不知如何下筆吧！如果你還是個學生，你可以說明 AI 對你未來想從事工作的影響，或是可能改變你未來想要就業的方向。

舉例來說，AI 技術可能使得企業不再需要工廠作業員（factory worker）。因為越來越多的公司和企業開始採用自動化和機器學習技術來自動化日常的業務流程和決策（adopt automation and machine learning to streamline their business processes and decision-making）。例如，在製造業（manufacturing）中，AI

技術可以幫助企業優化生產線，提高生產效率，並減少人為錯誤（help optimize production lines, increase efficiency, and reduce human error）。因此，原本在這行業當中從事這些工作的人，未來被企業需求的機會就愈來愈少了（There will be fewer and fewer opportunities of being demanded by businesses or factories in the future）。

另外，以醫療產業（medical industry）來說，AI 技術可以幫助醫療專業人員快速而準確地診斷和治療疾病（help medical professionals diagnose and treat diseases quickly and accurately），也可能使得醫療人員的需求降低。以生活層面來說，你可以舉「自動駕駛（autonomous driving）」的未來趨勢。目前汽車業中已經開始廣泛應用（It has already been widely used in the automotive industry）了。自動駕駛技術可以提高交通安全，減少交通事故，並減少對人力資源的需求（enhance traffic safety, reduce accidents, and decrease the demand for human resources）。

作文範例

Artificial Intelligence (AI) is a revolutionary technology that has the potential to greatly change our life. It has made significant advances in various fields such as healthcare, transportation, and finance, and has the potential to improve our daily lives in countless ways. As a factory worker, I'm of course worried about my future career, because it helps optimize production lines, increase efficiency, and reduce human error, so there will be fewer and fewer opportunities of being demanded by businesses or factories in the future. I think I need to rethink about my career path and acquire new skills to stay competitive in the job market. However, AI can also create new job opportunities, so it's important to stay informed and adaptable to the changing job market.

人工智慧（AI）是一項革命性的技術，有可能大大改變我們的生活。它在醫療保健、交通和金融等各領域都已有重大的進步，且可能以很多種方式改善我們的日常生活。身為一名工廠工人，我當然擔心自己未來的飯碗，因為它有助於優化生產線、提高效率、減少人為錯誤，所以未來被企業或工廠需求的機會會越來越少。我認為我必須重新考慮我的工作方向並學習新技能，以期能在就業市場上保持競爭力。然而，人工智慧也可以創造新的就業機會，因此隨時吸收新知並適應不斷變化的就業市場非常重要。

延伸學習

本題也可能要你對於 AI 技術的優缺點來做論述，以下補充可能帶來一些負面影響（negative impact）：

❶ 失業問題（unemployment）：人工智慧可能會取代（replace）某些工作，例如製造業、物流、客服（as manufacturing, logistics, and customer service）

等工作。這可能會導致失業率的上升（a rise in unemployment），對社會經濟帶來不利影響（have adverse effects on the economy）。

❷ 隱私問題（privacy issues）：人工智慧需要大量的資料來訓練和學習（AI requires large amounts of data for training and learning.），但這些資料可能包含個人隱私資訊。如果這些資訊被濫用或洩露（misused or leaked），將對個人帶來極大的損害。

❸ 偏見與歧視（bias & prejudice）：人工智慧可能會反映其訓練資料中存在的偏見（reflect biases that exist in its training data），例如種族歧視或性別歧視（racial or gender biases）等。這可能導致人工智慧做出不公平的決策，對某些群體造成不利影響（result in unfair decisions being made by AI and negatively impact certain groups）。

❹ 安全問題（security issues）：人工智慧系統可能被駭客鎖定或被濫用（be targeted by hackers or misused），例如使用惡意演算法攻擊其他電腦系統，或使用人工智慧技術進行網路釣魚（using malicious algorithms to attack other computer systems or using AI technology for phishing）等。這些可能導致資料洩露、個人隱私受損等問題。

❺ 生活層面的衝擊（impact on our daily life）：人工智慧可能會改變社會結構和人們的生活方式（change social structures and people's ways of life），導致一些社會問題，例如孤獨、社交隔離（loneliness and social isolation）等。

第一部分 朗讀短文

T10P1.mp3

New York, commonly referred to as simply NY, is one of the most populous cities in the United States and in the world. It is located in the northeastern region of the country. Known as a global hub for finance, fashion, art, and entertainment, NY is home to well-known landmarks such as the Statue of Liberty, Central Park, Times Square, and the Empire State Building. With its bustling streets, diverse culture, and endless attractions, New York is a must-visit destination for travelers from all over the world.

****

One way to build self-confidence is to spot negative self-talks and replace them with positive words of self-assurance. It's also important to set realistic goals and work towards achieving them, as accomplishing tasks can help increase feelings of confidence. Another strategy is to step out of your comfort zone and try new things. Finally, take good care of yourself by eating healthily, exercising regularly, and getting enough rest. With patience and effort, anyone can develop a strong sense of self-confidence.

答題解說

這兩篇分別是關於「紐約市」以及「培養自信心」的小短文。首先,第一篇提到的專有名詞,像是 Statue of Liberty、Times Square、Empire State Building... 等,每一個大寫的字都要發重音,其中 Statue(雕像)發音是 [ˋstætʃʊ],第二個字母 t 發 [tʃ] 的音;Times Square 的 Times,雖然字尾有 s,但後面的字(Square)也是 [s] 的音開頭,所以 Times 的字尾 [s] 不發出聲音,另外,Square(方形廣場)雖然音標是 [skwɛr],但 [sk] 兩個無聲子音在一起時,[k] 要發有聲的 [g] 音。其他應注意發音的部分,包括 hub(字母 u 發 [ʌ] 的音)、well-known(ow 發 [o] 的音)、bustling(u 發 [ʌ] 的音,-stling 中的 t 不發

音）。至於冠詞 the 的發音，請注意如果後面的接「母音開頭」的單字，the 要發 [ði] 的音。適當的節奏和速度是朗讀的重要元素。不要急促地朗讀，也不要太慢，要根據文章的內容和情感選擇適當的速度和節奏。

對於一個「有意義的群組」，請注意「一氣呵成」，讓語句的自然流暢，避免出現不當的斷句或卡頓的情況。例如第一篇中 the most populous cities in the United States and the world，以及第二篇中 to spot negative self-talks and replace them with positive words of self-assurance，兩者都是 be 動詞後面的主詞補語。不過，如果一個結構中的詞組是有逗號（,）來區隔時，那就必須在逗號的位置稍作停頓，像是第二篇的 by eating healthily, exercising regularly, and getting enough rest。同樣地，兩個句子之間（以句點區隔）也當然必須在句點的位置些微停頓。另外，請注意音量和音調的變化，以使文章更生動有趣。在闡述文章的核心觀點和情感時，像是 by eating healthily, exercising regularly, and getting enough rest 可以加強「每一項」字詞要強調的重點部位。類似情況顯示於以下標有顏色的單字，請盡可能唸得比較響亮，以及出現「|」的地方，請稍作停頓，試著讓自己融入短文的情境中。最後，也請注意字與字之間該連音（含「消音」）的部分（以下畫底線），像是 referred to、most populous、located in、With its、must-visit、words of、self-assurance、important to、feelings of、out of、good care、of yourself⋯等。

New York, | commonly referred to as simply NY, | is one of the most populous cities in the United States and in the world. It is located in the northeastern region of the country. Known as a global hub for finance, | fashion, | art, | and entertainment, | NY is home to well-known landmarks | such as the Statue of Liberty, | Central Park, | Times Square, | and the Empire State Building. With its bustling streets, | diverse culture, | and endless attractions, New York is a must-visit destination | for travelers from all over the world.

****

One way to build self-confidence | is to spot negative self-talks and replace them with positive words of self-assurance. It's also important to set realistic goals and work towards achieving them, | as accomplishing tasks | can help increase feelings of confidence. Another strategy | is to step out of your comfort zone and try new things. Finally, | take good care of yourself | by eating healthily, | exercising regularly, | and getting enough rest. With patience and effort, | anyone can develop a strong sense of self-confidence.

第1回
第2回
第3回
第4回
第5回
第6回
第7回
第8回
第9回
第10回

紐約，通常簡稱為 NY，是美國和世界上人口最多的城市之一。它位於美國東北部地區。紐約以金融、時尚、藝術和娛樂等的全球中心聞名，它擁有許多著名地標，如自由女神像、中央公園、時代廣場和帝國大廈等。紐約的街道熙熙攘攘，文化多元，吸引著來自世界各地的遊客，是一個必訪的旅遊勝地。

****

建立自信心的方法之一是，找出負面的自我對話並以積極的自我肯定語句取代之。同樣重要的是，設定實際可行的目標並朝著實現目標的方向去努力，因為完成任務有助於提高自信心。另一項策略是走出自己的舒適區，並嘗試新的事物。最後，照顧好自己、健康飲食，定期鍛鍊以及充足的休息。付出耐心和努力，任何人都可以培養強烈的自信心。

關鍵字詞

be referred to as phr. 被指稱為…，被視為… **populous** adj. 人口眾多的 **global hub** n. 全球中心 **entertainment** n. 娛樂 **be home to** phr.是…的家，擁有… **well-known** adj. 著名的 **landmark** n. 地標 **statue** n.雕像 **liberty** n. 自由 **square** n. 方形 **empire** n. 帝國 **diverse** adj. 多元的 **endless** adj. 無盡的 **must-visit** adj. 必去的，必訪的 **destination** n. 目的地 **spot** v. 發現 **replace... with...** phr. 以…取代… **self-assurance** n. 自信 **realistic** adj. 實際的，寫實的 **accomplish** v. 完成 **strategy** n. 策略 **comfort zone** n. 舒適區

T10P2.mp3

第二部分 回答問題

1. **Who's your favorite actor or actress? Why do you like him or her?**

誰是你最喜歡的男演員或女演員？ 你為什麼喜歡他／她？

答題解說

首先，要確保自己可以把喜歡的演員名字說對！如果沒把握把外國人的名字說正確，你可以直接選台灣的演員，然後直接以中文發音說出名字也可以。比方說，如果你講不出 Leonardo DiCaprio 全名，你可以說 Leonardo of the famous classic movie Titanic；或是 Julia Roberts of *Pretty Woman*（《麻雀變鳳凰》的茱莉亞・羅伯茲）。一般來說，一位電影或電視明星受歡迎的原因（用來說明你為什麼喜歡他們）包括：

❶ 演技（acting ability）：許多人欣賞明星的原因是他們的演技，包括能夠將一

個角色詮釋得很好、可以將情感表現得很好（interpret characters, express emotions in an excellent way）…等。

❷ 外貌（physical appearance）：很多人欣賞明星的原因是因為他們的外貌，包括身材、面容、氣質（physique, facial features, and overall demeanor）等。

❸ 個性（personality）：有些人欣賞明星的原因可能是因為他們的個性，包括幽默風趣、善良正直、領袖魅力（humor, kindness, integrity and charisma）等。

回答範例 1

Andy Lau is my favorite actor because of his ability to embody a wide range of characters. From action-packed roles to emotional dramas, he always manages to seize his audience with his natural charisma and superb acting skills. He is truly a talented artist and a joy to watch on screen.
劉德華是我最喜歡的演員，因為他能夠體現各種角色的能力。從動感十足的角色到情感戲，他總能以天生的魅力和精湛的演技俘獲觀眾的心。他確實是一位才華橫溢的藝人，在銀幕上看著他是一種享受。

回答範例 2

Julia Roberts has been one of my favorite actresses since I first saw her in *Pretty Woman*. It's her stunning performance that captures my heart. With her brilliant smile, natural charm, and undeniable talent, I believe she'll continue to be a beloved figure in the entertainment industry.
自從我第一次在《麻雀變鳳凰》中看到茱莉亞・羅伯茲以來，她一直是我最喜歡的女演員。正是她令人驚嘆的演技俘獲了我的心。憑藉她燦爛的笑容、自然的魅力和無可否認的才華，我相信她會一直成為娛樂圈中備受喜愛的人物。

關鍵字詞

embody v. 賦予…形體，體現　**a wide range of** phr. 各種各樣的…　**character** n. 人物，角色　**action-packed** adj. 動感十足的　**seize** v. 抓住，擄獲　**charisma** n. 非凡的個人魅力　**superb** adj. 非凡的　**acting skill** n. 演技　**artist** n. 藝人　**stunning** adj. 令人驚嘆的　**capture** v. 俘獲，捕捉　**brilliant** adj. 燦爛的　**charm** n. 魅力　**undeniable** adj. 無可否認的

延伸學習

在英文文文法中，有一些名詞本身是有「性（gender）」的區別。例如，代表「男／雄性」的 man（男人）、father（父親）、husband（丈夫）、cock（公雞）、son（兒子）、uncle（伯父）、king（國王）、sir（先生）、monk（和

253

尚）...等。代表「女／雌性」的 woman（女人）、mother（母親）、wife（妻子）、hen（母雞）、nun（尼姑）...等。

另外，名詞字尾如果加 -ess，代表「女／雌性」，例如，actor（演員）→ actress（女演員）、host（主人）→ hostess（女主人）、poet（詩人）→ poetess（女詩人）、prince（王子）→ princess（公主）、god（神）→ goddess（女神）、waiter（侍者）→ waitress（女侍者）等。

2. **What subject did you dislike most in school? Why?**

你在學生時代時，最討厭那個科目？ 為什麼？

答題解說

還記得在學校時，各個科目的英文怎麼說嗎？英文（English）、數學（Math）這兩個單字，你可能都很熟了，如果沒把握其他科目可以說得正確，就用你最有把握的字彙吧！其他科目的英文是：國文（Mandarin Chinese）、歷史（History）、地理（Geography）、物理（Physics）、生物（Biology）、自然（Natural Science）、社會（Social Studies）、化學（Chemistry）、健康教育（Health）、體育（Physical education / PE）、工藝（Crafts）、家政（Home Economics）、音樂（Music）…等。答題時間 15 秒，不要多花時間去思考「我究竟最不喜歡哪一科」這種問題喔！第二個問題等同於 Why did you dislike this subject most? 或 Why did you dislike this subject most?，每個科目有它的特性和目的，這部分你只要講個兩句話就可以了。如果覺得還要去想科目的特質太麻煩，可以說，因為某某科的老師說話很兇、常常給學生考試……等。

回答範例 1

Math was my least favorite subject when I was a junior high school student. I struggled with understanding mathematical concepts and dreaded every math class. However, over time, I began to realize the importance of math in the exams of further studies later and started being interested in this subject.

當我還是個國中生時，數學是我最不喜歡的科目。我在理解數學概念這方面吃盡了苦頭，每次上數學課我都感到害怕。然而，隨著時間過去，我逐漸意識到數學在我往後升學考試的重要性，且對這個科目有興趣了。

回答範例 2

I disliked Physics and Chemistry most when I was in junior high school because it requires a lot of memorization and problem-solving skills that didn't come naturally to me. Furthermore, the abstract concepts and formulas were overwhelming and difficult to understand without proper guidance and practice.

我在學生時代時最討厭理化，因為它們要背的東西很多，且需要解題能力，這些能力是我與生俱來就沒有的。還有，抽象的概念和公式可能會令人不知所措，如果沒有獲得適當的指導和練習，是很難理解的。

第 1 回
第 2 回
第 3 回
第 4 回
第 5 回
第 6 回
第 7 回
第 8 回
第 9 回
第 10 回

關鍵字詞

least favorite adj. 最不喜歡的　**struggle with** phr. 費力地做…；難以搞定…　**concept** n. 觀念　**dread** v. 害怕　**over time** phr. 隨著時間過去　**Physics and Chemistry** n. 理化（物理與化學）　**memorization** n. 記憶力　**problem-solving skill** n. 解題技巧　**abstract** adj. 抽象的　**formula** n. 公式　**proper** adj. 適當的　**overwhelming** adj. 壓倒性的，難以忍受的　**guidance** n. 指導

延伸學習

subject 當名詞時，可以表示英文文法中的「主詞」。例如：The subject of this sentence is "Tom".。此外，在學術領域中，它也可以表示一個主題或領域。例如：

❶ The subject of the painting is a beautiful landscape.（這幅畫的主題是美麗的風景。）

❷ The subject of today's lecture is history.（今天講座的主題是歷史。）

❸ The subject of my research is the effect of social media on mental health.（我的研究主題是社交媒體對心理健康的影響。）

❹ The subject of this book is economics.（本書的主題是經濟學。）

3. **Do you like to live alone, or live with roommates or your family members? Why?**

你喜歡一個人住，還是和室友或家人住在一起？為什麼？

答題解說

無論你是學生或上班族，無論是在外租屋或是住家裡與家人同住，都可能感受到一些優缺點。但有時候是沒得選擇的（have no choices but to...）。比方說，經濟狀況比較不好的人，可能會選擇有室友跟你一起負擔房租及生活費用（share rent and living expenses），或者有社交和互動機會，可以和室友一起聊天、做飯、看電影等，減輕孤單和寂寞感（social and interaction opportunities, being able to chat, cook, watch movies, etc. with roommates, reducing loneliness and isolation）等。但缺點可能是容易產生衝突與不和，有時需要遷就和妥協（sometimes need to compromise and meet halfway），不能完全按照自己的生活方式和節奏過日子（unable to completely follow one's own lifestyle and pace）等。若有時間的話，可以相對地補充獨自居住的優點。像是更大的隱私

和個人空間，可以有更多的時間和空間專注於自己的工作或興趣（more privacy and personal space, allowing for more time and space to focus on work or hobbies）等。

I like to live alone, though now I live home with my parents. Sometimes my mother nags me about trivial things and my father is too worried about my future. I just want more privacy and personal space to focus on work or hobbies.

我喜歡一個人住，雖然我現在和父母同住。有時候媽媽會因為一些瑣事來嘮叨我，而爸爸也很擔心我的未來。我只是想要更多的隱私和個人空間來專注於工作或愛好。

I think living with one or two roommates would be better for me. I have rented a small studio apartment and lived alone for about 5 years. Sometimes I feel lonely and isolated, and I want more social and interactive opportunities.

我認為有一兩個室友一起同住對我來說會比較好。我租一間小套房一個人住，差不多有 5 年了。有時我感到孤獨且孤立，我想要更多的社交和與人互動機會。

alone adv. 獨自一人地　**nag** v. 嘮叨　**trivial** adj. 瑣碎的　**privacy** n. 隱私
personal adj. 個人的　**studio apartment** n. 小套房　**lonely** adj. 孤獨的
isolated adj. 被孤立的　**interactive** adj. 互動的

在英文裡，租屋時所指的「套房」和飯店裡的「套房」是不一樣的。租屋的「套房」是有衛浴或廁所和房間，英文是 a (small) studio apartment。但如果是在一間公寓租一間有廁所的房間來住，就只能說 I share an apartment with others.。英文裡有 suite 這個字，注意它的唸法和 sweet 一樣，不是 suit 喔！這個字在字典中會看到「套房」的解釋。但 suite 指的是有一個小客廳或會客區的房間。所以在飯店裡這種就是比較大的房間，像蜜月套房、總統套房等。不然一般的房間就叫 guest room。

4. **What if you constantly had more workload than you can afford?**

   如果你經常承受超出自己所能負擔的工作量，你會如何？

題目的 What if...? 是「萬一⋯怎麼辦？」或是「如果⋯，你會如何？」的意思。

workload 是「工作量」，afford 是「負擔得起…」。

如果你還是個學生，對於這類出社會工作時會遇到的問題，可以先如實說明自己目前的身分等狀況，然後陳述以後自己要是遇到這類問題會如何處理即可。一般來說，回答本題的方向有：

❶ 與主管或同事進行溝通，協商哪些工作可以延後處理（communicate with your supervisor or colleagues to negotiate which tasks can be delayed）。

❷ 向主管或同事請求協助，或詢問是否有其他同事可以幫助分擔工作（inquire about whether other colleagues can help share the workload）。

❸ 與主管進行溝通，讓他們了解情況（communicate with your supervisor to make them aware of the situation），看是否需要重新調整工作分配，或增加人力支援，以減輕工作負擔（reassign tasks or increase human resources support to reduce the workload）。

回答範例 1

I'm still a student now. But if I encounter such a problem in the future, I think I'll solve it by myself first. I'll try to prioritize tasks based on their importance and urgency. If I still suffer from heavy workload, I'll ask for assistance from my supervisor.

我現在還是個學生。但如果以後遇到這樣的問題，我想還是先自己解決。我會試著把工作按照優先順序和緊迫性排列。如果還是承受著繁重的工作量，我會向我的主管尋求協助。

回答範例 2

For me, work doesn't mean the whole of life. So if I encounter this problem, I'll definitely let my supervisor aware of it and see if there are any other solutions. I won't make myself work under great stress. In short, maintaining a healthy lifestyle is crucial.

對我來說，工作並不是生活的全部。所以如果我遇到這樣的問題，我一定會讓我的主管知道，看是否有其他解決辦法。我不會讓自己在巨大的壓力下工作。簡言之，保持健康的生活型態相當重要。

關鍵字詞

encounter v. 遇到　**solve** v. 解決　**prioritize** v. 優先考量…　**urgency** n. 急迫性　**heavy workload** n. 繁重的工作量　**ask for assistance from** phr. 尋求…（某人的）協助　**the whole of life** n. 生活的全部　**supervisor** n. 主管　**solution** n. 解決辦法　**under great stress** phr. 在巨大壓力下　**maintain** v. 維持

延伸學習

當我們想要表達自己正承受很大的壓力時，可以使用以下英文來表達：在比較正

式的口語中，我們可以說 I'm so stressed out/wound up.，或是較為正式的說法：I'm under a lot of pressure/stress.。此外，我們也可以使用「工作 + almost + stresses me out / drives me crazy」的慣用語句，來表達自己感到壓力非常大或快要崩潰了。

另外，如果想要表達自己真的太過勞累，可以說 I'm really overworked。若是已經超過下班時間，但仍在繼續工作到很晚，可以說 I'm working overtime。透過這些英語表達，能夠更清楚地表達自己的狀況，讓對方能夠更能地理解和幫助自己。

5. Would you take a trip alone? Why or why not?

你會一個人去旅行嗎？為什麼？

答題解說

本題答題時間 15 秒，原則上三句話（一般長度）就可以結束了。「一個人的旅行」是一種特別的人生體驗，而本題可以針對其優缺點來發揮。當然，你也可以以自身的經驗為例。比方說，當時因為剛失戀（had just broken up with boyfriend/girlfriend）了，想要一個人出去散散心（go outside and cheer oneself up）；或者當時在繁重的工作（heavy workload）結束之後，想要擺脫工作壓力和煩惱（get rid of the stress and worries from work），然後在獨自旅行的過程中，獲得更多的時間和空間，思考自己的人生方向、價值觀和興趣愛好（have more time and space to think about one's direction in life, values and interests）…等。因此，無論自己是否曾經獨自旅行，如果對於獨自旅行抱持肯定態度，可以參考以上答題方向。如果抱持否定態度，你也可以說獨自旅行比較孤單，缺乏社交和安全感（lonely, lacking in social support and security），而且在旅行中遇到問題或困難時，沒有其他人的支持和幫助，容易感到無助和焦慮（may experience feelings of helplessness and anxiety when faced with problems or difficulties during one's trip without the support of others）…等。

回答範例 1

Yes, I used to take an individual trip to Japan several years ago when I had just broken up with my boyfriend. Though sometimes I felt a bit lonely during the trip, I got inspired and could ultimately recover from the lost-love depression shortly after the trip.

是的，幾年前我和男朋友剛分手時，曾經獨自去日本旅行過。雖然在旅途中有時會感到有點孤獨，但我得到了一些啟發，且最終能夠在結束旅行後沒多久，就從失戀的抑鬱中復原。

回答範例 2

No, I wouldn't travel alone, because I prefer to share the experience and memories of traveling with others, and enjoy the fun and excitement of traveling together. Moreover, traveling alone may require more planning and preparation, which could be challenging for me.

不，我不會一個人去旅行，因為我比較喜歡與他人分享旅行的經歷和回憶，一起享受旅行的樂趣和刺激。此外，獨自旅行可能需要更多的計畫和準備，這對我來說可能是個挑戰。

關鍵字詞

individual n. 個人的　**break up with sb**. prep. 與某人分手　**lonely** adj. 孤獨的　**inspired** adj. 獲得啟發的　**ultimately** adv. 最終　**recover from** phr. 從…復原　**depression** n. 憂鬱，抑鬱　**prefer to-V** phr. 較喜歡…　**preparation** n. 準備工作　**challenging** adj. 具挑戰性的

延伸學習

individual 和 single 都是相當常見的字彙。以下是兩者主要的區別：

❶ single 通常指一個人或物品，它是一個總體的概念，而 individual 則更指一個獨立的、明確的實體。例如：

There was a single chair in the room.（房間裡只有一張椅子。）

We need to consider the individual needs of each student.（我們需要考慮每個學生的個別需求。）

❷ single 常用於描述某人的婚姻狀態，表示「單身的」，而 individual 則沒有這個含義。例如：John was still single at the age of 35.（約翰在 35 歲時還是單身。）

❸ single 可以指某種類型的東西只有一個，比如說 a single book 表示「只有一本書」，而 individual 則沒有這種用法。

6. **How did you get acquainted with your boyfriend or girlfriend? Talk about your experience.**

你是怎麼認識你的男友或女友的？談談你的經驗。

答題解說

acquaint 是個英檢中級單字，這個動詞表示「使認識」，get acquainted with sb. 的意思是「與某人結識／認識」。而針對與男朋友、女朋友或交往對象（dating partner = somebody you're dating/seeing）如何認識的回答，可以說透過派對、聚會、活動等社交場合（through parties, gatherings or events），或

現在很流行的網路交友（online dating），有許多交友軟體或社交媒體平台（dating apps and websites）。

如果你現在是單身且沒有交往對象（single without a dating partner），可以談談過去如何認識交往對象，或從來沒談過戀愛的話，可以藉由上述提示，希望未來可以認識一個什麼樣的對象。

如果你是已婚的（married）呢？當然你也可以談談過去如何認識另一半（the better half），或是過去任何一位交往對象。請注意，本題是要你談談過去的經驗，所以不用拘泥於任何一個交往對象喔！

回答範例 1

I met my girlfriend on a blind date arranged by an acquainted auntie last August. Originally I wasn't in favor of meeting a dating partner on such an occasion. But later to my surprise, she and I hit it off immediately and had a great time together. We have been dating ever since and I'm grateful for my auntie's warm-hearted help. Sometimes it pays off to step out of your comfort zone and take a chance on love.

我去年八月透過一位相識的阿姨安排的相親中，認識了我的女朋友。本來我是不太喜歡透過這種場合找對象。但後來，令我驚訝的是，我和她一拍即合，並一起度過了愉快的時光。從那以後我們就保持交往關係，我很感謝我阿姨的熱心幫忙。有時候走出你的舒適區，並抓住愛情的機會是值得的。

回答範例 2

I don't have a dating partner now, but I'm trying to look for one through a famous online dating platform. I hope I can find someone who shares similar interests and values with me, and someone who I can build a genuine connection with. Although online dating can be challenging, I'm open to putting myself out there and taking a chance. I believe that with patience and perseverance, I'll eventually meet someone who I can see a future with.

我現在沒有交往對象，但我正試著透過一個知名的交友平台尋找中。我希望我能找到一個與我有相似興趣和價值觀的人，以及一個可以與我建立真正關係的人。雖然網路交友可能沒那麼容易，但我還是願意給自己一個機會試試看。我相信只要有耐心和毅力，我終會遇到一位可以看到未來的人。

關鍵字詞

blind date n. 相親　**acquainted** adj. 認識的　**originally** adv. 原本，最初　**in favor of** phr. 贊同，偏好　**dating partner** n. 交往對象　**hit it off** phr. 一拍即合　**immediately** adv. 立即　**be grateful for** phr. 感激⋯（某件事）　**warm-hearted** adj. 暖心的，熱心的　**pay off** phr. 值得　**take a chance on** phr. 抓住⋯的機會

dating platform n. 交友平台　　**genuine** adj. 真正的　　**connection** n. 關係，連結　　**be open to** phr. 對…保持開放態度　　**perseverance** n. 毅力　　**eventually** adv. 最終

延伸學習

date 這個字除了表示「日期」之外，常用來指「情侶或是愛人之間的約會」。另外，date 也可以指人，表示「約會的對象」，屬於比較口語的說法，正式或書寫時一般用 dating partner。另外，date 當動詞時則表示「在約會／交往」或「與…（某人）約會／談戀愛」，前者為不及物動詞，通常主詞是 A +B 或複數（代）名詞，而後者是及物動詞，用法是 A + date + B，而 date 也可引伸為「交往」的意思。例如：

❶ I had a date with my boyfriend yesterday evening.
（我昨晚跟我男友約會。）

❷ Phil phoned me last night, and we're going on a date this evening.（Phil 昨晚打電話給我，我們今晚要約會。）

So come on, tell us, who's your date this evening?（所以，來，告訴我們你今晚的約會對象是誰？）

❹ How long have you been dating John?（你和 John 交往多久了？）
另外，be together、go out、see somebody 也可以表示「交往」或「（男女之間的）在一起」。例如：

❺ Lisa and Chris have been together for three years.（Lisa 和 Chris 在一起三年了。）

❻ They had been going out for six years before they got married.（他們在結婚前交往了六年。）

❼ We have been seeing each other for about three months.（我們差不多交往三個月了。）

7. **If you suddenly become very rich, what will you do and what changes will be made to your life?**

如果你突然變得非常富有，你會做什麼，且你的生活會有什麼改變？

答題解說

想像自己中了大樂透或突然繼承了一大筆遺產，突然變得好有錢了，會做什麼、生活會有什麼變化？一般來說，這問題取決於個人的價值觀、生活方式和目標。你可以說，想買很多奢侈品和名牌、高級車輛、珠寶（luxury goods and brand-name items, high-end vehicles, jewelry）等，或者環遊世界，去看看世界知名

261

景點（go traveling around the world, pay visits to some world-renowned attractions），至於「生活會有什麼改變」的回答，你可以簡單說生活會變得非常快樂、無憂無慮、不需要再煩惱錢的問題（carefree, needless to worry about money again）。

回答範例 1

If I suddenly become very rich now, I think I'll keep a low profile and maintain my current lifestyle. For example, I have a car, but I won't see the need to upgrade it to a luxury one. Instead, I would invest my newfound wealth wisely and use it to achieve my long-term goals. Being content with what I have and living modestly is a value that I hold dear and would continue to uphold even if my financial situation changes.

如果我現在突然變得非常富有，我想我會保持低調，並維持我現在的生活方式。比方說，我有一輛車，但我不會認為有需要升級成豪華名車。相反地，對於我新獲得的財富，我做明智的投資，並加以運用來實現我的長遠目標。知足常樂，謹慎地過生活是我珍惜的價值觀，即使我的財務狀況發生變化，我也會繼續堅持。

回答範例 2

To be frank, I've been hard up for money since I was young. I have been eager to become rich and dreamed about living in a big mansion. So if I suddenly became very rich, I'd definitely use the wealth to improve my own and my family's lifestyle. Besides, I would go explore the world, traveling, adventuring, or experiencing various cultural activities such as attending music festivals, visiting some wonders of the world, and more. Last, I'd also invest my money in stocks and real estate.

坦白說，我從年輕時就很缺錢。我一直渴望變得富有，夢想著住進大豪宅。所以如果我突然變得非常有錢，我肯定會用這些財富來改善我自己和家人的生活。此外，我會去探索這個世界、去旅行、去冒險或體驗各種文化活動，比方說參加音樂節、去看看世界奇景等。最後，我還會將錢投資在股票和房地產。

關鍵字詞

keep a low profile phr. 保持低調　**upgrade** v. 升級　**luxury** adj. 豪華的　**newfound** adj. 新獲得的　**long-term goal** n. 長遠目標　**be content with** phr. 對…感到滿足　**modestly** adv. 謹慎地，適度地　**hold dear** phr. 珍惜　**uphold** v. 握住，抓緊　**be hard up for** phr. 苦於缺少…　**mansion** n. 大豪宅　**wonder of the world** n. 世界奇景

延伸學習

說到「一夜致富（become/get rich overnight）」，中樂透（win the lottery）可能是一種狀況。通常我們講到「彩券」時，最常使用的是 lottery，這是個英檢中

高級單字。它是所有彩券的通稱。那為什麼我們常說「樂透」而不說「彩券」呢？那是因為 lottery 這個字源自於 lotto，「樂透」其實是 lotto 的音譯。

「中」這個動詞其實非常簡單，就是用 win 這個字。例如：The poor guy won the lottery and became an overnight millionaire.（那窮小子因為中了樂透而一夕致富。）如果要說中了多少錢，那就要用介系詞 in 來搭配 lottery，例如：I won 5 million dollars in the lottery.（我中了五百萬元樂透獎金。）要注意的是，不能說 buy a/the lottery，買樂透其實是只買「樂透彩券」，如果只講 lottery，代表憑彩券兌獎的「遊戲」，所以英文用法上一定要加上 ticket 才正確。例如：I am used to buying a lottery ticket every month.（我每個月習慣買張彩券。）

8. **Your friend Gary was recently dumped by his girlfriend and is still in low mood now. Say something to encourage him!**

你的朋友蓋瑞最近被他的女友甩了，現在仍心情低落。對他說些鼓勵的話吧！

答題解說

dump 這個動詞是英檢中級單字，但要是一時聽不出來，可以從後面的 by his girlfriend 和 in low mood 來判斷，應該不難猜出本題要問你什麼事。如何給予「情場上的失意者」一些鼓勵呢？首先，你要當作 Gary 現在就坐在你面前，或者你打電話給他，正要開始說話。你可以說，失戀需要一定的時間來恢復（allow yourself time to process the breakup），所以不要太過著急，給自己充足的時間來處理自己的情感（give yourself sufficient time to deal with our own feelings）。另外，失戀是一個很好的機會來重新審視自己，瞭解自己在關係中可能犯過的錯誤，並嘗試修正這些錯誤（a great opportunity to take a fresh look at yourself, to examine the mistakes you may have made in this relationship, and try to fix them）。最後，鼓勵他重新尋找愛情，舊的不去新的不來，下一個會更好（Encourage looking for a new love; out with the old and in with the new; the next one will be better）…之類的話，都可以派上用場。

回答範例 1

I'm sorry to hear that you broke up with your girlfriend, and I know it could be a difficult and painful experience. As a saying, "Out with the old and in with the new," I encourage you to look for a new love, which, I think is the best and quickest way to heal from the breakup. But remember to take good care of yourself, and stay positive and optimistic about the future. You're not alone and I'll be always here with you.

我很遺憾聽說你和女朋友分手了，我知道這可能是一段艱難而痛苦的經歷。俗話說，「舊的不去新的不來」，我鼓勵你尋找新的愛情，我認為這是走出失戀陰影

的最好、最快的方法。但記得要照顧好自己，並對未來保持積極樂觀的態度。你不會是孤單的，我會一直與你同在。

Maybe it's unacceptable to you, but there are things you can do to make your life better. Firstly, it's important to take the time to process your emotions and allow yourself to cry hard. Pull your heart out to your friends or family. Secondly, focus on self-care activities like exercise or hobbies you enjoy. Lastly, keep yourself open to new opportunities. What I just want to say is, be kind to yourself and give yourself the time and space you need to heal.

也許這對你來說是無法接受的，但你可以做些事情讓自己好過一些。首先，花點時間來處理你的情緒並讓自己大哭一場，這是很重要的。向朋友或家人傾訴。其次，專注於自我保健的活動，例如鍛煉身體或喜歡的嗜好。最後，對於新的機會保持開放的態度。我想說的是，要善待自己，並給自己時間和空間去療傷。

關鍵字詞

break up with phr. 與…（某人）分手　**painful** adj. 痛苦的　**heal** v. 治療　**breakup** n. 分開，分離　**positive** adj. 積極正面的　**optimistic** adj. 樂觀的　**unacceptable** adj. 無法接受的　**process** v. 處理　**emotion** n. 情緒，心情　**cry hard** phr. 用力哭，大哭一場　**put one's heart out to sb.** phr. 向某人傾訴　**keep oneself open to** phr. 對於…保持開放態度

延伸學習

朋友失戀時，除了做一個好的傾聽者（listener），，也可以適時向朋友表達你的支持、同理，讓他們知道他們並不孤單。例如：

❶ I'm here for you.（有我在。）

❷ I'm here for as long as you need me.（只要你需要我，我一直都會在。）

❸ I'm always a phone call away.（你隨時都可以打電話給我。）

除了給予支持，也可以表示同理（empathy），讓朋友覺得有人懂他們的心情。例如：

❹ I can only imagine how you're feeling.（我完全可以想像你現在是什麼感受。）

不過要注意的是，有些 NG 的話，看似展現同理心，說出來可能適得其反：

I knew this would happen.（我就知道這種事會發生。）

Anyway, I never liked him / her anyway!（反正我從來都不喜歡他 / 她！）

朋友深陷悲傷情緒，可以讓他們知道難過、悲傷是沒有關係的：

❺ It's okay to be sad.（難過沒有關係。）

第 1 回
第 2 回
第 3 回
第 4 回
第 5 回
第 6 回
第 7 回
第 8 回
第 9 回
第 10 回

❻ This might take time.（可能需要一段時間。）

同時也要避免用過於責怪的口吻，像是：

Get over it!（你要放下！）

Don't be such a crybaby.（別哭哭啼啼的。）

9. **What's the best luck you've ever had so far? Talk more about it!**

目前為止你遇到過最幸運的事是什麼？多談一下吧！

答題解說

一般人遇到過最幸運的事情當然是因人而異了，如果你不想在考試的時候停頓太久的時間去想自己遇到過什麼幸運的事，以下包含可以「多談一點」的內容，供您參考：

❶ 獲得理想的工作機會或獲得提升（land a dream job or get promoted）：這樣的幸運讓人感到自己的付出得到了肯定，而且自己的生活品質也得以提高（feel validated for their hard work and it improves the quality of my life）。

❷ 遇見對的人（meet the right person）：遇到自己的終生伴侶或最要好的朋友。這樣的幸運讓人們感到自己被愛和關心（make me feel loved and cared for），同時也可以增加自己對生活的幸福感和滿足感（increase my happiness and satisfaction with life）。

❸ 中獎（win the lottery）：這類突然的好運氣（sudden stroke of good luck）包括贏得彩票、獲得獎金、偶然遇到了名人（winning the lottery, receiving a bonus, or bumping into a celebrity）等。這樣的幸運讓人感到興奮和高興，並可能改變自己的生活（This kind of luck can make me feel excited and elated and may even change my life.）。

回答範例 1

The luckiest thing that ever happened to me is finding my better half. I was going through a tough time in my life when I met her. She brought joy and love into my life, and we have been inseparable ever since. We share a deep connection and understand each other very much. Together, we have created a life full of adventure, happiness, and support. I consider myself lucky every day to have found someone who loves and supports me unconditionally.

我遇到過最幸運的事就是找到我的另一半。在我遇見她的同時，我正經歷一段人生的艱難時期。她為我的生活帶來了歡樂和愛，且從那時候起我們就形影不離。我們有著深厚的關係，且非常了解彼此。我們一起創造了充滿冒險、快樂和支持的生活。我每天都覺得自己很幸運，能夠找到一位無條件愛我、支持我的人。

The best luck I've ever had is being born into a loving and supportive family. From a young age, I was surrounded by the love of my parents who encouraged me to pursue my dreams and provided me with the support and resources I needed to succeed. I realize how fortunate I am to have such a strong support, and I am grateful for them every day. Their love and guidance have been significant in my personal growth, and I will always cherish the bond we share.

我最幸運的就是出生在一個充滿愛和支持的家庭。從小，我就一直被我父母的愛包圍著，他們鼓勵我追求自己的夢想，並為我提供成功所需要支持和資源。我了解擁有如強大的支持是多麼幸運，我每天都對他們心存感激。他們的愛和指引我個人成長意義重大，我將永遠珍惜我們擁有的這份關係。

關鍵字詞

happen to sb. phr. 發生在某人身上　**better half** n. 另一半　**tough time** n. 艱難時期　**inseparable** adj. 不可分的　**ever since** phr. 從那時候起　**unconditionally** adv. 無條件地　**be born into** phr. 出生在…（某個家庭　**supportive** adj. 支持的　**resource** n. 資源　**fortunate** adj. 幸運的　**grateful** adj. 感恩的　**cherish** v. 珍惜　**bond** n. 關係

延伸學習

luck 這個單字可能很多小學生都知道是「運氣」。也常聽到 Good luck! 用來祝福對方。但如果你聽到有人說 Just my luck.，別以為那是在說自己很幸運，其實意思剛好相反：有點用自嘲的口吻說「我一向都這麼衰／運氣很背」。例如：They sold the last ticket five minutes before I got there - just my luck!（在我到達那裡的 5 分鐘前，他們賣掉了最後一張票 — 我運氣真背！）

另外，有個片語叫作 luck of the draw，你以為是「幸運抽中」嗎？錯了，它是「全靠運氣」的意思。draw 是抽籤，意思是「如同抽籤一樣全憑運氣」。例如：We met simply by chance. It was just luck of the draw that we could be together.（我們會遇見純屬偶然。我們能在一起是命運的安排。）

最後來學一句與 luck 有關的好話，可以用來安慰人：Better luck next time（下一次會更好。）例如：I'm sorry to hear that you failed your driving test. Better luck next time!（很遺憾你沒考過駕照，不過祝你下次成功！）

10. Do you agree or disagree to death penalty? What are your reasons?

你同不同意死刑的存在？你的理由是什麼？

答題解說

penalty 是個英檢中級單字，而 death penalty 就是「死刑」的意思，相當於 capital punishment，也是本題的關鍵字詞。本題是個大家都知道的爭議性（controversial）話題，不過有些考生可能對於用英文回答這樣的問題感到有些吃力。以下提供一些回答的方向以及符合程度的相關用語：

❶ 同意（agree）的理由：死刑是最嚴厲的刑罰（most severe punishment），有助於對嚴重犯罪起遏制作用（may prevent some individuals from committing serious crimes），如恐怖主義、謀殺（terrorism and murder）等，進而減少這些嚴重罪行的發生，以及避免罪犯再次犯罪（prevention of repeat offenses），保障社會安全和公共利益（ensure social security and public interests）。

❷ 不同意（disagree）的理由：可能存在司法錯誤（judicial errors），因為法官的主觀因素（subjective factors of the judge）等原因，誤判或冤案（wrongful judgment and misjudged case）等是經常發生的。另外，死刑的執行（implementation of death penalty）可能存在殘忍或不人道待遇（cruel and inhumane treatment）等問題。

回答範例 1

I agree to death penalty because it serves as a weapon against serious crimes and gives justice to the victims' families. However, it should only be used in cases of extremely evil crimes where the evidence is beyond doubt. It is crucial to ensure that the criminal has received a fair trial and is not falsely accused. Additionally, efforts should be made to improve the criminal justice system and address the root causes of crime to reduce the need for such extreme measures.

我同意有死刑，因為它可作為打擊嚴重罪行的武器，並還給受害者家屬一個公道。但是，它應僅適用於罪大惡極、證據確鑿的案件。確保罪犯得到公正審判而不被誣告，這是很重要的。此外，應努力改善刑事司法制度並解決犯罪的根源，以減少對此類極端措施的需求。

回答範例 2

I disagree to death penalty because it is a punishment impossible to change. It runs the risk of killing an innocent person. Moreover, the justice system is not necessarily reliable, and there is always the possibility of a wrongful judgment due to factors such as racial bias, flawed evidence, etc. Besides, the death penalty also raises moral concerns, as it involves the state taking the life of an individual. Instead, it can be replaced by, for example, life imprisonment without any opportunities for prisoners to leave prison.

我不同意有死刑的存在，因為這是一種無法改變的懲罰。它存在著殺死無辜者的風險。而且，司法制度也不一定可靠，且總是有因種族偏見、證據不足等因素造成誤判的可能性。此外，死刑也會引起道德問題，因為它涉及國家剝奪一個人生命的問題。反而是，比方說，以囚犯沒有任何出獄機會的終身監禁取而代之。

關鍵字詞

death penalty n. 死刑　**agree/disagree to sth**. phr. 同意／不同意…（某件事）　**serve as a weapon against...** phr. 作為…的武器　**crucial** adj. 重要的　**ensure** v. 確保　**criminal** n. 罪犯　**fair trial** n. 公正審判　**falsely accused** adj. 被誣告的　**criminal** adj. 刑事（案件）的　**justice system** n. 司法制度　**address** v. 解決　**root cause** n. 根源　**extreme** adj. 極端的　**run the risk of** phr. 存在著…的風險　**innocent** adj. 無辜的　**reliable** adj. 可靠的　**wrongful judgment** n. 誤判　**racial bias** n. 種族偏見　**flawed** adj.有瑕疵的　**moral concern** n. 道德問題　**life imprisonment** n. 終身監禁　**prisoner** n. 囚犯

延伸學習

criminal 是個相當常見的單字，它是從 crime（罪）這個字衍生而來。如果要表示「犯人」，就是用這個字。但請注意，criminal 是「已經確認犯了罪的人」，也就是已經被法院的法官（judge）宣判有罪（pronounce a sentence）的人，如果是被檢察官（prosecutor）「起訴（prosecute）」的人，稱為 suspect，也就是還沒被判刑，只能算是「嫌疑犯」。另外還有一個屬於 GRE 等級的單字，叫作 culprit（被告，肇事者，犯人），它同時具有 criminal 和 suspect 的意思，只是法律上講究明確的概念（是否經司法審判確認），所以比較不會用這個字。如果要用比較簡單的單字來說 culprit，你可以用 bad guy 或 wrongdoer 就可以了。

接著我們再來認識 offender 這個字。你應該學過 offend（冒犯，觸怒；犯罪），後面加 -er 就變成「人」了，那麼它就是「犯罪者」的意思，其實就是 criminal 的概念，只是一般用在「非刑事重罪」的人，比較常用來表示「冒犯者，違法者」。

最後，要知道的是，在法律用語中，犯了什麼罪的人，也有不同的字來代表他們。比方說：謀殺犯是 murderer，縱火犯是 arsonist，強暴犯是 rapist，綁匪是 kidnapper，通緝犯是 the wanted…等。

第 1 回
第 2 回
第 3 回
第 4 回
第 5 回
第 6 回
第 7 回
第 8 回
第 9 回
第 10 回

第三部分 看圖敘述

T10P3.mp3

答題解說

雖然題目有提示你從四個點去回答問題，但如果每個點你只能回答一句話，這樣的內容是絕對不夠的。所以請先從圖片本身去掌握這張照片的主題，然後根據 where、who、why、what... 等架構來充實你的內容。若對於圖片中的人事物相關英文沒有太大把握的話，試著用代名詞或自己有把握說得正確的詞彙來表達。如果一時之間腦袋空白，不知道如何開口說的話，可以用 Well, what can I say about the picture? I think... 這類說法來佔用一點時間。

1. 照片裡的人在什麼地方？

   一開頭你可以說 It is pretty obvious that this picture was taken...，或是 If I'm not mistaken, this photo was taken...，接著放上地方副詞片語，像是 in a shopping mall（在購物中心）或是 outside the shopping mall（在購物中心門外）。如果只是說「他們在室外／室內」（They are outdoors/indoors.）之類的，分數可會打折扣喔！

2. 照片裡的人在做什麼？

   提到「人」的部分時，你可以先提有多少人（There are an old couple and a young couple...，或是 There are four people in the picture...），這裡的

couple 也可以用 pair of lovers 取代。接著提到他們可能的身分或關係。比方說，The young man could be the son of the old couple and the young woman their daughter-in-law....，或是 The young and old couples may not get acquainted with each other. They maybe just visitors to the shopping mall...，然後繼續說明他們正在做的事：They are taking a leisurely walk outside the shopping mall... 或是 They are just done with shopping and taking a carefree walk in the mall...

3. 照片裡的人為什麼會在那裡？

我們可以從照片拍攝地點，以及當中人物的行為、動作來判斷他們為什麼會來這地方。例如，你可以先說明，可能是因為之前得知商場有特賣會之類的活動而前來購物：It's possible that they were drawn in by the advertised weekend sales or the festive atmosphere of the mall...。

4. 如果尚有時間，請詳細描述圖片中的景物。

你可以從這張照片給人的一個感覺著手，例如，你可以繼續補充說：It's heartening to see people of different generations coming together and finding joy in a common activity...，或者 they may have got a great bargain on some desired products, and have spent a carefree afternoon exploring the shops and enjoying each other's company。

回答範例

It is quite obvious that this photo was taken at a shopping mall. There are an old couple and a young pair there. I guess the old and the young pairs are not acquainted with each other. All of them are just weekend visitors to this shopping mall where there may be many products going on sale. From the joyful smiles on their faces, I'm sure that they have managed to get great bargains on some desired products, and have spent a carefree afternoon exploring the shops and enjoying each other's company. Both the old and young pairs are walking happily with their hands full. While it's unclear whether the people in this photo are related or strangers, they are all united by their shared experience of shopping at the mall. It's possible that they were drawn in by the advertised weekend sales or the festive atmosphere of the mall. To me, it's heartening to see people of different generations coming together and finding joy in a common activity.

顯然，這張照片是在一家購物中心拍的。那裡有一對老夫婦和一對年輕夫婦。我想這對老少夫婦是不相識的。他們都是週末前來購物中心的遊客，那裡可能有很多產品正在打折。從他們臉上洋溢著歡樂的笑容，我相信他們已經成功地買到一些優惠且心儀的商品，並在彼此的陪伴下度過了一個無憂無慮的下午。這對老少

第 1 回
第 2 回
第 3 回
第 4 回
第 5 回
第 6 回
第 7 回
第 8 回
第 9 回
第 10 回

夫妻都滿手大包小包，歡喜地走著。雖然不清楚這張照片中的人彼此有關係或是陌生人，但他們都在這個商場有著共同的購物經歷而聚在一起。他們可能是被廣告宣傳的週末促銷活動，或是商場的節慶氣氛所吸引前來。對我來說，看到不同世代的人聚在一起並且在共同的活動中找到快樂，這是令人開心的。

關鍵字詞

shopping mall n. 購物中心　**be acquainted with** phr. 與…（某人）相識　**on sale** phr. 拍賣／折扣中　**bargain** n. 好價錢，討價還價　**desired** adj. 心儀的　**carefree** adj. 無憂無慮的　**company** n. 陪伴　**with one's hands full** phr. 滿手大包小包　**draw in** phr. 將…吸引過來　**festive** adj. 節慶的　**atmosphere** n. 氣氛　**heartening** adj. 令人開心的　**generation** n. 世代

延伸學習

當你手上提著一堆東西，聽到別人要你過來幫忙拿個什麼東西時，在中文裡我們通常會說：「拜託，我沒手了／我沒有手可以拿東西了！」那麼這句話的英文怎麼說呢？可千萬別說成 I don't have hands! 或 I have no hands! 了，因為在外國人聽來的意思是，你沒有手（只剩下腳），可會讓人回頭看著你的手而偷笑了！正確說法是：My hands are full.。這句話字面上的意思是「我雙手都滿了」，也就是我拿滿東西，沒辦法再幫忙拿別的東西了。另外，這句話也可以引申成「很忙碌」的意思。例如：

❶ My hands are full today; I can't go out with you.（我今天超忙；我沒辦法和你出去。）

❷ I can't leave now; my hands are full with my own work.（我現在沒辦法離開；我手頭上一堆工作要做。）

❸ Don't bother me. I have my hands full now.（別煩我。我現在很忙。）

台灣廣廈 國際出版集團 Taiwan Mansion International Group

國家圖書館出版品預行編目（CIP）資料

NEW GEPT 新制全民英檢中級口說＆寫作題庫大全 /國際語言
中心委員會、席菈著. -- 初版. -- 新北市：國際學村, 2023.05
面； 公分
ISBN 978-986-454-283-3
1.英語 2.讀本

805.1892   112004457

🌐 **國際學村**

NEW GEPT 新制全民英檢中級口說＆寫作題庫大全
完整10回試題，掌握最新出題趨勢（附擬真試題本＋口說測驗「考場真實模擬」與「解答範例」QR碼線上音檔）

作　　者／國際語言中心委員會・席菈　　編輯中心編輯長／伍峻宏・編輯／許加慶
　　　　　　　　　　　　　　　　　　　　封面設計／曾詩涵・內頁排版／菩薩蠻數位文化有限公司
　　　　　　　　　　　　　　　　　　　　製版・印刷・裝訂／皇甫・秉成

行企研發中心總監／陳冠蒨　　　　　線上學習中心總監／陳冠蒨
媒體公關組／陳柔彣　　　　　　　　數位營運組／顏佑婷
綜合業務組／何欣穎　　　　　　　　企製開發組／江季珊

發　行　人／江媛珍
法 律 顧 問／第一國際法律事務所 余淑杏律師・北辰著作權事務所 蕭雄淋律師
出　　版／國際學村
發　　行／台灣廣廈有聲圖書有限公司
　　　　　　地址：新北市235中和區中山路二段359巷7號2樓
　　　　　　電話：（886）2-2225-5777・傳真：（886）2-2225-8052
讀者服務信箱／cs@booknews.com.tw

代理印務・全球總經銷／知遠文化事業有限公司
　　　　　　地址：新北市222深坑區北深路三段155巷25號5樓
　　　　　　電話：（886）2-2664-8800・傳真：（886）2-2664-8801
郵 政 劃 撥／劃撥帳號：18836722
　　　　　　劃撥戶名：知遠文化事業有限公司（※單次購書金額未達1000元，請另付70元郵資。）

■ 出版日期：2023年05月　　ISBN：978-986-454-283-3
　　　　　　2024年07月2刷　　版權所有，未經同意不得重製、轉載、翻印。

Complete Copyright © 2023 by Taiwan Mansion Books Group.
All Rights reserved.

NEW GEPT
新制全民英檢
10回試題完全掌握最新內容與趨勢！
中級 寫作&口說題庫大全
—○ 試題冊 ○—

全書MP3一次下載

http://booknews.com.tw/mp3/9789864542833.htm

「iOS 系統請升級至 iOS13 後再行下載，
下載前請先安裝 ZIP 解壓縮程式或 APP，
此為大型檔案，建議使用 WIFI 連線下載，以免占用流量，
並確認連線狀況，以利下載順暢。」

第一回　寫作能力測驗答題注意事項

1. 本測驗共有兩部分。第一部分為中譯英,第二部分為英文作文。
   測驗時間為 40 分鐘。

2. 請利用試題紙空白處背面擬稿,但正答務必書寫在「寫作能力測
   驗答案紙」上。在答案紙以外的地方作答,不予計分。

3. 第一部分中譯英請在答案紙第一頁作答,第二部分英文作文請在
   答案紙第二頁作答。

4. 作答時請勿隔行書寫,請注意字跡清晰可讀,並保持答案紙之清
   潔,以免影響評分。

5. 測驗時,不得在准考證或其他物品上抄題,亦不得有傳遞、夾帶
   小抄、左顧右盼或交談等違規行為。

6. 意圖或已經將試題紙攜出試場者,五年內不得報名參加本測驗。
   請人代考者,連同代考者,三年內不得報名參加本測驗。

7. 測驗結束時,須立即停止作答,在原位靜候監試人員收回全部試
   題紙及答案紙,清點無誤後,宣佈結束始可離場。

8. 應試者入場、出場及測驗中如有違反上列規則或不服監試人員之
   指示者,監試人員得取消應試資格並請其離場,且作答不予計
   分。

全民英語能力分級檢定測驗

中級寫作能力測驗

本測驗共有兩部份。第一部份為中譯英，第二部份為英文寫作。測驗時間為 40 分鐘。

一、中譯英 (40%)

說明：請將下列的一段中文翻譯成通順、達意且前後連貫的英文。

　　　　陸地上的大眾交通工具在我們日常生活中扮演著極其重要的角色。在台灣，它是數百萬人彼此之間每天相互聯結的生命線。同時，它也建立起繁榮的社區、創造了就業機會、緩解了交通擁擠並造就更清潔的環境。比較普遍的交通運輸工具包括火車、公車、捷運、輕軌、計程車、接駁車等。這些運輸工具除了方便，也更環保。此外，在高油價的時代，乘坐大眾運輸工具也是個不錯的選擇。

二、英文作文 (60%)

請依下面所提供的文字提示寫一篇英文作文，長度約 120 字（8 至 12 個句子）。作文可以是一個完整的段落，也可以分段。（評分重點包括內容、組織、文法、用字遣詞、標點符號、大小寫。）

提示：每年找工作的人多如過江之鯽，尤其是在畢業季。除了本身學經歷之外，要找到一份理想的工作，面試時的表現是最重要的。有時候，一份好的職缺會吸引眾多競爭者，因此第一步就是撰寫一份完善的履歷，否則連第二關的面試、考試的機會可能都沒有。如何在求職過程中有好的表現、脫穎而出，您認為應如何做足功課，或者有哪些秘訣呢？

3

全民英語能力分級檢定測驗中級寫作能力答案紙

5

10

15

20

25

30

35

40

第一回　口說能力測驗答題注意事項

1. 本測驗問題由耳機播放，回答則經麥克風錄下。分朗讀短文、回答問題與看圖敘述三部分，時間共約 15 分鐘，連同口試說明時間共需約五十分鐘。

2. 第一部份朗讀短文有 1 分鐘準備時間，此時請勿唸出聲音，待聽到「請開始朗讀」2 分鐘的朗讀時間開始時，再將短文唸出來。第二部分回答問題的題目將播出 2 遍，聽完第二次題目後要立即回答。第三部份看圖敘述有 30 秒的思考時間及 1 分 30 秒的答題時間，思考時不可在試題紙上作記號，亦不可出聲。等聽到指示開始回答時，請您針對圖片盡量的回答。

3. 錄音設備皆已事先完成設定，請勿觸動任何機件，以免影響錄音。測驗時請戴妥耳機，將麥克風調到嘴邊約三公分處，聽清楚說明，依指示以適中音量回答。

4. 評分人員將根據您錄下的回答（發音與語調、語法與字彙、可解度及切題度等）作整體的評分。您可利用所附光碟自行測試，一一錄下回答後，再播出來聽聽，並斟酌調整。練習時請盡量以英語思考、應對，考試時較易有自然的表現。

5. 請注意測試時不可在試題紙上劃線、打「√」或作任何記號；不可在准考證或其他物品上抄題；亦不可有傳遞、夾帶小抄、左顧右盼或交談等違規行為。

6. 意圖或已將試題紙或試題影音資料攜出或傳送出試場者，視同侵犯本中心著作財產權，限五年內不得報名參加「全民英檢」測驗。請人代考，連同代考者，三年內不得報名參加本測驗。

7. 測驗結束時，須立即停止作答，在原位靜候監試人員收回全部試題紙且清點無誤後，等候監試人員宣布結束後始可離場。

8. 入場、出場及測驗中如有違反規則或不服監試人員指示者，監試人員將取消您的應試資格並請您離場，且作答不予計分，亦不退費。

全民英語能力分級檢定測驗

中級口說能力測驗

T01.mp3

請在 15 秒內完成並唸出下列自我介紹的句子：

My seat number is（座位號碼後 5 碼）, and my registration number is（考試號碼後 5 碼）.

第一部分：朗讀短文

　　請先利用一分鐘的時間閱讀下面的短文，然後在二分鐘內以正常的速度，清楚正確的讀出下面的短文，閱讀時請不要發出聲音。

　　Every year in Taiwan, about 200,000 students graduate from colleges or universities, with the average age of them 22 to 24. Approximately twenty percent of these graduates will study further for a master degree or go abroad for further studies, while 60% of them will enter the workforce, though nowadays the job market has always been competitive.

　　　　　　　*　　　　　　　　*　　　　　　　　*

　　Mr. Roberts went to a fancy restaurant last week to have a date with a pretty lady he was recently acquainted with. It was crowded inside and they had waited for about one hour before a waitress took them to a table. When the lady made her orders, hesitantly and slowly, the waitress looked annoyed and impatient. This made Mr. Roberts a bit upset, because he thought the waitress should not bear such an impolite attitude. He decided to make a complaint with the restaurant owner.

第二部分：回答問題

　　這個部分共有 10 題。題目已事先錄音，每題經由耳機播出二次，不印在試卷上。第一至五題，每題回答時間 15 秒；第六至十題，每題回答時間 30 秒。每題播出後，請立即回答。回答時，不一定要用完整的句子，但請在作答時間內儘量的表達。

第三部分：看圖敘述

下面有一張圖片及四個相關的問題，請在一分半鐘內完成作答。作答時，請直接回答，不需將題號及題目唸出。

首先請利用 30 秒的時間看圖及問題。

提示：
1. 照片裡的人在什麼地方？
2. 照片裡的人在做什麼？
3. 照片裡的人為什麼會在那裡？
4. 如果尚有時間，請詳細描述圖片中的景物。

請將下列自我介紹的句子再唸一遍：

My seat number is（座位號碼後 5 碼）, and my registration number is（考試號碼後 5 碼）.

第二回 寫作能力測驗答題注意事項

1. 本測驗共有兩部分。第一部分為中譯英,第二部分為英文作文。
   測驗時間為 40 分鐘。

2. 請利用試題紙空白處背面擬稿,但正答務必書寫在「寫作能力測
   驗答案紙」上。在答案紙以外的地方作答,不予計分。

3. 第一部分中譯英請在答案紙第一頁作答,第二部分英文作文請在
   答案紙第二頁作答。

4. 作答時請勿隔行書寫,請注意字跡清晰可讀,並保持答案紙之清
   潔,以免影響評分。

5. 測驗時,不得在准考證或其他物品上抄題,亦不得有傳遞、夾帶
   小抄、左顧右盼或交談等違規行為。

6. 意圖或已經將試題紙攜出試場者,五年內不得報名參加本測驗。
   請人代考者,連同代考者,三年內不得報名參加本測驗。

7. 測驗結束時,須立即停止作答,在原位靜候監試人員收回全部試
   題紙及答案紙,清點無誤後,宣佈結束始可離場。

8. 應試者入場、出場及測驗中如有違反上列規則或不服監試人員之
   指示者,監試人員得取消應試資格並請其離場,且作答不予計
   分。

全民英語能力分級檢定測驗

中級寫作能力測驗

本測驗共有兩部份。第一部份為中譯英，第二部份為英文寫作。測驗時間為 40 分鐘。

一、中譯英 (40%)

說明：請將下列的一段中文翻譯成通順、達意且前後連貫的英文。

　　　一個人的溝通協調能力，往往是能否將問題有效處理的關鍵。這不僅包括與他人交談時的態度，還有自我情緒控制的能力——千萬別輕易地情緒失控。善於溝通的人往往在職場上也更容易成功，且在各種社交場合中也會是個較受歡迎的人。

二、英文作文 (60%)

請依下面所提供的文字提示寫一篇英文作文，長度約 120 字（8 至 12 個句子）。作文可以是一個完整的段落，也可以分段。（評分重點包括內容、組織、文法、用字遣詞、標點符號、大小寫。）

提示：隨著全球疫情逐漸趨緩、邊境解封以及各種防疫措施的鬆綁，國內熱門餐飲店或特色餐廳等，也都看到人潮的回籠，有些餐廳甚至會遇到一位難求的狀況。請分享過去在餐廳用餐的美好或不愉快的經驗。

全民英語能力分級檢定測驗中級寫作能力答案紙

第一部份請由第 1 行開始作答，請勿隔行書寫。　　　　　　第 1 頁

TEST 02

5

10

15

20

第二部分請翻至第 2 頁作答

11

25

30

35

40

第二回 口說能力測驗答題注意事項

1. 本測驗問題由耳機播放，回答則經麥克風錄下。分朗讀短文、回答問題與看圖敘述三部分，時間共約 15 分鐘，連同口試說明時間共需約五十分鐘。

2. 第一部份朗讀短文有 1 分鐘準備時間，此時請勿唸出聲音，待聽到「請開始朗讀」2 分鐘的朗讀時間開始時，再將短文唸出來。第二部分回答問題的題目將播出 2 遍，聽完第二次題目後要立即回答。第三部份看圖敘述有 30 秒的思考時間及 1 分 30 秒的答題時間，思考時不可在試題紙上作記號，亦不可出聲。等聽到指示開始回答時，請您針對圖片盡量的回答。

3. 錄音設備皆已事先完成設定，請勿觸動任何機件，以免影響錄音。測驗時請戴妥耳機，將麥克風調到嘴邊約三公分處，聽清楚說明，依指示以適中音量回答。

4. 評分人員將根據您錄下的回答（發音與語調、語法與字彙、可解度及切題度等）作整體的評分。您可利用所附光碟自行測試，一一錄下回答後，再播出來聽聽，並斟酌調整。練習時請盡量以英語思考、應對，考試時較易有自然的表現。

5. 請注意測試時不可在試題紙上劃線、打「√」或作任何記號；不可在准考證或其他物品上抄題；亦不可有傳遞、夾帶小抄、左顧右盼或交談等違規行為。

6. 意圖或已將試題紙或試題影音資料攜出或傳送出試場者，視同侵犯本中心著作財產權，限五年內不得報名參加「全民英檢」測驗。請人代考，連同代考者，三年內不得報名參加本測驗。

7. 測驗結束時，須立即停止作答，在原位靜候監試人員收回全部試題紙且清點無誤後，等候監試人員宣布結束後始可離場。

8. 入場、出場及測驗中如有違反規則或不服監試人員指示者，監試人員將取消您的應試資格並請您離場，且作答不予計分，亦不退費。

全民英語能力分級檢定測驗

中級口說能力測驗

T02.mp3

請在 15 秒內完成並唸出下列自我介紹的句子：

My seat number is（座位號碼後 5 碼）, and my registration number is （考試號碼後 5 碼）.

第一部分：朗讀短文

　　請先利用一分鐘的時間閱讀下面的短文，然後在二分鐘內以正常的速度，清楚正確的讀出下面的短文，閱讀時請不要發出聲音。

　　The so-called "youth" shouldn't be just considered the time in someone's life when they are young. It is actually not just a time of life, but a state of mind; it is not a matter of rosy cheeks, red lips or flexible limbs; it should be full of strong will, creative imagination, rich in vigor of love; it should be able to keep you curious and energetic. The "youth" state of mind can be cultivated by embracing curiosity, creativity, and a passion for learning.

＊　　　　　　　　　＊　　　　　　　　　＊

　　Everyone may have some moments in life when they miss someone so much that they just want to take them from their dreams or memories to the real life, and hug them for real! Dream what you want to dream; go where you want to go; be what you want to be, because you have only live once. Don't let fear or doubt hold you back from experiencing all the beauty and wonder the world has to offer.

第二部分：回答問題

　　這個部分共有 10 題。題目已事先錄音，每題經由耳機播出二次，不印在試卷上。第一至五題，每題回答時間 15 秒；第六至十題，每題回答時間 30 秒。每題播出後，請立即回答。回答時，不一定要用完整的句子，但請在作答時間內儘量的表達。

第三部分：看圖敘述

　　下面有一張圖片及四個相關的問題，請在一分半鐘內完成作答。作答時，請直接回答，不需將題號及題目唸出。

　　首先請利用 30 秒的時間看圖及問題。

提示：
1. 照片裡的人在什麼地方？
2. 照片裡的人在做什麼？
3. 照片裡的人為什麼會在那裡？
4. 如果尚有時間，請詳細描述圖片中的景物。

請將下列自我介紹的句子再唸一遍：

My seat number is（座位號碼後 5 碼）, and my registration number is（考試號碼後 5 碼）.

第三回　寫作能力測驗答題注意事項

1. 本測驗共有兩部分。第一部分為中譯英，第二部分為英文作文。測驗時間為 40 分鐘。

2. 請利用試題紙空白處背面擬稿，但正答務必書寫在「寫作能力測驗答案紙」上。在答案紙以外的地方作答，不予計分。

3. 第一部分中譯英請在答案紙第一頁作答，第二部分英文作文請在答案紙第二頁作答。

4. 作答時請勿隔行書寫，請注意字跡清晰可讀，並保持答案紙之清潔，以免影響評分。

5. 測驗時，不得在准考證或其他物品上抄題，亦不得有傳遞、夾帶小抄、左顧右盼或交談等違規行為。

6. 意圖或已經將試題紙攜出試場者，五年內不得報名參加本測驗。請人代考者，連同代考者，三年內不得報名參加本測驗。

7. 測驗結束時，須立即停止作答，在原位靜候監試人員收回全部試題紙及答案紙，清點無誤後，宣佈結束始可離場。

8. 應試者入場、出場及測驗中如有違反上列規則或不服監試人員之指示者，監試人員得取消應試資格並請其離場，且作答不予計分。

全民英語能力分級檢定測驗

中級寫作能力測驗

本測驗共有兩部份。第一部份為中譯英，第二部份為英文寫作。測驗時間為 40 分鐘。

一、中譯英 (40%)

說明：請將下列的一段中文翻譯成通順、達意且前後連貫的英文。

　　　　海倫下個月就大學畢業了。她大部分同學們都在準備考研究所，也有一些人正在找工作。另外，有些人準備出國深造，而有些男生準備去當兵，但她卻有別的計畫。海倫打算先到國外打工一年。她不僅能獲得寶貴的工作經驗，還能存到一筆錢。

二、英文作文 (60%)

請依下面所提供的文字提示寫一篇英文作文，長度約 120 字（8 至 12 個句子）。作文可以是一個完整的段落，也可以分段。（評分重點包括內容、組織、文法、用字遣詞、標點符號、大小寫。）

提示：你聽過色彩心理學嗎？其實色彩可以反映出一個人的性格。喜歡什麼顏色，就表示有什麼樣的性格。例如，喜歡黃色的人比較外向；喜歡白色的人比較不接受妥協，且多是完美主義者。你喜歡什麼顏色呢？你覺得自己是什麼個性的人呢？

全民英語能力分級檢定測驗中級寫作能力答案紙

第一部份請由第 1 行開始作答,請勿隔行書寫。 第 1 頁

5

10

15

20

TEST 03

25

30

35

40

第三回　口說能力測驗答題注意事項

1. 本測驗問題由耳機播放，回答則經麥克風錄下。分朗讀短文、回答問題與看圖敘述三部分，時間共約 15 分鐘，連同口試說明時間共需約五十分鐘。

2. 第一部份朗讀短文有 1 分鐘準備時間，此時請勿唸出聲音，待聽到「請開始朗讀」2 分鐘的朗讀時間開始時，再將短文唸出來。第二部分回答問題的題目將播出 2 遍，聽完第二次題目後要立即回答。第三部份看圖敘述有 30 秒的思考時間及 1 分 30 秒的答題時間，思考時不可在試題紙上作記號，亦不可出聲。等聽到指示開始回答時，請您針對圖片盡量的回答。

3. 錄音設備皆已事先完成設定，請勿觸動任何機件，以免影響錄音。測驗時請戴妥耳機，將麥克風調到嘴邊約三公分處，聽清楚說明，依指示以適中音量回答。

4. 評分人員將根據您錄下的回答（發音與語調、語法與字彙、可解度及切題度等）作整體的評分。您可利用所附光碟自行測試，一一錄下回答後，再播出來聽聽，並斟酌調整。練習時請盡量以英語思考、應對，考試時較易有自然的表現。

5. 請注意測試時不可在試題紙上劃線、打「√」或作任何記號；不可在准考證或其他物品上抄題；亦不可有傳遞、夾帶小抄、左顧右盼或交談等違規行為。

6. 意圖或已將試題紙或試題影音資料攜出或傳送出試場者，視同侵犯本中心著作財產權，限五年內不得報名參加「全民英檢」測驗。請人代考，連同代考者，三年內不得報名參加本測驗。

7. 測驗結束時，須立即停止作答，在原位靜候監試人員收回全部試題紙且清點無誤後，等候監試人員宣布結束後始可離場。

8. 入場、出場及測驗中如有違反規則或不服監試人員指示者，監試人員將取消您的應試資格並請您離場，且作答不予計分，亦不退費。

全民英語能力分級檢定測驗

中級口說能力測驗

T03.mp3

請在 15 秒內完成並唸出下列自我介紹的句子：

My seat number is（座位號碼後 5 碼）, and my registration number is
（考試號碼後 5 碼）.

第一部分：朗讀短文

　　請先利用一分鐘的時間閱讀下面的短文，然後在二分鐘內以正常的速度，清楚正確的讀出下面的短文，閱讀時請不要發出聲音。

　　Our boss wanted each of us to take a public-speaking training lesson. Both the management and staff members were asked to decide whether these lessons will be taken during normal working time or outside office hours. According to the result of our recent survey, almost 90% of employees wanted to take the training lesson during the normal working time. No more than 9% of them were willing to sacrifice their after-work hours.

　　　　　　*　　　　　　　　　　*　　　　　　　　　　*

　　In our company, we offer three different programs for employees who have young children. We have a day care center for infants from 3 months to 36 months. We also hire child-care staff to take care of them. In addition, we have a special sensory integration program for these young children. This will help them grow up well and improve the capability of their five senses. If any of you, new comers, need these services, please let me know at once so we can get you an application form.

第二部分：回答問題

　　這個部分共有 10 題。題目已事先錄音，每題經由耳機播出二次，不印在試卷上。第一至五題，每題回答時間 15 秒；第六至十題，每題回答時間 30 秒。每題播出後，請立即回答。回答時，不一定要用完整的句子，但請在作答時間內儘量的表達。

第三部分：看圖敘述

　　下面有一張圖片及四個相關的問題，請在一分半鐘內完成作答。作答時，請直接回答，不需將題號及題目唸出。

　　首先請利用 30 秒的時間看圖及問題。

提示：
1. 照片裡的人在什麼地方？
2. 照片裡的人在做什麼？
3. 照片裡的人為什麼會在那裡？
4. 如果尚有時間，請詳細描述圖片中的景物。

請將下列自我介紹的句子再唸一遍：

My seat number is （座位號碼後 5 碼）, and my registration number is （考試號碼後 5 碼）.

第四回　寫作能力測驗答題注意事項

1. 本測驗共有兩部分。第一部分為中譯英，第二部分為英文作文。測驗時間為 40 分鐘。

2. 請利用試題紙空白處背面擬稿，但正答務必書寫在「寫作能力測驗答案紙」上。在答案紙以外的地方作答，不予計分。

3. 第一部分中譯英請在答案紙第一頁作答，第二部分英文作文請在答案紙第二頁作答。

4. 作答時請勿隔行書寫，請注意字跡清晰可讀，並保持答案紙之清潔，以免影響評分。

5. 測驗時，不得在准考證或其他物品上抄題，亦不得有傳遞、夾帶小抄、左顧右盼或交談等違規行為。

6. 意圖或已經將試題紙攜出試場者，五年內不得報名參加本測驗。請人代考者，連同代考者，三年內不得報名參加本測驗。

7. 測驗結束時，須立即停止作答，在原位靜候監試人員收回全部試題紙及答案紙，清點無誤後，宣佈結束始可離場。

8. 應試者入場、出場及測驗中如有違反上列規則或不服監試人員之指示者，監試人員得取消應試資格並請其離場，且作答不予計分。

全民英語能力分級檢定測驗

中級寫作能力測驗

本測驗共有兩部份。第一部份為中譯英，第二部份為英文寫作。測驗時間為 40 分鐘。

一、中譯英 (40%)

說明：請將下列的一段中文翻譯成通順、達意且前後連貫的英文。

> 有一句話說，「金錢象徵著你對別人的價值。」一個作家有多優秀，看他賣了多少本書，拿了多少版稅。一個畫家有多成功，看他的畫值多少錢。各行各業的成功幾乎都是如此。如果有一個畫家宣稱自己很成功，但他的畫作沒人買單，那只是自我滿足而已。

二、英文作文 (60%)

請依下面所提供的文字提示寫一篇英文作文，長度約 120 字（8 至 12 個句子）。作文可以是一個完整的段落，也可以分段。（評分重點包括內容、組織、文法、用字遣詞、標點符號、大小寫。）

提示：網路商店的商品價位不必去承受商店租金或店家雇用店員的成本，一般來說都會比實體店面便宜一些。但也容易出現一些交易糾紛。假設你今天在網路上買的東西是防冒品，請寫一封電子郵件向店家抱怨並要求合理補償措施。

全民英語能力分級檢定測驗中級寫作能力答案紙

第一部份請由第 1 行開始作答，請勿隔行書寫。　　　　　第 1 頁

5

10

TEST 04

15

20

第二部分請翻至第 2 頁作答

25

30

35

40

第四回 口說能力測驗答題注意事項

1. 本測驗問題由耳機播放，回答則經麥克風錄下。分朗讀短文、回答問題與看圖敘述三部分，時間共約 15 分鐘，連同口試說明時間共需約五十分鐘。

2. 第一部份朗讀短文有 1 分鐘準備時間，此時請勿唸出聲音，待聽到「請開始朗讀」2 分鐘的朗讀時間開始時，再將短文唸出來。第二部分回答問題的題目將播出 2 遍，聽完第二次題目後要立即回答。第三部份看圖敘述有 30 秒的思考時間及 1 分 30 秒的答題時間，思考時不可在試題紙上作記號，亦不可出聲。等聽到指示開始回答時，請您針對圖片盡量的回答。

3. 錄音設備皆已事先完成設定，請勿觸動任何機件，以免影響錄音。測驗時請戴妥耳機，將麥克風調到嘴邊約三公分處，聽清楚說明，依指示以適中音量回答。

4. 評分人員將根據您錄下的回答（發音與語調、語法與字彙、可解度及切題度等）作整體的評分。您可利用所附光碟自行測試，一一錄下回答後，再播出來聽聽，並斟酌調整。練習時請盡量以英語思考、應對，考試時較易有自然的表現。

5. 請注意測試時不可在試題紙上劃線、打「√」或作任何記號；不可在准考證或其他物品上抄題；亦不可有傳遞、夾帶小抄、左顧右盼或交談等違規行為。

6. 意圖或已將試題紙或試題影音資料攜出或傳送出試場者，視同侵犯本中心著作財產權，限五年內不得報名參加「全民英檢」測驗。請人代考，連同代考者，三年內不得報名參加本測驗。

7. 測驗結束時，須立即停止作答，在原位靜候監試人員收回全部試題紙且清點無誤後，等候監試人員宣布結束後始可離場。

8. 入場、出場及測驗中如有違反規則或不服監試人員指示者，監試人員將取消您的應試資格並請您離場，且作答不予計分，亦不退費。

全民英語能力分級檢定測驗

中級口說能力測驗

T04.mp3

請在 15 秒內完成並唸出下列自我介紹的句子：

My seat number is（座位號碼後 5 碼）, and my registration number is（考試號碼後 5 碼）.

第一部分：朗讀短文

　　請先利用一分鐘的時間閱讀下面的短文，然後在二分鐘內以正常的速度，清楚正確的讀出下面的短文，閱讀時請不要發出聲音。

　　Many health experts have called for further research on "long COVID," because in fact, it occurs in 10 to 20 percent of all cases. As the CECC has said that more than half of the population in Taiwan used to be infected with the virus, the government should also shift some of its attention and resources to understanding, preventing and providing treatment for long COVID.

　　　　　　＊　　　　　　　　　　＊　　　　　　　　　　＊

　　Personal details, such as your address, date of birth, telephone number and bank account information should never be disclosed online unless you use a trusted source. When you're shopping online, it's important to only purchase from web pages that have URLs starting with "HTTPS", which indicates the site is secure. If your detailed information gets into the wrong hands, they can be used for identity theft or fraud.

第二部分：回答問題

　　這個部分共有 10 題。題目已事先錄音，每題經由耳機播出二次，不印在試卷上。第一至五題，每題回答時間 15 秒；第六至十題，每題回答時間 30 秒。每題播出後，請立即回答。回答時，不一定要用完整的句子，但請在作答時間內儘量的表達。

第三部分：看圖敘述

　　下面有一張圖片及四個相關的問題，請在一分半鐘內完成作答。作答時，請直接回答，不需將題號及題目唸出。

　　首先請利用 30 秒的時間看圖及問題。

提示：
1. 照片裡的人在什麼地方？
2. 照片裡的人在做什麼？
3. 照片裡的人為什麼會在那裡？
4. 如果尚有時間，請詳細描述圖片中的景物。

請將下列自我介紹的句子再唸一遍：

My seat number is (座位號碼後 5 碼), and my registration number is (考試號碼後 5 碼).

第五回 寫作能力測驗答題注意事項

1. 本測驗共有兩部分。第一部分為中譯英,第二部分為英文作文。測驗時間為 40 分鐘。

2. 請利用試題紙空白處背面擬稿,但正答務必書寫在「寫作能力測驗答案紙」上。在答案紙以外的地方作答,不予計分。

3. 第一部分中譯英請在答案紙第一頁作答,第二部分英文作文請在答案紙第二頁作答。

4. 作答時請勿隔行書寫,請注意字跡清晰可讀,並保持答案紙之清潔,以免影響評分。

5. 測驗時,不得在准考證或其他物品上抄題,亦不得有傳遞、夾帶小抄、左顧右盼或交談等違規行為。

6. 意圖或已經將試題紙攜出試場者,五年內不得報名參加本測驗。請人代考者,連同代考者,三年內不得報名參加本測驗。

7. 測驗結束時,須立即停止作答,在原位靜候監試人員收回全部試題紙及答案紙,清點無誤後,宣佈結束始可離場。

8. 應試者入場、出場及測驗中如有違反上列規則或不服監試人員之指示者,監試人員得取消應試資格並請其離場,且作答不予計分。

全民英語能力分級檢定測驗

中級寫作能力測驗

本測驗共有兩部份。第一部份為中譯英，第二部份為英文寫作。測驗時間為 40 分鐘。

一、中譯英 (40%)

說明：請將下列的一段中文翻譯成通順、達意且前後連貫的英文。

　　一般對於單身或結婚的選擇有著各種優缺點的爭論。這個爭議性話題最常被討論的是陪伴、責任和生活方式這三方面。在過去，很少人會否認「婚姻是人生必經之路」的說法。而如今，這句老話已受到許多不婚族的挑戰。他們認為婚姻，甚至有無自己的後代，都只是一種人生的選擇。

二、英文作文 (60%)

請依下面所提供的文字提示寫一篇英文作文，長度約 120 字（8 至 12 個句子）。作文可以是一個完整的段落，也可以分段。（評分重點包括內容、組織、文法、用字遣詞、標點符號、大小寫。）

提示：無論是小孩子、青少年或是成人，朋友在每個人的生活中都是相當重要的。有句話說「近朱者赤，近墨者黑（If you live with a lame person you will learn to limp.）」學習如何結交好的朋友，並遠離不好的朋友，也是一門重要的人生課題。請提出自己對於「朋友」的看法。

全民英語能力分級檢定測驗中級寫作能力答案紙

第一部份請由第 1 行開始作答，請勿隔行書寫。　　　　　　第 1 頁

5

10

15

20

25

30

TEST 05

35

40

第五回　口說能力測驗答題注意事項

1. 本測驗問題由耳機播放，回答則經麥克風錄下。分朗讀短文、回答問題與看圖敘述三部分，時間共約 15 分鐘，連同口試說明時間共需約五十分鐘。

2. 第一部份朗讀短文有 1 分鐘準備時間，此時請勿唸出聲音，待聽到「請開始朗讀」2 分鐘的朗讀時間開始時，再將短文唸出來。第二部分回答問題的題目將播出 2 遍，聽完第二次題目後要立即回答。第三部份看圖敘述有 30 秒的思考時間及 1 分 30 秒的答題時間，思考時不可在試題紙上作記號，亦不可出聲。等聽到指示開始回答時，請您針對圖片盡量的回答。

3. 錄音設備皆已事先完成設定，請勿觸動任何機件，以免影響錄音。測驗時請戴妥耳機，將麥克風調到嘴邊約三公分處，聽清楚說明，依指示以適中音量回答。

4. 評分人員將根據您錄下的回答（發音與語調、語法與字彙、可解度及切題度等）作整體的評分。您可利用所附光碟自行測試，一一錄下回答後，再播出來聽聽，並斟酌調整。練習時請盡量以英語思考、應對，考試時較易有自然的表現。

5. 請注意測試時不可在試題紙上劃線、打「√」或作任何記號；不可在准考證或其他物品上抄題；亦不可有傳遞、夾帶小抄、左顧右盼或交談等違規行為。

6. 意圖或已將試題紙或試題影音資料攜出或傳送出試場者，視同侵犯本中心著作財產權，限五年內不得報名參加「全民英檢」測驗。請人代考，連同代考者，三年內不得報名參加本測驗。

7. 測驗結束時，須立即停止作答，在原位靜候監試人員收回全部試題紙且清點無誤後，等候監試人員宣布結束後始可離場。

8. 入場、出場及測驗中如有違反規則或不服監試人員指示者，監試人員將取消您的應試資格並請您離場，且作答不予計分，亦不退費。

全民英語能力分級檢定測驗

中級口說能力測驗

T05.mp3

請在 15 秒內完成並唸出下列自我介紹的句子：

My seat number is（座位號碼後 5 碼）, and my registration number is
（考試號碼後 5 碼）.

第一部分：朗讀短文

　　請先利用一分鐘的時間閱讀下面的短文，然後在二分鐘內以正常的速度，清楚正確的讀出下面的短文，閱讀時請不要發出聲音。

　　Life is short and sometimes in a messy and ever-changing world. Precious things can easily become lost. Frequently, circumstances out of our control cause loss, and our own choices may cause us to lose the things that mean the most. Each of us has different needs and priorities in life, but we share one thing in common: the absence of certain things in our lives can make us feel that our lives are incomplete.

　　　　　　*　　　　　　　　　*　　　　　　　　　*

　　Many of us take it for granted that we live safely, until something life-changing happens because our health is at risk. With good health, anything is possible. Without it, you can feel hopeless and helpless for the future. To be healthy means to take care of your emotion, body and soul. Don't be ignorant of what your body is telling you. Eat healthy and exercise daily to minimize preventable illnesses and the stress that may be keeping you from enjoying life.

第二部分：回答問題

　　這個部分共有 10 題。題目已事先錄音，每題經由耳機播出二次，不印在試卷上。第一至五題，每題回答時間 15 秒；第六至十題，每題回答時間 30 秒。每題播出後，請立即回答。回答時，不一定要用完整的句子，但請在作答時間內儘量的表達。

TEST 05

第三部分：看圖敘述

下面有一張圖片及四個相關的問題，請在一分半鐘內完成作答。作答時，請直接回答，不需將題號及題目唸出。

首先請利用 30 秒的時間看圖及問題。

提示：
1. 照片裡的人在什麼地方？
2. 照片裡的人在做什麼？
3. 照片裡的人為什麼會在那裡？
4. 如果尚有時間，請詳細描述圖片中的景物。

請將下列自我介紹的句子再唸一遍：

My seat number is（座位號碼後 5 碼）, and my registration number is
（考試號碼後 5 碼）.

第六回　寫作能力測驗答題注意事項

1. 本測驗共有兩部分。第一部分為中譯英，第二部分為英文作文。
   測驗時間為 40 分鐘。

2. 請利用試題紙空白處背面擬稿，但正答務必書寫在「寫作能力測
   驗答案紙」上。在答案紙以外的地方作答，不予計分。

3. 第一部分中譯英請在答案紙第一頁作答，第二部分英文作文請在
   答案紙第二頁作答。

4. 作答時請勿隔行書寫，請注意字跡清晰可讀，並保持答案紙之清
   潔，以免影響評分。

5. 測驗時，不得在准考證或其他物品上抄題，亦不得有傳遞、夾帶
   小抄、左顧右盼或交談等違規行為。

6. 意圖或已經將試題紙攜出試場者，五年內不得報名參加本測驗。
   請人代考者，連同代考者，三年內不得報名參加本測驗。

7. 測驗結束時，須立即停止作答，在原位靜候監試人員收回全部試
   題紙及答案紙，清點無誤後，宣佈結束始可離場。

8. 應試者入場、出場及測驗中如有違反上列規則或不服監試人員之
   指示者，監試人員得取消應試資格並請其離場，且作答不予計
   分。

全民英語能力分級檢定測驗

中級寫作能力測驗

本測驗共有兩部份。第一部份為中譯英,第二部份為英文寫作。測驗時間為 40 分鐘。

一、中譯英 (40%)

說明:請將下列的一段中文翻譯成通順、達意且前後連貫的英文。

台灣的交通擁擠是眾所皆知的大問題。在許多城市,道路常常擁擠不堪,特別是在上下班時間和週末假期,交通堵塞更是難以避免。加上車輛與行人互爭道路空間,交通事故也時有所聞。此外,台灣的公共運輸系統雖然完善,但仍難以負荷高峰時刻的客流量。

二、英文作文 (60%)

請依下面所提供的文字提示寫一篇英文作文,長度約 120 字(8 至 12 個句子)。作文可以是一個完整的段落,也可以分段。(評分重點包括內容、組織、文法、用字遣詞、標點符號、大小寫。)

提示:社群媒體扮演著極為重要的角色。有些人認為社群媒體對我們的溝通技巧和建立有意義關係的能力有負面影響。你同意還或是不同意這樣的說法?請舉例說明並佐證來支持自己的立場。

全民英語能力分級檢定測驗中級寫作能力答案紙

5

10

15

20

第二部分請翻至第 2 頁作答

25

30

35

40

第六回　口說能力測驗答題注意事項

1. 本測驗問題由耳機播放，回答則經麥克風錄下。分朗讀短文、回答問題與看圖敘述三部分，時間共約 15 分鐘，連同口試說明時間共需約五十分鐘。

2. 第一部份朗讀短文有 1 分鐘準備時間，此時請勿唸出聲音，待聽到「請開始朗讀」2 分鐘的朗讀時間開始時，再將短文唸出來。第二部分回答問題的題目將播出 2 遍，聽完第二次題目後要立即回答。第三部份看圖敘述有 30 秒的思考時間及 1 分 30 秒的答題時間，思考時不可在試題紙上作記號，亦不可出聲。等聽到指示開始回答時，請您針對圖片盡量的回答。

3. 錄音設備皆已事先完成設定，請勿觸動任何機件，以免影響錄音。測驗時請戴妥耳機，將麥克風調到嘴邊約三公分處，聽清楚說明，依指示以適中音量回答。

4. 評分人員將根據您錄下的回答（發音與語調、語法與字彙、可解度及切題度等）作整體的評分。您可利用所附光碟自行測試，一一錄下回答後，再播出來聽聽，並斟酌調整。練習時請盡量以英語思考、應對，考試時較易有自然的表現。

5. 請注意測試時不可在試題紙上劃線、打「√」或作任何記號；不可在准考證或其他物品上抄題；亦不可有傳遞、夾帶小抄、左顧右盼或交談等違規行為。

6. 意圖或已將試題紙或試題影音資料攜出或傳送出試場者，視同侵犯本中心著作財產權，限五年內不得報名參加「全民英檢」測驗。請人代考，連同代考者，三年內不得報名參加本測驗。

7. 測驗結束時，須立即停止作答，在原位靜候監試人員收回全部試題紙且清點無誤後，等候監試人員宣布結束後始可離場。

8. 入場、出場及測驗中如有違反規則或不服監試人員指示者，監試人員將取消您的應試資格並請您離場，且作答不予計分，亦不退費。

41

全民英語能力分級檢定測驗

中級口說能力測驗

T06.mp3

請在 15 秒內完成並唸出下列自我介紹的句子：

My seat number is （座位號碼後 5 碼）, and my registration number is （考試號碼後 5 碼）.

第一部分：朗讀短文

　　請先利用一分鐘的時間閱讀下面的短文，然後在二分鐘內以正常的速度，清楚正確的讀出下面的短文，閱讀時請不要發出聲音。

　　Everyone knows it's important to bear a positive and optimistic attitude toward life, though life doesn't always turn out the way we expected. We are not able to avoid frustrating results. Optimism means you treat people and things around you with an open-minded, tolerant, and accepting attitude. Even if you are getting into trouble, you can have the willpower to adjust your mood. For optimistic people, it's not that there are no troubles in his life, but that they are able to turn obstacles into motivation.

*　　　　　　　*　　　　　　　*

　　In our daily life, we are always tempted by various things. Once you become famous, you may not let go of fame; when you become rich, you may not give up seeking wealth; if you have a lover, you won't let him or her go even when they want to. When you are running your own business, you don't want to let it go bankrupt. The more you have, the more you want.

第二部分：回答問題

　　這個部分共有 10 題。題目已事先錄音，每題經由耳機播出二次，不印在試卷上。第一至五題，每題回答時間 15 秒；第六至十題，每題回答時間 30 秒。每題播出後，請立即回答。回答時，不一定要用完整的句子，但請在作答時間內儘量的表達。

第三部分：看圖敘述

　　下面有一張圖片及四個相關的問題，請在一分半鐘內完成作答。作答時，請直接回答，不需將題號及題目唸出。

　　首先請利用 30 秒的時間看圖及問題。

提示：
1. 照片裡的人在什麼地方？
2. 照片裡的人在做什麼？
3. 照片裡的人為什麼會在那裡？
4. 如果尚有時間，請詳細描述圖片中的景物。

請將下列自我介紹的句子再唸一遍：

My seat number is（座位號碼後 5 碼）, and my registration number is（考試號碼後 5 碼）.

第七回　寫作能力測驗答題注意事項

1. 本測驗共有兩部分。第一部分為中譯英，第二部分為英文作文。測驗時間為 40 分鐘。

2. 請利用試題紙空白處背面擬稿，但正答務必書寫在「寫作能力測驗答案紙」上。在答案紙以外的地方作答，不予計分。

3. 第一部分中譯英請在答案紙第一頁作答，第二部分英文作文請在答案紙第二頁作答。

4. 作答時請勿隔行書寫，請注意字跡清晰可讀，並保持答案紙之清潔，以免影響評分。

5. 測驗時，不得在准考證或其他物品上抄題，亦不得有傳遞、夾帶小抄、左顧右盼或交談等違規行為。

6. 意圖或已經將試題紙攜出試場者，五年內不得報名參加本測驗。請人代考者，連同代考者，三年內不得報名參加本測驗。

7. 測驗結束時，須立即停止作答，在原位靜候監試人員收回全部試題紙及答案紙，清點無誤後，宣佈結束始可離場。

8. 應試者入場、出場及測驗中如有違反上列規則或不服監試人員之指示者，監試人員得取消應試資格並請其離場，且作答不予計分。

全民英語能力分級檢定測驗

中級寫作能力測驗

本測驗共有兩部份。第一部份為中譯英,第二部份為英文寫作。測驗時間為 40 分鐘。

一、中譯英 (40%)

說明:請將下列的一段中文翻譯成通順、達意且前後連貫的英文。

> 　　道歉是一門藝術,需要有真心誠意和細緻的技巧。首先,道歉要明確承認自己的錯誤並且展現慚愧之情。其次,要傾聽對方的感受,並尋求解決之道。最後,要付諸實際行動,展現改變的意志。道歉不僅是彌補錯誤,更是重建信任的機會。

二、英文作文 (60%)

請依下面所提供的文字提示寫一篇英文作文,長度約 120 字(8 至 12 個句子)。作文可以是一個完整的段落,也可以分段。(評分重點包括內容、組織、文法、用字遣詞、標點符號、大小寫。)

提示:無論你是學生或上班族,或許有過在外租屋的經驗,但一般來說,租屋前自己最好先做些功課,到時候才不會遇到太多問題。你認為租房子時,應該注意那些事情,請發表你的看法。

全民英語能力分級檢定測驗中級寫作能力答案紙

第一部份請由第 1 行開始作答，請勿隔行書寫。 第 1 頁

5

10

15

20

46

25

30

35

40

第七回　口說能力測驗答題注意事項

1. 本測驗問題由耳機播放，回答則經麥克風錄下。分朗讀短文、回答問題與看圖敘述三部分，時間共約 15 分鐘，連同口試說明時間共需約五十分鐘。

2. 第一部份朗讀短文有 1 分鐘準備時間，此時請勿唸出聲音，待聽到「請開始朗讀」2 分鐘的朗讀時間開始時，再將短文唸出來。第二部分回答問題的題目將播出 2 遍，聽完第二次題目後要立即回答。第三部份看圖敘述有 30 秒的思考時間及 1 分 30 秒的答題時間，思考時不可在試題紙上作記號，亦不可出聲。等聽到指示開始回答時，請您針對圖片盡量的回答。

3. 錄音設備皆已事先完成設定，請勿觸動任何機件，以免影響錄音。測驗時請戴妥耳機，將麥克風調到嘴邊約三公分處，聽清楚說明，依指示以適中音量回答。

4. 評分人員將根據您錄下的回答（發音與語調、語法與字彙、可解度及切題度等）作整體的評分。您可利用所附光碟自行測試，一一錄下回答後，再播出來聽聽，並斟酌調整。練習時請盡量以英語思考、應對，考試時較易有自然的表現。

5. 請注意測試時不可在試題紙上劃線、打「√」或作任何記號；不可在准考證或其他物品上抄題；亦不可有傳遞、夾帶小抄、左顧右盼或交談等違規行為。

6. 意圖或已將試題紙或試題影音資料攜出或傳送出試場者，視同侵犯本中心著作財產權，限五年內不得報名參加「全民英檢」測驗。請人代考，連同代考者，三年內不得報名參加本測驗。

7. 測驗結束時，須立即停止作答，在原位靜候監試人員收回全部試題紙且清點無誤後，等候監試人員宣布結束後始可離場。

8. 入場、出場及測驗中如有違反規則或不服監試人員指示者，監試人員將取消您的應試資格並請您離場，且作答不予計分，亦不退費。

全民英語能力分級檢定測驗

中級口說能力測驗

T07.mp3

請在 15 秒內完成並唸出下列自我介紹的句子：

My seat number is（座位號碼後 5 碼）, and my registration number is
（考試號碼後 5 碼）.

第一部分：朗讀短文

　　請先利用一分鐘的時間閱讀下面的短文，然後在二分鐘內以正
常的速度，清楚正確的讀出下面的短文，閱讀時請不要發出聲音。

　　The internet is constantly evolving, with new terms emerging that reflect
the changing digital landscape. Some recent additions include "doxxing"
referring to the act of publicly exposing someone's personal information online,
"deepfake" meaning the use of AI to create realistic fake videos, and "cancel
culture" which describes the phenomenon of people being publicly blamed and
excluded for controversial views or actions. As the internet continues to shape
our lives, we can expect more new terms that reflect its impact on society.

*　　　　　　　　*　　　　　　　　*

　　Living in a dormitory can offer several advantages. Firstly, it allows
students to be in close proximity to their academic environment, which can
enhance their educational experience. Secondly, dorms provide a sense of
community and facilitate the formation of new friendships. Additionally, living
in a dorm can provide students with access to resources such as on-site advice
and study groups. Finally, dorm living can also be cost-effective, as room and
board costs are usually much lower than those of renting off-campus apartments.

第二部分：回答問題

　　這個部分共有 10 題。題目已事先錄音，每題經由耳機播出二
次，不印在試卷上。第一至五題，每題回答時間 15 秒；第六至十
題，每題回答時間 30 秒。每題播出後，請立即回答。回答時，不一
定要用完整的句子，但請在作答時間內儘量的表達。

第三部分：看圖敘述

下面有一張圖片及四個相關的問題，請在一分半鐘內完成作答。作答時，請直接回答，不需將題號及題目唸出。

首先請利用 30 秒的時間看圖及問題。

提示：

1. 照片裡的人在什麼地方？
2. 照片裡的人在做什麼？
3. 照片裡的人為什麼會在那裡？
4. 如果尚有時間，請詳細描述圖片中的景物。

請將下列自我介紹的句子再唸一遍：

My seat number is（座位號碼後 5 碼）, and my registration number is （考試號碼後 5 碼）.

第八回　寫作能力測驗答題注意事項

1. 本測驗共有兩部分。第一部分為中譯英，第二部分為英文作文。測驗時間為 **40 分鐘**。

2. 請利用試題紙空白處背面擬稿，但正答務必書寫在「寫作能力測驗答案紙」上。在答案紙以外的地方作答，不予計分。

3. 第一部分中譯英請在答案紙第一頁作答，第二部分英文作文請在答案紙第二頁作答。

4. 作答時請勿隔行書寫，請注意字跡清晰可讀，並保持答案紙之清潔，以免影響評分。

5. 測驗時，不得在准考證或其他物品上抄題，亦不得有傳遞、夾帶小抄、左顧右盼或交談等違規行為。

6. 意圖或已經將試題紙攜出試場者，五年內不得報名參加本測驗。請人代考者，連同代考者，三年內不得報名參加本測驗。

7. 測驗結束時，須立即停止作答，在原位靜候監試人員收回全部試題紙及答案紙，清點無誤後，宣佈結束始可離場。

8. 應試者入場、出場及測驗中如有違反上列規則或不服監試人員之指示者，監試人員得取消應試資格並請其離場，且作答不予計分。

全民英語能力分級檢定測驗

中級寫作能力測驗

本測驗共有兩部份。第一部份為中譯英，第二部份為英文寫作。測驗時間為 40 分鐘。

一、中譯英 (40%)

說明：請將下列的一段中文翻譯成通順、達意且前後連貫的英文。

英文單字並不需要死記硬背，可以運用各種技巧幫助自己更有效地學習。例如，可以使用單字卡、聯想法、背誦歌曲歌詞等方法，增加單字的印象深度。同時，每天多閱讀英文文章以及聽英語音檔，也有助於強化單字的記憶。

二、英文作文 (60%)

請依下面所提供的文字提示寫一篇英文作文，長度約 120 字（8 至 12 個句子）。作文可以是一個完整的段落，也可以分段。（評分重點包括內容、組織、文法、用字遣詞、標點符號、大小寫。）

提示：保持良好身材也可以保持身體的健康、加強心理層面的健康並提高自信心。此外，良好的身體狀態可以使人更有活力和耐力，進而更有意願參與各種活動，提升生活品質。你認為保持良好身材的方法有哪些呢？

全民英語能力分級檢定測驗中級寫作能力答案紙

第一部份請由第 1 行開始作答，請勿隔行書寫。　　　　　第 1 頁

5

10

15

20

第二部分請翻至第 2 頁作答

TEST 08

25＿＿＿＿＿＿＿＿＿＿＿＿＿＿＿＿＿＿＿＿＿＿

30＿＿＿＿＿＿＿＿＿＿＿＿＿＿＿＿＿＿＿＿＿＿

35＿＿＿＿＿＿＿＿＿＿＿＿＿＿＿＿＿＿＿＿＿＿

40＿＿＿＿＿＿＿＿＿＿＿＿＿＿＿＿＿＿＿＿＿＿

第八回 口說能力測驗答題注意事項

1. 本測驗問題由耳機播放，回答則經麥克風錄下。分朗讀短文、回答問題與看圖敘述三部分，時間共約 15 分鐘，連同口試說明時間共需約五十分鐘。

2. 第一部份朗讀短文有 1 分鐘準備時間，此時請勿唸出聲音，待聽到「請開始朗讀」2 分鐘的朗讀時間開始時，再將短文唸出來。第二部分回答問題的題目將播出 2 遍，聽完第二次題目後要立即回答。第三部份看圖敘述有 30 秒的思考時間及 1 分 30 秒的答題時間，思考時不可在試題紙上作記號，亦不可出聲。等聽到指示開始回答時，請您針對圖片盡量的回答。

3. 錄音設備皆已事先完成設定，請勿觸動任何機件，以免影響錄音。測驗時請戴妥耳機，將麥克風調到嘴邊約三公分處，聽清楚說明，依指示以適中音量回答。

4. 評分人員將根據您錄下的回答（發音與語調、語法與字彙、可解度及切題度等）作整體的評分。您可利用所附光碟自行測試，一一錄下回答後，再播出來聽聽，並斟酌調整。練習時請盡量以英語思考、應對，考試時較易有自然的表現。

5. 請注意測試時不可在試題紙上劃線、打「√」或作任何記號；不可在准考證或其他物品上抄題；亦不可有傳遞、夾帶小抄、左顧右盼或交談等違規行為。

6. 意圖或已將試題紙或試題影音資料攜出或傳送出試場者，視同侵犯本中心著作財產權，限五年內不得報名參加「全民英檢」測驗。請人代考，連同代考者，三年內不得報名參加本測驗。

7. 測驗結束時，須立即停止作答，在原位靜候監試人員收回全部試題紙且清點無誤後，等候監試人員宣布結束後始可離場。

8. 入場、出場及測驗中如有違反規則或不服監試人員指示者，監試人員將取消您的應試資格並請您離場，且作答不予計分，亦不退費。

全民英語能力分級檢定測驗

中級口說能力測驗

T08.mp3

請在 15 秒內完成並唸出下列自我介紹的句子：

My seat number is （座位號碼後 5 碼）, and my registration number is （考試號碼後 5 碼）.

第一部分：朗讀短文

　　請先利用一分鐘的時間閱讀下面的短文，然後在二分鐘內以正常的速度，清楚正確的讀出下面的短文，閱讀時請不要發出聲音。

　　News media plays a vital role in shaping public opinion. It provides a platform for reporting on current events and issues, enabling people to stay up-to-date. However, in recent times, the media has gradually become biased to reporting and tried to incite hatred. They have also created a flood of misleading information. Despite these challenges, news media remains a crucial part of our society, and it is important for journalists to maintain their integrity and uphold moral reporting standards.

*　　　　　　　　　　*　　　　　　　　　　*

　　Sports are regarded as part of our lives, whether we're playing them or watching them. They promote physical fitness and provide us with a healthy outlet for our competitive instincts. From football and basketball to tennis and swimming, they not only teach us important life skills such as teamwork, discipline, and dedication but also bring people from different cultures and backgrounds together. Whether you're a professional athlete or just a weekend warrior, sports can enrich your life in countless ways.

第二部分：回答問題

　　這個部分共有 10 題。題目已事先錄音，每題經由耳機播出二次，不印在試卷上。第一至五題，每題回答時間 15 秒；第六至十題，每題回答時間 30 秒。每題播出後，請立即回答。回答時，不一定要用完整的句子，但請在作答時間內儘量的表達。

第三部分：看圖敘述

　　下面有一張圖片及四個相關的問題，請在一分半鐘內完成作答。作答時，請直接回答，不需將題號及題目唸出。

　　首先請利用 30 秒的時間看圖及問題。

提示：

1. 照片裡的人在什麼地方？
2. 照片裡的人在做什麼？
3. 照片裡的人為什麼會在那裡？
4. 如果尚有時間，請詳細描述圖片中的景物。

請將下列自我介紹的句子再唸一遍：

My seat number is（座位號碼後 5 碼）, and my registration number is（考試號碼後 5 碼）.

第九回 寫作能力測驗答題注意事項

1. 本測驗共有兩部分。第一部分為中譯英,第二部分為英文作文。測驗時間為 40 分鐘。

2. 請利用試題紙空白處背面擬稿,但正答務必書寫在「寫作能力測驗答案紙」上。在答案紙以外的地方作答,不予計分。

3. 第一部分中譯英請在答案紙第一頁作答,第二部分英文作文請在答案紙第二頁作答。

4. 作答時請勿隔行書寫,請注意字跡清晰可讀,並保持答案紙之清潔,以免影響評分。

5. 測驗時,不得在准考證或其他物品上抄題,亦不得有傳遞、夾帶小抄、左顧右盼或交談等違規行為。

6. 意圖或已經將試題紙攜出試場者,五年內不得報名參加本測驗。請人代考者,連同代考者,三年內不得報名參加本測驗。

7. 測驗結束時,須立即停止作答,在原位靜候監試人員收回全部試題紙及答案紙,清點無誤後,宣佈結束始可離場。

8. 應試者入場、出場及測驗中如有違反上列規則或不服監試人員之指示者,監試人員得取消應試資格並請其離場,且作答不予計分。

全民英語能力分級檢定測驗

中級寫作能力測驗

本測驗共有兩部份。第一部份為中譯英，第二部份為英文寫作。測驗時間為 40 分鐘。

一、中譯英 (40%)

說明：請將下列的一段中文翻譯成通順、達意且前後連貫的英文。

當與他人發生爭執時，很重要的是保持冷靜與沉著。不要讓情緒控制你的行為，因為這可能會讓事情變得更糟糕。在辯論中，要尊重對方的觀點，不要打斷他們的發言，而是先讓對方說完。當你有自己的觀點時，務必清晰地表達出來，但要注意措辭，不要使用攻擊性的言語。

二、英文作文 (60%)

請依下面所提供的文字提示寫一篇英文作文，長度約 120 字（8 至 12 個句子）。作文可以是一個完整的段落，也可以分段。（評分重點包括內容、組織、文法、用字遣詞、標點符號、大小寫。）

提示：為了讓民眾能夠更有效地與國際接軌，並增進國家的國際競爭力與文化多樣性，政府近年來著手推動「雙語國家政策」，而「全英語授課（English as a medium of instruction, EMI）」就是這項政策的一環。請以此為題，說明你是否贊成全英語授課及理由。

第一部份請由第 1 行開始作答,請勿隔行書寫。 第 1 頁

5

10

15

20

_____

_____

_____

_____

25_____

_____

_____

_____

_____

TEST 09

30_____

_____

_____

_____

_____

35_____

_____

_____

_____

_____

40_____

第九回 口說能力測驗答題注意事項

1. 本測驗問題由耳機播放，回答則經麥克風錄下。分朗讀短文、回答問題與看圖敘述三部分，時間共約 15 分鐘，連同口試說明時間共需約五十分鐘。

2. 第一部份朗讀短文有 1 分鐘準備時間，此時請勿唸出聲音，待聽到「請開始朗讀」2 分鐘的朗讀時間開始時，再將短文唸出來。第二部分回答問題的題目將播出 2 遍，聽完第二次題目後要立即回答。第三部份看圖敘述有 30 秒的思考時間及 1 分 30 秒的答題時間，思考時不可在試題紙上作記號，亦不可出聲。等聽到指示開始回答時，請您針對圖片盡量的回答。

3. 錄音設備皆已事先完成設定，請勿觸動任何機件，以免影響錄音。測驗時請戴妥耳機，將麥克風調到嘴邊約三公分處，聽清楚說明，依指示以適中音量回答。

4. 評分人員將根據您錄下的回答（發音與語調、語法與字彙、可解度及切題度等）作整體的評分。您可利用所附光碟自行測試，一一錄下回答後，再播出來聽聽，並斟酌調整。練習時請盡量以英語思考、應對，考試時較易有自然的表現。

5. 請注意測試時不可在試題紙上劃線、打「✓」或作任何記號；不可在准考證或其他物品上抄題；亦不可有傳遞、夾帶小抄、左顧右盼或交談等違規行為。

6. 意圖或已將試題紙或試題影音資料攜出或傳送出試場者，視同侵犯本中心著作財產權，限五年內不得報名參加「全民英檢」測驗。請人代考，連同代考者，三年內不得報名參加本測驗。

7. 測驗結束時，須立即停止作答，在原位靜候監試人員收回全部試題紙且清點無誤後，等候監試人員宣布結束後始可離場。

8. 入場、出場及測驗中如有違反規則或不服監試人員指示者，監試人員將取消您的應試資格並請您離場，且作答不予計分，亦不退費。

全民英語能力分級檢定測驗

中級口說能力測驗

T09.mp3

請在 15 秒內完成並唸出下列自我介紹的句子:

My seat number is（座位號碼後 5 碼）, and my registration number is （考試號碼後 5 碼）.

第一部分：朗讀短文

　　請先利用一分鐘的時間閱讀下面的短文，然後在二分鐘內以正常的速度，清楚正確的讀出下面的短文，閱讀時請不要發出聲音。

　　Making a good impression is crucial, whether it's during a job interview, a first date, or when you meet someone new. It is also important to be confident, friendly, and sincere. Dressing appropriately for certain occasions, using good posture, and maintaining eye contact are also key factors. Additionally, showing interest in the other person by actively listening and asking thoughtful questions can make a big impact. Remember to be yourself and stay positive, as a positive attitude can be infectious and help leave a lasting impression.

*　　　　　*　　　　　*

　　Painting is a form of visual art that involves applying color to a surface, such as canvas, paper, or wood. It expresses ideas or emotions through the use of different colors and techniques. Paintings convey a sense of mood or atmosphere. Artists throughout history have used painting as a means of communicating, documenting historical events, and expressing their creativity. Today, painting continues to be a popular form of artistic expression and a valued part of many cultures around the world.

第二部分：回答問題

　　這個部分共有 10 題。題目已事先錄音，每題經由耳機播出二次，不印在試卷上。第一至五題，每題回答時間 15 秒；第六至十題，每題回答時間 30 秒。每題播出後，請立即回答。回答時，不一定要用完整的句子，但請在作答時間內儘量的表達。

第三部分：看圖敘述

下面有一張圖片及四個相關的問題，請在一分半鐘內完成作答。作答時，請直接回答，不需將題號及題目唸出。

首先請利用 30 秒的時間看圖及問題。

提示：
1. 照片裡的人在什麼地方？
2. 照片裡的人在做什麼？
3. 照片裡的人為什麼會在那裡？
4. 如果尚有時間，請詳細描述圖片中的景物。

請將下列自我介紹的句子再唸一遍：

My seat number is（座位號碼後 5 碼）, and my registration number is
（考試號碼後 5 碼）.

第十回　寫作能力測驗答題注意事項

1. 本測驗共有兩部分。第一部分為中譯英，第二部分為英文作文。測驗時間為 40 分鐘。

2. 請利用試題紙空白處背面擬稿，但正答務必書寫在「寫作能力測驗答案紙」上。在答案紙以外的地方作答，不予計分。

3. 第一部分中譯英請在答案紙第一頁作答，第二部分英文作文請在答案紙第二頁作答。

4. 作答時請勿隔行書寫，請注意字跡清晰可讀，並保持答案紙之清潔，以免影響評分。

5. 測驗時，不得在准考證或其他物品上抄題，亦不得有傳遞、夾帶小抄、左顧右盼或交談等違規行為。

6. 意圖或已經將試題紙攜出試場者，五年內不得報名參加本測驗。請人代考者，連同代考者，三年內不得報名參加本測驗。

7. 測驗結束時，須立即停止作答，在原位靜候監試人員收回全部試題紙及答案紙，清點無誤後，宣佈結束始可離場。

8. 應試者入場、出場及測驗中如有違反上列規則或不服監試人員之指示者，監試人員得取消應試資格並請其離場，且作答不予計分。

全民英語能力分級檢定測驗

中級寫作能力測驗

本測驗共有兩部份。第一部份為中譯英,第二部份為英文寫作。測驗時間為 40 分鐘。

一、中譯英 (40%)

說明:請將下列的一段中文翻譯成通順、達意且前後連貫的英文。

　　　尊重他人是建立良好人際關係的重要基礎。我們應該學會欣賞他人的價值觀、文化背景和生活方式,且避免評論或批評他人的行為或選擇。在日常生活中,我們可以從小事做起,如不打擾他人、不侵犯他人的私人空間,也不以言語或肢體威脅或攻擊他人。只有從自己做起,才能營造出和諧的社會環境。

二、英文作文 (60%)

請依下面所提供的文字提示寫一篇英文作文,長度約 120 字（8 至 12 個句子）。作文可以是一個完整的段落,也可以分段。（評分重點包括內容、組織、文法、用字遣詞、標點符號、大小寫。）

提示:近年來,人工智慧（AI）與機器人學習技術發展迅速,而大家也開始有所關切:AI 未來是否會影響自己的工作,或是對於自己生活上會產生什麼影響。請寫一篇短文論述你對這項技術的看法。

全民英語能力分級檢定測驗中級寫作能力答案紙

第一部份請由第 1 行開始作答，請勿隔行書寫。　　　　　　第 1 頁

5

10

TEST 10

15

20

第二部分請翻至第 2 頁作答

25

30

35

40

第十回　口說能力測驗答題注意事項

1. 本測驗問題由耳機播放，回答則經麥克風錄下。分朗讀短文、回答問題與看圖敘述三部分，時間共約 15 分鐘，連同口試說明時間共需約五十分鐘。

2. 第一部份朗讀短文有 1 分鐘準備時間，此時請勿唸出聲音，待聽到「請開始朗讀」2 分鐘的朗讀時間開始時，再將短文唸出來。第二部分回答問題的題目將播出 2 遍，聽完第二次題目後要立即回答。第三部份看圖敘述有 30 秒的思考時間及 1 分 30 秒的答題時間，思考時不可在試題紙上作記號，亦不可出聲。等聽到指示開始回答時，請您針對圖片盡量的回答。

3. 錄音設備皆已事先完成設定，請勿觸動任何機件，以免影響錄音。測驗時請戴妥耳機，將麥克風調到嘴邊約三公分處，聽清楚說明，依指示以適中音量回答。

4. 評分人員將根據您錄下的回答（發音與語調、語法與字彙、可解度及切題度等）作整體的評分。您可利用所附光碟自行測試，一一錄下回答後，再播出來聽聽，並斟酌調整。練習時請盡量以英語思考、應對，考試時較易有自然的表現。

5. 請注意測試時不可在試題紙上劃線、打「√」或作任何記號；不可在准考證或其他物品上抄題；亦不可有傳遞、夾帶小抄、左顧右盼或交談等違規行為。

6. 意圖或已將試題紙或試題影音資料攜出或傳送出試場者，視同侵犯本中心著作財產權，限五年內不得報名參加「全民英檢」測驗。請人代考，連同代考者，三年內不得報名參加本測驗。

7. 測驗結束時，須立即停止作答，在原位靜候監試人員收回全部試題紙且清點無誤後，等候監試人員宣布結束後始可離場。

8. 入場、出場及測驗中如有違反規則或不服監試人員指示者，監試人員將取消您的應試資格並請您離場，且作答不予計分，亦不退費。

全民英語能力分級檢定測驗

中級口說能力測驗

T10.mp3

請在 15 秒內完成並唸出下列自我介紹的句子：

My seat number is（座位號碼後 5 碼）, and my registration number is
（考試號碼後 5 碼）.

第一部分：朗讀短文

　　請先利用一分鐘的時間閱讀下面的短文，然後在二分鐘內以正
常的速度，清楚正確的讀出下面的短文，閱讀時請不要發出聲音。

　　New York, commonly referred to as simply NY, is one of the most
populous cities in the United States and in the world. It is located in the
northeastern region of the country. Known as a global hub for finance,
fashion, art, and entertainment, NY is home to well-known landmarks such
as the Statue of Liberty, Central Park, Times Square, and the Empire State
Building. With its bustling streets, diverse culture, and endless attractions,
New York is a must-visit destination for travelers from all over the world.

　　　　　　　　*　　　　　　　　　　*　　　　　　　　　　*

　　One way to build self-confidence is to spot negative self-talks and
replace them with positive words of self-assurance. It's also important to set
realistic goals and work towards achieving them, as accomplishing tasks can
help increase feelings of confidence. Another strategy is to step out of your
comfort zone and try new things. Finally, take good care of yourself by
eating healthily, exercising regularly, and getting enough rest. With patience
and effort, anyone can develop a strong sense of self-confidence.

第二部分：回答問題

　　這個部分共有 10 題。題目已事先錄音，每題經由耳機播出二
次，不印在試卷上。第一至五題，每題回答時間 15 秒；第六至十
題，每題回答時間 30 秒。每題播出後，請立即回答。回答時，不一
定要用完整的句子，但請在作答時間內儘量的表達。

第三部分：看圖敘述

　　下面有一張圖片及四個相關的問題，請在一分半鐘內完成作答。作答時，請直接回答，不需將題號及題目唸出。

　　首先請利用 30 秒的時間看圖及問題。

提示：
1. 照片裡的人在什麼地方？
2. 照片裡的人在做什麼？
3. 照片裡的人為什麼會在那裡？
4. 如果尚有時間，請詳細描述圖片中的景物。

請將下列自我介紹的句子再唸一遍：

My seat number is（座位號碼後 5 碼），and my registration number is
（考試號碼後 5 碼）.

學習筆記欄